Warrior

Blue

a novel by

Kelsey Kingsley

Copyright

To Audrey Hepburn—

For being everything good and right in this world.

I wish I could've known you,

But since I can't, I guess I'll just admire you, instead.

A Note From the Author

DEAR READER,

In 2018, when I released Daisies & Devin, I relished in how much I enjoyed writing it. I called it a book for me, a selfish passion project, and the same rings true for Warrior Blue. Maybe even more so.

I began writing this book on my phone, after I had my gallbladder removed and couldn't get on the computer for a month. The idea had been buzzing around inside of my brain for years, but let me tell you something about those passion projects … They're scary. Because the truth is, I love writing and releasing books that I know you, dear reader, will love. I love knowing that what I write will put a smile on your face, but when it's something I'm writing for myself, how the hell am I supposed to know if you'll love it, too? And the answer is: I can't. I can't possibly know, and that's what makes them terrifying.

But I wrote it, anyway, and dear reader, I'm not sure I've ever been more proud of a book. Because while writing this story, I fell in love with Blake Carson. I felt for him hard and the twists and turns Fate handed to him. But even more than that, I hurt for him, and believe me when I say, living in his head was a difficult task that I didn't recover from gently.

To be honest, I'm not sure I'll ever fully recover from this book.

I'm not sure I ever want to.

Kelsey

Prologue

IT WAS A beautiful picture.

Taken just before Christmas Eve Mass, in 1990-something. The smiling parents, still so in love even after years of marriage. The attractive pair of identical twin boys, no older than nine, stood in front of them. There was fire in those boys' eyes, burning with life and promise, their Mom and Dad beaming with undeniable pride.

This was a family. This was love.

It really was a beautiful picture, a favorite even.

Yet pictures are nothing but memories. Fragments of time captured to be stuck in a frame or an album, to spark joy or nostalgia or cause an indescribable surge of pain.

Now this picture sparked nothing but broken promises and broken hearts. All thanks to me.

And the guilt was getting heavy.

Chapter One

"**D**O YOU HATE your brother, Blake?"

"I never said I hated my brother."

"But you implied it." Dr. Vanessa Travetti lowered her notepad and pen to her lap. She peered at me from over her black-framed glasses, and if she hadn't sufficiently pissed me off with that asinine question, I would've been all about this hot librarian thing she was giving off today.

"*How* exactly did I imply it?" I sneered, leveling her with my steely glare.

"You tell me."

Leaning back against the overstuffed armchair, I crossed my arms and kept my eyes trained on her. "You know, Doc, I really hate when you play these fucking mind games with me."

Her glossy pink lips quirked with an obvious amusement she never intended to show. She quickly remedied the slip-up with a hasty shake of her head. "What mind games, Blake?"

I thrust a hand toward her and shouted, "*Those* mind games! Everything I say, you respond with another goddamn question. Trying to weasel some bullshit out of me that doesn't even exist. Why do I hate my brother ..." I scoffed, shaking my head. "I never fucking implied that I hate my brother. All I said was, I've been taking care of him for most of my life, and I'll continue to take care of him for the rest of it. How the hell is that the same as saying I hate him?"

Head canted and lips pursed, Dr. Travetti clasped her manicured hands over her notepad. "Do you understand that it's not *what* you said, but *how* you said it?"

"There you go again with the fucking questions."

"Why are you getting so defensive?"

I unraveled my arms and pounded a fist against the arm of the chair. "Because you're putting words in my mouth! I never said I hated my fucking brother. Do I hate that I'm strapped with the burden of dealing with him for the rest of my life? Yes. Do I hate that I can't make a goddamn decision for myself, without having to think of him first? Abso-fuckin'-lutely. But don't you dare tell me that I hate *him*, Doc. Because I don't."

"Why do you come here every week, Blake?"

I narrowed my eyes at the unrelated inquiry. "What the hell does that have to do with anything?"

She shrugged. "You don't have to come here—"

"You *know* I have to come here."

Holding up a finger, she shushed me and went on, "Nobody is forcing you to come here. You could find yourself another therapist, and if I'm reading into your thoughts inaccurately, then maybe you should. So, why *do* you come?"

"*Why*?" I answered exasperatedly.

"Yes."

"Because ..." My voice trailed off as I shook my head and turned to look out the window. Just down the street was my brother's daycare. I wondered what he was doing right now. Maybe eating a snack, or perhaps finishing the craft project he and his friends had been working on this week. It was more likely that he was giving his teachers a hard time, but I liked to think he wasn't making other people miserable. I liked to think that side of him was reserved only for our parents and me.

"Blake?"

Returning my attention to Dr. Travetti, I asked, "Huh?"

"Why do you come?" she repeated insistently albeit gently.

"Because, Doc," I continued with a heavy sigh and a shrug, "who the fuck else would I talk to?"

"Another therapist," she suggested lightly, offering a vague smile.

I shrugged again and canted my head with a helplessness I didn't want her to see, while hoping so badly she would notice. "Yeah, but I chose you first. Why the hell would I start going to someone else now?"

***

6

"Jake," Miss Thomas spoke softly as she knelt beside the long table. "Your brother is here to pick you up."

Jacob "Jake" Carson looked up from his drawing to sweep his gaze across the room. His eyes searched until they pinned themselves on me, standing in the doorway of his daycare classroom. His grin spread across his smudged, stubbled cheeks, and I made a mental note to give him a shave when we got back to our parents' place.

"Blake!" There weren't any volume controls on my brother and he always spoke too loudly. A few of his classmates turned to face me with irritation and curiosity.

"Hey, buddy," I said, making sure to speak quietly in the hope he'd eventually learn the difference between outdoor and indoor voices. "Time to go home. Go get your stuff."

At six foot two, Jake was as tall as he was clumsy. He scrambled to get up from his chair with the grace of an ice-skating elephant, with his feet kicking the legs of the table to jostle the pencils and crayons. I tried not to chuckle as every pair of eyes turned to glare at him with *how dare you* exasperation.

"That's Blake, my brother," Jake told Miss Thomas. He kept his eyes on her as he walked backward, in the direction of his cubby. "Blake looks just like me but we're not the same. He can drive and he has a job. We're not the same."

Miss Thomas nodded with delightful intrigue, pretending as though she hadn't already seen me a thousand times. "I bet you can do things that Blake can't, though," she offered, shooting me a small smile.

7

I stuffed my hands inside my pockets while slowly moving to stand beside his daycare teacher. Jake prattled on about his own personal talents. He might not be able to drive, but the guy could put a puzzle together quicker than anybody I know. And if you put a Lego set in front of him, there was no stopping him from showcasing his architectural skills.

"How was he today?" I asked quietly.

This was all part of the routine. Every day, I picked him up, and every day, I asked Miss Thomas how he was. Every day, she gave me the same response.

"Good!" Miss Thomas answered with too much enthusiasm. I read right through that bullshit and my eyes said so. Her exuberant expression wilted and she shrugged. "You know Jake. He has his moments."

Moments. Jake's life was a patchworked tapestry of *moments.* Good moments, bad moments. Moments in which he brought me to the brink of insanity and made me question every decision I'd ever made. And moments that made me hate myself more than I could ever hate him—*take that, Travetti.*

"He gave you a hard time?"

Miss Thomas faltered, eyes wide as though she'd said something she shouldn't have, before she shook her head. "No, not really. But he did get into a fight with Mr. Scott."

"A *fight*?"

I turned my glare on Jake. He was shrugging his Red Sox windbreaker on and telling Mr. Scott for the billionth time that he couldn't do zippers. Mr. Scott—the other teacher in the room—didn't seem to have any issues with my brother presently, so whatever issues they might've had earlier, clearly weren't lingering.

"Well, it wasn't a fight, per se," Miss Thomas corrected. "Jake had a bit of an accident earlier—"

"What kind of an accident?" I asked, and Miss Thomas grimaced apologetically. I immediately recognized that look and understood just what kind of accident she was referring to. "Ah," I muttered with a nod.

"He wasn't too happy about being cleaned up."

"Yeah," I replied. "He never is."

"We put his dirty clothes in a plastic bag. They're in his backpack."

"Thanks," I tried to say without muttering and without the niggling embarrassment I often felt for Jake. The embarrassment he never felt for himself.

Jake bounded over, zipped up and ready to go. His Mickey Mouse backpack was looped securely over both shoulders and his hands gripped the straps. His chocolate-covered grin was that of a five-year-old boy, an attribute frozen in time, while his body continued to age along with mine. We would be thirty-four this year, in just a month, and I was the only one of us to feel it.

"We going home, Blake?"

I smiled patiently at my brother and nodded. "Yeah, buddy. We are. Just ..." I grabbed a wet wipe from a container near the door and gripped his chin in my palm as I swiped gently at his face. The chocolate faded, leaving behind the adoring expression of my big brother, born two minutes before me. I laid a hand on the top of

9

his head and ruffled his thick brown mop of hair. "There we go. All set."

Miss Thomas wished us a good day and gave Jake a big hug. "I'll see you tomorrow, okay?"

"Bright and early, right?" Jake asked, grinning wide with anticipation.

"Bright and early," she repeated, and we left the building.

***

Our parents, Paul and Diana Carson, lived in Beverly, Massachusetts. Still in the same colonial farmhouse they had moved into right after getting married forty years ago, and after all those years, it was still painted the same shade of sunny yellow. The drive from Salem was a quick one, less than ten minutes, and as usual, I wished it'd been longer, *a lot* longer, but there was no chance I'd ever move further away.

"Will you let me give you a shave before I head home?" I asked my brother as we pulled onto the dirt driveway.

Jake nodded with his gaze affixed to the house. "Sure, Blake. Sure."

I pulled in a preparatory breath and turned the car off. With just about everything, Jake was always initially agreeable, but the execution was regularly a battle. He didn't handle change well, even if it was something as simple as removing three days' worth of scruff from his face and neck.

"Come on, buddy," I said, before climbing out and rounding to his side. I grabbed his backpack while he got out and waited patiently for me to lock up. We walked up the porch steps, and like every other day, our mother pulled the door open before I could take my keys out.

"There's my boy," she said, welcoming Jake inside with outstretched arms. He fell into her embrace, wrapping her in a hug that nearly swallowed them both. "How was your day today, huh? Was it good?"

He nodded against her shoulder. "It was good."

"That's great," she replied, patting his back. "Mickey missed you today," and at the sound of his name, Jake's lumbering idiot of a dog trotted over to the open door.

Jake released Mom immediately and pushed his way into the house to drop down and land on the living room floor with a laugh. Overgrown boy and dog rolled in a tumble of fur and long limbs while my mother addressed me with a tight smile. She crossed her arms over her chest and for just one fraction of a second, I wished she would just hug me the way she hugged my brother. Like *I* was a child trapped in a man's body, unburdened by adulthood and the truth about the world and her god.

"Are you staying for dinner?" she asked, probably out of obligation and not out of want.

I stepped inside and hung Jake's backpack on a hook beside the door. "I guess I could, if you have enough. I actually thought I'd give him a shave—"

"Dad can do it," she brushed me off with a shake of her head.

"But I always do it."

11

"Well, you don't always have to," she insisted brusquely. "Dad is perfectly capable, if you, for some reason, can't do it."

"You know it would be a battle if someone else did it," I retorted, my patience wearing thinner by the second.

"Oh, come on," she rolled her eyes, "it's *always* a battle, regardless of who does it, and you know that."

"Yeah," I shot back, sufficiently irritated, "and it'll be even *more* of one if—"

"Hey, why is it I always have to catch the two of you fighting?" Dad intervened, stepping into the living room from the kitchen wearing a strained grin. He worked a dishtowel around his hands and nudged his chin in my direction. "Hey, Blake. How's it going?"

"Great," I muttered, raking a hand through my hair and turning to watch Jake scrub his hands over Mickey's furry face.

"I was just telling Blake that you're *perfectly* capable of shaving Jake's face," Mom said to Dad, her tone so full of aggravation, I thought she might explode.

With a glance toward Dad, I saw the grin slip from his face, just as I thought it would. He pinched his lips and shrugged stiffly. "Yeah, yeah, sure. I could do that, if Blake was too busy or something." He shifted his eyes toward me and asked, "Are you too busy?"

"No," I shook my head and shot Mom a glare tinged with triumph and disdain, "I'm fine."

A thick discomfort swallowed the room in the way it always did. We were always so quick to irritate each other, so quick to fill the extensive spaces between us

12

with even more distance, packed tight with tension. I immediately felt stifled and a desperation for just a single breath of air wrapped its cold hands around my throat. I needed to get out. I needed to get back to Salem and back into my house, miles away from this place and the suffocation. Turning from my parents, I reached down to lightly rap my knuckles against Jake's shoulder, to instruct him to get upstairs and into the bathroom. But when he looked to me with an oblivious innocence, completely unaware of the lack of oxygen and enough silent threats to smother us all, I pulled a smile and decided to force my way through dinner. For him.

There wasn't anything I wouldn't do for him. Not when I owed him my life.

***

"Okay, buddy, I think you're all set," I said, rinsing his razor in the sink.

He sat shirtless on the toilet, with speckled remnants of shaving cream dotted around his jaw, neck, and cheeks. He watched me intently as I laid the razor on the vanity and grabbed a towel from the back of the bathroom door. It was as though he was trying to memorize the tasks I knew he'd never perform himself.

"Maybe next time, I can shave by myself," he told me. As he always did.

I smiled as I patted his face with the towel. "Yeah, maybe," I replied with a nod.

"You shave by yourself, right?" he asked, furrowing his brows as he tried to work through the quandary he seemed to face on a regular basis: *why can't I do the things Blake can?*

"Yeah," I said, nodding and then lifting my hands to my face, "but I don't, do I?"

He seemed to forget the question at hand as his lips spread into a grin. He shook his head. "You're hairy," he stated simply. "I wanna be hairy, too."

I scoffed playfully, shaking my head. "You can't be hairy."

"Oh, yeah?" he taunted, the grin never leaving his face. "Why not?"

"Because nobody would be able to tell us apart, that's why." I grabbed his shirt and playfully tossed it at him. It landed in his lap as his smile widened with enthusiasm.

He pulled it on and shouted, "Yes, they *would*!"

I laughed at the exasperation in his tone. "We look the same, dude!"

When his head popped through, he made no attempt to hide his eye roll. "We wear different clothes, duh."

"Well, maybe if *I* shaved to match *you*, I'd start to dress like you, too," I teased, quirking a brow. "I'd get myself some Mickey Mouse shirts, a Red Sox jacket …"

"No way!" He was nearly hysterical now, laughing boisterously and throwing his head back. "You don't even like baseball!"

I shrugged. "Hey, I used to be into it. Maybe if I shaved—"

A knock on the door stopped my words and I asked, "What's up?"

"Keep it down in there," Mom ordered from the other side. "Your father is trying to sleep."

Jake's eyes grew childishly wide, scared that we'd been caught laughing and having fun. I took a quick glance at my watch. It was barely eight o'clock at night, and I knew there was no way my dad had gone to bed this early. But I didn't call her out on her joy-killing bullshit, and instead replied, "Yeah, sure. Sorry."

I listened until her footsteps had reached the end of the hall before I rolled my eyes and flapped my hands mockingly. Just to make Jake smile, to hear his laugh again. Because I loved my brother, and nothing made me happier than seeing him happy. Even in these small, nearly insignificant ways.

Take that, Doc.

Chapter Two

I LIVED IN A warm and cozy three-bedroom house in suburban Salem, just blocks away from the town's life source. I welcomed the somber calm that I only felt here, within the town's force field. Close enough to be there for my brother when he needed me, with just enough distance to feel removed from my parents and the place I grew up.

The ghosts here were a lot friendlier than the memories at home.

My bones felt heavy from the interaction with my parents. They always did, every single day, but tonight, I was also left with a weariness I wasn't used to. Maybe it'd been my session with the good doctor, setting a different tone for the rest of the day, but something felt off, unbalanced, and I slogged my way toward the kitchen for a beer.

I didn't typically like to drink on a weeknight, but every so often, it was nice to take the edge off.

With a cold bottle in one hand and my phone in the other, I dropped into one of the two chairs at the table and looked across at the other, empty chair. I remembered when I'd bought the set a year ago, to replace the two worn-out tray tables I kept in the living room. I had told Dr. Travetti about that weekend. About the yard sale I'd stopped at and how I'd snagged the table and chairs for a song. When I'd shown her a picture, she just asked if I was going to buy anymore chairs, to which I had asked, "Why?"

I tipped the bottle back to my lips while my eyes remained trained on that chair. Sometimes I liked to imagine what it'd be like to sit across from someone who wasn't my mirror image, knowing very well that could never be anything more than a fantasy. Being Jake's brother was a full-time job, and one that didn't offer health benefits or a paycheck. Hell, I could barely carve out enough space in my life for my actual job that I needed to pay the bills. So, how the hell could I manage a relationship of any kind, with responsibilities like that holding me back and weighing me down?

Sighing, I resigned to browsing through my phone while finishing the beer. First things first, I checked my email and found a message from someone looking for some new ink. The message was short and vague, and I hated vague. I was very particular about the work I'd do, agreeing mostly to custom pieces and only making a few exceptions, and vague gave me absolutely nothing to work with. Never mind that I make it very clear on every social media outlet that I prefer a detailed description of the requested piece.

Scrunching my nose with disparagement, I shook my head, already suspecting this wasn't a job I'd end up taking. But still, I tapped out a quick message to request more info, even including my cell number, in case they'd prefer to speak directly. I sent the message away, then drained the beer before standing up from my small, two-person table.

In the heaviness brought on by the deafening silence of night, I didn't expect the phone to begin ringing from behind me. I peered over my shoulder at the lit screen, at the unknown number, and considered letting it go to voicemail. It was already late, and I needed to get some sleep. Five AM would be here before I knew it, and the routine of my day would begin all over again. But my better judgment was shushed by curiosity, and I reached for the phone, answering it before I had another chance to think twice.

"Blake Carson," I answered curtly.

"Hi!" came an upbeat, feminine voice on the other end. "So sorry if it's too late to call. I just got an email from you, with this number included, so I thought I'd—"

"It's cool. Don't worry about it," I interjected lightly, as my lips curled into a smile I knew was condescending. I hated being judged by superficial aspects of my being, and I hated even more to be a hypocrite. But, there was a certain type of person who was interested in my work, and if I was judging by her voice alone, this girl didn't fit the bill. Not by a long shot.

"Oh, good." The words were carried by a sigh of relief. "I'm really sorry I was so vague in my email. I was so excited it completely slipped my mind to tell you what exactly I wanted."

18

I took a seat at the table again and leaned back in the chair. "It's all right," I said, raking a hand through my hair and leaving it at the base of my neck. "So, what did you have in mind?"

"Well, actually, I was hoping I could come down to the shop tomorrow and show you."

The sigh that pushed through my nose was haughty. The statement matched her tone. This girl was interested in something she'd seen online, a shot she'd snagged from Google or Pinterest. Something that had probably been superimposed onto someone else. And now she wanted me to put it on her, and that was never going to happen.

Clearly, this was a waste of both of our time.

Still, this was my livelihood and there wasn't any sense in earning myself a bad review. So, I made the quick albeit difficult decision to remain cordial.

"You could," I told her, "but, if I'm being honest, I rarely do anything other than custom pieces. So, if you want, you can come in for a consultation and I could draw something up inspired by it—"

"Oh, um, I'm really looking to have this exact tattoo done, so ..."

My jaw ticked as her voice trailed off with her words hanging on the thick, tense air. "Okay. So, what I can do is, take a look at what you'd like to do, and then recommend you to one of the other artists at the shop. What style is—"

"Um," she interjected awkwardly, "actually, I really need this done by you, specifically."

19

I scrubbed a hand over my bearded jaw. I wouldn't argue with her and wouldn't allow my pride to mar my reputation as a professional, but it was obvious I'd need to put my foot down with this one. It happened occasionally, but damn, I hated it. It was a real test of my patience and I dealt with that enough as it was with my family.

"O-kay," I drawled, patronizingly, before putting her on speakerphone to open my phone's calendar. "I have a cancellation at nine o'clock tomorrow morning. The rest of the day is pretty booked-up, so unless you wanna come in another day—"

"No, that's fine," she said, her voice breathy with relief. "I really appreciate you making time for me."

"Yep," I replied shortly. "What's your name?"

"Audrey."

"Audrey?" I confirmed questioningly, my fingers hovering over the phone's keyboard.

"Yes. Like Audrey Hepburn."

I typed her name into my calendar. "Okay, Audrey. I'll see you tomorrow morning."

"Thank you so much. I'm really looking forward to it," she answered. I had no idea what this woman looked like, but I could picture her smile in the airiness of her words. So light and delicate, as curved and bubbly as a girl's handwriting. She probably dotted her i's with hearts and signed her name with a smiley face, and I could've kicked myself for my condemnatory smirk.

"Me, too," I lied, already predicting this would be a massive waste of my time. But at least it was in the morning. I'd get it over quick and go on with my day. No harm done. "Have a good night."

"You, too, Blake."

***

"Come on, Jake. Time to wake up." I opened the blinds in my brother's room, allowing the morning sunlight to stream across his Mickey Mouse comforter. "Gotta get you to school before you're late."

Jake mumbled something unintelligible and pulled the blanket over his head. I gently wrenched it from his hands and pulled it back.

"I don't wanna get up," he whined and pushed at my hands before rolling over. "Go away, Blake. I don't wanna get up."

"I know, buddy," I sympathized. In all of our lives, Jake had never been a morning person, and I felt guilty every day for waking him up. But someone had to get him up and get him to school, and since my parents would never do it without the battle of the century taking place, that someone had to be me. "You want some oatmeal for breakfast?"

"No way, José," he protested and rolled over again. "Go away."

"How about some fruit? An apple, or a banana, maybe?"

Jake finally rolled to face me. In his grasp, he held his ratty stuffed dog, Mutty. Sometimes, when his forehead crumpled with concern or the creases around his eyes deepened, it was easy to forget the challenges

21

he'd been burdened with. But in these moments, I could easily look beyond his exterior and toward the child within. When his mouth twisted into a pout like this, like he was four instead of almost thirty-four, it was hard to remember that this was my older brother albeit by two minutes.

"Banana with sugar?" he asked.

I raised an eyebrow and bargained, "Will you get up?"

"Uh-huh." He pulled himself into a seated position to prove he was good on his promise.

I crossed his bedroom to grab the clothes I'd laid out for him. "Will you get dressed?"

"You betcha." Jake held out his arms and I handed him the clothes.

"Okay. Then a banana with sugar, it is." I left his room and headed downstairs to the kitchen.

Mom and Dad sat at the table with coffee cups and cellphones in hand, playing the part of a picturesque American couple in their 60's, living comfortably in the 21st century. While my routine was to get my brother out of bed and to daycare before I headed to work, this was theirs.

Must be nice.

I grabbed a banana from the bowl of fruit on the table and went in search of the sugar. It'd been in the same spot my entire life, but today, when I needed it, it seemed to have gone missing.

Addressing my parents with a sigh, I asked, "Where'd the sugar go?"

Mom turned from her phone and pointed toward a white canister right in front of me. "Right there."

"These are new," I commented, opening the one clearly labelled Sugar. I felt like a moron for even missing it in the first place.

"Mom picked them up from the store a couple days ago," Dad said. "Nice, aren't they?"

"Not my style, but yeah, they're nice," I said, nodding as I grabbed a knife to slice the banana into a bowl.

Mom scoffed and shook her head. "Always have to throw your two cents in."

"Huh?"

Laying her phone down, she leaned back in her chair and pinned me down with a steely glare. "You can't just say, 'Yeah, Mom, they're nice.' You just *have* to add something negative. Why does it matter if they're not *your* style, Blake? You think I don't know that?"

"No," I muttered, pressing my lips into a thin, terse line.

"Okay. So, then why do you have to *say* it?"

I canted my head and gritted my teeth. My slicing quickened and became more aggressive. "I … don't know, Mom. Guess it's just all a part of my charming personality."

She uttered a disgusted noise and turned away from me. "Always negative. Always sarcastic," she mumbled under her breath and picked up her phone.

"Maybe I should put that on my resumé."

"Blake," Dad warned, shaking his head.

I turned away to grab a spoon and roll my eyes. Snippy retorts nagged at my tongue, but I didn't say anything more. I kept my lips sealed as I dusted the banana slices with sugar, giving my mother the opportunity to either fire back or accept the miniscule scrap of peace I'd offered by staying quiet.

Much to my surprise, she chose the latter.

Jake entered the kitchen with his sneakers on the wrong feet. I was about to say something as I placed his breakfast on the table, when Mom pointed it out first. She finished by saying, "Honestly, honey, are you ever going to learn? You're almost thirty-four years old, for crying out loud!"

My lips twisted with a hot anger as I ordered my brother to sit down and eat, before I dropped to my knees to help fix his shoes. He laughed innocently at my mother's probably well-intentioned jab. She never meant to be nasty toward him—she saved that for me, the negative, sarcastic, problematic son—but I couldn't help feeling the overwhelming need to defend him. To point out that he was *never* going to learn, no matter how old he got. And to ask her why she felt the need to rub it in his face, when he was all too aware of how different he was.

But I said nothing, choosing to keep the peace, until after Jake had eaten his breakfast and we were heading out the door. Mom gave Jake a hug, kissed his cheek, and wished him a good day, and as she turned to head back into the kitchen, she casually said, "You better drive safe, Blake, I swear."

She instructed me to drive safely every damn day, and I normally mumbled an agreement before getting out of there. But today, she'd thought to add that extra oomph with the "I swear." It felt like a threat, an attack, and I stopped with my hand on the door.

"When the hell have I ever been in an accident?" I foolishly asked, shaking my head with disgust.

Turning slowly on her heel, she cocked her head with a wash of incredulous disgust blanketing her features. "I'm going to pretend you didn't just ask me that," she spat at me before rushing into the kitchen, leaving me alone with the gaping hole in my chest neither of us would allow to heal.

***

"You look like shit," my co-worker and friend, Celia, eloquently pointed out as I hurried through the back door of Salem Skin.

"It's been a fuckin' day," I explained gruffly, dropping my leather jacket on the back of the couch in our breakroom.

"It's nine in the morning," she laughed, crossing her arms and smirking.

"And that should tell you how shit's been going for me, so don't piss me off," I threatened in jest.

She nodded with sympathy and tipped her head toward the front of the shop. "Well, it's about to get even better. Girl walked in about fifteen minutes ago asking for you. Said she made an appointment with you?"

I groaned under my breath and scrubbed a hand over my chin. I'd completely forgotten about the consultation I'd scheduled with that chick, Audrey. "Oh, shit," I muttered, shaking my head. "Yeah, we talked last night."

Cee smirked and her eyes crinkled with amusement. "Well, good luck with *that*. She's a freakin' *Barbie* doll, man."

"That bad, huh?"

"Let's just say, I don't envy you."

I grumbled a thanks and left the breakroom to head toward the front of the shop. Gus, my boss, sat at the counter with an issue of *ModInk* in hand. He lifted his head at the sound of my heavy footsteps and nodded a greeting before shifting a glance toward the young woman sitting on the couch. With her legs crossed, one foot swinging carefree in the air, her face was downturned as she scrolled through her phone. I couldn't discern from the angle what her features looked like, but from where I stood, it was clear she was attractive. Gus's eyebrows raised when he looked back to me, a suggestive glint in his eyes, and I smirked as my head shook.

She might've been pretty, but I knew, from the pastels she wore and the pink manicure on her long nails, she wasn't my type.

Casually stuffing my hands in my pockets, I took another step toward her. "Audrey?"

She lifted her eyes from the phone and smiled brightly at the sight of me. Hastily stuffing her phone in her bag, she rose to her feet and extended a hand. "You must be Blake! Hi! It's so nice to meet you."

I had to bite back my chuckle as I enveloped her palm in mine. "How's it goin'?"

"Good!" she exclaimed, nodding and pinning me to the spot with her powder blue eyes.

I would never say that I'd never seen eyes that color before—that'd make me a liar—but it was their shape and size that struck me dumbfounded. They were round and big, wide open as if she were always surprised by something. Like a deer perpetually caught in the headlights. There was something almost comical and cartoonish about them, and I might've even laughed, had they not suited the rest of her face so well. Her heart-shaped face and straight nose. Her full, bottom lip and the emphasized curve of her Cupid's bow. A small, pointy chin sat just above a long slender neck, leading the way to an exposed and delicate collarbone.

I didn't allow my gaze to wander below her neckline, I was a professional and composed myself as one. But she was the type of pretty you didn't find yourself facing every day, and while I'd never say I was attracted to her, I couldn't argue that she was irrefutably gorgeous.

"So, you said you had something in mind," I said, clearing my thoughts and releasing her hand.

"Oh, yes," she quickly replied, reaching into her bag to retrieve a piece of paper. As she began to unfold it, I spotted the colorful wings of a typical butterfly design. And somehow, I managed to quell my shudder.

"No. I don't think this is gonna work."

Her hands froze as those big, blue eyes met mine. "Oh, but um, I thought—"

"I'm sorry," I said, shaking my head. "I won't do it. I'll see if Celia wants to take a look, but otherwise, I really don't want to waste anymore of my time. Or yours."

From behind me, I listened as Gus cleared his throat. "Hey, uh, Blake? You wanna come chat with me for a second?"

I held in my groan, closing my eyes for a brief second, before turning. "Yeah, just give me a—"

"Actually, right now would be a really good time." He stood from the desk, holding my glare as he headed toward his office.

Pulling in a deep breath, I groaned and made a sharp right into the closet he called an office. "What's up?"

"Close the door, will ya?" I did as I was told and before I could get in a word, Gus continued. "Blake, I get you have your thing, and I've always been really cool about it. But it wouldn't kill you to get down off your high horse. You know. Just every now and then."

"My high horse?" I snorted, crossing my arms tightly over my chest.

"Yeah, your high horse," he repeated, his tone sharpening. "You know I like you, Blake. I love you, even. But I gotta tell ya, refusal to work with clients is not cool. We both have bills to pay."

"Come on, Gus," I groaned, shaking my head. "You're acting like I'm constantly turning people away. This chick brought in some Pinterest butterfly bullshit. Celia can do it."

"No, but turning *one* away looks like shit for the whole shop," he pointed out. "And that girl specifically

28

asked for you, so you're gonna make an exception this one time. Now, go out there and ink the prettiest damn butterfly you've ever done."

"You're killing me," I muttered, unwinding my arms and raking a hand through my hair.

"Yeah, maybe, but I'm still your boss. I'm allowed to kill you sometimes. Now, get out of here." And I decided, in that moment, that Gus was the devil and I was repenting for my abundance of sins. I sighed and left the office without another word. Audrey was still standing where I'd left her, with her hands clasped at the edge of the butterfly print.

"Let's go," I told her brusquely as I hurried past.

"O-oh," she stammered, collecting her purse and running to keep up with me. "We're doing it now? I thought you just wanted to look at it today."

"It'll be quick." I brought her to my station and aggressively wiped down my vinyl-covered chair with disinfectant. The willpower to not be a complete jerk was excruciating. "So, where are we putting it?"

"Oh, um, I was thinking maybe my hip?"

I looked at her exhaustedly. "I want you to be absolutely certain of where you're having me put this thing. No questions, no maybes."

"I thought you would give me your professional opinion," she admitted.

"Honey, you don't want my professional opinion."

Audrey's gaze narrowed curiously as she cocked her hip. "Why's that?"

"Because, in my professional opinion, you shouldn't be getting some Photoshopped crap you found on someone's Pinterest," I spoke frankly, struggling to keep my tone from sounding too snobby. "You shouldn't be getting some random butterfly because you think it's cute. You should be getting a one of a kind piece of art created specifically for you with your body and vision in mind, and—"

"It was my sister's," she cut in abruptly, her voice quiet and small. "She got it done by you a few years ago."

My gaze was still and blank as I stared at her. Sufficiently speechless, stunned, and stupefied. I took a gulp from my water bottle to wet my mouth, before asking, "Can I see that for a second?"

"Sure." She passed the picture to me and I studied it, trying my best not to let it show how much of a judgmental piece of garbage I suddenly felt like.

Only one half of the butterfly was colorful, while the other was grizzly. Splotched with black and grey, highlighted in white. I struggled to remember doing it and who I'd done it on. I did so many tattoos, it was hard to memorize them all. Hard to remember every meaning behind them. I didn't remember Audrey's sister, but I thought I might remember this tattoo. It was a transitional piece, I think. Meant to symbolize a change in her life, I think—or maybe not. *Fuck.* What did it mean? I couldn't recall and I immediately felt embarrassed for it.

I cleared my throat and rubbed a hand over my mouth. "Where does your sister have it?"

"Oh, my sister is dead."

At the blunt statement, my eyes shot up to meet hers. "Fuck. I'm sorry."

Audrey waved a hand and shrugged nonchalantly. "It's okay. Anyway, it was on her shoulder. So, maybe I should get it there, too?"

I chuckled and let my eyes soften. "Is that where *you* want it?"

She smiled almost bashfully. "Actually, I really wanted to get it over my heart, but I'm scared it'll hurt."

"It's going to, but the pain is temporary," I replied bluntly. "If that's where you want it to go, then that's where it should be. Nothing else will look right to you, and the last thing I want is for you to regret it."

A flicker of apprehension passed over her gaze before she toughened up and nodded. "Okay. Let's do it."

"All right. Let me just get the stencil drawn up. You can take a seat right here and we'll get started in just a few minutes."

***

"It's perfect," she announced, studying the wrapped tattoo in the full-length mirror. "Thank you so much."

"No problem." I tossed my black latex gloves into the trash. "Take your time. I'll meet you up front."

Celia snapped her gum and grinned at the sight of me. "Well, look who it is. The world's biggest asshole."

"Oh, fuck off," I grumbled as I shoved my way to the computer to calculate the cost of Audrey's tattoo.

"I only do originals," she mocked in a deeper voice. "Oh, wait, what was that? That *is* one of mine? Oops. My bad, har har."

"Cee, I'm gonna kick your ass in two seconds," I warned as Audrey came out from the back. She pulled her white sweater on, favoring her chest as she buttoned it up.

"How much do I owe you?"

"Well, I charge one-fifty an hour and we were working for three, so ..." A wash of guilt swept over me, remembering the way I'd treated her when I first saw her. Then, I shook my head. "You know what? Let's just call it fifty for the supplies."

Audrey looked absolutely flabbergasted. "What? No, I couldn't do that. I'll pay you for the three hours."

"Pay me for one, and we'll call it even," I haggled, offering her a smile.

Audrey sighed and pulled out her wallet. "Okay," she relented. "But, seriously, thank you so much. I really appreciate it a lot."

"I appreciate you not high-tailing it out of here when I was acting like a judgmental asshole."

I accepted her money and ran through the tattoo aftercare. Then, Audrey was out the door, with the familiar euphoria of fresh ink leaving its permanent mark on her skin.

I thought about that tattoo throughout the rest of my workday. I wondered about her sister, how she had died, and what brought Audrey in, years later, to have the butterfly done for herself. I regretted not asking her in the hours she'd spent in my chair. I'd been too self-absorbed in my own shame for jumping to conclusions based solely on her physical appearance. I hated so much when people did that to me, so why did I think it was okay to treat her in that manner?

It tormented me for the rest of the day. Thoughts of butterflies and assumptions. Siblings and stories. It kept me preoccupied and quiet while I worked, right until I snapped my gloves off for the final time that night.

"You're all set, man," I said to my last client of the day.

"You okay, bro?" he asked as he stood from the chair.

"Yeah," I assured him. "Just got some shit on my mind. How do you like it? We all good?"

He went to the mirror to assess my work and there he stood. Stunned. "Holy shit," he muttered, bicep proudly displayed. He marveled at the scythe and sword bordering the gritty black and white skull. "You are a legend," he gushed, unable to take his eyes off the tattoo.

"Glad you like it," I replied, brushing the compliment off. "I'm just gonna wrap you up."

"Yeah, yeah," he nodded, eyes still fixated on his reflection. "You ever think of opening your own place?"

"Nah," I lied, putting on a fresh pair of gloves and grabbing some plastic wrap for his arm.

"You're too good to be here, dude."

"Don't let my boss hear you say that. He's the one who taught me this shit."

"Well, the student surpassed the fuckin' teacher, that's for damn sure."

I smiled as I wrapped the fresh ink and tender skin in the plastic. I secured it with surgical tape and rang him up. A piece that big garnered a good tip, and I smiled at the wad of cash I'd accumulated throughout the day already in my pocket. I needed to go grocery shopping and with that money, it was going to be a good trip.

After work, I stopped at Jake's daycare to pick him up. I was surprised to find him in a good mood after such a long day, but, as reiterated by my brother, he had spent the time baking cookies with Miss Thomas and Mr. Scott. They had kept *Sesame Street* on the TV and allowed him to take over the table with their big box of Legos, and by the time I'd gotten there, he was the last guy left in the room.

"What are you doing this weekend, Jake?" Miss Thomas asked as I helped him into his windbreaker.

"What are we doing?" he asked me, watching intently as I pulled the zipper up to meet his chin.

I smiled, clapping my hands to his shoulders. "Come on, buddy. What do you do every weekend?"

"I watch cartoons and play with Mickey."

"Oh, boy, that sounds like fun," Miss Thomas said. "I bet you're excited."

"Mom loves having you home all day, right?" I said, grabbing his backpack.

"Yeah," he nodded fervently.

"And Mickey loves that you don't have to leave," I added pointedly.

"Mickey is my dog," Jake told Miss Thomas. "He's a Golden Retriever. Blake doesn't let him come over like me because he says he'll shit all over the house."

Miss Thomas snorted as I patted his shoulder and led him to the door. "What'd I tell you about filters, buddy?"

"Enjoy your weekend, guys," she called after us.

I knew Jake would enjoy the weekend with his dog and our parents. He always had a good time with the Lego sets our father picked up for him. He loved going on walks with Mom and Mickey. And I knew he especially enjoyed not waking up in the morning. But I was convinced nobody enjoyed the weekends more than me, when I was granted the sanctity of silence for a little over twenty-four hours. When I could kick my feet up, relax, and pretend my life wasn't controlled by the needs of my twin brother.

And sometimes, I even allowed myself to not feel guilty about it.

Chapter Three

IT WAS TOO EARLY to hit up the poetry club I frequented on the weekend. So, I spent that time babying my bike, giving the Harley the attention I wished I could give it during the week. With Nine Inch Nails filling the garage, I gave it a bath, polished the chrome, and wiped down the leather seat. I remembered when I bought the old girl, nearly ten years ago, with the promise that I'd get the chance to ride on a regular basis. That was before I accepted the realities of my life and before I really understood the responsibilities I'd always be saddled with.

After the bike was clean, and with some time left, I pulled out my phone to call Celia. She also got the weekends off and answered on the first ring.

"Hey, it's not really a good time," she said in a harsh whisper.

"What do you mean, not a good time?" I scoffed lightheartedly. "A good time for what? You don't even know why the hell I'm calling."

Cee snorted. "Well, I have a feeling it has something to do with an extracurricular activity you only get to partake in when you don't have your brother to deal with."

I laughed, pushing my dark hair back with a hand. "Guilty."

"Yeah, see I know you, Blake. You're predictable as fuck." She laughed again but I heard the regret in her voice, and I wished I hadn't called. "Seriously, I'd invite you over, but I have the kids tonight."

"I thought it was your ex's weekend." I seemed to recall a conversation from earlier in the week.

"It was, but he's got something to do for work, so he asked if I'd trade weekends." She sighed into the phone and said, "You know what? If you really wanted to do something, you could come by later—"

"Nah, it's cool," I quickly replied, not wanting to impose or put myself in an awkward position.

"You sure? 'Cause once the kids are in bed, I wouldn't turn away some company. As long as you kept that mouth of yours shut."

I considered the possibility. I'd never been to Cee's place while her kids were around. At six and four, she didn't want to complicate things by having her friend with occasional benefits around while they were, and I didn't blame her. I had too much on my plate as it was. The last thing I needed was to confuse a couple of kids who would never have a chance of calling me Step Daddy.

But still, it had been a while since I'd gotten laid, maybe two or three months, and those had been a few long months of unrelenting responsibilities and unending self-love before I passed out for the night. The company of another body sounded more like a necessity and less like a simple human pleasure, so I nodded thoughtfully and replied, "Yeah. Okay. Text me when they're asleep and I'll come by."

***

The highway wind whipped around me on the way to the club. Dusk had settled over Massachusetts in streaks of orange and pink, with dark clouds laying across the sky in silhouettes of black and shadow. I pulled into the parking lot and parked the bike into a spot. Judging from the amount of cars, there was a good turnout tonight. Good for the club, not so good for me. I didn't like the place too crowded. Didn't like the potential for attention. But this was more fruitful than any therapy session I'd had so far.

I took the stairs to the basement and was greeted by the bouncer, a big guy I never bothered to learn the name of. He nodded a familiar greeting at the sight of me and I offered one in return. Dim lights and the smell of nag champa greeted me in a calming embrace and I inhaled, breathing it in before heading over to the bar. I would only ever indulge in one drink—I was driving, after all—but I needed it tonight. Just one would be enough.

With an IPA in hand, I wandered to a darker corner of the already dark club and slumped into a chair wedged against the wall. In my black leather jacket and jeans, I was instantly submerged in the shadows, becoming a part of the darkness and not an obstacle inside of it. I could hide here for the night if I wanted, listening and deciding, and nobody would know I was there. It felt safe.

"Good evening, everyone," the club owner said, standing underneath the spotlight. "So glad to see such a crowd here tonight. We welcome all readings, as long as the work is original. Just put your name on the list and no cutting in line. The first poem of the night will be read by yours truly ..."

I tapped my fingers soundlessly on the table as she read her work. I always tried to keep my personal opinions at bay—it never felt like the place—but it was difficult to not scoff at the stereotypical prose of blackened tears and black-winged birds carrying the soul off to whatever afterworld there may or may not be. It was uninspired and lacking, and I was bored.

Luckily, the readings improved. I enjoyed a beautifully written sonnet about a tree, and another about a first love gone astray. I marveled at the talent of a young man with a broken heart clearly displayed on the sleeve of his shirt. And then, just when I thought I might put my own name on the list, the next reader stole my breath and dried my tongue.

"Hi everyone," she spoke into the mic. "This is my first time coming, but a couple of my cousins convinced me, so ... here I am. My name is Audrey and this poem is called Windswept."

As she read a short poem, about the dusty petals of a dandelion floating without control, I wondered if it was at all possible that it wasn't her, the woman I'd met a few days ago at the shop. Audrey wasn't an unpopular name, and this woman could've just looked similar. But I was fooling myself. The tattoo, faintly pink around the edges and beginning to scab, was displayed proudly on her chest. It was crisp and unmistakable, and I was desperate to hide from it, to sink into the wall behind me and disappear entirely.

She left the stage and headed in my direction, and my heart pumped noisily in my throat. There was no way she could see me—right? I was shadowed, lurking in the dark like a creep, but it was possible she'd seen me walk in—right? She could've noticed me sit down. She could've mustered the courage to approach me, once the adrenaline from being on stage took control. Did I *want* her to speak to me? The clamminess of my palms told me no, absolutely not, but the hopeful pitter-patter of my heart resounded with absolution and I held my breath. Waiting. Hoping. Dreading. Needing. This was my chance to find out about that tattoo, what it's story was, what brought her here to my little underground hideout.

But before she made it to me, she abruptly sat down two tables away, in the company of two other women. My heart sank with relief and the unsettling sensation of despair.

Later on, after the last poem had been read, I headed to the Harley with a relentless nagging in my brain, reminding me that I hadn't read my poem. I had written it and wanted to read it, to release it and throw it away, but I hadn't, in fear that Audrey would at once realize I was there and want to speak to me. But, I wanted her to. I wanted her to talk to me. Fuck, I wanted to talk to *her*, to ask my questions, to ask her out, to ask her into my bed, and ...

No. It was better she didn't. My life was too complicated, too busy, and consumed, and it would never work out well for anybody. Not me, and certainly not her. So, I hurried quicker and hoped to escape.

"Hey!"

It was her voice. That friendliness and airy lilt, threatening to turn on the light, and I took a glance over my shoulder. But she hadn't been talking to me. It was someone else, presumably one of her aforementioned cousins, and I breathed out the relief and breathed in the disappointment as I went to climb on the back of my bike and take off for Cee's place.

***

"Jesus, Blake," Cee groaned in protest, and I rolled to the side, unable to hide my frustration. "Aggressive, much?"

"Sorry," I muttered with defeat, sitting up and draping my arms over my knees.

"What's up with you tonight?" She lit a cigarette to add to the scent lingering in her sheets and in her hair. I never liked the smell of cloves and smoke much, and maybe that was another reason we would never have more than the occasional hook-up. But it was still so uniquely her, and I breathed in that smoke, finding comfort in knowing I was here. With Cee, and not back at the club with Audrey.

"Nothing," I lied, not wanting to get into it.

"Yeah, okay," she drawled around an eye-roll. "How many times have we slept together?"

"I don't know," I shrugged.

"Yeah, me neither," she laughed lightly through her nose, "but it's been enough for me to know you always get off, and tonight, you didn't. So, what's up?"

I didn't want to get into it. There was no reason to, and what the hell would I say, anyway? That seeing the chick with the butterfly tattoo had shaken me up so thoroughly, I couldn't come? It was absurdly pathetic, not to mention completely uncharacteristic of me to let something so meaningless bother me, so I merely lifted a hand and waved it flippantly.

"It's just been a long week, I guess," I said, offering her an explanation that wasn't entirely a fabrication of the truth. "I thought this would help me relax, but I guess not." I glanced over my shoulder at her with her dreadlocks fanned out against the pillow. I mustered a smile and added a genuine, "Sorry."

Clipping my shoulder with her knuckles, she replied, "Hey, you still got me off, so there's nothing for you to be sorry for," and she laughed.

"You're welcome," I drawled, chuckling.

"Maybe you just need to sleep. I mean, when was the last time you got some really, *really* great sleep?"

I shook my head. "I don't even know."

Her hand laid against my shoulder and her clawed fingers squeezed gently. The touch was that of a friend and I found a gentle comfort in it as I sighed. "Then maybe that's all you need."

"Maybe," I replied, nodding and wishing it was that easy.

"Anyway, um, I actually wanted to talk to you about something," she said, removing her hand from my shoulder.

No conversation starting that way ever went well. "Yeah?"

"I wanna start dating again," she blurted out, finally putting the cigarette to her lips.

I shrugged and turned toward the door. "Okay. Good for you."

"So, I'm no longer available for booty calls," she further explained before taking a puff and holding the smoke in her lungs.

Laughing, I shook my head. "Was tonight a parting gift or some shit?"

"God, no!" she shouted, voice strained by tense lungs, and clapped a hand over her mouth as she coughed, startled by the volume of her own voice and her eyes went wide. Lowering her hand slowly, she repeated in a hiss, "No. Jesus Christ, Blake, of course not."

"I was kidding, Cee, it's fine."

"I'm sorry," she added quietly.

"Really. It's cool," I assured her, masking the sting of rejection with a chuckle.

"You know, maybe you should find someone, too," she suggested. "You're not getting any younger and you're a great guy. There's gotta be some little witch out there just dying to find her dark prince."

"Oh, yeah. They're just lining up," I chided sardonically. "But seriously, you know I can't make that shit work. I have too much going on and I can't focus on a relationship. Casual shit is best for me." Then I caught myself before I launched into a total pity fest. Before I could make her feel guilty for ending what we'd always known was a temporary thing. "But really, I'm good."

"You sure?"

"Yes," I stated firmly as I got out of bed to get dressed, unable to shake the loneliness that hung over me in the dark that had once felt so friendly.

Chapter Four

"HOW WAS YOUR weekend, Blake?" Dr. Travetti crossed her legs. She was rocking a yellow pantsuit today and with her tall, lean frame, it gave her the unmistakable resemblance of a pencil.

"It was okay."

"What did you do?" She laid her clipboard against her lap and tapped the end of the pen against the metal clip.

I shrugged, leaning forward to plant my elbows to my knees. "Cleaned the bike, called Celia—"

"Celia?"

"I've told you about Celia. She's my friend. I work with her."

"I know," she said. "But why did you call her?"

"To hang out, I guess. Why?"

Dr. Travetti wasn't buying that bit of bullshit. She knew my history with Cee. "To hang out, or to have sex?"

I released a heavy sigh and shook my head. "Does this seriously matter right now?" She scribbled something onto the first sheet of paper and I lowered my brow with scrutiny. "What was that?"

"Just writing, Blake. Keep telling me about your weekend."

"No, I'm curious. What did you write?"

Laying the pen back down on the board, she folded her hands and leveled me with a glare. "Tell me something, Blake. Why did you immediately get defensive when I asked if you called Celia to have sex?"

"Because it's irrelevant, and none of your business."

"It was a simple question. An innocent one, at that."

"I don't know why the hell it matters if I call my friend for sex or not. It was a mutual agreement between us, and she doesn't want to anymore, anyway so—"

"Why doesn't she want to?"

I lifted a hand and dropped it angrily to the arm of the chair. "Once again, Doc, none of your business—"

"You brought it up, Blake."

I groaned in reply. "Whatever," I muttered dismissively, then added, "And if you *really* wanna know, she wants to start dating again, so that's the end of our thing."

"That bothers you," she assessed. "Did *you* want to date her?"

I scoffed and shook my head. "Hell no. Cee and I are friends and co-workers. That's all. Yeah, I mean, we hooked up every now and then, but there's nothing more than that between us."

"Then, what bothers you about her dating someone?"

I furrowed my brow. "I don't know."

"But it does bother you."

"Yeah, I guess it does a little," I relented.

She waved a hand toward me. "Well, try to explain it to me."

I unburdened myself with a huff and pressed my back to the chair. "You know, Doc ..."

"Try, Blake," she encouraged gently. "You only bring these things up when I know you want to talk about them, so just try."

Raking my fingers through my hair, I looked up to the ceiling and without a second thought, I began to speak. "I don't know. I guess maybe I feel a little rejected. A little frustrated, too. I thought we had a good thing going. I mean, we've been doing this shit for years. We always kept the sex from getting between our work relationship and how rare is that? I don't even think Gus suspected anything. We kept that shit separate. But now, she decides she wants to date people, and I get it. She doesn't wanna have to explain her fuck buddy to them, that's fine, but what am I supposed to do? I know that makes me sound like a selfish prick, but I mean, seriously. It's not like we fucked regularly or anything, but every now and then, the mood struck, and we were there for each other. But now ..." I shrugged with defeat.

"Now you feel alone," she finished for me.

"Yeah," I concluded as my gaze traced the outline of crown molding. "I guess that's it."

"Are you jealous?"

Bringing my attention back to her, I laughed darkly. "*Jealous*? Of who?"

"Celia? Or … whoever she ends up dating?"

I laughed again. "Nah, I'm not jealous. I told you. I don't feel like that about her."

"No," Dr. Travetti said sternly. "I meant, are you jealous that she might have someone soon, and you don't?"

"Hell no." I snickered, tipping my head back again.

"Why is that so hard to believe?"

"Because I don't want someone."

There was a long pause, too long, and I looked back to the good doctor to make sure she hadn't disappeared altogether. What I found was Dr. Vanessa Travetti, pursing her pretty lips and assessing me for too many seconds longer than I would've liked. She was picking me apart, playing her mind games, and the longer she watched, the more I wanted to yell at her. But before I could speak, she finally asked, "Do you want to know what I think?"

"Not really," I snorted a bitter chuckle. "But sure. Hit me."

She smiled fondly. "I think you *do* want someone. I think you have spent a very long time forcing yourself into thinking you don't, whatever be the reason, but deep down, there's a part of you that craves affection. That's why you turned to Celia in the first place. She's the closest thing you've had to an actual girlfriend, and—"

"I've had girlfriends before, Doc."

"When? In the time you've been seeing me?"

48

I shook my head, then shrugged. "I guess not since, uh … college, maybe? I don't know." I tried to conjure a vivid memory of my last girlfriend. She was a feisty little punk with a duo of tongue rings. Hot as fuck with a nice ass. But the moment she called my brother an idiot, I kicked her out of my car and out of my life.

"That's a long time ago, Blake," she answered gently. "And now that Celia is removing herself from serving that position in your life, I think you're realizing that you're going to miss it."

I barked with a laugh. "I turned to Celia because we were both horny as hell one night and we were both single. We were convenient for each other then, but now, we're not. She's got the opportunity to find someone, and I'm alone. It's always gonna be that way, so ... End of story."

Dr. Travetti lifted her head with intrigue. "Why did you say that?"

Why *had* I said it? I should've bitten my tongue. But then, wasn't this the very reason why I'd signed up for therapy in the first place? To talk to someone?

"Because." I brushed it off with a flip of my hand.

"Because why, Blake?"

"Because it's fucking true."

She nodded slowly. "Does this have to do with your brother?"

I gritted my jaw. "Don't bring him up again, Doc."

"But it does, doesn't it?"

"I don't know what you want me to say to that."

"I want you to tell me the truth. This is the safest place, Blake. I won't judge you."

49

"No, but you'll write some shit on your fucking clipboard, won't you?"

"I might."

"Well, isn't that the same thing?"

With an assertive smile, she picked up her board and tossed it gently across the coffee table to me. It landed in my lap and I furrowed my brow. "Now *you* have my clipboard. I have nothing to write on."

I hummed contemplatively. "Touché, Doc."

"Well?"

I read the lines she'd scribbled earlier. "*Defensive when talking about Celia. Angry? Jealous?*" I twisted my lips at the sight of those words. Seeing them written so plainly, in the good doctor's pretty script, drove them like spears through my skin and they pierced my heart with their pointy little T's and that arrowhead A.

"The truth is, Doc," I swallowed, resigning myself to speak a truth I never thought I'd utter aloud, "I've spent a long time being jealous of other people. Friends, relatives … It just felt really unfair, because you know, when I was a kid, shit was great, until it wasn't, and I'd start to watch these TV shows and movies for an escape. I'd find myself feeling so ridiculously jealous of fuckin' Ross Gellar, whose only real problem was whether Rachel was into him today or not. How pathetic is that?"

"Everybody does that, Blake. We all envision ourselves in scenarios foreign to us. The grass is always greener on the other side, or so they say—"

"Yeah, but see, Doc, for me? The grass is *actually* greener. It's bright and vibrant and fucking beautiful. I'm unbelievably jealous that Celia can go out and find herself a boyfriend. I mean, I'm happy as hell for her, wish her the best and all that, but I'm jealous that she doesn't have to worry about what her brother would think. How he'd react. If he'd throw a fit if something was set just a little off kilter in his life. Or ..." I wiped a hand over my mouth and shook my head. "Or fuck, what if the guy had a problem with her brother? What if this guy found out about him and ran for the fucking hills? Because that brother is a permanent fixture in her life, and she will have to care for him forever. That's not a choice she has, it's just the way it is, but that guy? He can leave. He can get as far away from it as he can, and he fucking *should* because dealing with that brother is exhausting and draining and so fucking *consuming*, never mind her parents, and ..." My words floated away as I stared at her, lips parted and breathing hard.

"Something tells me we're not talking about Celia anymore." Dr. Travetti offered me a small albeit sympathetic smile.

I wiped a hand over my face and allowed myself to chuckle. "Wow, Doc. What the fuck was your first clue?"

***

"What'd you end up doing on Sunday?" Celia asked with trepidation. She stood at my station, hip checked and arms crossed, as I cleaned and got things set up for my first client.

"I hung around the house," I answered without missing a beat. My morning session with Dr. Travetti had left me jarred, open and vulnerable. But I wouldn't let Celia know about that. "How was your day?"

"Good. I actually had a date after my ex picked the kids up for dinner," she replied.

"Wow," I muttered dryly. "You don't waste any time, huh?"

Her cheeks pinked slightly. "Actually, I, uh, already had the date planned. I just hadn't told you about it, 'cause I—"

"Didn't want me to be jealous?" I lifted a brow, uttering the inside joke I only understood after my session with the good doctor.

"Yeah, maybe." Celia grimaced. "So, uh … Are you?"

"Nope," I replied. Then for good measure, I added, "How did it go?"

"Great, actually." The thrill of potential love pricked at the corners of her lips. She had never looked at me that way. Nobody ever had. "We went and saw the new Marvel movie, grabbed some dinner, and went back to his place to chill."

Chill was code for fuck, or at the very least, mess around. Even though I knew Celia in the biblical sense, knew what she sounded like in the heat of the moment, I noted that it didn't bother me in the slightest that she had been intimate with someone else. It felt marginally triumphant, knowing for certain that I didn't in fact want her, if there'd been any doubt in my mind at all.

"He a good guy?" I met her eyes with sincerity, and she smiled, nodding.

"He is. He's sweet. Divorced with two kids."

I laughed. "Holy crap, Cee. *You're* divorced with two kids. If you guys get married, you could have some real *Brady Bunch* shit going on."

"Oh, God," she groaned and rolled her eyes playfully. "I'm not even close to thinking about another marriage."

The front door jingled open and I stood up from my stool. "First comes love, then comes marriage, then comes Cee with a baby carriage," I sang teasingly as I walked away.

"Shut your damn mouth! My tubes are tied!" Celia called back as I grinned to myself and entered the waiting area.

I'd been expecting my first client of the day, a guy named Felix, with a fondness for skulls. Another person who'd found my work through my Instagram account and had wanted something dark and gloomy permanently imprinted on their skin. That's who I had expected to find waiting on the old, brown leather couch, but who I found instead was a tall guy, about my height and with my shared affinity for black attire. Black, white, and shades of grey crawled from the collar of his jacket, covering his neck and creeping over the curve of his jaw and chin. He slid a pair of sunglasses off, revealing a small cross beside his left eye, and I watched as he took in the shots of art covering the walls.

"Hey, can I help you?" I asked, stuffing my hands into the pockets of my jeans.

The guy turned to face me and a cool smirk quirked his lips. He pointed toward a few of my more popular pieces and said, "This shit is absolutely sick. Yours?"

53

"Yeah, they're mine," I confirmed casually.

"So, you're Blake Carson." I nodded affirmatively in response and he stepped forward, hand extended. "It's awesome to meet you. I'm Shane Easton, editor for *ModInk Magazine*. Ever heard of us?"

ModInk was one of the leading publications showcasing body modification. If you were in the business, or at all interested in tattoos, piercings, or other realms of the body mod world, you knew of *ModInk*. Shaking Shane's hand, my heart hammered a mile a minute, beating much faster than was healthy. Still, I managed to keep my composure, as I smiled cordially and nodded.

"Of course. Been a fan for years," I replied coolly, while hoping my palm wasn't too clammy. "What brings you to Salem?"

"You mean other than the history and awesome shit to do?" He released my hand and took a step back. "I came to check you out in person, my man."

I crossed my arms and cocked my head. My resolve to remain cool and collected was slipping away by the second. "No way. How, uh ... how did you find my work?"

"Well, I was checking some stuff on Instagram," he said, pulling his phone from a pocket.

"Ah, of course," I replied with a nod. "You found my page."

"Well, no. Not exactly," he corrected, and turned his phone to me. "I found this one, and from there, I found *your* page."

I had to blink and clear my mind of the image before I could look at his phone again, just to be sure I'd seen it correctly. But when I opened my eyes, there it was, just as I had thought. The picture of a butterfly, one half beautiful in splashes of color and the other bold in black and white, gritty and dripping with morbidity. I had once forgotten I'd even tattooed this image onto anybody's body, and now, I couldn't seem to escape it.

"This piece is absolutely killer," he went on. "I mean, there are so many talented artists out there, and so many of them can adequately dabble in multiple styles. But this vision, the flow of the watercolor and the seamless transition into this sooty black and white ... I don't know. It's not exactly unique, but at the same time, it's nothing I've ever seen before. The craftsmanship, man ..." Shane laughed, shaking his head as he looked around the shop's waiting area. "I gotta be honest, I didn't expect to find you in a hole in the wall like this."

I was too in shock to laugh with him about the grungy, outdated state of the shop. Too startled to react. Shane's laughter waned as he tucked the phone back in his jacket pocket.

"Anyway, I was hoping you'd let me run an article about you in an upcoming issue of *ModInk*," he cut to the chase, eyeing me with hopefulness.

"Shit," I uttered. I heard footsteps approaching from behind me. Celia had overheard. "You're serious?"

"Fuck yes, man. I'd love to interview you and show off some of your work. And hey, if you have some free time, I have a bit of skin on my leg that's all yours." He patted his left knee and chuckled easily.

I knew what was being presented to me. It was an open door. The opportunities that awaited me over the threshold would change my life and leave me without a shred of down time for years to come. But fuck fuck FUCK! I also knew what that meant for my personal life. What would I do about Jake? How could I continue to closely care for him while experiencing a surge in my career? God, this was all I'd ever wanted and dreamed about, but the call of real-life responsibility had its hands tight around my neck, and it was choking the fucking life out of me.

"I'd be happy to get you in. How long are you here for?"

Shane grinned with the promise of fresh ink on the horizon. "I took the week."

"Awesome. I'll check my schedule and get you in sometime over the next couple of days."

"And that interview?" He was optimistic, but in that moment, I was the destroyer of hope.

I smiled apologetically. "Can I think about it?"

Shane was visibly taken aback and unsure of how to react. I imagined he didn't get turned down often and a *can I think about it* might as well have been a *no*. But he nodded and smiled diplomatically, accepting my answer with professionalism, and I headed back for my phone to check my schedule.

Celia followed.

"You'll *think* about it?" She hissed disbelievingly. "Have you completely lost your mind?"

"I think that happened a long time ago," I muttered dryly, grabbing my phone.

"Blake, seriously!"

"I didn't say no," I pointed out, tapping through my calendar.

"Yeah, okay. And my ex-husband didn't really fuck his secretary by letting her suck his dick."

I curled my lip with disgust. "What a clichéd douchebag."

"Yeah, he is, but whatever, we're not talking about him. We're talking about you, and you don't turn down *ModInk*, Blake. You don't fucking do that. You *need* this."

I narrowed my eyes. "You're not jealous?" My session with the good doctor came back to me in a rush of heat and embarrassment. I imagined a bright, tomato red, flourishing over my cheeks and dripping over my neck, giving me away and calling attention to the secrets I had shed before.

"Jealous?" She scoffed incredulously, shaking her head. "I'm not jealous, but I *am* going to be pissed if you don't grab that opportunity by the balls, you moron. You deserve this."

I was touched, but I wasn't convinced I deserved anything. So, I simply smiled gratefully and repeated, "I'll think about it," and before I could listen to her protests, I headed back up front to pencil Shane in.

***

Shane had given me the green light to design a fresh piece for him. He didn't want to provide me with any input or inspiration, and while the freedom was delicious and made my fingers itch with excitement, I couldn't deny the pressure it put me under. Whatever I did for him would undoubtedly end up on the *ModInk* Instagram page, at the very least, and my name would be known to the world of body modification and alternative style. I wanted this tattoo to be good. Fuck, I wanted it to be amazing—my best, even. And that was a stress I could've done without, especially while attempting to leave my parents' house as my brother threw a boisterous anger-fueled tantrum in his bedroom.

"You guys got this?" I asked Mom and Dad, just as a crash and the telltale sound of Legos scattering filled the stairwell. I groaned and faced the sound, as both my parents pinched their eyes shut with exhausted disdain.

"Go handle him," Mom demanded. I thought she was speaking to me, when I noticed her looking at Dad.

"What? We're watching this!" Dad gestured toward the TV. Funny, when he'd hardly paid attention to, whatever was playing, until he actually needed to do something. "Why don't you deal with him?"

"I deal with him all the damn time. You could pretend to be his father and do something, you know. Give me a freakin' break once in a while," she snapped, and I groaned loudly.

"Never mind," I growled, and stormed up the stairs to follow the sounds of combusting Legos.

I didn't bother to knock, just threw the door open, and found my brother close to tears in the center of his room. A multicolored storm of blocks laid at his feet and his fists clenched at his sides.

"What's going on in here?" I demanded to know.

Jake kicked at the pile of Legos and they scattered further over the carpet. "They wouldn't stick. I put them together and I put them together and they kept coming apart. They wouldn't stick. They're broken."

"They're not broken," I insisted. "Sometimes they just fit looser—"

"They're *broken*!" My brother turned on me with fiery rage, clenching his fists so tight they shook.

"Jake, buddy, they're not—"

"They're. BROKEN!" He broke the words with kicks of his feet and the blocks sprayed in every direction, hitting the walls like tiny plastic bullets. The tantrum wasn't unlike a toddler's, if the toddler was six-foot-two with impressive physical strength for someone who watched so much TV. I kept myself tougher, stronger, but Jake had the capability to do serious damage if he got the upper hand. And right now, he was close to that point. He was beyond reasoning. Too far gone.

I sighed and coaxed a calm when all my body wanted was to lash out in frustration. "Hey," I said, speaking in a soothing tone and stepping into the room, "you wanna go watch something on TV?" I reached out, seeking his shoulder. "We can put on Mickey, or maybe *Daniel Tiger*. I can get you a snack, if you—"

"No!" He swatted at my hand, knocking me out of the way. But I persisted, reaching out once again and meeting my mark. I squeezed his shoulder and felt the tension in his bones start to slip away. "We can have a snack and watch *Daniel Tiger*?"

"Yeah, buddy."

We stood in the middle of the mess he'd made not five minutes before when he was tyrannical and menacing. It was almost hard to believe this could be the same guy, now meeting my eye with a sweetness in its purest form.

"This room is a mess," Jake stated, so matter of fact, and I pushed myself to smile.

"Yeah, but we'll clean up later before I head home, right?"

"You betcha."

So, we sat on his bed with bowls of pretzels and *Daniel Tiger* playing on the TV. With my sketch pad on my lap, I managed to work on my concept for Shane, in between Jake's incessant questions and commentary. But all the while, one thought rang loud and clear in my mind. The same thing that I'd known to be true for a long time.

Jake would be with me forever, and as long as he was there, my life would be his. There wasn't room for anything, or anyone, else. And there never would be.

Chapter Five

I BOOKED A LAST-MINUTE session with Dr. Travetti the day of Shane's appointment, and after dropping Jake off at daycare, I barreled into the office with determination singeing my veins. My leather jacket was splattered with the beginning of a thunderstorm, my favorite weather, and on any other occasion, I would've found the dark clouds soothing. But today, I saw them as a premonition from a god I could never believe in.

"This is new," she declared, gesturing toward me before sitting in her chair.

"What is?"

"You coming in here unannounced."

I screwed my face with confusion. "Unannounced? I made an appointment this morning."

"You did?" Surprise widened her eyes and she quickly checked her phone, probably searching through her schedule. "Ah, you did. This is what I get for running late in the morning."

I snorted at her admission. "So, you're telling me the good doctor is human."

"More than you know," she said with a small, sad smile, revealing a side of herself I'd never seen before. I wondered if I'd ever see it again as she asked, "So, are you okay?"

The question was tied to a smile but full of concern, and I lowered my brows at the insinuation. "Why wouldn't I be okay?"

"Well, you gotta see that this is different for you, Blake. You're usually very regimented. You keep a strict schedule. You're very much a creature of habit, and you've been seeing me every Monday morning for the past two years, and suddenly, out of the blue, you need a last-minute appointment. So, back to my initial question—are you okay?" She smiled encouragingly without any glimmer of sadness and I missed it. That sadness had made her more relatable.

"Yeah, I'm fine ..." The assuredness in my voice wavered and she noticed.

"Are you?"

With a sigh, my elbows planted to my knees, the leather of my jacket creaking with the movement. "I think so?" I looked to her for corroboration and she laughed incredulously.

"I can't tell you if you're fine, Blake. But I do think something brought you in here, so ..." She shrugged innocently.

I turned my head and looked out the window. Her office was on the second floor of a building overlooking Derby Square in Downtown Salem. The cobblestone streets called my name within this historical town. It was where I granted my soul the permission to come alive when the sun set and the moon rose and my dreams breathed. If things were different, if *life* was different, this was where I'd open up my own shop. In the heart of the history of my favorite place on Earth.

If things were different ... Even with the use of an *if*, I felt I looked at it as an option, when I shouldn't be thinking it at all. It wasn't possible. It wasn't happening. It was no less improbable than the sun dropping from the sky at this very second, and the finality formed a lump in my chest that moved to my throat and made me shudder with defeat.

"Blake?"

I shook my head at the window, at Old Town Hall and the brick steps and the pedestrians with rain-dotted umbrellas. "Shit's been weird," I blurted.

"How do you mean?"

Turning from the rain and the cloudy sky, I elaborated. "Last week, some chick ..." I stopped myself, feeling instantly disrespectful to this woman I didn't know but remained haunted by, and I started over. "This woman, Audrey, emailed me, looking for a tattoo. Then, when she came into the shop the next day, I took one look at her and jumped to conclusions like a total dick. I never do that, I'm not a judgmental prick, but I said shit I shouldn't have. Yet, instead of walking out of there like a normal person, she stayed. She wanted this tattoo done by me specifically, because apparently, it was something I had designed years ago."

"You didn't remember it?"

I hesitated before shaking my head. "I didn't, and that in itself was embarrassing. I mean, I've been doing this shit for a long time, Doc, so naturally I'm not going to remember every skull or raven I put on someone. But this fuckin' thing ..." I scrubbed a palm over my scruffy face. "I feel like I should remember it because it's so *different*. To the best of my knowledge, it's the only piece I've done with color in it, the only one *ever*. I don't know why I'd even agree to doing it, based on that alone. It's not my style."

"You didn't ask?"

I shook my head. "I was too blindsided by what a fucking dick I'd been. I'm not usually that mean, you know? I'm an angry motherfucker, but I'm not *mean*. Not like that."

"Hm ..." Dr. Travetti wrote on her clipboard and I didn't get a chance to question what she was scribbling before she said, "Go on."

"Anyway, uh ... I've had a hard time getting this tattoo out of my head, and when I'm not thinking about it, it's following me. I mean, it's the craziest shit."

She lifted her head, tipped her chin, and asked, "What do you mean, it's following you?"

"Well, uh ... I saw her—Audrey—at the poetry club on Saturday."

"You saw her? Have you ever seen her there?"

I shook my head affirmatively. I would have noticed her before. "Nope."

"Interesting. Did you speak to her?"

"No." My response was too rushed, too brash, and Dr. Travetti tilted her head with question.

"But you wanted to."

"What? I didn't say that. Why do you always—"

Her head tipped in the other direction as a small smile stretched across her face. "Can you do me a favor, Blake?"

"What?"

"I'd like you to not get defensive for one session, and because this is a shorter one, I'd like you to try that today. Can you do that?"

I sighed and slumped into the chair. "Fine. I'll do my best to make you proud."

Her laugh was sniffed and quiet. "Thank you. Now, why didn't you talk to her?"

I shrugged as if I didn't know, but still I said, "Because what's the point?"

"The point is to make a human connection, and we've already established that you crave affection."

"And we've already established why that can't happen. There is literally no room in my life for that shit. And in any case, I didn't talk to her, so whatever. It's done."

"Okay," she concluded with a stiff nod. "So, why are you here then, if this happened on Saturday?"

I cut my fingers through my dark mass of hair. "Because on Monday, the editor for *ModInk* walked into the shop, and he wants to interview me."

Dr. Travetti cocked her head like a curious dog, and I explained why exactly that was an enormous deal. With wide, hopeful eyes, she said, "That's amazing, Blake! What an incredible opportunity."

"Yeah, it is. Except I have to turn him down. I know what would happen the second he puts my shit in that magazine, or hell, even on his social media. Business would pick up, and as much as the shop itself could use it, they wouldn't be coming for Gus, Celia, Kara, or Matt. They'd want *me*, which means longer hours, more work. I'd have to work weekends, and I need my weekends, Doc. I need ... I need my time, you know? So," I finished with a rueful sigh and a shrug, "I gotta decline."

"Sounds like you've made up your mind."

I nodded, unable to meet her eye. "Yeah. I'm doing his tat today, and I'll break the news to him."

"So, what do you need me for?"

I fidgeted with the zipper on my jacket, pulling it up and listening to the hum of metal clicking against metal. "I need you ..." The words caught in my throat and they died in a whisper.

"You ... need *me*?" The question was accusatory. Dr. Travetti pressed a hand to her chest, and I hurried to patch up the insinuation.

Clearing my throat, I said, "I need you to tell me I'm doing the right thing."

Sympathy wiped away her startled expression. Her eyes softened and her fingers clenched her pen. "You know I can't do that, Blake. I can help you find the answer, but I can't tell you what the answer is."

"But isn't that your job?"

Her smile was small and regretful. "It's not. But I can tell you, if you're questioning yourself this much, you might want to reconsider. Your intuition is telling you something and maybe you should be listening."

I scrubbed a hand over my face and raked my fingers through my hair. "You know, this wouldn't be such a fucking problem if it wasn't for that goddamn tattoo."

She cocked her head. "Why do you say that?" she asked, and I told her about how Shane had found out about me in the first place. Dr. Travetti took in the new piece of information and with a drawn-out sigh, she leaned back in her chair. "Blake, what do you think about signs?"

"Signs?" I snickered. "What do you mean? Like from God or some shit?"

"From God, from the universe ..." Her hand waved gracefully around in the air. "Wherever."

I laughed and shook my head. "Doc, I thought you were a woman of science, and then you gotta throw in some religious B.S.."

"*Is* it B.S.?"

I lifted my eyes, leveling her with a condescending glare. "Yes. Yes, it fucking is. Signs are bullshit. God is bullshit. The universe is bullshit. It's all *bullshit*."

"You're getting defensive again," she said pointedly.

"No. I'm not. I'm getting honest. None of us have a plan laid out for us by some almighty, mythical being. We're all mistakes on this mistake of a planet, floating through our lives of good shit and bad shit until we die. The end."

"That's very bleak, don't you think?"

I snorted and tipped my head back to assess the popcorn ceiling. "Can't spell Blake without bleak," I muttered under my breath.

"What's that?"

"Nothing."

With the sigh of the defeated, Dr. Travetti tossed her clipboard unceremoniously onto the coffee table and said, "I want you to read what I wrote."

"Oh, I have your permission?" I questioned condescendingly.

"Yes." She gestured toward the paper, and I leaned forward with a smirk I wasn't quite proud of.

Dammit, I really was being defensive and I wasn't proud of it. In fact, I felt like a child. But she'd struck a nerve with that God shit. The weak and desperate fell on God, while the realists see the world for exactly what it is. Is it depressing? Sure, but so is the brutal and tragic reality that some kids are born perfect, full of potential and promise, only to have their problematic brother steal it all away.

With a bored sigh, I lowered my gaze to the page, and there in bold black cursive, I read, "*Why won't he give himself a chance*?" The question was circled once, twice, and underlined, like this was the good doctor's purpose in life to answer this one, stupid question.

I looked back to her and asked, "What do you want me to say to this?"

She dropped her pen into her lap. "I want you to tell me why you live like this. Why you're so pissed off. Why you won't let yourself live your damn life."

"I already told you, my br—"

"You blame a lot on Jake, I know, and maybe that blame is justified to an extent. But you're not the only one in a situation like this, Blake, and many of those other people live their lives the best they can. So, what is it about *your* special situation that makes you different from them? Why is it such a struggle for *you* to live?"

Anger, rage, and the ever-persistent sting of guilt injected itself into my veins. It was hot, scorching, and I jumped from my chair, startling the good doctor. I stabbed my chest with a finger as I loomed over her, like the mythical being she apparently believed lived in the sky, and began to shout.

"Because what gives *me* the right to live? Tell me *that*, you know-it-all bitch! What gives *me* the fucking right to go about my miserable fucking life, finding *love*, finding *happiness*, finding success in whatever-the-fuck, when he had it all ripped out from under him?"

The smooth, slim column of her throat shifted with apprehension as she swallowed her shock. Her tongue flicked out, wetting her lips, and she asked, "But why is that your cross to bear, Blake? Why do you live your life like you're some prisoner to your brother?"

"Because nobody else will," I stated simply, knowing immediately that it was only partially the truth. So, with the need to speak more honestly and to spit the poison from my tongue, I added, "And because it's *my* fucking fault."

***

The needles jutted, in and out, in and out, threading the ink through the skin of Shane's calf. The tender, naked flesh tightened beneath my gloved fingertips, flinching involuntarily with every hastened prick. Hunched over his leg, I traced the lines with my machine, as he chatted with Celia about his time at *ModInk*.

"Wasn't it owned by your dad in the seventies?" she asked, her voice pulled taut with excitement. She'd never admit to fangirling over the guy, but she was totally swooning in the girliest of ways. I looked up from my work to smirk suggestively at her, and when she noticed, her eyes widened with a stern, silent warning to keep my big mouth shut.

"Yeah, it was," Shane answered. His voice held that euphoric quality a lot of people adopt when in the throes of receiving new ink. The haze. The high. I knew it well, and listening to him now, nearly breathless and serene, I was jealous. "He left it to me when he retired. That was nine years ago now. Crazy how fast time flies."

"I remember when you took over," she said. "The internet exploded. Nobody trusted you."

The room filled with Shane's short, gruff laugh. Like the memory still held insult for him. "Yeah, nobody likes change. But I'd like to think I've done a good job. I mean, I love my dad, but things had gotten pretty stale, in my opinion. He didn't like to take many risks, you know? He was very set in his ways, in the styles he liked, and didn't want to venture outside of it."

Celia winced apologetically. "I remember. He showcased a lot of traditional artists, standard piercings, and not much else."

Folding an arm beneath his head, Shane nodded. "He was afraid of the controversy that might come up if he, I don't know, showed off a killer set of microdermals or subdermal implants. He didn't wanna piss off the reader base." He chuckled lightly. "The guy hated the idea of stepping on toes. He hates confrontation. Hell, you should see him on holidays. The family starts talking politics or religion, and he flees the scene."

"Sounds like my family," Celia laughed with him. Flirtation bled from the sound and I made a mental note to tease her about it later on.

But for now, I simply quipped, "Sounds like *every* family."

"God, isn't that the fucking truth," Shane muttered, shaking his head.

The needle dipped close to the ridge of his ankle bone and he flinched. I lifted my machine on reflex and flitted my gaze to his, making sure he was okay. "You good?"

"Yeah. Sorry, man." He smiled with the embarrassment of a guy trying to be tough but who couldn't shy away from the pain of needle hitting bone.

"No worries." I took the opportunity to wipe his skin of excess ink and blood and change my gloves. "Just a little more line work, and then we'll take a break before I start shading, okay?"

"Sounds good." He lifted a thumbs up. "I could use a smoke."

"If this guy gets too rough, don't be afraid to kick him in the face," Celia teased, rounding the table to brush her knuckles against my shoulder.

"Nah, I'm good. No pain, no gain, right?" A chuckle rumbled from Shane's chest as he eyed Cee with half-hooded lids. I knew carnal interest when I saw it, and I smirked privately, dipping my head to return my attention to my work.

"So, Blake, how long have you been tattooing?"

The realization that I'd forgotten about the interview laid over me like a too-hot blanket. "Hey, uh, Shane ..." I leaned away from the table, sat straight on my stool, and pulled my gloves off before scratching at my ear. "I forgot to mention ... about the interview ..."

Lifting on his elbows, Shane said, "Dude, I caught the drift with your vow of silence over the past hour."

Celia's laugh burst from beside me. "Oh, don't take it personally. He's usually a mute while he works."

"Not always," I muttered in defense.

"No, it's cool," Shane cut in with a smile. "You get in the zone, I understand. But seriously, don't worry about the interview. I'll get you another day. I'm just trying to make conversation. Unless you'd really prefer to stay silent, in which case Cee and I can continue shooting the shit."

Cee. My ears pricked at the warm familiarity in his tone as the stolen nickname dropped from his mouth. He smiled at my friend, his eyes meeting hers, and when her cheeks blotched in a new shade of red, I knew any other prospects on Celia's horizon had been forgotten. Maybe even for good.

I bowed my head and set back to following the lines, drowning my thoughts in the hum of the machine. "I've been tattooing since I was sixteen," I told him.

"Sixteen, huh?"

Celia pulled over a chair. "Gus took him on as an apprentice before he even finished high school, after he'd

72

been fucking around with a tattoo machine in his buddy's basement."

I nodded. "Yep. That's about right."

"When did you jump on board?" he asked her, stealing the opportunity to learn something about her.

"Oh, I started working here, when was it? Ten years ago?" Cee turned the question on me, and I nodded.

"Just about."

"There are two other artists here, Kara, Gus's daughter, and her husband, Matt, but they're usually here on weekends or evenings," she added, looking back to Shane.

"But this guy is the talent," he complimented.

Celia's pride was burnt by the comment. I saw it in the faint wilt of her smile. "It's why Gus won't ever let him leave. He'd never get any business."

"Oh, knock it off," I grumbled. "You're good."

She rolled her eyes in my direction. "Right. I'm *good*. But my skills are a dime a dozen. Yours, though? You have your own style. People come to you looking for original work—"

"Because that's what I do," I laughed, grabbing a paper towel to wipe down Shane's leg.

"Right! And the clientele knows it! Me? I get the walk-ins."

"Nothing wrong with that," Shane chimed in.

"No, there's not," she agreed. "And it's good work. I love it. But Blake? He's wasting his potential."

Reverting to silence, I cleaned off the muddied mess of crimson and ink from his skin now raised and blotched with irritation. I hummed with satisfaction at the sight, at

73

my crisp handiwork, and rolled away to toss my gloves and used paper towel in the trash.

"Okay, man. Break time."

With a stretch, he sat up and favored his leg as he lowered his feet to the floor. "So, why don't you get out of here and open your own place? You would explode, man."

"Yeah," I nodded in melancholic agreement. "It'd be nice, but it's not in the cards right now. Maybe someday," I lied.

Celia offered an acknowledging, sympathetic smile as Shane remained in the clueless dark.

It was better that way.

***

"You're all set," I announced. "Lemme just grab a picture for my Instagram."

After scouring Shane's Instagram page and learning he was a big classic horror movie buff, I had decided to immortalize an ode to horror on the outside of his calf and managed to create something fresh and different. I'd mulled over the design for hours until deciding on a geometric piece framing a gritty shot of classic Nosferatu. Sketchy cobwebs and stippling decorated the surrounding negative space, fading elegantly into the neighboring tattoos.

"Fucking sick, man," Shane marvelled, struggling to catch a good glimpse of his leg in the position he was in. "You're an absolute master of your craft. I hope you know that."

"Thank you," I accepted the compliment graciously while those inner demons reminded me that I didn't deserve good things like talent and praise. I grabbed my phone and snapped the shot, making a mental note to put it up later.

"Do you mind if I throw it up on my social media?" Shane asked.

I swallowed as the temptation to tell him that, yes, I did mind bubbled up in my throat. It jittered against my tongue, demanding to be said, but I bit back the words and pushed a smile. "Of course not."

"I'll give you credit," he assured me, and my smile waned.

"Just give the shop credit," I instructed him, and he studied me with disbelief for a moment before shrugging.

"It feels like a crime to not mention you by name, but yeah, sure. Okay."

I refused his money, and he refused to accept a freebie. So, I told him the shop's hourly rate and low-balled the amount of time we'd been working. But even still, Shane stuffed seven hundred-dollar bills into my hand and told me to keep the change. It felt like robbery, but he insisted, and I tried to accept the hefty tip graciously and failed.

"Can I give you a piece of advice?" he asked, but I had a sneaking suspicion it wasn't up for debate.

"Sure," I said, wiping down my table.

"The great ones never get anywhere living on modesty," he told me, pulling on his jacket.

One side of my mouth curled upward into a pained half-smile. "The great ones are trying to get somewhere. I'm just trying to pay my bills."

He narrowed his eyes and pursed his lips. I was under the microscope of his scrutiny for two seconds longer than comfortable, and I turned away to clean the counter.

"You really have no idea how good you are, huh?" I remained silent as he smirked. "Man, I'm gonna feel honored as fuck to have known you before you made it big," he stated confidently, and I looked over my shoulder to remind him, like a broken fucking record, that I was never going to make it big. But when I met his eye, he only winked. "I'll be in touch, Blake."

"Take care." I offered him a brief nod of my chin as I dissected that wink. What the fuck did that mean? What shit was he going to pull?

As he left, the paranoia settled in my stomach as a balled-up bundle of nausea and nerves. So heavy and tight, I worried myself to the point where my gut turned sour. My heart crashed against the fragile walls of its cage, desperate to break open to freely jitter with nervous dread and anticipation. My mind rewound and settled bitterly on that one thing that had started this all.

The game changer.

The plan ruiner.

That fucking butterfly tattoo.

I wished I could go back all those years, to when Audrey's sister had walked through the door of the shop. To that moment when she'd asked me to draw up a design, something completely different from my other work. And I wished I had said no.

Chapter Six

DAYS PASSED BEFORE Shane said anything on social media. But on Saturday it popped up at the top of my Instagram feed, along with the notice that I'd gained over a hundred new followers in less than an hour. He had mentioned the shop, as promised, but he'd also mentioned me.

My first reaction was to lash out in anger. I deliberately instructed him not to do that. I didn't want the attention. And I didn't want the forty new messages and requests for appointments. But then, as I read the comments and the contents of my inbox, I felt the first dose of praise zing at my veins and I learned just how easily it would be to become addicted.

Without Jake around to remind me of why it was a bad idea to share my work, I allowed myself the hours of solitude to bask in the glory of being good at my job—fuck, scratch that, it was my *passion*. No guilt. No self-deprecation. Just good old-fashioned pride. This was the work that fueled my life. It was my happy place, and dammit, it felt good to be appreciated for it.

I took the Harley out to the club that night. I was in a rare mood, a good one, and I put my name on the list without hesitation. Tonight, I'd read, and I'd let myself be proud for that, too.

When my turn came around, I approached the microphone with confidence. It had been weeks, maybe even more, since I last read one of my poems at the club. Poetry wasn't a constant in my life, I didn't always feel the need to write. But, every now and then, I felt the call and the pressure of vile verbiage, and I gave in.

I didn't announce my name to the audience of sordid faces and I didn't tell them the title, because it didn't have one. I never titled my poems, never gave them the respect. They were a release, mental fecal matter meant to be expelled, and nothing more.

So, I read.

A butterfly,
Born on the ground,
A crawling mess of fibers and legs.
We see it change,
We see it turn,
We see the transformation,
From fibers and legs to beauty and wings,
And we stare,
Awed,
Bewildered,
Entranced by its beauty.
But who stares at the caterpillar?
Ugly.
Disgusting.

Grub.
We spew these hateful words,
Shun the fibers and legs,
Until it is beautiful.
But is it not still a butterfly?
I was born beautiful.
Perfect pink toes,
Perfect blue eyes.
Perfection has a heavy cost,
And I paid the price.
Watch me grow,
Watch me transform,
See me change.
Scribble the ugliness on your paper,
Let it process,
Save it for later.
Godless.
Hateful.
Angry.
But am I not still human?
Am I not still a metaphorical butterfly?
A butterfly, but in reverse.

I stepped away from the mic and stuffed the torn-off sheet of paper into a pocket. I didn't care if I crumpled or destroyed it. It didn't matter—I never meant to keep it, anyway. I didn't keep any of them.

A hushed applause resounded through the club. Heads bobbed with approving nods, though I didn't need their approval or praise, much like with my tattoos. But it did feel nice, good even, to think that maybe some people knew where I was coming from. That empathized and maybe even understood.

I moved my way back to my seat, ready to grab my jacket and make a run for it, when a hand laid against my back.

"Blake?"

The sweet melody of her voice was a ray of light, a slender stream of brightness through a pin-pricked hole in a never-ending canopy of dark. I froze on the spot, unable to move an iota of an inch. She'd rendered me speechless, motionless, and if it weren't for the vibration of my heart, I would've assumed I was dead.

She rounded to stand before me. Shit ... When I'd seen her a week ago, how had I not noticed then what a sight she was? Sure, I'd noticed she was attractive, but now, in this new light, she left me awestruck. White-gold hair gleaming underneath the grey light of the club. Pale blue eyes taking on a navy hue in the shadows. If I believed in a heaven, I could've been convinced that she'd fallen, an angel with fractured wings.

At the thought, my eyes dipped to a glint of silver hanging from a chain around her neck. The cross twinkled with every rise and fall of her chest, and I forced my disappointment down to the pit of my stomach. To turn and sour and haunt me later.

"Oh, hey." I said, regarding her with the kindest smile I could muster.

"Hey!" She grinned, showing off wide rows of white teeth. She extended her fair hand, and I hesitated. I didn't deserve to touch her, to soil her pristine skin, but I accepted and lightly held her hand in mine as she said, "Audrey. I don't know if you remember—"

"I do," I cut in without hesitation, nodding. That tattoo etched into her chest, its black wings peeking out from the neckline of her pink t-shirt, had haunted my thoughts and world for over a week. There was no way I could mask my recognition now.

"Sorry for bothering you," she apologized needlessly. "I just saw you read that poem and had to tell you, it's beautiful. A little sad, but definitely beautiful."

"Thanks," I said, but I also wanted to correct her. It wasn't beautiful. It was me, my thoughts, and there was absolutely nothing beautiful about the shit crawling around inside my brain.

Beneath the dimmed lights, I watched a faint pink blush creep its way up her neck and blossom in springtime flourish over her cheeks. It was cold, the middle of October in Salem, and the cockles of my stony heart echoed with a deathly winter chill, but this woman reminded me of flowers and newborn animals. Of warmth, sunshine, and color.

"Are you here with anyone?" she asked.

"Nah," I answered, uncomfortable that she'd asked.

With a flutter of her hand, she gestured toward a table. "My cousins and I are over there, if you want—"

"I was actually just leaving."

The abruptness of my response rendered her momentarily speechless. Her mouth was frozen in a pink O that shouldn't have made me think lewdly, yet it did. I thought of her, on her knees, dirtying up those light-colored jeans. *This is why I can't find someone*, I thought, sending a message out to Dr. Travetti. I'm filthy, soiled, and I'd only ruin someone else. Especially someone like her.

"Oh, okay," she finally spoke. "Can I walk you to your car, then?"

"I rode my motorcycle," I corrected her, as if it mattered, and began to walk away. "It was nice seeing you again, Aud—"

"Hold on," she called to me, before telling someone else, "I'll be right back."

I listened for her footsteps. Hoping she was following, hoping she decided to stay behind. I moved quicker toward the stairs that would lead me to the sidewalk, tricking myself into believing she wasn't behind me, until I heard her say my name again.

"Blake! Goodness, you walk fast."

I didn't want to be a dick. Honestly, I didn't. So, I made myself stop. I allowed her to catch up, and when she did, she smiled up into my eyes.

"Sorry," I muttered in a voice so low, it seemed nearly sinister to my ears.

"It's okay."

I didn't want her to walk with me outside into the parking lot. I didn't want her to see the bike that only came out to play once a week, when my brother wasn't my responsibility. I didn't want her light to seep anymore into the fractured seams of my life, but I did nothing to stop her as she followed me up the stairs.

I pulled a breath of cool air into my lungs and closed my eyes. Audrey did the same, as if she was mocking me. Or maybe it was also her way, to appreciate the chill of a sunless night.

"It's beautiful tonight," she commented quietly. "I love the fall."

"So do I."

She laughed lightly. "Oh, I'm so surprised." There was sarcasm in her tone and when I looked to her, I saw that her bottom lip was trapped between her teeth, just begging for the permission to smile. "And don't tell me ... Your favorite color is black."

My lips curled in a reluctant smile. "I can't imagine what your first clue was."

Audrey shrugged. "Oh, I don't know ..." She took a step back and dragged her scrutinizing gaze over my leather jacket, jeans, and boots. All black.

I chuckled, averting my eyes toward my bike. Gleaming beneath a lamp and begging me to hop on and take it home. Home. Haven. Away from people and Audrey and that tattoo ... That fucking tattoo ...

My eyes flicked back to the sharp black lines, teasing me from beneath her collar. The cross hung above them, playing in multiple contrasts. Darkness and light. Hell and Heaven. Evil and good. Standing there, I then felt the analogy applied to us as well. Her, in pink and denim. Me, in black and nothing but. Her, wearing the symbol of Christ. Me, wearing the anger of the damned.

What was a woman like her doing with the brand of the devil on her chest, disguising itself as art?

"I'll let you leave," she said apologetically. "I just wanted to thank you again for the tattoo. I'd been wanting to get it done for a while, but I was kinda scared, so I put it off. But I'm so glad to have it now. It feels like it's always belonged there."

"I'm glad," I replied with a single nod.

"I wasn't sure I'd feel like that," she admitted airily. "I thought I'd regret it. You know? I don't have any other tattoos, so I wasn't sure what it'd be like after it was done. I mean, once it's there, it's really *there*. It took my cousins to convince me ..."

She prattled on nervously, and my eyes dipped to her mouth. Her lips moved; her voice as gentle as the breeze around us. Her lip gloss reflected the light, glittering with multicolored sparkles, emphasizing the rounded curve of her bottom lip and the subtle dip of her Cupid's bow. I stopped listening to her speak and focused on those lips, so pronounced in structure but so temptingly soft in appearance. My mind wandered, wondering what her lip gloss tasted like and if it would glide against my lips or create a tacky barrier that would only make me frustrated and angry.

"... you know what I mean?"

I lifted my eyes back to hers. Shame burned my cheeks, realizing I had no idea what she'd just said, and I smiled through the humility. "Sorry. What did you say?"

"Oh." She dropped her gaze to the sidewalk and her shoes, before clearing her throat. "Um, I was just saying that I really love the tattoo."

That wasn't all she had said, and I knew it. I felt guilty. I felt like a pervert. But I pushed myself to smile genuinely as I replied, "I'm glad."

"You truly have a gift, Blake," she said softly, and fuck, I hated when people said that. It implied that it was intentionally given, that it wasn't just a silly, stupid fluke. But I said nothing as she went on, "You make people feel whole."

Oh, if only she knew what a crock of shit that really was. I broke my brother, robbing him of any chance he'd have at being his own artist. I drained the love from my mother's heart and stole the happiness from my dad. I was a leach, a parasite, and I was paying for it with my life.

And that's why I needed to leave. To remove myself from her presence and get away from the twinkling sparkle of her lips and the taunting glint of that cross around her neck.

With a curt nod and an agonizing smile, I stepped backward. "I really need to get going," I brushed her off, pushing her away with my words, and she nodded hastily.

"Oh, of course, yeah. Get home safe, okay? Have a good night."

"Thanks, you too."

We parted ways and I moved swiftly toward the Harley. I was so close, ready to swing my leg over the seat and get the hell away from there, when a thought wedged itself between my resolve to leave and the need to stay.

What the fuck does it mean?

I thought I had let it go. I thought it no longer mattered. But with the sudden popularity of my work on Instagram and all of it leading back to that stupid fucking tattoo, the curiosity was back with a wild vengeance and I felt my lips move before I could remind myself of why this was such a bad idea.

"Audrey, wait!" I called to her and turned around to see her glance over her shoulder. "I have a question."

"Yeah?"

I approached her this time, moving slowly and breathing evenly. Pulling the air in and out of my lungs, as though I was convinced it'd be the last time I'd savor the sweetness of the autumn air. She stood beneath the glow of a streetlamp that illuminated her in an ethereal glow. Her white-blonde hair pulled in the rays and put them back out into the world, shining like a beacon to be found, and I was a moth to her flame. Involuntarily succumbing to its glow.

"This is crazy," I said more to myself, "but I've been wondering, why did your sister get that tattoo? What does it mean?"

Her lips stretched into a smile. "I think you kinda already know."

"Huh?"

"It's life and death," she explained frankly, never allowing her smile to wilt. "Or, as you put it, a butterfly, but in reverse."

Chapter Seven

I STOOD, RIGID, with my spine locked, to keep my legs from buckling from beneath me. Had I known it already? Had I understood it's meaning when I wrote that damn poem? Had I remembered it, somewhere in my subconscious, from when I'd tattooed it to her sister's body? That was all possible, all feasible, but hearing her say the words, those *exact* words ...

The good doctor's voice sounded in my ear, reminding me of signs, and the growling hellhound in my head scared her away.

I nodded in response, unable to speak around a tongue too dry and heavy. So, I let my eyes do the talking, and let my stance tell her I was intrigued and wanted to know more.

Audrey shrugged, her smile now sad, as she said, "It was supposed to be a, uh, metaphor for her life, I guess."

I was hungry now, as Dr. Travetti had said. Starving for a connection, for affection. Famished. I pinned her with my gaze and nodded again, eagerly, feeling an immediate connection to this dearly departed sister of hers. One I had touched with my art and machine.

"Sabrina ... My sister ..." Audrey took a deep breath, as if to prepare herself. "She was born with a congenital heart defect, but we didn't know about it until we were older and it'd already progressed to the point where the doctors knew she was going to die."

What I wanted to say was, we all die. We all get sick, get old, get run over, and we all die. But instead, I tethered myself to her offered confession, a simple piece of twine, and felt that desperation for a connection sigh with satisfaction.

"I'm sorry," I replied.

"It's okay." She said the words so calmly, so sincerely, like it really was okay that her sister's heart had been diseased and gave out. I didn't understand that, how she could be so accepting, when I still hadn't learned to accept my brother's fate of perpetual childhood.

I crossed my arms, warding myself and reclaiming the conversation. "So, how exactly was it a metaphor?"

"Well, she began her life with so much beautiful possibility and potential, and by the time she was diagnosed, it was very black and white, you know? Live and die."

"Isn't that everybody's life?" I countered with a question I never intended to ask. I faltered with a swallow and felt immediately like an asshole. "Sorry."

"Don't apologize," she said gently. "I like your vibe."

The compliment was abrupt and unlike the others I'd received recently, and I did react to this one; I scoffed.

My *vibe*? I didn't have a vibe. "Vibe" seemed like a descriptive word they slap on you in high school, tacked onto a clique or subculture. Goth vibe. Punk vibe. Jock vibe.

I don't have a vibe. I'm just me. Vibeless Blake.

"Okay," I replied flatly. My tone should've thwarted her, should've ended the conversation, but instead, she smiled brightly as she asked, "Will you please stay for a drink?"

"I really have to get home," I insisted, but my resolve was fading with the strength of her hope.

"Just one, I promise. I have a poem I'd really like you to hear."

"So, a drink and a poem?" I narrowed my eyes and looked toward the stairs I'd just come from. This seemed like a bad idea. Nothing good was ever going to come from this. I'd told the good doctor as much countless times, and now I was telling myself. This was bad, but she felt good, and I wondered if I could afford to let a little bit of that into my life. Just for tonight. Just to see how it felt to do something selfish, for myself.

Just once.

***

"Girls, I want you to meet Mister Blake Carson."

Two blonde women wearing pastels and flashing pearly white teeth turned to face me. Their broad smiles wilted slightly at the sight of my exterior, and I'd be lying if I said the feeling wasn't painfully mutual. If I'd known

I would be sharing a drink with the Stepford Wives, I might have declined.

"Blake, these are my cousins and best friends, Regina and Nicole." Audrey pointed to each of the ladies, and with each introduction, they waved with waggling fingers.

"Nice to meet you," I said, not yet sure if I was lying.

Audrey's hand lifted and laid against my leather clad bicep. I glanced down to her smooth, porcelain skin and white-tipped fingernails, stark against the black backdrop of my jacket. The gesture was friendly, strictly platonic, but again, all I could wonder was, why the hell would she want to spend any time with me?

"We're just going to the bar to grab a drink and then we'll be back. Can I get you girls a refill?"

"Water for me," Nicole answered. She turned to Regina and drawled, "I'll pretend it's wine while you guys enjoy yourselves."

"Tell David to keep his dick to himself and you won't get knocked up again," Regina quipped dryly before regarding Audrey. "What are you drinking?"

"Oh, I don't really know ..." Audrey shrugged. "I was thinking maybe a, uh—"

"Oh, come on, Audrey." Nicole snorted, lifting her almost-empty glass of water to her lips. "We all know you're just gonna order another Manhattan."

Regina's gaze met mine. "She only started drinking like, a year ago, and all she knows to order is a Manhattan."

Audrey laughed lightheartedly through her embarrassment, wearing her blush with pride. "I led a very sheltered life, okay?"

"Jeez, it wasn't *that* sheltered. You went away to college, for crying out loud," Nicole shot back, eyes wide and glinting with laughter.

"And I spent the whole time studying!" Audrey's defense was shrill and coated with laughter. I wasn't sure at what point I began to smile, but now I was grinning and really relaxing in the company of these women I'd just met.

"What are you getting, Blake?" Regina asked.

"Oh, uh," the sound of my name caught me off guard and I collected my thoughts, "I'll probably get a Sam Adams."

"I've never had one of those," Audrey admitted, tipping her head in a way that made her look so innocent.

"You haven't had one of anything," Nicole grumbled with an eye roll.

"Except a Manhattan," Regina added pointedly.

I smiled at Audrey's cousins before turning to her. "It's a lager. It's, uh ..." I shrugged. "It's a little crisper compared to beer." Audrey's cheeks turned a deeper shade of pink and I assessed, "You've never had beer before."

"Winner, winner, chicken dinner," Regina answered, poking at Audrey's side. "Sam Adams sounds good. I'll have one of them."

I walked with Audrey to the bar at the back of the club. She glanced at me with an apologetic glare and said, "Sorry about them."

I waved it off. "They're fine."

The bartender sauntered over and asked, "What can I get ya?"

Before Audrey could speak, I answered, "Two Sam Adams, a water, and a Man—"

"Make that three Sam Adams," Audrey interrupted with an assertive lift of her head. When she caught my curious glance, she simply said, "It's a night for trying new things."

I found it funny how little she knew about me and how out of left field this all was, and yet, she could utter a statement so true. Hell, this entire day had been about embracing situations outside of my comfort zone. It was nice, exciting even, and I was already dreading Monday morning, when my usual routine would commence.

But that was over a day away. Right now, I was here, with the woman bearing the very tattoo that had haunted me for over a week. This was nothing more than a delightful coincidence, presented to me amidst the chaos of my life, and I made the choice to just enjoy it. Whatever it was, and whatever came from it. Because it was one night, that was all, and living my life for myself for one night wouldn't kill me.

When the bartender brought over our drinks, I lifted a glass to her and said, "To trying new things."

Audrey lifted hers warily, eyeing the lager within, as she clinked the glass against mine. "To trying new things."

***

Audrey walked toward the mic without trepidation, owning the stage with light. I couldn't remember the poem she had read the week before—wasn't it something about a flower? A dandelion, maybe? It annoyed me now that I couldn't remember it in the same way I couldn't get that damn butterfly out of my head. But something whispering in my heart told me it was unlikely I'd forget what she was about to read tonight. This poem, whatever it was, would remind me forever of that one time I stepped outside the lines and permitted myself to live.

"Hi, everyone," Audrey practically sang to the crowd. "I call this one New Skin."

She cleared her throat and took the sheet of paper from her pocket. Then, she read.

> *This skin is mine.*
> *A gift from my mother,*
> *My father,*
> *From God.*
> *One size fits me,*
> *And no one else.*
> *It has burned,*
> *It has paled,*
> *It has protected,*
> *And it has failed.*
> *It has grown,*
> *It has shrunk,*
> *But what have I done for it?*
> *This gift, my skin,*

What have I given,
When it's given so much?
Think, I think, think some more.
The answer is obvious,
The answer is her,
The missing half to my duo.
A little pain, a little time,
And now, thanks to him,
I am whole again,
A patchworked person,
Of new skin and old.

The room murmured with approval and applause as Audrey bowed graciously and slipped from the stage. Nicole and Regina nodded, smiling with pride, as their hands clapped. I should've applauded her. I should've done something, anything, to express a hint of acknowledgment, yet I couldn't. I was stunned and startled, in complete awe over her ability to write something so profound about skin of all things. And then there was the mention of—I'm assuming here—me, and that shook my heart so much, I looked beyond the mention of God.

She had written something about me. Was it possible that I'd haunted her as much as she'd inadvertently haunted me?

And what did it mean if I had? My brain swarmed with the usual words—*coincidence, accident, mistake*—but my heart clung to something else, something that had me shaking my head and wanting to curse.

I finished off my Sam Adams and stood from the table. Regina and Nicole turned to stare at me, and I smiled apologetically.

"I really gotta get going," I said, and Audrey came to stand beside me.

"Do you really need to leave now?" Worry tied her words together, her eyebrows tipped with concern. "Can we maybe—"

"I really have to go," I repeated, firmer. "I gotta wake up early, but this was fun."

I wished her cousins a good night before making my escape. I hurried through the club, even as a new reader went to the stage, but I wasn't caring about etiquette or manners. I cared only about getting away from a woman that I hardly knew, who was making me think things I had firmly set myself against years ago.

When I reached the sidewalk, I realized I'd been followed. I groaned internally, squeezing my eyes and turning around. "Look, I really—"

"What did you think?" she interrupted meekly, and I opened my eyes.

"What?"

"My poem. I wanted to know what you thought."

I cocked my head, suddenly frustrated and ready to be done with this night of trying new things. "It was good," I answered half-heartedly, hoping it'd be good enough.

But Audrey smiled and saw through my bullshit. "Tell me what you really think. Please?"

"Why?"

"Because your opinion matters."

I scoffed, finding it hard to bite my tongue and keep the demons buried beneath my skin. "No. It really doesn't."

Audrey cocked her head and stared at me with too much sincerity, emotion, and way too much affection and care for someone who didn't even know me. "Of course, it matters, Blake."

I was crumbling, succumbing, as my shoulders relaxed and my hands found the confines of my pockets. With a begrudged sigh, my shoulders shrugged and I said, "You're talented. That's what I think."

Audrey smiled and released a sigh of relief. "Thank you. I'm sorry, I was just so blown away by yours, I needed to know what you thought of mine."

I nodded. "I get it."

"I'll let you go, now that I've made myself seem like a psychopath." She laughed nervously with self-deprecation, as one hand tucked a strand of fly-away platinum hair behind her ear.

"You're fine," I assured her. "I'm just not very good company."

The apples of her cheeks were highlighted in a glowing shade of pink as she said, "And I come on too strong."

I let my lips curl into a smile. "You're fine," I repeated, and she replied, "So are you."

Chapter Eight

MY PARENTS HAD invited me over for Sunday dinner, and while I normally wouldn't have welcomed any extended amount of time with them, I was in desperate need of a distraction from my night with Audrey.

I hadn't slept well Saturday night, with thoughts of her and poetry and otherworldly eyes keeping me from finding a deep slumber. And Sunday morning hadn't proven to be much better, with the regular stream of new Instagram followers coming in, constantly reminding me of what had started it all—that girl and her tattoo.

To say I'd been shaken was an understatement.

I walked into the house and was welcomed by the warm and fragrant scents of pot roast, asparagus, and garlic mashed potatoes. They triggered my nostalgia, remembering a time when my parents regularly cooked these family dinners. That was so long ago, a lifetime even, but now I remembered those times like they'd happened yesterday. Back then, the house had been full of laughter and love. Not a single one of us had any reason to be unhappy. But that was before.

Now, the scents were there, but the laughter was missing. The love was stifled and damn near nonexistent. The house moaned beneath my feet with every ounce of agony my family had felt for the past couple of decades, and I recalled a moment from a few years ago, where I'd wondered, if I'd ceased to exist, whether it would make it all better.

I shook that thought away and walked into the dining room, where I found my father wrapped in an awkward conversation with Jake. Their interactions always left Dad with a pained expression on his face, like he'd rather lay on a bed of hot coals than engage in any way with my brother. I hated him for it—Jake couldn't help the way he was, and he was still the man's son. Dad could've made more of an attempt to treat him like it. But I didn't expect he ever would.

"Oh, look!" Dad exclaimed, turning to face me with relief and gratitude. "Blake's here!"

Jake's face lit up at the sight of me. "Blake, I gotta show you the new plane Dad got me! You gotta see it! You wanna see it now?" He began to stand from the table when Mom bustled into the room, wielding a plate of asparagus and a bowl of potatoes.

"You'll sit down right now, Jakey. No Legos until after dinner," she commanded. Her eyes lifted to mine momentarily as she placed the dishes down. "Hi, Blake."

"Hey, Mom."

"Glad you could make it." Her tone was so dull and curt, she felt more like a stranger and less like my mother.

"You need any help in there?" I nudged my chin toward the kitchen.

"Um," she stilled awkwardly, wiping her hands on her shirt, "well, I guess you could cut the meat, if you don't think you'll hurt yourself."

"I can manage."

She looked skeptical but didn't say anything as I followed her into the kitchen. I set to work carving the roast, while she busied herself by fetching a pitcher of iced tea from the fridge and taking it to the dining room. She made sure that she wasn't alone with me for any length of time. It was just as well; we'd only argue, anyway.

When I was finished, I carried the platter of meat to the table, only to find Jake meandering around the room and my mother relentlessly scolding him for not sitting down. He stopped at the table and grabbed a banana from the bowl of fruit and proceeded to tap it against the wall.

"Jacob!" Mom shouted, smacking her hand against the tabletop. The glasses and dishes rattled with the impact and Dad winced. *Coward.*

In a battle for control, Jake continued to stand by the wall, tap tap tapping the banana until the tip was chipped and ruined.

"Jacob, if you don't sit down right now—"

"Hey, buddy," I finally intercepted, rounding the table to take the banana from his hand. His stare was centered on the bowl of fruit and he reached for another piece, an orange, but I was quicker. Dropping the banana on the floor, I reached for both his hands and held them in mine. "Hey. Look at me."

Jake turned and met my gaze. His eyes flitted up to the crown of my head, and they dropped again. I saw in them the mirrored reflection of my own, along with an anger, a cool helplessness, and my gut was surrounded by dread. Call it a twin connection, intuition, whatever— I didn't need to ask my parents to know he'd had a bad day.

"You okay, buddy?" I asked.

"He's fine," Mom answered for him, exhaustion evident in her tone.

"We had a bad morning," Dad added. "Mickey got sick, and Jake—"

"Mickey's not sick!" Jake wrenched his hands from mine and grabbed the orange from the bowl, throwing it across the room. "Mickey's fine! He's not sick!"

"Really, Paul, you had to get him started again?" Mom hissed. I quickly glanced over my shoulder to catch her palms laying over her face and her shoulders hunched forward.

Jake was on a rampage now. He was squeezing another orange in his fist, breathing heavily and close to tears. Ignoring his mood or what he might do to me, I stepped forward and wrapped my arms around him. I hugged him tightly, felt his body's tension drop, before his arms went limp at his sides and he shuddered with a sob.

"M-Mickey's not sick, Blake," he cried against my shoulder.

"No, he's not, buddy. Mickey's fine."

"He threw up, but he's not sick."

I nodded, rubbing my hand in small, soothing circles between his shoulder blades. "I know, Jake. It's okay."

Mom and Dad sat, silent and staring, as I calmed my brother down. It's how it'd always been. Dad would pretend everything was fine, while Mom would get frustrated, and it'd be up to me to fix it. And sure, they hadn't purposely dropped the responsibility into my lap. But maybe it was simply that I was the only one who could settle his mind and bring him back to reason. I did wonder though, if it pissed them off that they were rendered so useless by me, of all people.

I asked Jake if he was ready to eat, or if he wanted to take a moment to breathe in his room. He chose to be alone, to find his happy place with his blocks, and I let him leave, much to my mother's disapproval. Now, alone with Mom and Dad, I sat at the table and resumed the motions of dinner, taking and cutting my food, as they kept their eyes on their empty plates.

"Aren't you guys hungry?" I finally asked, stuffing my face with a heaping forkful of potatoes.

"He's out of control," Mom blurted, and my eyes darted to bore into hers.

"Huh?"

"Your brother!"

"He's no different than he's always been," I defended him in a way that also felt like I was defending myself.

"And what does that tell you, Blake?" she snapped, instantly heated and vengeful.

"You tell me, Mom. You're the one bringing it up."

"Well, it tells me he's not getting any better! You wanted him in that damn school, and what good is it doing?"

"You want him to hear you talking about him?" I gritted out bitterly.

"Come on, Blake. He doesn't even understand what we're saying," Dad brushed it off, shaking his head.

"Oh, no?" I laughed darkly. "He's not a fucking idiot, Dad."

"Blake, watch your mouth," Mom snapped, her tone cracking like a whip, and I slumped against the back of my chair, shaking my head and wishing I hadn't come. Wishing there was some way, *any* way, for the two of them to leave the two of us alone.

Dad sighed, folding his hands on the table. "We've just been wondering if we're shelling out the money for this place for nothing. That's all. No reason to get so defensive."

Defensive ... The good doctor had accused me of being defensive, and hell, maybe I was. But Jake was being attacked, and shouldn't I defend *him*?

"He's fine," I replied with finality, turning back to my food. I popped a piece of pot roast into my mouth and chewed, but I wasn't tasting it. The only flavor in my mouth was the bitterness of accusation, because between the lines, between every one of their words, was the reminder that I had failed my brother.

"Well, we're not sure he is," Mom said, her tone cold.

I dropped my fork, submitting to my anger as I turned my attention back to her. "Why? Huh? Why all of a sudden? It's been almost ten fucking years, so why now?"

Mom shook her head and turned to my father as she shoved away from the table. "I need some air. I can't talk to him when he gets like this."

"Oh, for fuck's sake, Mom." I rolled my eyes and shook my head.

Without a reply, she left the house, closing the door noisily to ensure I knew she was gone. Left alone with my father, I decided I wouldn't be the first to speak. I wouldn't give him that satisfaction. I steepled my hands and stared ahead, at the wooden china cabinet, so clean and bright. It made me think of my own furniture and how much more comfortable I was with all that black paint and dark wood. My mind wandered to what felt like every criticism my parents had ever shot my way. They hated my style. My tastes in clothing, furniture—even my career. I was the rebel, and they were the disapproving parents, waiting for their boy—their only *normal* child—to grow out of his little phase.

I shook my head, sending the thoughts away. I was too fired up, too angry, and making something out of nothing. I needed to calm down and go the fuck home. But how could I when Jake was upstairs, also trying to calm down? I needed to be there for him. I needed to fight for him.

"Blake."

I closed my eyes to the cabinet. "Dad. I think I'd really prefer to not talk right now. Okay?"

He sighed but wouldn't budge. "This wasn't meant to be an attack. We've given it plenty of time. But it's not helping, and—"

I turned to him with fire in my eyes. "So, what, then? What do you want to do with him, huh? You want him to sit in this fucking house doing nothing all day, like he used to?"

Dad's throat moved with a deep, slow swallow. "We were thinking we should look into other options."

"Oh, yeah? Like what? What other options have you thought of that I haven't already considered?"

"Maybe an assisted living facility, or—"

"You want to send him away?" My hands dropped to the table with a thud and I stared at my father while the anger burned my eyes. Tears I'd never let fall formed, and I blinked them away.

"Not *away*, Blake." Dad scoffed and ran a hand over his balding head. "For Pete's sake, you make it sound like we want to get rid of him or something."

"Oh, I know that's *exactly* what you want," I accused, shaking my head. "You don't even deal with him now!"

He shook his head but I couldn't miss that blink of shame that passed over his eyes. "Blake, he's out of control. These tantrums are hard to deal with and you know it."

"I don't seem to have any problem calming him down."

Narrowing his eyes, he jabbed, "Well, that's great for you, but you're not with him all the time, are you?"

"Maybe I should be," I snapped back. "Maybe he should come live at my place. Then the two of you could be done with both of us. How would you like that?" I hardly knew what I was saying, but as the words spilled out of my mouth, the more I liked the idea.

"Well, we think this is the option we should explore," he replied curtly, not even entertaining the thought of Jake living with me. But why not? He'd be happy there. I'd even allow that damn dog to live under my roof if it meant Jake would be out of this house for good.

"And you know what *I* think?" Dad spoke, proving he wasn't quite finished.

"Oh, here we go," I muttered.

"Knock it off," he scolded me. "This angsty, *the world hates me* attitude of yours was acceptable when you were sixteen, but guess what, pal? That ship sailed a long time ago. You're a man in your thirties, for crying out loud, and it's about time you acted like one and owned up to your bullshit. You can start by shutting your big mouth and listening to me right now."

He pointed at me from across the table. "*You* are not Jake's parent; we are, your mother and I. I know how much you love your brother and how much you take responsibility for him. But you've done so much—*too* much, if you ask me. We're thinking maybe it's time we tried something different for a while. And maybe we could all use a break," he lowered his finger and tapped my arm, "including you."

Scoffing, I shook my head. "A break ..." I nearly choked on the concept and scrubbed a hand over my face. "I don't want a break, Dad."

"You're miserable."

"I'm fine."

He folded his arms on the table. "Are you? When was the last time you went out, Blake? When was the last time you had a girlfriend?"

"I went out last night," I grumbled between my teeth.

He sighed, rubbing the palm of his hand against his chin. "You know what I mean. You're still young. You don't need to carry the world on your shoulders like you owe it something. Live a little, for once."

He rubbed his hand against my arm and patted. It was the period on the sentence. The end. He stood up, looking down at the pot roast with regret.

"Sorry about dinner," he muttered apologetically.

"It's okay," I brushed it off, shrugging. It wasn't the first time one of Jake's outbursts had spoiled a family meal and it probably wouldn't be the last.

"I'm going to talk to your mother," he announced, standing from the table. "Maybe she's calmed down."

"Okay."

"You're a really good kid, Blake. You have a big heart," he added hurriedly, like he'd been harboring the sentiment and needed to say it aloud before he combusted. Then, he scurried from the room, leaving me alone.

I didn't feel like a good kid, and even more than that, I didn't feel like a good brother. My parents had seen my efforts as an experimental failure, and hell, they were right. I'd failed them, and more importantly, I had failed him.

You're fine.

So are you.

Last night with Audrey felt light-years away. I held onto the memory now, gripping onto the frayed edges of something I knew I wasn't. I wasn't fine, and I wasn't good. I was a poser, a failure, a miserable excuse of a man.

Live a little.

The voice of my father echoed, clattering around in my brain with his plea. Get a life, get laid, get a girlfriend. Did they think they were doing this for me? Did they think they were doing me any favors by sending my brother away? Because what they failed to realize was, Jake needed me as much as I needed him.

I didn't know who the hell I was without him.

***

"You hungry, buddy?" I leaned against the doorframe of Jake's room, watching him build a Lego castle. Jake nodded his response, too in the zone to respond verbally. "You wanna eat in here tonight, so you can keep building?"

Excitement lit the dark in his eyes, and he grinned, big and happy. "You betcha!"

I nodded, smiling. "Just for tonight though, okay?"

I went to the kitchen and made a plate of food for him. When I returned, Jake was sitting on his bed, TV remote in hand. He was changing the channels, finding something to watch while he ate, and when he landed on *Toy Story*, the remote was dropped to the bed.

"Don't make a mess, okay? Mom and Dad will kill me." I set the plate on his nightstand as he nodded. "You need anything else?"

He shook his head and started to eat, when he stated, "They want to give me away."

Jake was a lot more perceptive than my parents realized sometimes, and I cursed under my breath that he'd heard.

"It's okay, buddy. They were just talking."

"You want me to go, too?" His eyes, identical to mine, lifted and pinned me to the place I stood.

"No, Jake. I don't want you to go."

He studied me quietly, as though he could see the uncertainty in the statement. My words had been flimsy, unsure, and I hated the thought that he could tell.

"You're yellow," he stated, his tone flat and unmoving, before turning his attention onto his food. He focused on eating and watching the movie, and I left the room.

Back at home, I went to my room and grabbed the book I kept about aura colors. I flipped through the pages in search of yellow, and when I found it, I read through the different shades and their meanings. Jake would never be specific. He would never discern if my color was dark or light. But it didn't matter as my eyes fixated on one word.

Hope.

Chapter Nine

"YOU SEEM TENSE today," Dr. Travetti commented breathlessly. She had been running late again, and I was already seated in her office when she'd arrived. I watched her as she situated her mug of coffee on the table between our chairs.

"I bet you paid big bucks to develop those killer people-reading skills," I muttered sardonically, crossing my arms and slouching in my chair.

"Oh, I love when we start the session off with some sarcasm. I know it's gonna be a good day."

I nodded approvingly as my lips curled into a smirk. "Nice, Doc. I'm teaching you well."

A moment of silence passed as she sat and crossed her legs, assuming her professional position. I liked her more when she was rushing and out of breath. When she was more relatable, more human. I thought, if I was a therapist, that's what I'd do. None of this suit-and-tie, stick-up-the-ass bullshit. I'd get on the level of the people, meet at a cafe or some shit, and talk like a friend and less like a doctor.

But I'd never be a therapist. I couldn't even save myself—how the hell could I save someone else?

"So, I was thinking," she began, finding a comfortable place in her chair, "maybe we could pick up where we left off last time. Our session was so short, and I had to cut you off so abruptly ..."

"I'd rather not," I replied curtly.

"Well, I really thought we started to make some progress, so I thought ..." She shrugged innocently.

I shook my head persistently. "You know, Doc, I'd really rather talk about my shit-show of a weekend, if that's okay with you."

"Oh," she gestured for me to continue, giving me the floor, "of course. Go ahead."

"Shane mentioned me on Instagram and got me a whole lot of attention. Then, I went to the club and read one of my poems," I told her.

Her eyes widened with intrigue. "You've never shown me one of your poems."

"I don't keep them," I informed her with a nonchalant shrug. "I write 'em and toss 'em out."

"That's pretty sad," she commented.

I snickered. "Why is that sad?"

"You're never proud and want to keep them?"

"Nope."

"Okay," she nodded slowly, absorbing. "What made you decide to read this one, then?"

"I liked it."

"What was it about?"

"Myself. And that tattoo."

"I see. And did you see that woman ..." Her eyes dropped to her clipboard as she thumbed through the sheets of paper. "What was her name? Audrey?"

I cocked my head, suddenly suspicious. "How did you know I saw her again?" Had she been there, too?

"Just making an educated guess," Dr. Travetti replied, smiling gently. "So, what exactly was so terrible about your weekend? This all sounds fine to me."

"Well, first of all, I didn't *want* to see Audrey."

"You didn't?"

"Hell no. That's the last thing I wanted." Her lips trapped between her teeth as she eyed me with suspicion. I laughed easily. "What the hell is *that* look for?"

"Oh, nothing." Dr. Travetti dropped her gaze to the lapel of her jacket and brushed an invisible piece of lint away. "I just think you *did* want to see her."

"Oh, really?" I challenged. "And what makes you think that?"

She raised her eyes to mine, challenge igniting a fire within. "Because you read a poem that you never intended to keep, and it just so happened to be a poem about the tattoo you put on her. You sent out a Bat Signal for her, and she answered the call."

I chuckled at the reference. "Doc, I never would've pegged you for a *DC* girl."

She smiled fondly. "I'm a *Marvel* fan, personally, but I have a soft spot for Batman."

With a nod, I pointed at her. "Keaton or Bale?"

"Ooh ..." Dr. Travetti sucked in a breath and tipped her head back. "That's a tough one, but if I had to pick, I'd say Keaton."

I pushed forward with my fist extended. "Same, Doc."

With a laugh, she pounded her knuckles against mine. "How was your encounter with Audrey this time?"

Settling back in my chair, I considered the question. I remembered the push and pull of my desire to be in her presence. The internal battle. "It was hard."

"Hard?"

"Yeah," I sniffed and turned to look out the window. "It was nice, until I thought about what I was doing, and then I wanted to get the fuck out of there."

She nodded, slow and steady. "And why do you think you felt like that?"

I knew what she was doing. She wanted me to look deep within, to chisel out the secrets from the darkest corners of my heart, and then reveal them to her. Because it was her job to figure me out and fix me. But I already knew the answer to her question, and without hesitation, I stated, "Because I don't deserve nice things, and Audrey is ..." I blew out a drawn-out breath. "Well, she's a nice thing."

"And this brings us back to our last session. You don't give yourself a chance. You don't allow yourself to feel good, proud, happy ..." She shook her head and tapped the tip of her pen against the clipboard. "We need to—"

"I'm not done telling you about my weekend."

113

She sighed and shifted her gaze to the clock ticking away on the wall. "Okay, I'm sorry. Continue."

I swallowed and hurried to speak before she could weasel her way in again. "I had a good time with Audrey while it lasted, and then I got the fuck out of there before I could do anything really stupid. And you know, I started to regret that the next day, on Sunday. I started asking myself, why couldn't I hang out some more? But then, I went over to my parents' place for dinner. Jake threw a fit, you know, I told you about his mood swings."

"Yeah, you've mentioned them," she nodded sympathetically.

I gripped the back of my neck with a sweaty palm. "It'd apparently been a continuation of something that had been going on all day, and my parents told me they think he needs to be put into a *place*," I spat with disgust.

"What kind of place?"

A sour taste flooded my mouth as I choked out, "An assisted living facility or some shit."

Dr. Travetti eyed me with concern and sympathy. "You don't agree."

"No, I don't fucking agree."

"Why?"

My palms clapped to the chair's leather arms and my fingers dug into the upholstery. "Because he's fine! He likes his teachers; he likes the daycare. He needs a routine, and we have one, and I don't know what the hell it'll do to him to change."

"Are you more concerned about him, or you?"

"What?" I balked, flabbergasted. "Him!"

114

"Are you sure about that?"

I thrust forward, mashing my elbows to my knees as I pointed at the good doctor and her pantsuit and that know-it-all mouth of hers. "Don't act like you know better about this than me, Doc, you understand me? I know Jake better than *anyone*. I know what he needs, I know what he wants, and I know how to deal with him. He needs *me*, okay? Not some fucking strangers at a place that's gonna treat him like a nuisance. He needs *me*."

I pushed my back into the chair and tucked my shaking hands into my lap. I returned my glare to the window and the world outside. To a sunny autumn day and pedestrians free to live their lives as they saw fit.

"Blake."

"Yeah, Doc?" My voice scraped against my throat and I wanted to claw at my flesh, to relieve the itch. To feel something other than this relentless tugging at my heart that hurt so goddamn badly.

"Let's do something, okay?"

I smirked at the sky. "Isn't it against the rules for a doctor to *do something* with a patient?"

"Very funny," she drawled. "No, seriously, let's try an exercise."

"Yeah, fine. I'll play."

"Excellent. Okay. I'm going to ask you a question, and you're going to answer with the first thing that comes to mind."

I laughed. "How is this different than what we always do?"

"Because you're not going to contemplate your answers for once."

I sighed and turned away from the window, fixing my glare on hers. "Okay, fine. Let's do it."

She picked up her pen and placed the tip on the paper. "Why do you hate religion?"

"Just a week or so ago, you asked me why I hated my brother. Now, you're accusing me of hating religion. Maybe you're the hateful one here, Doc."

Exhaustedly, her pen flopped to the paper. "*Do* you hate your brother?"

"No."

"Do you hate religion?"

"Yes."

"So, it's not simply that you don't believe in anything; it's a hatred."

I nodded. "Yes."

"Why?"

And so, I told her that a god who was good, a god that was just, would never have allowed a horrific accident to happen to someone as talented and wonderful as Jake was. That a god painted to be so righteous and fair would've instead punished me, the bad egg, the black sheep. Dr. Travetti wasn't expecting the answer, her surprise made evident in her wide-eyed stare and softly parted lips. I wanted to ask what she had assumed I'd say. That I'd had an awful upbringing in the Church? That my parents shoved the Lord and His book down my throat until I couldn't recite a passage without gagging on my own tongue?

"So, you blame God for what happened to Jake."

"No," I corrected her with a lift of my finger. "I don't believe there *is* a god. I'd have to believe in something to blame him or her, or whatever."

"But your disbelief is derived from hate and anger."

"What does that matter?"

Dr. Travetti shook her head. "It doesn't. I'm just making sure I have everything straight. So, because you can't blame God for what happened to your brother, because God doesn't exist, you blame yourself."

"There's only me to blame, Doc," I agreed with a nod. "It's all my fault. All of it."

"When did this start?"

"Start?" I laughed, dark and bitter. "Doc, I caused the fucking accident that—"

"No, I got that. But at what point did you decide you were going to punish yourself for as long as you live?"

I wedged my bottom lip between my teeth and bit down hard. A hint of copper flooded my taste buds as I hesitated to answer. Dr. Travetti leaned forward and met my eye.

"Blake, what happened?"

I stood up, moving away from her eyes, and paced the room. "There wasn't one pivotal moment, Doc. Lightning didn't strike one day and I just decided, hey, I'm going to be miserable for the rest of my fucking life. It was just, I don't know, a compilation of shit that just kept piling up. I realized my mother was angry all the time and my dad couldn't even look at Jake anymore." I faced her with a melancholic smile. "They were way different before the accident, they were awesome, but one stupid decision changed everything. And that was my doing, you know? And it all felt so wrong. Like, I was growing up, and he wasn't. I had a girlfriend, and he never would. I graduated high school, and he couldn't remember basic addition and subtraction. I learned to drive, and he could barely ride a fucking bike."

"You were leaving him behind," she assessed softly.

I turned to her, thrusting my hands out. "Yes! I was! And how the fuck is that fair? Why should I get to go out and live my life, when I'm the fucking reason he can't live his? It's fucking bullshit!"

I dropped back into the chair. "People used to always tell me it's awesome that I have a twin, that it's so cool I have someone who looks just like me and knows what I'm thinking all the time or some bullshit like that. But then, he got hurt, and now, when people meet him, all I get is sympathy. Like, *poor Blake, look at what he has to live with. This guy looks just like him, but he still wets the fucking bed.* People still compare us, the way they used to, but there's no fucking comparison anymore. And that's when I started to realize that ... sometimes it blows to be a twin, and that if I had never fucked up ... if I never even *existed* ... he would've had a fighting chance." My throat tightened and my voice broke. Fucking hell, was I actually going to cry?

Dr. Travetti put her pen down and clasped her hands over her knee. "I think we've done enough for today," she concluded in the most anticlimactic way possible. I nearly snickered and rolled my eyes, because after a performance like that, I'd hoped for more. An applause, a tear—something.

"But, Blake?"

118

"What, Doc?"

"This was the most critical session we've ever had; I want you to realize that. You've been coming to me for years, and we have never made as much progress as we have today."

"Oh, I'm so thrilled," I muttered dryly.

"Well, you can be sarcastic all you want, but I really am. Thrilled, I mean." She offered me a genuine smile, and I tried to return the gesture.

"Well, Doc," I stood up and pushed my hair back against my scalp, "it's been—"

"I have an assignment for you this week."

I gaped at her. "You're giving me homework now?"

"Yes." Her mouth lifted in a little smile. "I want you to find Audrey and ask her out."

I gawked at this smirking woman. "What the fuck? Why would I do that?"

"Because you like her."

"That's a stupid fucking reason," I grumbled with a roll of my eyes.

Dr. Travetti tipped her head and met my gaze with sincerity. "But what better reason is there?"

Chapter Ten

"**H**EY, BLAKE, what do you wanna get for lunch?"

"Whatever, it doesn't matter," I grumbled, tracing the lines of a sternum piece. The dude under my needle flinched every five seconds and I was about ready to send him home with a half-finished tattoo.

"Come on. Do you want Chinese? Or uh, we could order from—"

"Cee," I interrupted with an exasperated huff. "Just decide what you want, and we'll get it, okay?"

"Fine, jeez ..." She shot me with a sour look and turned away to head back up front.

I shook my head and continued to work, diving headfirst into the hum and vibration of my machine. I coaxed my lungs to breathe, to settle the tension winding me up tight and leaving my shoulders rigid. I listened to the music playing from the sound system, Marilyn Manson's "Coma White," and drowned in my work. Until my client moaned and shifted beneath my hands and my reflexes sent me upright in a flash.

This was the fourth time in twenty minutes and my patience was wearing thin.

"You okay?" I asked, keeping my tone even and calm.

Ryan was his name and he smiled apologetically. "Yeah, man, sorry."

"You wanna take a break?" I offered, hoping he'd accept, and to my delight, his eyes lit with gratitude.

"Really? We can do that?"

"Yeah, sure, let's take a breather." I rolled backward to the trashcan and pulled my gloves off as Ryan sat up.

"I didn't think it'd hurt so much," he admitted, grimacing.

"Anything right over bone can be pretty tough," I informed him, brushing my annoyance away with sympathy and understanding.

"I feel like a wuss."

I stood up and clipped my knuckles against his shoulder. "Nah, you're fine. Give yourself a few minutes and we'll get going again."

I left him at my station and went up to the desk to find Celia. She had her nose in a takeout menu from Bonchon Chicken, refusing to look up when I approached.

"Cee," I coaxed, tapping my fingers on the countertop.

"Go away, Blake. You're being a whiny bitch today and I don't wanna deal with your shit."

I chuckled lightly. "I deserve that."

"Oh, good. I'm glad you know you're being an asshole. That makes me feel so much better."

I folded my arms and peered over the counter's ledge at her. "I'm sorry. I had a shitty session with my therapist this morning, and—" I caught myself and stopped talking. I'd never admitted to my therapy before and nobody knew. Celia made that evident by the shocked expression she revealed as she glanced up at me.

"Wait, you're in therapy?"

"Uh, yeah ..." Uncertainty coated my voice and I scrubbed a hand through my hair.

"Why didn't I know this?"

I shrugged. "I don't know ... I guess it just never came up."

"How long have you been going?"

"Um, a couple years."

"A couple *years*?" She dropped the menu and gawked at me. "I mean, it's none of my business, but how have you been seeing a therapist for years without telling me?"

I laughed tightly through my shame and humiliation. "It's really not a big deal, Cee."

"No, it's not, but ... I don't know. It's just weird you've never mentioned it. I'm like your best friend."

I cocked my head at the declaration. My best friend? Celia and I had been working together for years, developing a strange relationship based on craft, casual conversation, and the rare occurrence of sex. She was one of the few people to know Jake, to know my moods, to know *me*. Yet, I had never thought of her as my best friend before. Maybe I'd never thought that I deserved a best friend. Maybe I never thought I could have one, with my world being the way it was. But turns out, it had happened anyway, and it was fine.

You're fine.

So are you.

"Sorry," I said again, unsure why.

"It's okay," she brushed it off. "Anyway, you want chicken? I'm in the mood for Bonchon."

"Bonchon's good," I agreed.

"Cool. You want your usual? I'll pick it up while you finish up in there."

"That works for me." I reached over the counter and ruffled her dreadlocks. "Thanks, Cee."

"You're welcome," she mumbled, and I headed back to work, feeling just a bit happier and lighter.

I have a best friend.

***

"Blake, Blake," my brother ran down the stairs from his bedroom in a hurry, clutching a Blu-ray disc in his hand. I turned from opening the front door to give him my attention.

"What's up, buddy?"

"It won't play. I keep putting it in and it won't play. You gotta fix it, Blake. Fix it."

"Okay, let me see."

He thrust the disc into my hand and I didn't need to look closely to see hundreds of tiny scratches etched into its surface. It was his favorite movie, *Gremlins*, and I knew he'd have a fit if I told him it was broken. "You know what, Jake? I think I'm gonna need to fix this tomorrow, okay? It's gonna take too long right now and I gotta get home."

He eyed me with worry and a dash of panic. "But you're gonna fix it? I need it fixed, Blake. Can you fix it?"

"Yeah," I assured him, making a mental note to stop at the store the next day to grab a new one. "I'm gonna fix it tomorrow."

"Pinkie swear?" He held up his pinkie and offered it to me.

"Pinkie swear," I nodded, wrapping my finger around his.

He breathed a sigh of relief, but his eyes remained on the ruined disc in my hand. I tucked it gently into my pocket before laying my hand on his shoulder, squeezing reassuringly.

"Did you brush your teeth?" I asked.

"Uh-huh."

"You sure?"

His eyes looked to the ceiling, studying the paint and light fixture as he ran through the sequence of the night. "I went to the bathroom, peed, and brushed my teeth."

"Okay, go back upstairs and into bed. I'll find another movie for you to watch before I head home."

"I wanna go home with you," he told me, and I noted that in all the years I'd lived outside of this house, he had never said that before. Never expressed an interest in leaving these walls.

"Maybe you can sleep over one day this week," I offered.

"I wanna sleep over every night."

With those words ringing loudly in my head, I coaxed him back into his room and under the covers. I put on *The Goonies* and after saying goodnight once again, headed home way later than intended. All to take care of him. To do the things my parents wouldn't.

Lying in bed, I browsed social media. Since Shane's mention, the hype had died down, which hurt with a faint flick against my ego. It was a reminder that the world we live in today, is full of people with short attention spans and the need for instant gratification. But I moved on just as quickly. It was for the best. I'd gotten a handful of new clients, and that was fine. A handful was manageable, for now. Soon, if my parents had their way, I wouldn't need to devote any time to Jake. No more picking him up, no more dropping him off. No more staying late at my parents' place to help care for him.

The thought was a knife, thrust deep between my ribs. Scraping bones, piercing my heart, digging deep until I thought I'd die. What the hell would I do with myself, if he wasn't around? What the hell would I do with all my time?

I posted a picture of Ryan's tattoo from earlier today. The dagger against his sternum had been painful but worth it, he'd said, and I was pleased with the work. Delicate lines and heavy shading created the image of something that could've been used in the darkest of fairy tales, and I nodded with self-approval.

I continued to browse the pictures on my feed. Tattoos done by Cee, Gus's daughter Kara, and a few other shops in the area. But, it didn't take long to grow bored with the posts from the few people I followed, and my attention was drawn toward browsing other black ink tattoo artwork.

The artists I found from around the world were brilliant and masterful at their craft. They received great amounts of praise in the comments, their follower counts were plentiful, and I could only imagine that their list of clients kept them in very comfortable lives. They deserved it and their art spoke for itself. But the more I browsed, the more it occurred to me that, while they were excellent, so was I. I don't think it'd ever dawned on me before, that my skills were easily on par with some of the greats. And wouldn't I be able to do more for Jake, and myself, if I was making more money? Maybe I could even convince Mom and Dad to let him stay with me, if I could prove myself to be a more reliable support. But even if my parents insisted on putting him in a facility, which I would fight tooth and nail, I could at the very least ensure he'd be put in a suitable one ... If I was making more.

My wandering mind drove my fingers to find Shane's Instagram page. The picture of his tattoo I'd done was liked well over a thousand times, with nearly four-hundred comments of praise. There wasn't a single bit of negativity from what I could see and a sensation I hadn't felt in a long time, maybe ever, swelled in my chest and overflowed, sparking the prick of tears against my eyes.

I was proud. Absolutely and completely proud of something that I'd created.

I could feel like this all the time, I thought. Hell, I *should* feel like this all the time. It felt good, and didn't I at the very least deserve that? To feel proud and good about my work?

Without a moment's hesitation, I opened my inbox, found my conversation with Shane, and typed out a message: *Hey, man. So, I was thinking about that interview. If the offer still stands, I'd love to do it. Give me a call. Hoping to hear from you soon. – Blake*

Chapter Eleven

JAKE WAS AT my place for a sleepover when my phone rang. It was Shane and I couldn't miss his call. So, I answered, hoping Jake could contain himself long enough for us to have a conversation. But I should've known better. Shortly after the formalities were out of the way, my brother was badgering me with desperation, and my patience was wearing thin.

"Blake, Blake, Blake." Jake had my name on repeat, trying to grab my attention, and in a huff, I pulled the phone from my ear.

"Jake. Buddy. I need you to be a little patient right now, okay? I'm on the phone." I sighed at the blank expression on his face and said into the receiver, "Sorry about that, Shane."

He chuckled and replied, "It's all good. I have kids, myself."

"Oh, uh—"

"Blake, Blake, I need—"

I groaned and finally shouted, "Jake! Please, give it a rest, okay? Give me *two* minutes!"

I don't know what I'd been thinking, taking this call in the house. I should've stepped outside. Jake had zero understanding of patience or of the concept that I could too busy for him, and the constant interruptions were not only frustrating but embarrassing as well.

When he opened his mouth to speak again, I hurried into my room and shut the door behind me, locking it for good measure.

"Fuck. I'm really sorry. I thought it wouldn't be a problem talking here, but if it'd be easier, maybe I should give you a call when I'm at work."

"No, no, it's cool. Seriously." He was nothing but friendly, and I relaxed a little before he added, "How old?"

My brows lowered as I sat on the bed. "Huh?"

"Your son, how old is he?"

My head lifted with the realization that he thought Jake was my kid. "Oh, no, I don't have any kids," then I stopped myself. "Well, not exactly. That's my brother, Jake—Jacob."

"Oh! My bad, man. So, your brother is younger, right?"

Shane was making innocent, casual conversation. It was no different than how you'd get to know anybody else. But for me, these questions felt intrusive and invasive. I wanted to ward them off and defend myself, tell him it was none of his goddamn business. But Dr. Travetti was right, I get too defensive when I don't need to be, and so I took a deep breath instead.

"Uh, well, no. Not exactly. He's my twin brother." Immediately I realized how ridiculous and confusing that

129

sounded, and I scrubbed a hand over my face before explaining, "He's disabled."

Shane's surprise was blatantly apparent as he replied, "O-oh, sorry, dude. I didn't realize."

I shook my head and felt the cocktail of irritation and embarrassment creep over my neck and onto my face. "It's fine."

"Maybe we'll talk about that in your interview," Shane suggested, and I began to sweat, despite the window being cracked open. "I mean, if that's cool with you. I'm just curious to know how that has affected your art."

My jaw clamped shut and my molars ground together. "I'd rather not. I don't talk about it much."

"Oh, yeah, of course," Shane hurried apologetically. "Sorry, I shouldn't have mentioned it. That was a dickish move."

"It's cool," I muttered, laying my forehead in my palm.

"Anyway, so I'm heading back up to Salem in a couple of weeks to hang out with Cee, sometime around Halloween. Would you be able to get together then for the interview?"

I nodded to the nothing surrounding me in my room. "Yeah, that works for me."

"Awesome, man. I'm looking forward to it. Thanks so much for reconsidering, by the way. I'm fucking excited. The response from the ink you did on my leg has been insane."

I grunted my acknowledgement. "Yeah, I've been watching on Instagram. Pretty crazy."

Shane laughed boisterously. "You're so casual, man! God! I feel like I could tell you Ozzy fuckin' Osbourne wanted to get ink from you and you'd just be like, yeah, that's cool. You have a crazy vibe, I fucking love it."

I narrowed my eyes toward the wall. Nobody had ever mentioned my *vibe* before, and now, two people in less than a week had said something. It was a coincidence, I knew that. Life was all just a pile of accidents and coincidences that sometimes made sense and at other times, total chaos. But right now, I could distinctly feel my brain start to tip toward a belief in more. I shook my head to get that crazy shit out of there as quickly as I possibly could.

"Yeah, so anyway," he went on. "I guess I'll give you a call in a couple of weeks. Sound good?"

"Sure, yeah. That sounds great."

"Awesome. You take care, Blake. Can't wait to make this shit happen with you."

We hung up after our quick good-byes and with the sudden silence, I could hear Jake shuffling around and breathing outside my door. I sighed, thrusting my fingers into my dark hair, and granted myself two more seconds just to breathe. This ... Life ... In an instant, it just felt so heavy, laying on my back and weighing me down. I wanted to double over, collapse under its heft and give up.

But if I didn't take care of things, nobody would. So, I pulled in a breath, pushed myself to my feet, and opened the door.

"What's up, buddy?"

With big, worried eyes and a pout fixed to his lips, he looked like a lost, abandoned dog. Like I'd shut him out, never to let him back in, and the guilt of that, of putting something—myself—above him, left me burdened with a fresh bout of shame. I waited for him to respond, and when he didn't, I wrapped an arm around his shoulders and sighed.

"Come on, let's go make dinner. What are you in the mood for?"

"Miss Thomas said she eats breakfast for dinner. She's wrong. You can't eat breakfast for dinner."

I snorted, leading the way into the kitchen. "You can eat breakfast whenever you want, man. So, is that what you're saying? You want pancakes for dinner? 'Cause I'm totally down for pancakes."

"Okie dokie."

I opened the fridge. "Okie dokie. Pancakes, it is."

***

"We're gonna stop at Jolie Tea on the way to school, okay?" I said, parking the car.

Jake checked his digital watch. "I'm going to be late. I don't want to be late."

"We have almost an hour before school starts, buddy. You won't be late," I assured him, as we got out of the car. I gripped his bicep and steered him toward the sidewalk. "And hey, maybe I'll get you one of their cookies."

"Cookies aren't for breakfast."

"Yeah, but you already had breakfast," I reasoned. "This is like, a snack before lunch."

"Snacks should be tasty and healthy."

I shrugged casually. "Okay, fine. Sorry I tried to be a nice brother."

We walked through the door of the quaint shop. The delicate scent of freshly brewed tea wafted along the air, and I smiled at the familiar faces behind the counter.

"My favorite brothers!" Mindy exclaimed, her ponytail bobbing as she moved to the register. "What can I get for you guys today?"

"Hey, Min. I'm out of my tea," I told her as Jake stood obediently beside me.

"So, you need four ounces of vanilla Earl Grey, right?"

"You know it," I replied with a smile as I heard the door jingle open from behind me.

"Anything else?" Mindy asked as Stella, the other employee, assisted the next customer, saying, "Good morning! What can I get for you?"

"No, I think that's everything," I said.

"You sure? No macarons for this guy?" She smiled sweetly at Jake, who responded with a shy curl of his lips.

He began to speak, then Mindy went to respond, but my ears weren't picking up on their brief correspondence. Instead they'd pricked at the soft melody of the other voice in the shop, and I turned my head, acutely aware of that sound.

"Hey, can you recommend a good green tea? My cousins have been going on and on about this place but I only drink—" Before she could finish her thought, Audrey noticed me staring and her eyes brightened with the spread of her grin. "Oh, my God, Blake! Hi!"

"Hey," I replied, swallowing hard and wishing I'd picked another day to stop by and grab my tea.

She cocked her hip and continued to grin. "You know, I never would've pegged you for a tea drinker."

Another swallow before I cleared my throat. "Oh, no?"

She shook her head. "Definitely not. I totally would've thought you'd be a coffee guy. Black, no sugar," she said in a mocking tone, deep and sultry. Her playfulness should've been catching, but my legs and feet begged for me to leave, and their urgent message to my brain kept me from smiling along with her.

Because this wasn't a Saturday night when I was allowed my time to be myself, vibe-less Blake. This was the middle of the week and a part of my routine that offered zero opportunity for this. Social pleasantries. Casual conversation. I had to work. I had Jake.

"Nope, not into coffee," I muttered, curling my lips in a curt, dismissive smile before turning my attention back to Mindy and Jake. He was scarfing down a macaron and I raised an eyebrow. "What happened to no cookies in the morning?"

"I made him an offer he couldn't refuse," Mindy replied, smiling fondly at my brother. "It's on me."

"Thank you," I said gratefully.

"Let me just get your tea and I'll ring you up."

"Awesome," I replied, and thanked her again.

I watched as Mindy hurried around the small shop, purposely keeping my gaze from settling on the short, blonde woman beside me. To look at her would've been to grant myself the permission to settle deeper under her spell. I couldn't have any of that. My mind would be liable to think further into signs and the possibility of Fate—*fuck you for planting* that *seed, Dr. Travetti.*

But even as I refused to look at her, I still listened. She was buying a cup of their Ocean Breeze green tea, iced, and a variety sampler of other green teas they had to offer. She yammered on about how much she just loved green tea and how she preferred its light flavor over the strength of black teas. The suggestion that she'd maybe enjoy a white tea bit at my tongue, begging to escape, and I was satisfied when Stella took the words right out of my mouth.

"Oh, I've never had a white tea!" Audrey exclaimed enthusiastically.

Mindy glanced over her shoulder as she weighed out the loose tea. "Blake, didn't you really enjoy one of our white teas over the summer?"

I ground my fingernails into my palm, angry that I'd been dragged once again into conversation with this woman. But a smile masked my irritation as I replied, "Oh, yeah, it was the strawberry white. Jake really liked it."

"That's right," Mindy responded with a smile. "Then you drank it all on him. Remember that, Jake?"

"Blake drank all the tea," Jake laughed with more exuberance than necessary. "He said he didn't like it and then he drank all the tea."

He clapped his hands as he laughed, and I laid a hand on his shoulder to settle him down. My eyes shifted toward Audrey, not wanting her to judge or scrutinize, as unholy as that would've been for a good, cross-wearing girl like her. Not that it'd ever stopped Christians from passing unfair judgment before. Yet, when I looked at her, I saw nothing but affection and acceptance in her pale blue eyes. That simple piece of twine I held onto thickened and pulled me in closer, further into her energy and radiating light.

"Who's this good-looking guy?" she asked, addressing Jake with the kindest smile I would never deserve.

I hesitated before saying, "This is my brother, Jake."

"Hi, Jake," she said, extending her delicate hand. He observed her fingers for a moment, unsure of what to do, and I leaned into him.

"Buddy, you shake her hand. Remember?" And solely for demonstration purposes, I took Audrey's hand in mine and shook, unsuccessfully ignoring the sprinkle of electricity that encouraged the hairs along my arm to stand on end. "See? Like this."

Audrey smiled and released my hand to try again with my brother. He accepted this time and shook her arm aggressively. She laughed, a sweet sound, as I gripped Jake's wrist to still his assault.

"Whoa, man. You wanna *shake* her hand, not dismember her."

"What's your name? I'm Jake," he said, ignoring me and the fact that I'd already told her his name.

"It's very nice to meet you, Jake. My name's Audrey."

Jake nodded, looking from her to me and back to her. He was watching us both intently, staring studiously with that look he got sometimes. The look that told me he knew something and was unable to verbalize it in the way he'd like to, in a way I'd understand. I wanted him to stop. I wanted to shake him and tell him to knock it off, because there was no reason he should be looking at her that way. There was nothing to see here and nothing to dissect. She was nothing more than a traveler, passing through my life more times than welcome, and I needed him to stop looking at her right now.

"Blake," he said, gripping my shoulder and shaking me with urgency. "Blake."

"What's up, buddy?" I asked, passing Mindy my debit card.

"I like her color. She's yellow. Pretty yellow. Like flowers. She's like a *flower*, Blake."

I stilled at the innocent analogy. There was beautiful simplicity in the comparison. She really was a flower, beautiful and seemingly untouched by the ugliness this world could offer. It was all the reason I needed to grab my bag from Mindy, thank her, and hurry out of there with my brother in tow. Just to get the hell away from her, to keep her beautiful and unsullied by me.

Outside, I hurried Jake along, insisting that we were going to be late for school, even when we had plenty of time to spare. It didn't surprise me when I heard the quickened gait behind me and her voice. Her fucking voice.

137

"Blake! Wait up!"

I pretended to ignore her when my brother turned. "Hi, Audrey!" he shouted, waving his arm, and I hadn't wanted to punch him so much since we were kids.

I slowed our walk to let her catch up and she appeared at my side. "Hey, where are you headed?"

"Walking this guy to school," I said astutely.

"Oh, wow, I bet you like going to school, huh, Jake?"

"Yeah, yeah, I do. My teacher likes Mickey Mouse," Jake replied with an eager nod.

"Do *you* like Mickey Mouse?"

"Oh, Mickey is my favorite. My dog is Mickey, too. He's a Golden Retriever and he's a real good boy."

Audrey smiled. "I love dogs. I used to have one … Well, actually, he was my sister's dog, but she passed away and so did he."

"Passed away means dead," Jake replied bluntly and I glared at him with narrowed eyes.

"Jake. Come on, man."

Audrey surprised me by wrapping her hand around my arm as much as it would go. Her hands were so small, so delicate. So fragile, I could break her. "No, it's okay," she told me gently. Then, addressing Jake again, she said, "Yes. Passed away means dead."

"Dead means gone. Gone forever," he muttered somberly, furrowing his brow to work through the feelings he didn't quite understand. "Daisy died. Daisy's gone forever."

"Who's Daisy?"

I sighed, growing increasingly impatient with this exchange. "Daisy was our dog growing up."

"Ah." Audrey nodded sympathetically. "That's true, Jake. Dead does mean gone, but not necessarily gone forever. Daisy went to Heaven, and one day you'll see her—"

"So, was there something you wanted?" I cut her off, leveling her with a stony glare that didn't seem to affect her whatsoever.

"Oh! Yes, sorry," she waved her hand flippantly, as though embarrassed she'd gotten away with herself. "I wanted to ask what that meant, about the color. He said he liked my color."

I could steer her away from the conversation of spirituality, but it was more difficult to divert her attention from this when she'd already heard.

I encouraged Jake to wander ahead but close enough that I could keep an eye on him. The instructions put more intrigue into Audrey's watching stare and I took a deep, preparatory breath, knowing there'd be more questions to follow the initial explanation.

"One of the symptoms of Jake's condition, is that he associates colors with people," I said, keeping my voice low.

It had been the oddest thing. I remembered him in his hospital bed, and I remembered my parents, so afraid that he'd never talk or walk again. I remembered the shock that resounded throughout the room when he finally did speak, to let me know my color was red—angry. I'd been so angry at nobody but myself. Not scared, not worried. Just angry and so, so bitter. I was only ten and too young to feel so much hate. But those first words—"*You're red, Blake.*" Nobody knew what they meant at the time. Nobody knew what to think. But we had clambered toward his bed, crowding around him with hugs and smiles.

I wished now that our brief moment of happiness and relief had lasted longer.

"Wow," she responded, astonishment in her eyes. "So ... he sees auras?"

I shrugged. "Whatever you want to call it."

"Well, what do *you* call it?"

I snorted. "I call it a symptom."

Audrey hummed contemplatively. "*I'd* call it a gift. A very special one. Not many people are given intuition like that. He's lucky."

This conversation wasn't going the way I had anticipated. "*Lucky*?" I scoffed as my eyes drifted to my brother. Thirty-four years old, six-foot-two, and jumping from puddle to puddle along the sidewalk. "I'm not sure where you get lucky from that."

Audrey gaped at me, a flash of anger darkening her gaze. "What an awful thing to say."

Startled by the harsh bite in her tone, I lowered my brows and glared right back. "Uh, excuse me?"

Pointing ahead at Jake, now fidgeting with his fingers and peering across the street at a Labrador walking with its owner, Audrey said, "Not only is he unburdened by the harsh reality of the world around him, but he has the gift of honest intuition and a brother who obviously adores him. That is the very definition of lucky, Blake, and it breaks my heart that you could actually look at him and say something like that."

Her statement felt like a slap in the face, and I was instantly ashamed. "I guess that's one way to look at it," I said thoughtfully.

Audrey smiled then and changed the subject. "I'm actually a little surprised to find that you're a twin."

I stuffed my hands into my pockets. "Why?"

"Because," she said, shrugging shyly and watching her feet, "Sabrina was *my* twin."

My toe caught a crack in the sidewalk, and I stumbled, reaching out to steady myself against a storefront. Audrey grabbed my arm in her hands and asked, "Are you okay?"

"Yeah," I said, righting myself. "Uh, so you're a twin, huh?"

"Yep," she nodded. "We weren't identical, like you guys, but we looked alike enough."

I was behaving like an idiot as I remained silent and let the moment process. I pretended to be distracted by Jake, watching him drag his finger along the storefront windows, while I found myself thinking a question I hadn't thought in decades.

What does it all mean?

It meant nothing, of course. It was just another coincidence to toss onto the ever-growing pile. But the thought felt natural, racing around my mind as we walked closer to Jake's daycare. Would she continue to walk with me, after he was dropped off? Would she follow me to work like a lost puppy, desperate to be taken in?

Lost. I'm *the one who's lost.*

"Has he always been like this?"

Audrey's voice fractured my thoughts and I turned to her abruptly. "Huh?" She gestured toward Jake and my flesh prickled with immediate defense. "No," I spat out. "He hasn't. Why?"

Unfazed, she smiled toward my brother. "He's incredibly sweet. Is it just you two?"

"No. Our parents are alive."

"Do they live with you?"

I wrinkled my nose. "What is this, an interrogation?"

Audrey's laugh was brighter than the sun. "No! Oh my gosh, you're so—"

"This is our stop," I cut her off, as we neared Jake's daycare.

Her eyes glanced toward the building and I thought I noticed a glimmer of recognition sparkle in her eyes, but it disappeared quicker than I had time to react. "Oh, okay. I'll wait here for you, if you don't mind."

I minded. I minded so much, my brain screamed with obscenities and my bones tensed beneath my skin. But outwardly, I shrugged nonchalantly, as if I didn't care. Like I didn't want her to get the hell away from me. Like I didn't want her to burrow in the palm of my hand so I could carry her with me everywhere.

"Yeah, sure. I'll just be a couple minutes."

She gave Jake a hug and wished him a good day, before perching herself on the cobblestone wall and pulling out her phone, averting her attention until I'd return. I took just a second to look at her light washed

142

jeans, the white Adidas on her feet and the baggy
lavender sweater hanging over her slender frame. She
reminded me of the girls in high school, so many years
ago. The ones who held themselves out of my reach,
exchanging dirty glances and whispering insults. Freak,
goth, creep. They had wanted nothing to do with me, and
that was just fine, the feeling had been mutual. They
were fake, ingenuine, plastic, and plastic breaks. Plastic
melts to reveal the ugly wiring beneath the surface.

Yet, while Audrey reminded me of them
aesthetically, something told me the resemblance stopped
at the surface. And I knew, if she continued to wait, if
she continued to walk by my side to work, I would likely
want to see her again. Just as the good doctor instructed.
And, I would do it while ignoring the warnings that she
was light, she was good, and that I was the darkness
looming in the near distance, just dying to snuff her out.

***

"Wasn't that Butterfly Tattoo Chick?" Cee asked, her
eyes trained on the front window. Together we watched
Audrey walk away, her feet moving along the air,
practically floating with every step.

"Yeah."

Before Audrey could disappear, she waved one last
time, wiggling her fingers with optimistic flourish and
smiling like our walk had been a journey through
Disneyland.

"What the hell are you doing with Butterfly Tattoo Chick?" Celia turned her attention on me, her lips stretching in a judgmental smirk.

"I bumped into her at Jolie Tea."

Cee narrowed her eyes and crossed her arms. "So?"

I hadn't mentioned to Celia the frequent circumstantial coincidences regarding the so-called Butterfly Tattoo Chick. I'd kept that shit to myself and Dr. Travetti—nobody else needed to know. But now, we'd been seen together, and I didn't know how to hide it anymore. I didn't even know if it should be hidden, period.

"I've sort of seen her a couple of times," I casually mentioned, shrugging for effect.

"Sort of? What, you're *friends* with her?" Celia laughed incredulously. Then, laughing harder, she waved her hands and added, "Wait, wait ... Are you *screwing her*?"

"I'm not screwing her," I muttered through gritted teeth.

"So, then you're friends."

I shook my head and headed toward my workspace. "Not friends either."

Celia followed me. "So, what, you just happened to take a beautiful autumnal walk together for no particular reason?"

"Yep."

"God, you're so full of shit, Blake."

She could think I was full of shit all she wanted. I didn't care what she thought, and I proved my point by ignoring her statement and setting up for my first client of the day. Cee just continued to stand there, watching me through scrutinizing eyes, until finally she snickered and headed across the shop to her own station.

"So, is this about me and Shane?"

That grabbed my attention and I turned to glare at the back of her head. "What?"

"Shane asks me out, I cut you off, so … what? You need to find someone else to get your fix?"

I laughed, disbelieving. "You're high, Cee."

She shot a glance at me over her shoulder. "Not high, smart-ass. I'm just trying to figure out what the hell you'd be doing with *Barbie*."

There was a genuine glint of concern in her eyes, between her words and in the twitch of her lips. Celia was my friend. A former friend with benefits, sure, but she was still my friend, first and foremost. She thought this was a backslide, a strange cry for help in the form of a preppy girl with a butterfly inked to her chest, instead of the small of her back, and suddenly I felt I owed Cee an explanation.

"I bumped into her at the poetry club," I said. "She writes, too."

"Oh," she replied, genuinely surprised. "That's cool."

"Yeah. We ran into each other again at Jolie Tea this morning. She walked with me to Jake's daycare, and that's it." I shrugged nonchalantly, leaving out the fact that Audrey had asked me to meet her at the club on Saturday. The reminder fluttered my lids and forced my throat to swallow.

"Wait," Celia said, "she met Jake?"

145

"He was there," I replied.

"Wow," she muttered under her breath.

I dug deep between every letter of that three lettered word.

Wow. She wanted to ask how it went, Audrey's meeting with Jake.

Wow. Celia's first meeting with Jake a few years ago hadn't gone well. Jake didn't care for Cee initially. He thought she was too angry, dark and scary. She had a right to be—her husband and the father of her kids had screwed around behind her back. Of course she was angry. Red. But Jake hadn't liked it.

Wow. Perhaps she had the same thoughts as the good doctor. That there are no coincidences. Only signs and Fate. And my brother approved of this ray of sunshine that had somehow seeped into the gloom of his brother's life.

Wow. Wow wow wow.

Meet me on Saturday.

Audrey had asked me to write a poem to read. She would write one, too, she said. I was already nervous, and yet, I was also cautiously excited, too. I found myself looking forward to it. Looking forward to the warmth of the sun on a dark night in October.

Chapter Twelve

"WHAT ARE YOU doing tonight?" Mom asked out of obligation as Jake tried on his Halloween costume. He was going as *Daniel Tiger*.

"Going to the club," I told her, like it wasn't a big deal and like I wasn't meeting up with a woman. Was this a date? I hadn't figured that out yet.

Mom nodded, pursing her lips in the way that told me she was thinking. In the way I knew that she'd now say exactly what was on her mind. I hoped she wouldn't. Things had been even more tense between us since our failed family dinner. That was almost a week ago and we'd had several phone conversations since, but her tone had been tight and my spine had been rigid.

"Don't you miss going out during the week?"

I lifted my hand to the bridge of my nose and pinched. "Mom …"

"I'm just asking," she said, forcing an air of innocence into her tone. "I mean, limiting yourself to only going out on the weekends has to be rough."

"It's called being an adult, Mom."

"But wouldn't you like to have *options*? Remember when you were in college? You were out every other night, and you had friends, and—"

"I was a kid!" I scoffed incredulously.

"Yeah, and? Why should anything change?"

"Because I have a job," I laughed, shaking my head. "I have responsibilities."

"Well, if we find Jake a—"

"Mom," I closed my eyes and shook my head, "not now, okay?"

"I'm saying, *if*, Blake. *If* we find Jake a nice place, then maybe you could get out a little more." She nudged an elbow against me and said, "And hey, you're my only hope for grandchildren."

I laughed at her attempt at a normal mother-son conversation. The sound was damn near hostile to my ears. "Yeah, okay."

"I'm just saying, maybe you could meet a girl."

"You have no idea if I've met a girl or not already," I dared to mention, and why? Why had I done that? I wondered what Dr. Travetti would say about that come Monday.

Mom looked instantly startled and hopeful. "Have you?"

I crossed my arms tightly over my chest and shrugged. "I've seen this woman a couple of times," I answered honestly, not divulging the context in which I'd seen her.

"Wow," she mentioned, clearly taken aback. Her voice demonstrated shock and I struggled to find the happiness I thought I'd also hear. "Why haven't you said anything?" Ah, she was hurt.

"It's not serious, Mom."

"It's serious enough that you thought to mention it."

"I mentioned it because you won't get off my case," I said brusquely. "And because I wanted you to know that I'm quite capable of meeting people, even with Jake around."

She pinched her eyes shut and shook her head exhaustedly. "Okay, Blake," she sighed, dismissing me. And then, she walked away.

***

"You came!"

Audrey bounded toward me. It was a cold night and whatever top she wore was kept secret beneath her bright white coat. I wondered, though. What color was her shirt? And did it reveal the butterfly I'd carved into her chest? Could I make out the outline of her bra? Was she even wearing one?

I wondered what she'd say if she knew what vile things swarmed my brain. I wondered what she'd do.

"Of course I did," I answered, unsure of what to do. Should I hug her? Should I kiss her cheek?

Without giving me a moment to decide, Audrey wrapped her arm around mine and led me toward the steps down to the underground club. The contrast of our coats, black leather and soft white, was stark and alarming. We were the Yin and Yang, balance, and for the first time since meeting her, I wondered if maybe that could be a good thing.

After heading inside, she made a beeline to the reader list.

"Okay, you put your name down first," Audrey instructed, offering the pen to me.

"Why can't you go first?" I asked, eyeing the ballpoint skeptically.

"Because I want to make sure that we're *both* reading," she reasoned with an encouraging smile. She insistently tried to pass the pen into my empty hands. "Come on, Blake. Don't leave me hanging."

She was grinning at me, unbothered by my persistent scowl as I stared at the implement in her hand. Finally, I took it with a begrudging sigh and quickly scribbled my name on the first empty line.

"You can write mine down, too," Audrey said, her smile unrelenting, and so I put the tip of the pen to the line beneath mine. She watched as I scrawled her name in my trademark sloppy cursive. Chicken scratch, my mom always called it. She'd always thought I should practice neater handwriting, but Audrey's lips closed, hiding her teeth, and her smile shrunk to something smaller and more contemplative. "I like the way you write my name," she complimented.

"Huh?" I laid the pen down and stuffed my hands into the pockets of my jeans.

"Your handwriting is so pretty." Her fingers touched the dried ink and traced the A with her nail.

I couldn't help but laugh. "My mom hates it," I admitted. "She always complains that it's too messy."

Audrey looked up to smile into my eyes. "Messy can still be beautiful."

The simple statement immediately reminded me of those lame quotes girls came into the shop looking for. But this felt different and didn't feel like something she'd read online. It felt like something that was written on the spot and made special, just for me.

She thought my handwriting was beautiful—did she think *I* was beautiful? That seemed unlikely, but so did all of this, walking through the poetry club with her on my arm and finding a vacant table to sit at. She looked to me as though I was more than how I felt, like a gallant hero, or a noble gentleman. For a moment, I chose to play the part she seemed to squeeze me into and pulled out her chair.

"Thank you," she said gratefully, removing her coat to reveal her light blue top. Adorned in lace, it clung to her arms, and the hem blossomed out to hang loosely around her narrow hips. Her skintight jeans complemented it well, accentuating the length of her legs and the heels on her feet.

If I stared too long, I wondered too much. What the fuck was she doing here with me? Hell, what the fuck was *I* doing here with *her*?

"You look like you wanna run away," Audrey said quietly, hanging her coat from the back of the chair.

Was it that obvious? I forced a pained smile, and without answering her question, I asked, "Do you want something to drink?"

Her smile fell. "Um ... I guess a Manhattan?" Her voice was apologetic, and I remembered she wasn't familiar with drink ordering. "What are you going to get?"

"Probably a gin and tonic. Or maybe an Old Fashioned."

Audrey smiled then. "How about you just get me whatever you're getting?"

"What if you don't like it?"

She shrugged lightly. "How am I supposed to know if I like something if I don't try it?"

My head bobbed in a slow nod. "Good point. I'll be right back," and I headed toward the bar.

I ordered two gin and tonics and waited for them to be made. Every two seconds, I found myself looking back toward the table, to check on Audrey. To make sure she was still there. To remind myself that this was real. I wiped a hand over my dry lips and shook my head.

"You okay, boss?" the bartender asked, sliding the two glasses toward my waiting hands.

"Yeah, I'm good," I told him, leaving a few bills on the bar and taking the glasses. "Thanks."

But I wasn't good. I was shaken and in denial, expecting her to admit this was all a joke, an elaborate set up. Maybe it was an experiment the good doctor was conducting, to see how I'd react in the situation. All of it, an extravagant role-play scenario I wasn't aware of.

I headed back to the table and placed a glass in front of her before sitting down in the chair beside hers. She smiled sweetly and thanked me for the drink. I nodded and lifted my glass to my lips, but before I could take a sip, she asked, "What should we drink to?"

I allowed a light chuckle at the question. "We don't need to drink to anything."

"Do you drink a lot?"

I considered the question and then shook my head. "Not really. Maybe a couple drinks a week, I guess. Why?"

"Then, this is a special occasion," she declared. "So, we should drink to something."

And I actually gave it some thought. I lowered my glass and pursed my lips, ignoring the droning of the poet currently on the stage. I shook my head, coming up empty, and admitted, "I got nothin'."

Audrey tapped a finger against my wrist and said, "I know. We should drink to us."

"Us?" The word rolled sour against my tongue. *Us* felt like we were something, together, and that's not what this was. There was no *us*.

But Audrey nodded assuredly. "Yes, us. The better twins." She still wore that bright smile, but there was a darkness in those words, lacing between the letters and tying them tight, bringing them together. And that was something I understood. Darkness. I thrived in its shadows and knew its deepened corners well.

"What does that mean?" I asked, folding my arms and forgetting about my drink.

Audrey shrugged and wrapped her manicured fingers around the glass. "You know what I mean, Blake."

I shook my head. "No, I don't think I do."

"Jake became disabled, right?"

"Yes."

Her eyes met mine. "My sister became very sick."

Better. Burdened. Guilty. It was all the same, and then, I understood. I nodded solemnly and lifted my glass.

"To being the burdened twins," I corrected, using my own words.

But Audrey shook her head. "Not burdened, Blake. Just better," and her glass clinked against mine.

***

His face, like mine,
His height, the same.
But his mind is different,
And I'm to blame.
Starved and forbidden,
Unable to thrive,
They say it's a miracle,
He's even alive.
But what kind of god,
Shuns one of his own?
What kind of father,
Leaves his child alone?

Audrey waited at the table as I walked back, tearing up the poem as I went. An expression of horror blanketed her features as I returned. When I asked what that look was for, she questioned, "Why did you just do that?"

"Do what?"

"Tear it up!" she exclaimed exasperatedly, thrusting her hand toward my fist where the torn-up shreds of paper remained.

"What's the point in keeping it?" I countered, sitting down and grabbing my glass. It was my third drink. I never drank more than one, but tonight, it was three. Would there be a fourth?

"Because it's beautiful, Blake!" Audrey's volume had raised a bit since we'd arrived. It was also her third drink, and something told me she couldn't handle her liquor well.

I snickered. "No, it wasn't. My shit isn't beautiful."

Her face fell with a crushing amount of sorrow as her hand pressed against her chest. "Oh, Blake. You ... You are *so* beautiful. You're so talented and gifted and your words are ..." She shook her head, planting her hand against her chest again and again. "Your words are your heart, and it's broken, but it's not ugly. *You're* not ugly."

"You don't know what the hell you're talking about," I scoffed, leaning back in my chair. "Talk to my shrink. She'll tell you how ugly I am."

It was a challenge, almost spiteful and bitter, and I knocked the rest of my drink back in one gulp. Audrey didn't so much as flinch when I brought the glass back down to the table with a hollow *clunk*. I wanted her to react, I wanted to see her jolt and quake with every shred of who I am. It was then that I suddenly felt the urge to narrow my eyes, twist my lips, and lean further against the table. I stared directly into her eyes, hoping to finally shake her up, to let her see just how hideous I was beneath the surface—a bitter, hateful thief.

With my nose just an inch from hers, I asked, "What the hell do I have to do to make you leave me alone?"

"Do you *want* me to leave you alone?" Her tone remained even and calm, instantly sober as her eyes held mine with a patience I hated her for.

"I—"

"Next up, we have Audrey!"

In synchronized fashion, we turned toward the stage and the owner of the club, applauding and welcoming her to the mic. Audrey didn't let me finish what I was about to say as she stood up and told me she'd be back, before climbing the steps into the spotlight. I held my breath, holding in the belligerence, as she cleared her throat and pulled out a sheet of paper from her pocket.

"This one is called *He*," she spoke in her pleasant voice, not at all tipsy-sounding, and began to read.

> *He is heated,*
> *He is cold.*
> *He is subtle,*
> *He is bold.*
> *He is honest,*
> *He is lying.*
> *He's barely living,*
> *He is dying.*
> *He is gifted,*
> *He is blessed.*
> *He is angry,*
> *He's a mess.*
> *He is broken,*
> *He is fine.*
> *He is wanted,*
> *But he's not mine.*

I could have thought of a thousand ways to interpret that poem of simple words. Who was *he*? Was it someone I didn't know? Was it me? I thought it was about me. I *wanted* it to be about me, even if there was no reason for me to believe it was. She hardly knew me, how could she write something about a man she knew nothing about?

And yet, there was that feeling that this was all meant to be. That maybe she *did* know me, maybe somehow, in some way, she really did ... Fate. Signs. Written in the stars. God. Plans. I shook my head at the insanity and climbed from my chair to get a drink before Audrey could sit back down.

This would be my fourth drink. What the hell was I thinking? Is this what she drove me to do? To drink myself into a drunken stupor? With another gin and tonic in hand, I went back to the table and dropped myself down in the chair.

"Did you like it?" she asked, slowly sipping at what was left of her drink. She wouldn't meet my eyes and that only meant one thing.

"You wrote a poem about me." She nodded and I asked, "Why would you do that?"

Her gaze diverted to mine for one, two fractions of a heartbeat before dashing away again. "It's not obvious?"

"What are you talking about?"

She shrugged. Her finger ran a circuit around the glass's rim. Round and round and round ... I was in high school again, talking to a girl I liked, who maybe liked me, and dammit if it wasn't making my innards turn into a mess of warm putty. Dammit if I was too lost in gin and tonics to focus on anything but how awful this was and how she needed to stop this now before I couldn't.

"I like you, Blake," I found her saying, and I found myself laughing. It was a sinister, mocking sound and I shook my head toward the bar, just to look at anything but her.

"No, you don't."

"Yes. I do."

"No," my volume raised and my back hunched over the table, bringing my eyes only centimeters from hers. "You like the *idea* of me. You like the idea of having something to *save*, a fucking *project* to talk about at Church or whatever the hell it is you do."

"I don't go to Church," she quietly interjected.

"Whatever! You like the idea of spending a little time with someone nobody in your perfect little life would ever approve of. You like the idea of getting *fucked* by someone who might know what they're doing. Hell, I don't know what your reason is, but trust me, sweetheart; you don't like *me*."

And damn her, she didn't react. She continued to watch me, displaying an inhuman amount of tolerance and I couldn't take it anymore. I couldn't sit across from a woman who might as well have been a machine, if it weren't for the timely expanse of her chest with every breath she took, or the blink of her eyelids showing off the faintest glimmer of champagne eyeshadow. I couldn't fucking stand it and I knew that, not only was this a mistake, but I needed to get the hell out before I did something I'd regret. Something else. Something more.

I drank the rest of my drink in one choked gulp. I never drank this much and it was hard to swallow. I pulled myself up, snatched my jacket from the back of the chair, and hurried toward the stairs. I didn't look back, didn't pay attention to if she was following, didn't care if she was angry or hurt or crying or calling her cousins to bitch about the guy who'd just rejected her. All I cared about was getting home and getting away, *far* away, and I ran up to the street and out into the parking lot.

"Blake! Wait!"

Fucking hell. Fuck her. Fuck this. Fuck this town. Fuck *everything*. I clenched my fists, ignoring her voice and her feet against the pavement behind me. *Something* had to make this woman leave me the hell alone.

"Blake! Stop! Come on, *please* don't leave!"

Then, I did stop. I stopped and spun around on my heel. She stood there beneath a lamppost, her pristine white coat dragging along the dirty ground, and if that wasn't a fucking metaphor, I don't know what was. Signs. Premonitions. They were all displayed right there in her white coat, getting covered in dirt and mud.

"I need to leave," I stated, feeling like I'd used that line on her too many times and I was sick of it.

"But why?"

I shrugged, slapping my hands against my thighs. "Because if I don't get the fuck away from you, I'm not prepared to handle what's going to happen."

"What's going to happen?"

I scoffed with a shake of my head. "You sound like my shrink, answering questions with more fucking

159

questions." I looked back to her and stated bluntly, "If I stay, I'm going to try to fuck you, Audrey. That's what's going to happen."

Audrey was hard to move but she reacted then. Her throat bobbed and the apples of her cheeks deepened in their rosy hue. "Oh."

"I'm drunk," I reasoned weakly. "And I like you way too much. Neither one of those things ever should've happened, but whatever, here we are. And dammit, you make me so fucking mad, but that's only making it harder for me. So ... I need to get the hell out of here, and so should you."

"You shouldn't drive," she protested.

"I don't even fucking care at this point," I replied honestly, albeit foolishly, and her worried gaze made me groan. "Fine, fuck ... I'll get a cab or some—"

"Take a walk with me?"

"Are you fucking kidding me?"

She shook her head. "No."

"I just told you I want to fuck you, I said all of that shit in there, and you want to take a fucking *walk with me*?"

Audrey nodded as she pulled on her dirty coat. "Please?"

I raked a hand through my hair and looked over my shoulder at my bike. Reason told me I shouldn't climb on it and ride home. I was intoxicated, and as much as I didn't really care much about my own well-being at the moment, Jake still needed me, and that was enough.

So, I turned back to Audrey, and against my better judgment, agreed to her walk. Because I needed time to sober up. Because truthfully, I didn't want to go home just yet. But mostly because I so desperately wanted to believe that I could be worthy of someone like her.

Chapter Thirteen

O CTOBER IN SALEM meant tourism and a lot of it. The streets were crawling with tour groups and shoppers, witches and ghouls. It was equal parts good and bad. This was my favorite time of the year, and it brought a hoard of like-minded people to my town. I felt alive on those weekends, seeing the faces of those I knew genuinely appreciated the atmosphere. The awe in their eyes as they took in the architectural beauty, the sadness etched in the lines on their faces when they learned of its haunted history.

But then, there were those who I knew flocked to the cobblestone streets strictly for the thrill from mingling with the fabled ghosts. They weren't here to learn, to mourn, or to appreciate. They merely wanted to take some pictures, drag the kids through a couple of museums, and leave. That was the downside, and I scowled at a cluster of boozed-up sorority girls as they clicked their heels down the street and mocked their caped tour guide.

"How long have you lived here?" Audrey asked, making small talk and distracting me from my irritation.

"Where? In Salem?"

"Yeah," she clarified as we turned at Old Town Hall and took the steps through Derby Square.

"Since I was twenty-two."

"How old are you now?"

I narrowed my eyes and silently questioned why that even mattered. "I'll be thirty-four on the 31st."

"Get the heck out. You were actually born on Halloween?"

I nodded, feeling a bit smug. "The creepiness was bred into me."

"That's crazy!"

"Not really," I laughed. "My parents grew to hate Halloween pretty quickly. Not only did they have to take us trick-or-treating, but then they had to wrap presents, do the whole cake thing, have a birthday party ..." I shrugged. "It got easier when we got older. We only celebrate Jake now, so ..." Why the fuck wouldn't my mouth stop moving?

"You don't celebrate your birthday?"

I turned to look up at the window of Dr. Travetti's office. I'd know it anywhere, I looked through it so much, but now, it looked so different from the outside. Less like a prison and more like an intriguing piece of my town's history. Was that how Audrey saw me? Less like a bundled heap of pessimism and anger, and more like a source of curiosity?

"No," I answered flightily as we walked past the building. "That's my shrink's office."

"Why do you see a therapist?"

I turned my eyes on her and felt my mouth lift in a faint smile. "Why do *you* ask so many questions?"

She shrugged gently as we made our way through clusters of shoppers at the night market. "I want to know about you."

Scoffing, I barked a laugh. "I can't even begin to imagine why."

Again, she shrugged. "I told you that I like you. And I find you interesting."

I sighed and shook my head. "Okay, whatever. Uh ... Anyway, I stopped celebrating my birthday a while ago. No point."

Audrey narrowed her eyes, lit with laughter, and poked a finger at my side. "Hey! You didn't answer my question!"

"I'm not telling you why I see a therapist," I told her point blank.

"Okay, fair enough," she answered, backing down. "I saw a therapist for a while after my sister died. I questioned a lot of things and it really helped me to talk to someone."

I grunted with a nod. "Yeah."

"It was hard to hold onto my faith when I was deep in mourning." She spoke quietly, holding her hands to her chest. I watched as her fingers tucked between the lapels of her coat to tug the cross out. "It's hard not to question why such horrible things can happen to good people. Or how God could allow one of His own to suffer so much, when she had done nothing wrong."

I didn't mean to snicker but I did. It was a gentle sound, barely audible, but she heard it. She trained her eyes on me as we turned onto the sidewalk and asked what I was laughing at.

"I'm not laughing."

"You just did."

"No," I insisted weakly, but she knew better. So, I said, "I don't believe in any of that shit."

"Any of what shit? God?"

"Yep."

She nodded gently. "I figured. That's okay. You're within your right to believe what you want. Faith, to me, is a very personal thing. That's why I don't go to Church."

"Oh, thanks so much for your permission," I deadpanned.

"I didn't believe for a little while."

I don't know what made me ask, "What changed?"

Audrey smiled at the question, as though she could see phantom shreds of light seeping from between my cracks. She was all too eager to share her story as she welcomed herself to wrap an arm around mine. "For about a year after my sister died, I considered myself agnostic. I hoped there was more, you know—a god, an afterlife ... But it was hard to continue following my beliefs when I was in so much pain. It was like having a piece of my body removed and not being given anything to dull the ache."

I imagined living without Jake. I imagined him being gone, and not in the sense my parents were talking but *really* gone. I had almost lost him once, but he'd been stubborn. He wouldn't die. Instead, he stuck around, and even with as rough as it was, I'd prefer this life over not having him at all.

The thought immediately choked me up, and I shook my head, sending it away.

"But, then ..." She hesitated and eyed me skeptically. "Do you promise not to laugh?"

"Sure," I shrugged.

"I'm not sure I believe you."

I snorted. "That's fine. Don't tell me then." Pulling my arm from her grasp, I continued walking down the street with a boorishness I wasn't proud of, and Audrey hurried to keep up.

"Okay, I'll tell you," she relented easily. "I woke up one morning and, on my windowsill, was a butterfly."

I had heard about this, people seeing butterflies and thinking they were visitors from the beyond. A message. A sign. It was just another thing people told themselves to bring a tiny shred of comfort to their lives. And I understood it, sure, but it didn't stop it all from sounding completely absurd.

"I see," I muttered, not wanting to say anything else in fear I might actually laugh in her face.

"I know what you're thinking," she said. "You're thinking I'm insane."

"Not insane," I corrected.

"I wasn't *looking* for a sign from my sister," she insisted adamantly.

"Sure. I get it."

"No." She grabbed my arm with a surprising amount of force and turned me to face her. "You don't understand and you're not listening."

"Fine," I muttered, staring down into her eyes, a dark navy in the darkness. "So, tell me."

"That morning, I woke up to find a butterfly on the windowsill of my bedroom," she said, a firm and serious expression drawn on her face. "My window was open a crack, there was a small hole in the upper part of my screen that I'd been begging my father to fix for months, and somehow, this butterfly managed to find its way through the hole and down through the crack and onto the windowsill inside my room."

"Okay," I nodded, still unimpressed. This was what they did, religious people. People of faith. They try to convince you of the things you know to be false. They try to sway you toward their stance of blind belief in something that might as well be as impossible as the unicorns or mermaids. This was exactly why Audrey and I couldn't happen, this was exactly why this entire night was a bad idea, and yet, I remained standing there with her as she stared at me with an intensity that could've made me believe in the Easter Bunny if she looked long enough.

"It was *this* butterfly," she pressed and wrenched the neckline of her top lower to reveal the tattoo I had done on her. Her finger tapped the black, white, and gritty half and I shook my head.

"Okay?"

"It was a black Swallowtail," she went on. "I had *never* seen one of these in person before, it was Sabrina's

167

favorite, and it just happened to show up on my windowsill on the day I woke up with the love of God in my heart for the first time in years. You don't think that means something?"

I struggled to find the right thing to say, to tread lightly into a subject we were both passionate about, but from opposite sides of the fence. "I think it's a very nice coincidence," I said in a flat tone.

"Is it also a coincidence that I booked my appointment with you the day before?"

"Yes," I stated, unmoved, pulling my arm from her grasp.

I was still drunk, but I could already feel the effects of the alcohol wearing off. I could feel too much, think too much, and I needed something to take the edge off this fucking conversation. I turned from Audrey to begin walking again, steering my loose legs down the sidewalk. When she asked where I was going, I didn't reply. I didn't want to say it out loud. But I was going home, and I was taking her with me.

***

"Your house is so cute," she commented as we walked over the cobblestone pathway to the front door.

"Thanks," I grunted, although I would never have used that particular word to describe my home.

I patted myself down in search of my keys. "You put them in your pocket," she said lightly, and I tucked my hands into my jacket. Audrey shook her head. "No, they're, um ..." She reached out to touch one of the front pockets on my jeans and pulled her hand back just as quickly.

I dipped my hand in and found them there. "Thanks," I muttered again, as I slid the key into the door.

It was an old house, built in 1870. I didn't believe in ghosts, or that something as silly as an old house could serve as a vessel to harbor them, but I loved the history. I loved the creaks and groans in the floorboards, the way it shifted beneath my feet. It was heavy with the memories of time passed and lives lost. It's what I had wanted, ever since I moved into an old apartment on Essex years ago, and as soon as I had enough money, I snatched this place up.

Apart from Jake and tattooing, the house was one of the only things in my life I truly cared for, and I felt it showed. It was clean, repainted. The hinges were oiled, and the appliances were new. But now, watching Audrey step through the doorway and into the living room, it somehow felt tainted. Soiled, like the stains on her white coat. Unworthy.

I drew in a quivering breath and brushed past her into the kitchen, where I kept my liquor. It was there only because my parents and relatives occasionally gifted me with a bottle on Christmas, yet I seldom drank it. Most of the bottles remained sealed, and probably beyond their Best By date. But now, I perused the shelf of multicolored glass, in search of something to further take the edge off of this goddamn night.

Audrey walked in slowly behind me. Her footfalls were light and barely audible against the kitchen tile, save for the gentlest tap of her heels. Her steps whispered to me with warnings of her coming. Closer, closer, closer ...

"What are you drinking?" She was directly behind me now. I pulled in another breath, controlled and deep, as I pulled a bottle of Fireball whiskey from the shelf. I lifted the bottle over my shoulder, to show her the label. "Cinnamon? That sounds interesting."

"It's good," I told her as I grabbed a couple of glasses from a nearby cabinet. Then, as I opened the bottle, I realized what a presumptuous prick I was being. I needed the drink, not her, and yet, I had assumed and grabbed a second glass. "Do you want any?"

"Sure," she answered cheerfully.

I only poured a small amount into her glass, she wasn't staying and would have to get home. Being too inebriated was a recipe for disaster, no matter how you looked at it, so I kept that in mind as I poured some into mine.

I turned and passed her glass into her waiting palm. "Thanks," she said gently, and immediately pulled it to her lips. I watched her drink and thought about how pretty her mouth was. After she took a sip, she pressed her lips together, savoring the flavor. A bead of whiskey lingered on her bottom lip, and I would've greedily enjoyed it for myself, had her tongue not flicked out to capture it, as I stood there like a voyeuristic statue.

"Oh, wow," she gushed, looking down into the glass of liquid amber. "That's so good."

Her eyes lifted to mine and she watched me expectantly. There was a mingled blend of scrutiny and uncertainty chilling the flecks of silver in her icy rings of blue, and as she swallowed, the gradual shift of her throat revealed the presence of her nerves. I excited her with fear and danger, and wasn't that a fucking laugh? There wasn't a damn thing about me that was at all fearsome or dangerous, but here she was, standing before me in a façade of bravery, hiding the anxiety beneath.

I drank, needing my own dose of courage, and the hot, hot heat of the cinnamon and the alcoholic burn warmed my body instantly. It was comfortable and good, and in that comfort, I wondered if she could feel that way, too.

My gaze held hers as I put my glass on the counter and shrugged my jacket off. I laid it over the back of a chair before reaching out to take the buttons of her coat between my fingers. Audrey's breath tripped from her mouth as she dropped her stare to my hands. She stood there, pillar stiff, as I worked at the buttons, moving downward until there weren't any left and I could slip the coat from her shoulders. She turned soundlessly, allowing me to pull it off, and I laid it over mine.

It was a simple invitation, but a big step. I grabbed my glass and headed back into the living room, where I took a seat on the couch. Audrey, on the other hand, decided to continue her walk.

Touching her fingertips to the mantel, she looked at the pictures, all of Jake and me throughout the years. In a visual timeline, she watched us grow, seeing me change and him staying the same. She picked one up and studied it closer, allowing her smile to grow.

"You were so cute," she said, turning the frame to show me the picture I already knew so well. Jake and me, with our arms wrapped around our family's old dog, Daisy, an Old English Sheepdog with more hair than brains.

"What the hell happened, right?" I chuckled, studying my drink and glass.

"You look so much alike."

I laughed again, deep and surprisingly genuine. "Well, we *are* identical twins."

"I know that," she giggled lightly, and somewhere in this dark house, someone turned on the faintest of nightlights. "But you looked more alike then."

"Yeah, well," I shrugged, lifting the glass, "I grew a beard."

She laughed again and put the picture back on the mantle. "He doesn't live with you?"

"He doesn't. I pick him up for school in the morning and drop him off in the evening."

She nodded and continued to move around the living room. Eyeing the pictures and studying the art on the walls. She cocked her head at a gritty penned portrait of Jake and me, lying side by side in the yard. Mom had taken the original photograph a few years ago, after I had first bought the house. It was my favorite of the two of us, and I remembered that day in the sunshine. A moment of playful reprieve, when Jake tackled me to the ground and we rolled in the grass like we were kids.

"You're so talented," she uttered on a thin breath.

"Thanks."

Looking at me over her shoulder, she smiled weakly. "You don't believe it, though."

"I know I'm good at what I do," I offered. "I have skills, and I know how to use them."

She nodded, turning back to the drawing. "Yeah, you do, but it's your gift that allows you to capture the difference in your eyes with nothing but a pen."

I furrowed my brow. "What?"

She pointed at pen-Jake's eyes. "He's so happy, innocent and excited, but then, you ..." Her finger aimed at pen-me now. "You're smiling, but your eyes are so empty. Like you've given up and you're constantly reminding yourself to not care."

I sucked in a heavy breath of air. "Hm," I grunted and downed the rest of my drink.

"Hm," she mocked the sound, albeit lighter, and turned to walk toward me. She sat on the couch, one cushion away, and sipped lightly at her drink. "So, what do you want to do?" she asked.

"I don't know." That was bullshit. What I wanted to do was reach over, pull her hair, and thrust my lips against hers until she begged me to rip her clothes off and fill her soft body with the hardness of mine. She would've expected that, I realized, after my crass attempt at making her leave earlier at the club. But I couldn't say it now, not even with the extra liquor floating through my bloodstream. My tongue wouldn't move and my lips remained shut.

So, instead, she asked, "You know what *I* think we should do?"

"What?"

173

"I think we should talk."

And even though my body would've preferred to lay over hers and sink between her thighs, I swallowed those urges and nodded.

Chapter Fourteen

WITH GLASSES OF WATER now in hand, we sat on either end of the couch, facing each other while keeping at a safe distance. She watched me intently, listening with intrigue, and the way she nodded and replied made me wonder if I could possibly be the most interesting person she'd ever met.

"When did you first start tattooing?" she asked before sipping at her glass.

"When I was fifteen," I told her.

"Wow, isn't that young?"

Shrugging nonchalantly, I replied, "I guess. An old buddy of mine got his hands on a tattoo machine and we fucked around with it in his basement." For the sake of sharing, I lifted my left leg and crossed it over the opposite knee. Rolling up the leg of my pants, I pointed at the shitty, faded skull on my calf. "This was my first."

Audrey tipped forward just a bit, peering at the old ink, hiding between pieces of art much more impressive. "Your friend did this?"

"No. I did it."

Her eyes lifted back to mine. "Your first tattoo, you did on yourself?"

With another nonchalant shrug, I rolled the pant leg back down. "It was no big deal."

The bowed curve of her lips spread slowly and the brilliant blue of her irises twinkled in the living room light. I asked what that look was for and she answered, "It feels so ... wrong to be talking to you. Like, bad."

I snorted as I lifted my glass of water to sip. "I told you. I'm no good."

She shook her head. "No, I don't mean like that. I mean, you're like, one of those boys TV shows and movies always warned me about. The bad boy that always felt like an exaggeration of the truth. Like ... Kiefer Sutherland's character in *The Lost Boys*. But you're not an exaggeration. You're the real deal."

I laughed at that, taking a deep drink before placing the glass on the coffee table. "Your mom wouldn't approve, is what you're saying."

"Oh, no, I didn't mean it like that."

I dropped my gaze to the cross hanging against the frame of her collarbone. I imagined her upbringing and the judgments her family would make on me. But why the hell did I care, anyway? Just a couple of hours ago, I was saying whatever I could to make her leave me alone, and now I was wondering what her parents would think of me.

"Ask me something."

Tearing me away from those thoughts, I looked back to her. "Ask you what?"

"Anything."

I threw my whole body into another shrug. "I don't know ..."

Her smile was never waning as she readjusted herself on the couch. "Come on, you gotta be curious about *something*."

She was right about that. There were a thousand things I was desperate to know, anxious to find the answers to, but to ask would have been to admit the niggling doubts worming their way into my brain. Asking would be a confession of the distress I'd been feeling for the past couple of weeks, regarding beliefs I thought I had a handle on.

"Okay. What do you do?" I settled on with a flippant wave of my hand, as if to say, "There, happy?"

"I'm a preschool teacher," she answered with a pride I found endearing.

I laughed gently, not intending to and Audrey asked what was funny, and I admitted, "Because that's exactly the kind of job I would've pictured you having."

She smiled; her cheeks tinted a shade of embarrassment. "Yeah, I guess I play the part. Except," she outstretched her arms and glanced down to her shirt, "right now I'm missing the finger paint and glitter glue all over my clothes."

I chuckled, painfully aware of the dipping, swooping sensation happening in my stomach. The gradual descent of my heart, barely scraping the surface of something emotional. Testing it out and trying it on for size. Before, I had liked her appeal. I had liked what we could do together in my bed. But now, I found, I simply liked *her*. It was wrong in a thousand ways. She was wrong for me,

I was entirely wrong for her, but this attraction of my heart couldn't be quelled.

It didn't help when she looked up at me and smiled, her eyes twinkling and her lips shining. How could she look so put together while weaning a lingering inebriation? I imagined how I must look to her, red-eyed and fucked up. Messy hair and scruffy beard. Sweaty and dirty. My lips begged to meet hers, to say hello, to feel the contradiction between our skin. But I was filthy, and she was so, so clean.

"It's getting late," I found my mouth moving, unsure of the words.

She lifted her wrist to look at her watch. "Oh, wow, yeah. It's past midnight. That's crazy." Her eyes met mine once again. "Time flies when you're having fun, I guess."

My laugh erupted from my throat, bursting past my lips. "Oh, yeah. I'm loads of fun." I swiped my glass from the coffee table and took hers before standing and heading into the kitchen. "Should I remind you of the shit I said to you before? I'm a world class asshole."

I placed the glasses in the sink, and there were her footsteps again.

"You're not an asshole," she argued gently. "You're guarded, and abrasive, and way too hard on yourself. But you're not an asshole."

Guarded ... I spelled that word out in my mind, tracing the curve of the G with my fingertip against the sink's lip. I was guarded. The good doctor always said I was defensive with her, but actually, I was *always* defending. Myself, my faults, my brother.

Guarded.

What a perfect word to describe something so far from perfect.

"You should go," I muttered quietly.

I awaited her reply with dread. I wanted her to go so badly, but even more than that, I wanted her to stay. Cee had never stayed the night, and for once, I wanted the company. I wanted to witness the contrast of her skin against mine. I wanted to entangle my legs in the web of hers and catch myself in the lengths of her hair. I wanted to breathe in her scent as we fell asleep. But those reminders of why this was all a terrible idea wouldn't shut the fuck up, and I couldn't stop telling myself that the last thing she should want is me.

"Yeah," she breathed, and I exhaled with relief and regret, until she added, "but I don't want to."

I turned to face her with trepidation and anticipation, and before she or I could speak and stop this from happening, my hands were on either side of her face and my lips were on hers in the most impromptu first kiss. It wasn't magical and it certainly wasn't sweet. It was an urgent display of my desire in the middle of my kitchen, in a house she thought was cute.

I walked her backward until she hit the wall, never breaking the lock my mouth had on hers. To feel her hands in my hair was deliciously deviant. Her fingers wrapped within the strands in coordination with her lips, opening to accept my tongue, and I obliged with a needy and guttural groan. Every bit of warning was silenced by the sounds of our mouths, moving together in a dance of tongues and the crash of teeth, and every want I'd ever had aimed directly at her was spread blatantly across every one of my fingertips. They clasped at her face, thrust into her hair, and moved around to press firmly against the small of her back, to prove just how badly I wanted her.

Audrey whimpered into my mouth and her knees buckled, leaning further against me. "Blake?" she whispered, pulling her lips from mine.

"What?" The word scraped against my throat.

She opened her eyes and they dodged over my face before settling within my gaze. "Did you mean it when you said you'd try to fuck me?"

Hearing her repeat those words made it feel so much filthier, but I couldn't deny the truth in them. "Yes."

"I don't want you to try," she admitted bashfully as her cheeks pinked and her gaze dropped. "I just want you to do it."

I shook my head. "We shouldn't ..." But the statement was weak, because why shouldn't we? She was granting me permission, I liked her, she liked me ... What was so wrong about that, apart from every other little thing? But my dick didn't care about every other little thing. He didn't give a rat's ass if she was the very last person I should ever in my life find attractive, let alone sleep with, and right now, all I gave a shit about was what he thought.

So, I cut my protest short and hoisted her into my arms. I carried her with deliberation to my bedroom and kicked the door shut before dropping her to my bed. I didn't give her a chance to look around before laying beside her, to resume our kiss and gradually strip us of

180

our clothes. And when we were naked, I found that beneath all the black and pastels, we weren't very different. In nothing but our skin, we were both simply human, a lesson I was long overdue in learning, and even though my skin was significantly more decorated than hers, it felt the same.

"These are so beautiful," she commented in awe at my tattoos, marveling at my body as I struggled to convince myself I was worthy of hers. How was it right for someone to be so flawless? What the hell had I been thinking, laying my destruction across her chest?

"Not sure beautiful is the word for them," I muttered, kneeling on the bed before her and opening her legs.

"What would you call it, then?"

I shrugged. "They're just parts of my story."

Something in those words made her look up from my stomach to seek my gaze. "Maybe you'll tell me that story one day."

I nodded once, to neither confirm nor deny, as I crawled between her thighs and laid my body over hers. "Maybe."

With that final word, I hushed her with another kiss. I found myself within her easily, thrusting gently as to not destroy her, despite the feeling that I already had. She trembled like a virgin and moaned like a seasoned professional, kissing me ferociously and timing her thrusts with my own.

We fucked like we had fucked each other thousands of times before. We knew exactly when and where to touch, to kiss, to bite and to scratch, and for the first time in my life, my climax was partnered with another's. It was perfect, and incredible, and I wondered if I would black out just from the thought alone. Our timing was impeccable, and what a fucking joke that was.

Timing ...

Serendipity. Fate.

Signs.

I rolled away from her to stare at the ceiling, to remove myself from those thoughts and what we'd done. But Audrey rolled toward me, wrapping a leg around mine.

"I had thought about killing myself," I blurted out, and why? I don't know, I have no fucking clue. Maybe I was trying to prove how broken I was, how screwed up and bad. Or maybe I just wanted someone to know, and I wanted that someone to be her.

"What?"

"That's why I'm in therapy," I clarified. "You asked before, so I'm giving you an answer."

Her breath had stalled for a moment before she exhaled, long and winded. "Can I ask why?"

I bit at my lips, staring at the ceiling and deciding if I wanted to go that far. I remembered that night like it was yesterday, the night before I found Dr. Vanessa Travetti and gave her a call. My mind hadn't been clouded by a hazy depression or influenced by intoxication. The clarity had been startling, terrifying, as I held that bottle of aspirin, and I had dropped it to the floor, knowing I needed to talk to someone and let this shit out. Before I really did do something I couldn't undo.

"You don't have to tell me," Audrey relented.

I shook my head. "No, it's … it's okay. I just thought everything would be better if I wasn't around. I'm, uh, kinda the reason my family is so fucked up," and I realized she didn't know my family. She didn't know our tense and messy dynamic.

"Do you still feel that way?"

"No," I replied honestly.

"Good," she whispered softly, touching my shoulder with her lips. She laid her arm across my waist, pressing her cheek to my chest, before breathing a sigh against my heart.

And my heart sighed back.

Chapter Fifteen

GOOD SLEEP WAS as foreign to me as pride and self-acceptance. So, when I awoke with the unfamiliar sensation of being well rested, it was as if my entire body awoke with a sigh. How wonderful it was to face the window without dread. How peaceful it was to have her still coiled around my body in a cocooning embrace.

I allowed myself a smile, like I had forgotten my own life. I nuzzled my cheek against the top of her blonde head and coaxed myself to find that incredible sleep I'd had just minutes ago, my arm tightening around her shoulders. She unraveled with a dreamy sigh, sliding her hand from my chest to my waist, to hug me closer. Together, we neared the edge of deep sleep once more, and as my head grew heavier and my limbs grew limp, I was shaken by my phone.

As it vibrated on my nightstand, I thought for a moment that it was an alarm I'd forgotten to turn off. I grabbed the damn thing and peered at the screen through bleary eyes, ready to dismiss a reminder to wake up, when I realized it wasn't an alarm, but a call from Mom.

"Fuck," I muttered, unwinding my other arm from around Audrey's shoulders and sliding it out from under her. She protested with a groan as I sat up, cleared my throat, and answered hastily. "Hey, Mom," I said, feigning awareness and clarity in my tone.

"Did I wake you up?"

"Uh …"

"You sound hungover," she accused suspiciously.

Of everything I'd drank the night before, I could safely say my hangover wasn't derived from the alcohol. The sex, maybe. The girl, absolutely. But not the alcohol.

"No, I'm fine."

"Hm," she grunted with suspicion. "Okay. Well, I need you to keep an eye on Jake today. I have some stuff I need to do."

"Uh, s-sure." My eyes flitted toward Audrey, now wide-awake beside me, staring at me with question and lust.

She wanted me again, and I wanted her, but there wasn't time for that. She needed to get out, and she needed to get out *now*.

"We had an early day today, right, Jakey?" Mom went on. "We went to the store and ran a couple errands, and then we had brunch at this adorable little—"

"What time is it?" I asked both my mother and Audrey.

Audrey won the race to tell me. "It's twelve forty-five," she whispered.

185

Almost one? I rarely slept after seven. "Jesus, it's late," I said to the two of them. "How long until you're here, Mom?"

"Oh, um ... fifteen minutes, maybe?"

Fifteen minutes. It was enough time to get Audrey out of here and to make myself look as though I hadn't engaged in a night of sex and mind-numbing sleep. I calculated my plan down to the nanosecond and hastily told my mom I needed to go. I hung up and looked directly at Audrey, both menacingly and regretfully.

"You really need to go." And for good measure, I added, "Now."

Audrey nodded, standing from the bed to grab her clothes. "Yeah, I got that."

She sounded hurt and I didn't want that. I just wanted her to understand the very real possibility of my mother seeing her in my house and immediately assuming there was something more than a one-night stand and an unexplained attraction between us. So, I approached her steadily and laid a hand on her shoulder. My fingertips remembered her skin, her touch, and her voice from last night, curling sensually around my name, and I held back the urgency to take her mouth once again.

"My mom is on the way with Jake," I explained hurriedly, trying not to focus on the ticking clock and failing miserably. "She hasn't seen me with a woman in ..." When was the last time either of my parents had seen me with someone? It felt impossible that it could be years, but I was about to be thirty-four and my last serious relationship met its end when I was in my early twenties. Could it really have been that long? A *decade*?

"Well, it's been a long time," I concluded and mustered a smile to mask my embarrassment.

"Oh, I gotcha," she replied, nodding with instant understanding. "She'll start filling scrapbooks with wedding plans and baby names."

My skin scattered with goosebumps and my gut tied in a thousand complicated knots. "Yeah."

She moved away from my touch to get dressed and I dropped my hand to my side. She slipped her feet into her shoes that lifted her up a few more inches. In her tight-fitting pants and flowing top, she walked from my room to the bathroom, moving gracefully like a ballerina on a runway, and I thought, no woman had ever made a morning after look so glamorous.

"What is she like?" she called, and next came the telltale sign of liquid hitting porcelain. The woman had left the bathroom door open as she peed, too comfortable to care if I heard, and it felt stupid how much something so silly could leave my chest aching with need and desperation.

"Who?"

"Your mom."

She flushed the toilet and the faucet ran. I took that moment to stand in the open doorway, arms crossed and scowling in thought.

"My mom's okay," I replied simply.

"But?" My eyes met Audrey's and she smirked knowingly.

Chuckling softly, I shrugged. "We don't get along very well."

"Oh, I never would've guessed," she laughed, washing her hands before raking her wet fingertips through her hair. "Do you have an extra toothbrush?"

Soundlessly, I opened the medicine cabinet and grabbed one of the brushes my dentist kept me stocked with. She accepted it with a grateful smile, as I went on, "Things have been tense between us for a long time, but after ... after the accident, it always pissed me off the way my parents were handling it. I told them they should be doing something more for Jake than what they were doing at home."

"Which was?"

"Nothing," I stated bluntly, unsure of why I was shedding these truths to her like dry, brittle skin. "They weren't doing a damn thing for him. It was like, they became so fucking complacent when they realized he wasn't gonna go to Yale or some shit. They weren't giving him a chance to get better, in whatever way he could. So, when I was finally out of the house, I made a deal with them, that I'd get him into a program that would help him. You know, give him something to do, people to see. I thought it was the least I could do. And if I failed, then they could take over again, but under the agreement that *they* would find him help, instead of just going back to the way shit was before."

"I see," she replied softly, nodding. "That's common. I think sometimes parents can be complacent about these kinds of things. And it's usually not for lack of caring, but lack of knowledge. Not to mention, it's so overwhelming."

"Exactly," I muttered, pinching my lips and bobbing my head with agreement.

"So, I'm guessing that's kinda where you're at now, then."

"What was your first clue?" The question came out gruff and gritted, squashed between my teeth.

"All I asked was what your mom's like." She laughed, immediately lightening the mood, and I shook my head as I fought an unbeatable smile.

"Sorry. Touchy subject."

"I understand," she said, and somehow, I knew she meant that.

"Anyway, um ... my mom's a nice person. She means well." *Most of the time.*

Audrey smiled as she smoothed her hair out. "Well, for what it's worth, I think we would make beautiful kids."

I snorted, taken aback by the blunt statement. "Oh, you think so, huh?"

"Oh, yeah," she insisted, pulling her hair back into a bouncy ponytail. "I mean, your coloring and my eyes? They'd *have* to be gorgeous."

I looked to her eyes at the mention and even though I wouldn't say it—I could never say it—I knew she was right.

***

"Blake, this place is a wreck," Mom assessed with her hands planted firmly to her hips. She surveyed the living room as I hurried around, picking up a glass here and a coaster there, trying to erase the night before in haste. "I should've brought over some Clorox and Swiffers."

"It's not *that* bad." And it really wasn't. It might not have been the pristine standard she preferred but it could've easily been worse.

"What were you doing last night?" she pried, walking into the kitchen.

"Went to the club, came home, had a drink, went to bed." None of it was a lie, I told myself, and there was no need to divulge that I hadn't been alone.

"Hm." It was a short sound, one tainted in skepticism, and I rolled my eyes as I bent over and swiped a pillow from the floor. As I tossed it back on the couch, I noticed something, a shimmer of light on the coffee table, and I eyed it closely.

Audrey's necklace. Her cross.

My heart escalated to a gallop as I wondered, when had she taken it off? I couldn't remember, and I thought I surely would've noticed, I'd stared at her so much the night before. But upon closer inspection, I noticed the chain, delicate and silver, hadn't been unclasped but was broken. It must've fallen from her neck and neither of us had noticed. My chest thrummed at a frightening speed at what this could've meant, if it could mean anything at all. I imagined her god, otherworldly and mighty, sitting upon his throne and punishing her for spending her night with a devil like me. Just a wave of his almighty hand,

and there went the necklace, sent to the coffee table and left there to serve as a bad omen, a warning—a *sign*.

I swallowed as my blood chilled and rushed through my brittle heart. I didn't want to touch the damn thing, worried my flesh would burn and my bones would break. But, then there was my mother, and if she saw the fucking thing, the questions she would ask would break me more than some stupid piece of metal ever could.

I swiped it from the table and stuffed it into my pocket. My skin went unscathed and I was embarrassed by my own sigh of relief.

Jake walked into the room from the hallway, carrying his iPod in one hand and his enormous headphones in the other. He moved toward me with purpose and demanded, "Put on the One Foot Song."

"Oh, Jakey. Enough with that already. *Please*," Mom mumbled exhaustedly.

I took the iPod and glanced in her direction. "What?"

"That's all I've heard since yesterday. He wants me to put on the One Foot Song, and I have absolutely no idea what that even means. I never know what he's talking about."

"It's Walk the Moon, Mom," I muttered, scrolling through his collection of songs and pressing play. I took the headphones and fitted them over his ears. "There you go, buddy."

With a satisfied grin and a shouted thanks, he headed back to his room, bopping his head all the way. Mom wasn't as pleased as she came back into the living room to stand beside me.

"I really don't understand how you do it."

"Do what?"

"Handle him like that. I can't get through to him the way you can and it frustrates the living hell out of me."

For one fraction of a second, I wondered if this was her reasoning behind putting him in a group home. To punish me by taking him away, by stripping me of the only purpose I had ever truly found in my life. But I shooed it away. She wouldn't do that to me. My mother didn't understand me much, but she wasn't cruel because of it.

I shrugged apologetically. "It's just the way it is."

"It's the twin thing or whatever, I get it, but that doesn't make it any less unfair. I'm his *mother* and I never know what the hell to do with him."

"You could've called me," I reminded her, and she dismissed the thought with a flippant wave of her fingers.

"I already told you, I don't want to depend on you. You need your own life."

It was a funny thing. Not long ago, we'd had that conversation, about me living my life more for myself and less for Jake. At the time, I'd gotten defensive and pushed the very concept away. But now, I wondered about it, and whether it was at all possible to have a life outside of Jake. Hell, for all I knew, it could maybe include him, too. It only took a second to realize what had changed between then and now, as I felt the silver cross warming a spot on my leg from inside of my pocket.

It was Audrey. That's what had happened. And I wasn't entirely sure how to feel about that.

Chapter Sixteen

"YOU LOOK DIFFERENT today," Dr. Travetti commented, sitting down and adjusting her pant legs over the tops of her feet.

"Yeah, so do you," I commented, gesturing toward her. "Your hair's down."

She laughed lightly and touched the ends of her shoulder-length brown hair. "Too cold today to wear it up."

"Hm," I grunted and nodded thoughtfully. "It's beautiful today."

Her gaze softened. "Beautiful, huh?"

"Hell yeah. It really feels like autumn today. Cool, crisp ..." I glanced toward the window with a nod of my chin. "Fucking beautiful."

Dr. Travetti situated her clipboard on her lap and began to scribble. I sat up straighter, craned my neck, and tried to catch a glimpse of what she was writing. When she caught me spying, she smiled fondly, shaking her head.

"Don't be so paranoid," she gently scolded.

"I'm not. Just curious."

"Mm-hmm," she chided. She jotted for a few more seconds before lowering the pen. "So, tell me how your weekend went. What'd you do?"

My jaw clenched as my options were laid out before me. I could keep myself clammed up and keep all the secrets from my weekend in a little box of selfishness. But somehow, I felt I owed it to the good doctor to tell her. After all, she was the one who had encouraged me. She was the one who had listened to my relentless mumbling and grumbling for the past couple of years.

"I went out with Audrey," I confessed, and the admission brought my gaze to my lap, to watch my fingers as they clenched and pulsed.

Dr. Travetti was plainly excited, expressed with a clap of her hands and a joyful squeal. "Blake! That's great!"

"Wow, don't get too excited," I laughed uncomfortably. "I didn't ask her to fucking marry me or some shit."

"No, but you went out with her. That's huge. I'm so proud of you."

Proud. *Proud.* I repeated the word on a loop in my brain. I tried to remember the last time someone had told me they were proud of me. I came up empty, while my heart now puffed with pleasantries and goodness.

"So, tell me how it went."

I shrugged as I held onto that word—proud. "It was good, I guess. I was kind of a dick to her, but—"

"Why were you a dick?"

"Because I wanted her to leave."

"And why's that?"

A heavy sigh escaped my lungs as those feelings of good evaporated from my pores. "Because, Doc, I was drunk, and she doesn't deserve to spend her time with a piece of shit like me. And yet, I couldn't make her leave, no matter what I said to her. She wouldn't go away. So, we went for a walk and ended up at my place."

"Wow. Lots of highs and lows, huh?" And there she went, writing again.

"You could say that," I mumbled. "It was like ... like a yo-yo or some shit. One second, I didn't want her to leave and the next, I was two seconds away from shoving her out the door. And it was like that all fucking night until we ... uh ..."

"You can say whatever you want in here. You know that." Then she added, "Whatever you're comfortable with."

"I fucked her," I admitted, shoving a hand through my hair.

"And?"

My eyes widened as the corner of my mouth lifted in a smirk. "What the fuck, Doc? I never pegged you for a perv."

She laughed easily. "I'm not asking for details, unless you want to give them for whatever reason. I'm asking, how did it make you feel to sleep with her? What happened afterward?"

"It was nice," I admitted quietly. "And she stayed over. I've never had a woman stay over, so ...," I shrugged before repeating, "It was nice."

"That's great, Blake." Her tone was so soft and genuine, but there was something else that lingered there, between the letters and words. Sadness? Jealousy?

"Yeah, it was," I scoffed, diverting my gaze toward the window and Derby Square. "Until my mom called the next morning and reminded me exactly why I can't have *nice*. I can't have good sleep and good sex with a woman I like, because I have priorities and other shit going on. And then," I snickered, shaking my head, "there was the crap with her cross ..."

There was a pause in the good doctor's scribbling. "What about a cross?"

"I found her cross in my house. It must've broken off her neck or something. How the fuck am I supposed to take *that* shit?"

Leaning back against her chair, Dr. Travetti eyed me studiously. "What do you mean, how are you supposed to take it?"

"Doc." I thrust a hand toward the coffee table between us. "The goddamn thing was just laying in my living room. I can't even think of when it would've fallen off, but there it was, just waiting for me to fucking find it. That can't mean anything good ... right? Like, that's gotta be some bad omen bullshit right there."

"But I thought nothing means anything," she reminded me, a hint of challenge glinting in her eyes as she fiddled with the tip of her pen. "Everything is coincidental and meaningless."

"Well, yeah, but I mean ..." I cleared my throat and clasped my hands. "I'm just saying that, um ..." What the fuck *was* I saying?

196

I pressed my lips shut and studied my hands. The lines of ink, some of them faded, and the creases of my knuckles. My fingernails and palms. There wasn't anything inherently interesting about them, about the ink injected into layers of my skin or the lines coursing across my palms, but they were a distraction and I appreciated them for it.

"Blake?"

"Yeah." I traced the back of one hand with a finger. Round and round a raven's eyeball.

"I thought you didn't believe in signs."

"I don't," I insisted, but it was weak. My voice, my assurance, my resolve to denounce faith and all that comes with it—*weak*.

"Then, why are you shutting down?"

I glanced up at her from studying a speck of dirt beneath a nail. "Because I'm just thinking, if there *were* signs and there was some fucking god out there trying to tell me something, I might be convinced that this is one."

"I see," she replied with a nod. "And what do you think he'd be trying to tell you?"

"To stay the fuck away from her," I retorted without hesitation.

Dr. Travetti nodded astutely before narrowing her eyes. "Maybe. But let me ask you this, Blake. What are you going to do with it?"

"The cross?" She nodded, and I continued, "Well, I have to give the thing back to her, right? I mean, it obviously means something to her, so I have to find a way to give it back."

"And if you hadn't found the cross, would you be so inclined to see her again?"

I considered that for a moment. Would I? The sex was good, the sleep was great, but would I have found her for a round two? Would I have found her at all, to talk or to have a drink? There was no doubt in my mind that the answer was no, and I didn't have to say so. The two-lettered word was written plainly on my face and Dr. Travetti nodded.

"Okay. So, maybe the cross really *is* a warning, you could be right," she agreed, nodding. "Or maybe it's something else."

"Oh, yeah? Like what?"

"Maybe it's an invitation."

***

"Jake, buddy." I held out his backpack. "Come on, let's go."

Jake's resolve to pace the living room angrily continued, despite my pleading. "Not going. Not going today."

"*Why* aren't you going?"

"Miss Thomas is sick. She's not coming back. Miss Thomas is gone."

I sighed and pinched the bridge of my nose. Since picking him up from daycare Monday evening to waking him up this morning, I had heard about nothing except for how Miss Thomas had left school early. She had a sinus infection and had realized too late that she wasn't well enough to handle the likes of my brother and his pals. And that would have been fine, if Jake could handle change. But if one tiny thing was thrown off in his life, the turmoil was horrific.

"Miss Thomas isn't gone, Jake. She just needs to stay home for a couple of days while she gets better. She'll be back soon."

He shook his head fervently. "She's sick, she's gone. Never coming back. She's gone."

"Goddammit," I muttered under my breath, quickly realizing that the likelihood of him going to daycare today was slim to none. Our parents were both out all day, and he couldn't be left unsupervised. I'd have to watch him, which was fine, but what about work? I had three appointments today and couldn't cancel unless it was a real emergency, and was this *really* an emergency?

I considered the question, and then threw Jake's backpack on the couch. "Fine, don't go," I relented as I headed to the door. "Come on."

"Where are we going, Blake?"

"I don't care if you don't go to school," I told him, "but then, you're coming with me to work."

***

"What the hell is this, Blake?" Gus, my boss, crossed his arms and side-eyed my brother as he watched *Daniel Tiger* on his iPad. "This isn't Bring Your Brother to Work Day, man."

"I didn't have a choice. It was either that or call out." My eyes met his as I sat in my stool. "Which would you have preferred?"

Gus fought an eye-roll with a heavy-leaded sigh but didn't say anything. I was his cash cow, his protégé, and there was no way he'd prefer that I took the day off.

"So, what's he gonna do all day, then?"

"You're looking at it."

"This is it? He's just gonna watch shit on that thing?"

I frowned and squinted my eyes, defense bringing my blood to a steady bubble. "Yeah. That's it."

With another sigh and a shake of his head, he made his exit, murmuring as he walked away, "He better not get into stuff, Blake, or I swear ..."

"Knock it off, Gus."

"I'm just sayin', Blake. I like your brother, but I gotta run a business here."

"Uh-huh," I mumbled under my breath, and got ready for my first client.

As predicted, Jake kept to himself as I worked. He sat in the corner of my station, watching his videos and eating Goldfish crackers, and the only time he interrupted my work was to announce that he needed to pee. My clients didn't comment on his presence, but I noticed their questioning stares, glancing in the direction of the grown man with a *Mickey Mouse* t-shirt and iPad playing children's shows. More than once I wanted to tell them to mind their own business and to keep their eyes to themselves, but I bit my tongue and did my job.

The day went smoothly until we were ready to close, and the front door opened. Celia announced she'd handle it as I continued to clean up, and I listened as Cee went up front.

"Hey, is Blake around?"

That voice. I closed my eyes and took a deep breath, feeling my lungs swell and deflate like it'd been days since I last knew what air was.

"Uh, yeah, one sec," Cee answered questioningly, and she stuck her head into the back. "Hey, Butterfly Tattoo Chick is here."

"Oh," I replied sheepishly. "Okay."

"Why would she be here?" she whispered.

"I dunno," I lied, my throat rough and my voice graveled. "You can send her back."

"Or *you* can come up front."

I glanced over my shoulder and caught the glare of suspicion coming from my friend. "Send her back here, Celia."

With one last narrowed glance, she told Audrey to come back. I heard her footsteps before I saw her. Light and delicate against the dingy tile. I forced indifference into my veins as she walked toward my station, and then Jake looked up from his videos.

"Oh! Oh!" His face lit up instantly, emanating with an endearing exuberance. "Blake! Audrey's here! Audrey came!"

How he remembered her name, I didn't know, but I turned to face the object of his excitement. I studied her soft gait and her blonde hair, curled at the ends to trail over her shoulders and back.

"I see that," I answered under my breath.

"Hey, Jake!" It was as if I wasn't even there as she addressed my brother with her full attention. "I didn't expect to see you today. What a nice surprise!"

He jumped up from his seat, rushing toward her with urgent concern. "Audrey. Blake is working, but you can watch *Daniel Tiger* over here. You gotta be quiet. Blake likes it quiet, so *shhh*." He pressed a finger to his lips, as though he wasn't the one shouting just two seconds ago.

"Oh," she lowered her voice to a whisper. "I'm sorry. I didn't know. Thank you for telling me."

"I got *Daniel Tiger* over here, Audrey." He hurried back to his corner of the room and patted his seat. "You can be quiet and watch *Daniel Tiger* over here."

"Okay, that sounds great," she whispered. "But can you just give me a minute? I need to talk to your brother about something, okay?"

"Blake is my brother. We look the same because we're twins."

"Twins are so special, aren't they?" She grinned sweetly.

With their exchange happening before me, I felt like an intruder. But I couldn't look away. I watched them interact in a way I'd only seen my brother behave with me, and I sat there, stunned. At her ability to treat him like an equal, like there wasn't a damn thing wrong with him. And I continued to stare, even as Cee walked in and took a seat, obviously curious and eavesdropping.

"Special, yes," Jake agreed, nodding adamantly. "Special. I like Special K. I eat it sometimes for breakfast when I'm running late."

"It's a great cereal," she agreed. "Good for you, too."

Jake nodded. "Yeah, yeah. Audrey, I got *Daniel Tiger* over here. You can be quiet and watch *Daniel Tiger* with me over here."

"You know what, Jake? That sounds great, but can you just give me a minute?" Audrey asked again, gently reminding my brother of why she was there. "You go watch *Daniel Tiger,* while I talk to Blake and then I'll be right over." She smiled kindly, so patiently, and he nodded fervently.

"You'll be right over in just a minute," he repeated, and she nodded her clarification. Satisfied, he headed back to the corner of the room to grab his iPad, and Audrey turned to me.

"Hi, Blake," she said in nearly a whisper, as though we were exchanging secrets. As though we ourselves were a secret and the world was constantly trying to listen in.

"Hey, Audrey."

Suddenly shy, she smiled bashfully and lowered her hypnotic blue gaze from mine. "I feel bad for showing up here unannounced."

"Yeah, it's no problem. You actually caught me at a good time," I gestured toward my paper towels and bottle of disinfectant, "I was just cleaning up for the night."

"Oh, okay," she replied, sighing with relief. "I don't feel so bad then."

Something moved behind her and my trance was broken. I shifted my gaze to look at Cee and the scrutiny in her eyes. Suddenly, I didn't like her being there and seeing this, this moment that was somehow private and personal, and I stood up abruptly.

"You wanna step outside with me for a second? I need some air," I suggested.

Audrey's eyes lifted back to mine, looking startled as she nodded. "Yeah, sure."

"Jake," I said, "sit right there. I'll be back."

I turned to lead the way and Cee finally spoke, "You're gonna leave me alone with your brother?"

"He's fine, Cee. Just pretend he's one of your kids," I muttered and left the shop with Audrey on my heels.

Outside in the evening air, I sucked in a deep breath, filling my lungs and preparing my mind with the cacophony of cars and pedestrians surrounding us. Then, I turned to her, so spotless and perfect in her white coat.

I pointed to where I knew there'd been smudged stains against the stark white. "You had it cleaned."

She looked toward the spot I was referring to. "Oh, yeah. I just picked it up this morning." Her face turned and her smile zapped my chest. "Good as new."

"I'll give you the money for it."

"Oh, jeez, don't be ridiculous. It's fine."

I opened my mouth to protest, to insist that she take my money or my life or my anything she desired, but before I could make a complete ass of myself, she filled the air with her voice.

"So, I-I think I left something at your house, and I ..."

"Oh, right!" My hand pushed into a pocket to wrap around the delicate silver chain. I pulled it out and opened my palm. "Here."

The breath she released seemed to ease any bit of tension from her shoulders. "Oh, thank the Lord," she whispered, before meeting my eyes and saying, "Thank *you*."

"You're welcome. I found it in my living room."

"I was so worried it was gone forever," she admitted quietly, staring at the necklace in my palm.

"Well, um, you could've just bought another one. I mean, they're probably a dime a dozen, right?"

Her lashes drooped lower to her perfectly rosy cheeks as she stole the delicate silver from my hand. "It was my sister's."

I shut my stupid mouth and hung my stupid head. "Fuck. I'm sorry."

"It's okay. You didn't know."

I gestured toward her balled fist. "The chain was broken, but I took it to a jeweler yesterday and had it fixed."

The shushed admission struck her momentarily dumbfounded. She blinked for a moment and swallowed hard before opening her hand and silently inspecting her sister's sacred cross.

"Thank you," she whispered, her words ridden with emotion.

"Yeah, it's no problem."

She lifted her eyes back to mine. "I guess you don't have to pay for my dry cleaning after all. You've already done enough."

"Yeah, I guess so."

She nodded silently, then lifted the cross from her palm. I watched as she undid the clasp, new and strengthened with the better parts I'd paid for, and pulled it around her neck. Moments passed with her hands behind her neck before she laughed uneasily, and asked, "Can you help me with this? My nails are too long and I'm having a hard time gripping it."

"Oh, uh, yeah. Sure."

With a smile, she turned around, passing the ends of the chain to me with eager hands, and my fingers brushed hers as I took them. Sharp, electrocuting zaps of energy passed from my fingertips through my nerves and directly to my heart. Every ping and every surge ground my teeth and locked my jaw, as she lifted her hair from her shoulders and I clasped the necklace. My hands dared to linger a moment, barely grazing the nape of her neck, and my eyelids drooped at the reminder that I had kissed her there. I knew the taste of her flesh and the sound of her moan. I knew the flavor of her kiss and the wetness between her legs, and the thought pulsed in my groin and sent my hands away from the necklace to hang at my sides.

"Thank you." I heard her voice through the echo of my beating heart, and she turned to face me with a smile, her fingertips touching the cross delicately.

"Yeah," I replied, choked. "You're welcome."

"I guess we can go back inside now."

"Oh," I answered, taken aback. "I, uh … I thought you were just stopping by."

Audrey shrugged, her smile stretching her glossy pink lips. "I was. But I promised Jake I'd watch *Daniel Tiger*, and I really like that show."

***

Audrey hung out with Jake while I cleaned my space, collected my tools, and packed the autoclave to disinfect. She kept him company, kept him smiling as he reiterated the two episodes they had watched together. Every time I glanced their way, I tried to figure her out. I'd catch myself staring, entranced by her smile and confused by her desire to spend time with me. Jake, I could understand. He was sweet and endearing, but I had done everything in my power to force a hatred in this woman and I wasn't getting through to her. She was resilient, and she was beautiful.

After the two episodes had been watched, Audrey glanced at her watch and announced she needed to get going. She gave Jake a kiss on the cheek as he wrapped her in a suffocating hug, leaving me with only a smile and jealousy. Where was my kiss? Where was my hug? I watched her back as she walked toward the door with a big, stupid grin on my face, because I couldn't remember another moment in my life in which I'd been jealous of my brother.

The moment she was gone, Celia was ready with an interrogation, sitting at the front desk with a simpering smirk plastered to her face.

"So, you and Butterfly Tattoo Chick, huh?"

"Huh?" I feigned pointless cluelessness.

"I mean, talk about opposites attracting, am I right?" she teased, her pencil-thin, tattooed eyebrows jumping suggestively toward her hairline.

"I hate you," I muttered, chuckling lightly under my breath.

"For real though," she said, standing from the chair. "What's going on with that? I thought you weren't sleeping with her."

"I'm not—" I cut myself short and thought twice about denying it. "I don't know what's going on. It's just ... going, I guess."

"But you like her," she assessed, bobbing her head slowly. "Like, *really* like her."

Incredulous, I asked, "How the fuck do you know that?"

Cee's smile teetered somewhere between rueful and encouraging as she said, "Because you never looked at me the way you look at her."

"The way I look at her ..." I snickered, shaking my head.

"No, seriously, there's something different about the way you look at her," she laughed. "And it's fine, Blake. We knew what we were."

"We weren't anything," I admitted, wondering if I should feel guilty for that as I pressed my forearms to the counter. "We were hardly a *we*."

"No, I know, but it was what we needed, I guess." Her knuckles clipped my arm. "And hey, it was pretty good."

I chuckled. "Yeah," I nodded, agreeing. "It was good."

"But not like her, huh?"

I shook my head. "Not like her."

Chapter Seventeen

THE LOOKS EXCHANGED between Shane and Celia were anything but friendly. Heated glances. Flirty smiles. If it wasn't for her kids being at her place, I was certain he'd be spending the night in her bed. And as the place filled with pheromones and tension, I wished her ex would take them for the night.

"This is the best tea I've ever had," Shane declared, putting his steaming cup of vanilla Earl Grey down on the table. "I'm not even normally a tea guy, but this shit is good."

"Blake fanboys hard over Jolie's," Cee teased, glancing in my direction with a smirk.

"I like what I like," I shrugged unapologetically.

Shane took a bite of biscotti and crumbs sprayed against the tabletop. He muttered a "shit" as he quickly used a hand to sweep the mess into his palm. "Totally making an ass of myself today," he laughed nervously. A hint of blush swept over his cheeks as he quickly glanced in Cee's direction.

That was putting it lightly.

Shane had been running late this morning, which had been fine with me. With Jake still giving me a hard time about Miss Thomas being out of commission, the extra time to convince him to go to daycare was much appreciated. Then, Shane had announced his eventual arrival by spilling what little was left of his energy drink on the front desk of Salem Skin. The incident was followed by him tripping twice on our walk to Jolie Tea, not to mention the countless times he'd fumbled on his words.

The fact that all of these mishaps had happened while in the presence of Celia wasn't lost on me, and she wasn't much better. The woman was a mess of giggles, rosy cheeks, and flips of her dreadlocks.

Someone needed to get these two a fucking room. But in the meantime, I was ready to tell Cee to get lost while we conducted the interview, just to keep the guy focused.

"Okay. Let's do this," Shane began, wiping his hands on his skintight black jeans. He then pressed record on his phone and placed it on the table in front of me. "So, Blake, tell me how you got into tattooing."

I eyed the phone with uncertainty, feeling instantly on the spot, and Shane chuckled gently. "Pretend it's not there, man. Just talk."

"Easier said than done," I chuckled awkwardly, scrubbing a palm over my beard. "But, uh, okay, so ... I was a total art nerd when I was younger—"

"I'm sorry," Shane cut in, laughing. "I have a really hard time believing you were ever a *nerd*."

"Okay," I relented, shrugging. "Maybe *nerd* isn't the right word for it, but I was always into drawing. I drove my parents crazy, always filling up my sketchbooks faster than they could buy them. Then, when I was maybe twelve or so, my uncle came up from Florida. It was the first time I really paid attention to his tattoos. This guy's arms are covered, right, and I remember just sitting there in my parents' living room, checking 'em out, and I just remember thinking two things. One, that it was the most badass shit I'd ever seen in my life, you know, to be a living canvas. And two, that I could do so much better than the drawings he had on his arms."

Shane nodded, a grin slowly growing across his face. "So, really, you wanted to be a tattoo artist to fix your uncle's shitty tattoos."

I laughed and canted my head. "Well, I mean, it's all gotta start somewhere, right?"

"True that, brother. True that." He quickly glanced at the sheet of questions in front of him. "So, your work is very distinct, you definitely have your own style. Were you influenced by anybody?"

I sipped at my tea as I considered the question. "You know," I said, putting my cup down, "I've never really thought about that much. I've always just kinda done my own thing, you know what I mean? But now that you've asked, I think a lot of my style came from my love for this town and its overall eeriness, blended with some of the graphic novels I read when I was younger. I was a big fan of the gothic stuff. You know, *The Crow*, *The Sandman* … I loved that shit, and then when they turned

The Crow into a movie, forget it. The grittiness coupled with gothic romanticism ... I ate that shit up."

"Actually, now that you mention it, I can definitely see that influence in your work."

"Yeah, man. I fucking love it."

He laughed. "Although, dude, I gotta be honest. You mentioning romanticism is like a fuckin' oxymoron."

I couldn't help the laugh that barked from my chest. "Are you calling me unlovable?"

Cee's eyes shifted toward me as she smirked. "You are kind of a hard-ass," she jabbed.

Shane laid a palm over her arm and I thought her eyes might jump right from their sockets at the touch. "Nothin' wrong with being a hard-ass," he told her before turning his attention back on me. But his hand didn't move from her arm. "Nah, man. You're just a, uh … You're a *bad*ass, let's put it that way, and hearing you talk about romance gives you a softer vibe. It's not what I expected, but it's not a bad thing."

The interview continued with questions pertaining to my favorite artists and preferred ink brands. They were all innocent enough and nothing left my heart freaking out with bottled-up anxiety. When it was clear we were finishing up though, Shane threw a question at me that tensed my jaw and clenched my fists.

"Well, Blake, this has been awesome and really appreciated. Before I let you go, could you tell our readers what your plans for the future are? Any chance you're gonna open up your own place, or go on tour?"

The obvious answer was simple enough, two little letters and one short, easy syllable: *no*. But as I sat in my chair, surrounded by Jolie Tea customers, Cee, Shane, and so many possibilities, I found that I didn't want to say no. I didn't want to slam that door shut on my future when I hadn't even given it an opportunity to flourish. Would it kill me to be honest? Would it hurt me to admit what *I* wanted, without my responsibility to my brother getting in the way?

My heart raced as I shrugged. Sweat pearled at the base of my neck. "Well, uh, I'd love to open my own place someday. That's always been a dream of mine. It was always the goal."

Celia's eyes darted from Shane's hand, still on her arm, to my face in the matter of milliseconds. She hadn't expected that answer—who would?

"Dude, that'd be fuckin' awesome," Shane answered, nodding.

"Yeah," I agreed, nodding. I felt myself backpedaling, needing to close the window I'd let crack open. "But you know, we'll see what happens. Plans can always change."

Shane pocketed his phone and stretched his arm across the table, offering his hand. "Thank you for this, brother."

I clapped my palm against his and shook. "No problem."

"I'm gonna get my photographer up here this weekend to snap some pictures, and we'll get this piece ready for the December issue. You're gonna ring in the New Year with a shit-ton of new clients, I hope you realize that."

I chuckled gruffly. "I'm looking forward to it," I replied, only speaking half the truth.

"And that thing about opening up your own place …" He gripped my hand and lifted his mouth in a lopsided smile, before continuing, "That's in the cards, man. Nothing holding you back, except you."

***

I couldn't get those words out of my head for the rest of the day. *Nothing holding you back, except you.* They played on repeat as I picked Jake up from daycare and cooked him dinner. They continued to circle, as I threw his soiled sheets from the night before in the dryer and made his bed with a clean set. They kept going and going as I tucked him in and got his new copy of *Gremlins* playing before heading home.

Nothing holding you back, except you.

I *wished* I was one of those people, being held back by their personal qualms and a mental roadblock. If only I could simply power through, get myself over the proverbial wall, and continue the journey toward greatness. But what the hell was I supposed to do about the life forced upon me, the one that didn't give me a choice?

Except I *do* have a choice, I reminded myself. My parents had given me one. If I stopped fighting their suggestion to put Jake into a facility, if I even helped them to find one, I could get the ball rolling in my own life.

"Fuck," I moaned, laying my hands over my face and flopping back against my bed.

I felt like a traitor for considering it. Like a selfish piece of shit. This wasn't supposed to happen. I wasn't supposed to give up or give in. Was never supposed to steal from him and throw him away, like he was something to be used and trashed. But was it really giving up, if it was helping?

With a sigh, I grabbed my phone and dialed my mom's cell number. She answered on the third ring and I wondered if I'd woken her up.

"Hey," she said. "Did you forget something?"

"No ..."

"Oh," she replied curtly, then said, "I can't remember the last time you called me."

I studied the ceiling for a moment as I tried to remember the last time I'd called my mother and came up empty. "Huh. I guess you're right."

"Of course, I'm right. I'm your mother." She used the tone that I knew she thought was playful but instead just came across as obnoxious and superior.

I forced a chuckle and wished I'd called my father instead. "Yeah ..."

"Anyway," she went on with a sigh, "what's up?"

"Um, well, I was actually wondering how it was going with finding a place—"

"For Jake?" She cut me off, implying shock with her high-pitched tone. I couldn't blame her for being startled. After my initial reaction, she'd been hesitant to bring it up with me again.

"Yeah," I answered reluctantly.

"Oh, well, we found a couple of places we thought we'd look at. Your dad made an appointment to meet with the director at one of them next week, so I guess—"

"I'll go."

"You want to come?"

I nodded to the ceiling, affirming my resolve to go through with this. "Sure."

"I was hoping you would," she admitted. "You're so close to him, I wanted to get your approval before we settled on a place."

That word *settle* stuck out like a sore thumb and my brow furrowed with irritation. "We're not gonna *settle* on a place, Mom. We're going to find—"

"Blake. You know what I meant."

Stop being so defensive. I fixed my jaw and nodded. "No, I know. Sorry."

"Anyway, your father and I are going to watch a movie. So, I'll see you—"

"What movie?"

"Oh, um … That new Stephen King one, I think? Which one is it, Paul?" I heard Dad mutter something from not too far away and Mom said, "*It*. We're watching *It*. The remake."

I nodded with startled approval. "You like horror movies?"

"*Like* them? Honey, I *love* horror. How do you not know this?"

My lips turned and twisted with question. "I don't know."

She huffed with laughter. "I mean, come on. Where do you think *you* get it from?"

With well wishes for a good night and good rest, we hung up, and I wondered about that. Where *had* I thought I'd got it from? I guess I'd gone through my entire life just assuming I was the bad seed of the family, a heathen in black, or a rebel with a tattoo machine. Assuming that something had simply gone awry in my DNA and I'd ventured on my own toward the dark side. I'd never even considered that maybe I could've picked up on some things from my God-loving parents. I'd never taken any notice.

Maybe I was more like them than I thought.

Chapter Eighteen

SHANE HAD ARRANGED the photoshoot for Saturday. While I was happy for it to coincide on a day when Jake wasn't around, I found it odd that I still didn't want to go alone. It was my first time being professionally photographed. Well, outside of the mediocre point-and-shoot sessions for school pictures, conducted by some greaseball moonlighting as a photographer, and I was nervous.

Cee would be there, I knew that, but she wouldn't be there for me. She'd be hanging around, ogling Shane and waiting impatiently to get him back to her place. She'd be watching as *ModInk*'s photographer instructed me to stand this way and that, but she wouldn't be there for *me*. And hell, I didn't want her to be.

I wanted Audrey.

Perched on my bike, one block away from the shop, I stared at the phone in my hand. For one desperate moment, I considered calling Dr. Travetti, to ask her to come down as my groupie. To cheer me on and pump me up. But how fucking lame would it be, to ask my shrink to come, and all because I didn't want to call the girl I liked.

"Don't be a fucking pussy," I scolded myself in an angry grumble, as I hit her name in my contact list.

I almost hung up, but she didn't give me a chance. "Blake! Hi!"

My groan was coupled with my smile. How could she always sound so happy, like every day was Christmas and every moment was a gift?

"Hey, Audrey."

"How are you?"

"Um, good," I answered honestly. "How about you?"

"Well, I mean, it's Saturday and I don't have work, so obviously that makes it a great day." Her voice was full of smiles and laughter. "What are you up to?"

There it was. The opener. She'd given it to me, she'd made it easy, and I grabbed for it. "Actually, funny you ask. I had an interview the other day with *ModInk*—uh, it's this big tattoo magazine, and—"

"Oh, that's so cool!"

"Yeah," I agreed, nodding. "Today, they're doing a photoshoot down at the shop and I thought I'd ask if you, um ..." I felt like an idiot, pursuing the pretty girl who was so completely out of my league, she was practically in a whole other universe. My hand raked through my hair, and I pinched my eyes shut, knowing it now looked like crap and would need to be redone for the pictures.

"I'd love to," she answered, before I could ask. "I just need to do a couple things and then I'll come down. Would twenty minutes from now be okay?"

"Yeah," I replied in a voice so choked, I was surprised I could speak at all. "Yeah, that'd be fine."

For two seconds too long, there was nothing but air passing between us. Whispers of the mind, secrets of the heart, and I wished I knew what to say to take the awkwardness away. Hell, forget awkwardness—I wished I knew what to say, period. But Audrey … She always knew.

"I'm really excited to see you," she confessed quietly, making it seem easy to speak her mind.

The nature of my being wanted to scoff, insistent that there was no way she could possibly be excited about seeing me. But before I could give in to instinct, I found myself wondering what the good doctor would tell me to do. What would she tell me to say? Because it was Saturday, she wasn't working, but if she was, I'd take my bike over there right now and ask her to coach me in how to talk to pretty girls. But I was left to my own devices, so I took a deep breath, focusing harder on the saint in my heart and less on the devil in my brain.

Then, I replied, "I'm excited to see you, too."

***

"Okay, Blake. Stand just like that and look down. Right into my lens," Toby, the cameraman, instructed, crouching to the ground at my feet.

I felt like an idiot, standing outside the shop with my arms crossed over my chest, but I did as I was told without protest. I let my lids droop as I looked directly at the camera and Toby nodded with approval as he snapped a few shots.

"Perfect, awesome," he praised absentmindedly, shifting his heels and grabbing another shot from a different angle. "Look over here now—excellent. Great."

A few more clicks of the camera and he rose to his feet with a directing wave of his arm. "Lex, this damn wind is killing me. Can you fix his hair again?"

Toby walked away to change his lens and Lex the stylist came over with her damned comb in hand. As she reached to fuss with my hair for the umpteenth time, I took that as my cue to relax my arms and push a disgruntled sigh from my nose. My eyes shifted toward the cluster of familiar faces standing off to the side. Cee and Shane watched with amusement creasing their eyes and pulling at their lips, and I felt the temptation to tell them they wouldn't find it so funny if they were the ones with some strange woman raking their hair back. But I maintained my silence as my eyes fell on Audrey.

She had come by over forty minutes ago, when we had just started with the shoot, and I'd stopped everything to greet her with a sheepish grin. She had been so serious then, encouraging me to get back to work, but now, her pale blue eyes lit with laughter as she bit her bottom lip. Cee said something to her, and I saw Audrey's mouth move with her reply. Dammit, I wish I knew what they had said, because Audrey doubled over with an eruption of giggles and Celia clapped a hand over her mouth. They were laughing at me, I knew that much, and not even the defensive part of my brain could stop me from basking in the glow of that sound.

"Your girlfriend is cute," Lex commented, following my gaze.

I damn near jumped at the insinuation. "What? Celia's not my—"

"No, I know; Shane's into her. I mean the one in white. What's her name? Audra?"

"Audrey," I corrected. "And she's not my girlfriend."

"Ah." Lex brushed my hair back and strategically laid a few strands against my forehead before declaring, "Okay, Toby, he's good."

"He better be," Toby replied and came back to instruct me into a few other poses while I mulled over my brief exchange with Lex.

This thing with Audrey had begun coincidental, was damn near accidental, but it'd quickly become something close to habitual. We had exchanged numbers. We'd slept together. Hell, she had even spent the night. Everything about that was screaming *relationship* to me, yet I still wasn't sure that was what I even wanted. Maybe all I wanted was someone to fuck every now and then, now that Cee was clearly out of the picture. Maybe I just wanted someone to make me feel the way Audrey did when she was around.

Actually, she left me terrified.

Terrified of letting her in. Terrified of letting her go. Terrified of the day she'd finally open her eyes and see me for the person that I am—paranoid, surly, hateful.

Terrified.

"Okay, man. Let's move it inside," Toby instructed irritably. "This goddamn wind is pissing me off. I don't know how you guys can stand how cold it is."

"Cold?" I laughed, incredulous. "This isn't cold."

Toby's grey eyes met mine, unamused. "I'm from Virginia. Trust me. This is cold."

Audrey quietly sauntered over. "Cold is the middle of January in Minnesota," she jumped in, taking a place at my side. "This, right now, is *perfect*."

"Whatever you say," Toby snickered, shaking his head and heading inside.

Lex, Shane, and Celia followed closely behind, taking quick glances in our direction before disappearing into the sanctuary of the shop. Audrey and I were left alone for the first time since she'd arrived, and even as the cars drove by and the pedestrians passed, I felt wrapped and secluded in her energy. My mind settled and my lungs worked easily, breathing in the cool air and granting myself a moment to simply feel alive and good.

Audrey's head tipped back and her eyes met mine. In this position, I wanted to forget about the photoshoot and just spend the next twenty years of my life kissing her. But I stood there, frozen, just drowning quietly in her gaze.

"Cold," she snickered, breaking the silence. "This isn't cold."

I laughed at her eyeroll and playful demeanor. "Minnesota, huh?"

"Yeah. My whole family went on this big trip to Minneapolis when I was fifteen. They were so excited about the great deals they got, until they realized *why* they were so great."

Continuing to chuckle, I shook my head. "I bet that was fun."

She barely nodded as her eyes dropped to my lips. "Yeah. It was. I mean, it was freezing, don't get me wrong. But we had fun."

She wanted to kiss me, and hell, I wanted to kiss her. But my attention was pulled toward the window and I saw Toby pitching his umbrella lights while Lex laid out her supplies. My gut churned with apprehension, thinking about this and what it meant, and where it would take me. It was a good thing, only a good thing, but fuck, the rolling in my stomach was so uncomfortable, I wanted to run and forget about the whole damn thing.

"You okay?" Audrey asked, grasping my attention and tugging my gaze back to hers.

There she was, still wearing a smile even while her tone dripped with concern. She was the embodiment of calm, a soothing beacon to lure me into comfort, and what that meant, I wouldn't think about right now. I just needed her to be here, to work whatever power she had over me, and she was.

"Yeah." I nodded slowly. "I am."

For now.

***

With some equipment and a very small crew of people, Salem Skin had been transformed into a photography studio. Audrey and Celia had found themselves a seat on the waiting room's couch, while Shane directed Toby and Lex. Gus had perched himself at his daughter's station. He overlooked the process with a shit-eating grin plastered to his face, and I could only imagine the dollar signs prancing around in that brain of his. I couldn't even blame him, knowing the coverage the shop would get the moment the magazine hit the stands. Both of our pockets were going to be comfortably lined in cash and the confusing blend of emotions coalescing in my gut had become unbearable by the time we were finished.

"I am fucking *starving*," Shane declared with an exhausted sigh.

"Well, if y'all wanna grab something to eat, I'm finished here," Toby replied, packing his camera away before disassembling the umbrella lights.

"Thank fucking Christ," Shane muttered, pushing himself away from my counter as he asked me, "You wanna grab some food?"

With a quick glance at the clock, I noted the time. The poetry club was going to open in just an hour, and I knew that getting dinner would mean skipping an integral part of my routine. I'd been going to the club for at least six years, but I was also starving. To say I was conflicted was a big understatement.

So, I peeked through the open door at Audrey and nudged my chin toward her. "Hey, Audrey," I called, feeling her given name was somehow too impersonal but not knowing why.

She glanced my way, smiled, and instead of simply answering from where she sat, she patted Celia's knee and got up to walk my way, giving me her full attention. "Yeah?"

"What do you wanna do tonight?"

It was so presumptuous of me to ask her that. The question was one a man in a relationship might ask his girlfriend, and why I thought she'd even want to spend her night with me, I don't know.

"Well, what are my options?"

I scratched uncomfortably at the back of my neck. "Uh, well, I didn't know if you were going to the poetry club or not, so if you wanted to head over there, you could—"

"Okay, let me rephrase that. What are *you* doing tonight?"

Darting my eyes toward Shane, I found him busying himself by helping Toby pack up. Celia was occupied with her phone, Gus had gone into his office, and Lex had already left. Realizing I had a moment of wide-open privacy, I locked onto Audrey's gaze with my own.

"Shane mentioned grabbing dinner. I wasn't sure if you'd want to come, or if you had other plans, but if you wanted—"

"Blake," she stopped me, meeting my eyes with desperate sincerity. "I'm here, okay? I'm here."

It felt like it should've made me feel patronized, the slow, quiet, patient tone of her voice. It wasn't unlike the tone I used on my brother when he was out of control. But those two little words, "I'm here," pressed firmly against my heart, hugging and begging for access. I swallowed at the desperate need to doubt and defend, and my brain began to buckle and relent.

"Okay," I replied simply.

"So, you guys down for dinner?" Shane asked, brushing his hands against the thighs of his jeans.

"Yeah," I told him.

Shane hit me with two thumbs up before asking, "How about you, Toby?"

His nose wrinkled and he shook his head. "Don't take it personally. I'm just not into being the third wheel on a double date," he said, and surprisingly, I didn't feel the need to correct him.

Chapter Nineteen

LIVING A METICULOUSLY planned life with Jake, meant rarely straying outside of my own routine. Meals were always bought at the grocery store and cooked at home. But now, I was in a restaurant, surrounded by people who weren't members of my family, and I felt strange and out of place. At nearly thirty-four years old, eating in public shouldn't have been such a challenge. Yet I found myself fumbling foolishly with the cloth napkin and its enclosed utensils, as Celia and Shane discussed the menu items. For the first time ever, I wondered if Jake maybe was holding me back.

"Having a hard time over there?" Audrey's voice tore me from the difficult task of laying the napkin across my lap, and when I looked up, I caught the grin she struggling to contain.

"I feel like an asshole," I admitted, smoothing the fabric over my thighs and glancing around the restaurant to see if anybody had noticed.

"Don't get out often, huh?"

"Is it that obvious?"

She smiled and shrugged easily. "It's okay. I know the feeling."

I wished we were here alone, without Cee and Shane and a room full of tourists and drunkards surrounding us. I wished I could talk candidly about the traitorous thoughts cycloning through my mind, and with her, I felt I could. But not now.

"You drinking?" Shane asked, his chin tipped toward me.

"I dunno, man," I shrugged. We had walked to Rockafellas from Salem Skin, but I would still have to take the bike home. I didn't like the idea of leaving it overnight. That was a risk I'd taken last week and I didn't want to do it again.

"Come on, don't let me drink alone!" He was boisterous and full of laughter, as he dropped the menu exasperatedly. He bumped his shoulder against Audrey's. "What about you, Aud?"

"Um …" She lifted her menu and pointed to something. "I was thinking about this, but I don't know …"

Cee lifted in her chair to see what Audrey was pointing at. "Oh! The candy corn martini is freakin' incredible. Get that. You'll love it."

"Well, if I get a drink, you have to get one, too." I felt the toe of Audrey's shoe touch the side of my boot. "Just one?"

"Fine," I relented, unable to say no to her. How could I? "One."

But one turned into two, and two became three, and by the time the fourth round of drinks made it to the table, my mind was no longer on my bike. It was on the burger half-eaten in front of me, the breeze flowing in from the open door, and the bustling atmosphere. It was on the warm feeling in my belly, the woman who had put it there, and the cross laying against the split butterfly on her chest.

Her smile never left her lips and her laugh added melody to the restaurant racket. I leaned back in my chair, head cocked and eyes hooded, just watching as she talked to Celia and Shane like she wasn't the odd ball in her turquoise top and white jeans.

"I love these," she declared, holding up her fourth candy corn martini. "*So* much better than a Manhattan."

Shane clinked his tall glass of lager against the stout glass in her hand. "Yeah! Fuck Manhattan," he agreed with valor, then furrowed his brow. "Wait, are we talking about the city or the drink?"

"The drink," I chimed in, reaching out for my gin and tonic.

"Oh," he replied, raising his glass to his lips. "That's different, then."

"What do you have against Manhattan?" Cee asked him.

"Absolutely nothing," he laughed, shaking his head. "I was just going along with what she was saying to be nice."

Giggling, Audrey's eyes met mine as she explained, "Up until a few weeks ago, I had never had anything other than a Manhattan. And then, *this* guy," she reached across the table to nudge my hand with hers, "introduced me to the exciting world of alcohol."

I snorted. "You make it sound like I drink so much."

"Well, you drink more than I do!"

Shane watched the exchange with amused intrigue. "Wait, how did you two meet, anyway?"

My gaze dropped to the tattoo on her chest and I pointed toward it. "I have that thing to blame entirely for all of this shit," I grumbled, catching her eye and finding it impossible to fight my grin.

"Wait, what?" Shane peered closer, focusing on the image, and his eyes widened with recognition. "Whoa. Hold up. *You're* Butterfly Tattoo Chick?"

The rosy hue on her cheeks deepened as her lips dipped toward her martini. "Guilty."

Shane threw his hands into the air and tipped onto the back legs of his chair. "Get the fuck out of here. This is the craziest shit *ever*! Why didn't you tell me you were her? I could've gotten a few shots of the two of you together or something!"

My brow furrowed and Audrey asked between giggles, "Why?"

"Oh, Audrey, Audrey, Audrey ..." He draped his arm over the back of her chair and came in close to her ear, tipping his forehead toward her temple. He was crowding her and I saw the column of her throat shift with a swallow. He was one inch away from making her uncomfortable, and my fists were clenched against the table.

"Sweetheart. Do you know you're the reason why I even found this guy?" he went on. Then, he turned to face Cee. "Huh, come to think of it, I never would've met you, either."

Cee blushed, as Audrey replied, "I didn't know that."

"Fuckin' Fate, man," Shane muttered, releasing her from his grip and grabbing his pint glass. He raised it up into the air and said, "To Fate, for *making shit happen*."

Audrey and Cee raised theirs and repeated in unison, "To Fate."

The three pairs of eyes turned to me. Staring and waiting for my anti-religious resolve to buckle and break under the weight of peer pressure. But they weren't getting it from me. Not here, not tonight. But I did raise my glass in silence, letting the lip tap against Audrey's, and I downed my fourth drink, knowing there would be a fifth, all while two words echoed through my head.

To Fate.

***

"Well, kids," Shane announced, draping an arm around Cee's shoulders, "we're out of here."

"What are you guys gonna do?" Cee asked, flitting her gaze between Audrey and me.

"Oh, *I* know what they're gonna do," Shane teased, reaching out to jab between my ribs.

I snorted and brushed him off, while wondering if he was right. Would I sleep with her again? Fuck, I hoped so.

"Get home safe, guys," Audrey said, stepping forward to give Cee a hug.

"Yeah, you too," Celia replied, wrapping Audrey in a tight embrace. "I hope I see you again, pretty lady."

It was strange, witnessing Celia's purple dreadlocks blend against Audrey's platinum blonde hair. It should've been unnatural, just like my attraction to her. But somehow, it wasn't. Somehow it was as natural as my need for darkness and autumn, and it was driving me crazy that I couldn't make sense of it. So, I thought maybe it was time I stopped trying to and just accepted it for whatever it was.

Shane and Celia left us alone on the sidewalk in front of Rockafellas. I stuffed my hands into my coat pockets, and Audrey slipped her hand into the crook of my elbow.

"I guess we should get back to the shop," I declared. "I gotta get my bike."

"Nuh-uh. No way are you driving." She shook her head persistently.

"How am I supposed to get it home, then, Audrey? Huh?" I cocked a brow, challenging her with a tone teetering on playful.

"You'll get it tomorrow," she told me, tugging me along. "Right now, we're going for a walk."

"You and your walks," I chided.

"What's wrong with taking a walk?"

"I just know where they lead," I mused, nodding thoughtfully as we walked past a cluster of people dressed as zombie *Teletubbies*.

"Mm-hmm," Audrey hummed, stopping abruptly to slip her arms into my open jacket and around my waist. The city was alive with lights and sounds as her body pressed against mine. Rocking on the balls of her feet

233

and tipping her head back, she asked, "Will you kiss me, Blake?"

It was as if she knew I'd hesitate to show any sign of affection toward her in public. And if she'd been anybody else, I would've thought twice, but not with her.

Slowly, I snaked my arms around her waist, holding her to me as I brought my lips to hers. Audrey sighed, followed by a whimper, and I closed my eyes to open my mouth and taste the alcohol on her tongue. Her fingers gripped my shirt, clenching the fabric in a tight grasp as she teetered unsteadily on high heels and weak knees, and I moved one hand to her hair while the other held her waist tighter.

I was trapped in a euphoric bubble, tangled in her kiss, as the rest of the world disappeared. The storefront we stood against vanished, and the pedestrians and rushing cars were nothing more than fading white noise.

"Blake," she whispered, muffled by my lips on hers.

"Hm," I answered with a grunt, planting kiss after kiss to the corner of her lips, her cheek, behind her ear.

"Come back to—"

"BOO!"

Audrey's grip on my shirt strengthened as her mouth wrenched away from mine with a frightened gasp. Instinct had my arms wrapped around her in a protective hold as I looked up and searched frantically for the fucker who'd dared to burst our bubble, when my eyes landed on a kid of about eleven. He was dressed as Michael Myers and was accompanied by pint-sized versions of Freddy Kreuger and Jason Vorhees. Their costumes were excellent, and I appreciated them for a second before Michael pulled his mask off hastily.

"Sorry," he hurried, startled by my anger.

I softened my glare and lifted my mouth in a half smile. "It's cool. But only 'cause your costumes are awesome."

"Thanks!" He grinned and pulled the mask back on. "Happy Halloween!"

Audrey loosened her grasp and turned in my arms to appreciate them as they ran away to torment some other unsuspecting fool. She smiled and tipped her head against my chest.

"I love this town," she said with a wistful sigh.

"Me, too."

"Halloween is in a few days."

I nodded. "Yep."

"What are we doing?" She unraveled my arms from around her and took my hand.

"We?" I snorted, threading my fingers with hers and questioning if anything had felt this good before. If anything could feel this good ever again. "What's with this *we* bullshit?"

She nodded, eyelids heavy with booze and lust. "Yep, *we*. We're a *we* now."

My heart thumped annoyingly in my throat as I let her lead me. "Oh, we are, huh? When was I gonna know about this?"

Audrey's lips spread with her knowing smile. "Don't tell me you didn't already know."

Fate. God.

Signs.

"Fine," I relented. "I won't."

Slowly, we walked in silence for a few more seconds, quietly enjoying the air and ambience of a city we both shared a love for. Then, she tugged me down a residential street, over cracked sidewalks and beneath trees decorated in red and gold, and I realized I didn't know where we were headed.

We. I allowed a smile at the thought, squeezed her hand, and asked, "Where are you taking me?"

"I want you to see where I live," she answered.

"You live in Salem, too?"

Audrey nodded. "Yep."

"For how long?"

"Well," she released my hand and wrapped an arm around mine, "let me think. I'm twenty-six now, so—"

"You're twenty-six?" I interrupted.

Giggling, she pressed her cheek to my arm. "Yes, why? Does that matter?"

"Nah, not really. I just wasn't aware I was a fucking cradle robber," I groaned around a short chuckle, rolling my eyes toward the sky.

"You're not that much older than me," she giggled, hugging my arm.

"Old enough," I muttered.

Sighing, she continued, "Anyway, apart from the few years I was in college, I've been here my whole life."

"How have I not seen you before?"

Snickering, she shook her head. "You probably wouldn't have noticed me if you had."

I didn't say it, but that was bullshit. To not notice her would've been to ignore the sun. It was impossible.

We stopped at an old, red brick Victorian, trimmed in white with a black stained-glass door. The wrap-around porch was littered with wicker furniture and was decorated with cobwebs and hanging skeletons. An impressively realistic cemetery was set-up on the lawn among a handful of scattered bones and dead leaves.

I tucked my hands into my pockets, unable to contain my grin. This was my kind of place, not unlike my own, and I shook my head at the man I was weeks ago. The man who'd taken one look at her and made assumptions based on appearance alone.

"I think I misjudged you," I admitted sheepishly.

Leading me up the walkway, she replied, "Well, in your defense, I don't really look the part."

Then, as we stepped onto the porch, she lowered her voice and said, "Now, we have to be quiet. The house is broken up into a few apartments and they're light sleepers."

"Noted," I muttered with a nod, and she unlocked the door.

Inside, it was dark, save for a small lamp near the staircase, but even in the dim light, I knew it was a history buff's wet dream. Carved crown molding, scrolled newel post, and creaking hardwood floors. My mouth was practically salivating as I stood still, waiting for Audrey to lead the way, when I quickly heard another door open.

"Okay," she whispered, grabbing my arm. "This is my place."

I followed her through the door nearest the house's entrance and waited for her to turn on a light, but she never did.

Instead, she attacked, wrapping her arms around my neck and seeking my mouth with hers in the darkness. I stumbled, walking backward a few paces until my legs hit what I assumed was a couch, and I fell back.

"Please tell me you don't have a roommate," I mumbled between kisses as she fumbled with the buttons on my shirt.

"Nobody's here," she answered hurriedly, giving up on my shirt and moving to my jeans instead.

"Good."

I kicked my boots to the floor and moved my hands to assist her in undressing. I unzipped and unbuttoned my jeans, shoving them off, and then reached for the waistband on hers. In seconds, they were thrown to the floor, and with our underwear discarded with them, my body filled hers with fluttered eyelids and a sigh.

"Fuck," I exhaled, reaching up to press my palm to her cheek. "How can you feel so fucking good?"

I hadn't meant to ask the question. It just slipped out between my open lips and into her dark apartment as she worked against my body with lazy movements. But, now that it was out, I let it settle in my heart while she leaned forward and rested her lips once again on mine, to kiss me lazily while our hips moved in a perfect, slow rhythm.

The answer was so obvious to me, and it glinted like the cross around her neck. Whether it was Fate, God, or simply serendipity, it was *right*. Nothing but right.

Audrey and me. Us.
We.

Chapter Twenty

I T'S SUNDAY.

I woke up with the reminder screaming through my mind, loud and clear. Almost as loud as the banging resounding through the apartment.

My eyelids snapped open to a chandelier I didn't recognize, and my brow furrowed with immediate suspicion.

Where the fuck am I?

The confusion was fleeting as I felt Audrey move against me, and I noted we were both naked from the waist down. I chuckled through the sleep still rasping my throat, realizing we must've fallen asleep immediately after sex, and wondered if we'd ever sleep together without booze floating through our veins.

"Hey," I whispered, nudging her cheek with my knuckles. "Audrey."

"Hm?" She nuzzled her nose against my neck and hummed sleepily as her arm tightened around my shoulder.

The knock against the door persisted and then came a voice. "Audrey? Audrey, are you home?"

With a flash of platinum hair, Audrey sprang from the couch and threw my jeans and underwear over my bare legs and groin. "You have to get dressed," she hissed, demanding and scrambling to collect her own clothes. "Oh, Lord, what is she doing here *now*?"

She was talking to herself, muttering with worry and frustration, and I watched as she hurried to smooth her hair down.

"Oh, when have we done this before?" I snickered teasingly.

Audrey turned me to with pleading eyes as the banging continued. "*Please*, Blake. Put your pants on."

"I'm doing it," I muttered, pulling myself up and getting dressed.

"Okay," she breathed out, shaking out her hands. "I'm opening the door now." Another deep breath. "Okay, gonna do it now. Right now."

I lowered my mouth to her ear and asked, "Are you actually gonna do it, or should I?"

Wide-eyed, she turned her blue gaze on me and shook her head. "You better not."

"Then, I suggest you do it, because my hangover really isn't appreciating that fucking noise."

Nodding with understanding, she laid a hand against her temple, as though remembering just how much we'd both had to drink the night before. She moved slowly toward that damn door, two knocks away from being busted open, and unlocked it.

But right before she opened it, she turned to me with a nervous bite of her lip and said, "Brace yourself, okay?"

I crossed my arms over my chest and narrowed my eyes with scrutiny. "Why?"

"Just … brace yourself."

Before I could ask again what exactly she meant by that, she opened the door. I immediately saw the older woman, her dark hair pulled back in a ponytail, greying at the temples. She grinned with taunting acknowledgement at Audrey, her pale blue eyes twinkling, and I knew this must be Audrey's mom.

I backed further into the room at the knowledge, tightening my arms around myself. I didn't do this. I didn't meet parents. Hell, judging from previous experiences, the parents I *had* met didn't like me, even if those experiences were limited and from over a decade ago. I tried to imagine what the good doctor would have to say about all of this. No doubt, she'd make passive aggressive comments about putting the right foot forward or some shit like that.

"Oh, hi, honey. Were you sleeping?" Her mother's voice sounded like hers, if a little raspier. Her tone lilted with playful teasing, and the tension in my arms relaxed just a little. "I seem to remember someone telling me she'd call last night when she got home, but …"

"I'm sorry, Mom," Audrey groaned in reply, laying a hand over her face. "I got a little, um … distracted."

"Uh-huh. *Distracted.*" Her mother allowed a little laugh before sighing. "I didn't want to bother you,

242

honey. But *someone* didn't want to wait any longer before coming down."

Audrey's breath released from her lungs with a long-winded exhale that I was sure must've hurt. "Oh, uh, yeah. Okay."

She quickly glanced in my direction, worry laced between the hints of silver in her eyes. I couldn't decipher what was happening in her mind, or what was happening at all, until her mother said, "Get over here, Freddy. What did I tell you about playing with that plant? What did it ever do to you?"

As Audrey crouched to the floor, my heart raced toward panick territory as my eyes quickly scanned the living room. It'd been so dark the night before, I never noticed the toys littering the coffee table or the buckets of Lego stacked in the corner. But now I did, and I understood with clarity, Audrey had a son. My palms began to sweat as the realization seeped beneath my skin and chilled my veins, and I turned to see the little brown-haired boy appear in the doorway.

"Hey, pal," Audrey greeted him sweetly, successfully pushing any hint of a hangover or irritation from her voice.

"Mommy, Grandma doesn't have pancakes," he replied.

"Oh, here we go with the pancakes again," Audrey's mother muttered.

"What about pancakes?" Audrey asked, looking up to her mother, then back to her son.

"He wanted to have pancakes for dinner last night," her mom explained with a sigh and a shake of her head.

"I didn't have the stuff to make them, so this is all I've heard about since."

I couldn't help my chuckle, remembering Jake and our conversation about pancakes for dinner just a couple of weeks ago. The sound alerted Audrey's mother to my presence, and she gasped, laying her hand over her chest as she peered into the apartment.

"Oh!" she exclaimed and pinched her eyes shut. "I'm so sorry. I thought … Audrey, I thought you were alone. You should've said …"

Hurrying to stand, Audrey's hands waved with protest. "N-no, Mom, it's fine. Really." Then, she turned toward me, extending a hand in my direction. "This is Blake. Blake, this is my mom, Ann."

This is not what I do, I reminded myself, as I discreetly wiped my palm against my jeans and stepped forward. I extended my hand and said, "Hey, nice to meet you."

Ann tipped her head back to take me in before slipping her hand into mine and glancing at Audrey. Using her other hand to shield her mouth, she muttered quietly, "Wow, he's cute. I know you told me he was good looking, but he's *really* cute."

Audrey gaped at her mother and smacked her shoulder. "Mom!" she laughed, incredulous.

Releasing my palm, Ann casually shrugged. "What?"

Audrey glanced at me apologetically before turning back to her mom. "Uh, did you forget about Daddy?"

"I've been married forty years, honey. I'm faithful, but I'm not blind."

Freddy, forgotten at his mother's feet, eyed me warily as he tugged at her shirt. Now up close, I saw he must've been about four years old and was wearing a *Daniel Tiger* t-shirt and blue jeans. I couldn't help but smile, suddenly missing my brother.

I pulled in a deep breath, raking back my sex-and-sleep disheveled hair. I took the initiative and knelt to the floor, making sure to look him in the eye. To give him respect and gain his trust.

"Hey, Freddy," I said, extending my hand. "I'm Blake."

He looked at my hand suspiciously. "You have tattoos," he stated bluntly.

I turned my hand over and answered, "Well, what do ya know? I do."

"You have a lot."

I nodded my agreement. "Yes, that's true. I do have a lot."

"My dad has three tattoos," he informed me, standing tall. "How many you got?"

I cleared my throat at the mention of his dad, wondering who he was and why I hadn't heard about him. Hell, why hadn't Audrey mentioned she was a mother at all?

"Oh, man, you know, I don't know if I can count that high," I told him, and Freddy scoffed, rolling his eyes.

"*I* can count to twenty."

"That *is* pretty high," I appraised, then winced. "But I think I have a few more tattoos than that."

Freddy squinted his eyes at me and pursed his lips, holding tight to Audrey's shirt. He was a tough guy, protective, and I knew I liked him.

"Do you like Legos?" he asked.

I nodded. "I'm pretty awesome at building Legos, actually. My brother's a big fan."

"You wanna see mine?"

With that, he headed into the apartment toward the stack of Lego buckets, and I stood back up to face the adoring smiles of both Ann and Audrey.

"Can I talk to you?" I asked Audrey in a low tone that I hoped spoke volumes.

Understanding immediately, she swallowed and nodded slowly. "Yeah, sure." Then, addressing her mother, she said, "We'll be right back, Mom."

We stepped outside, moving from the foyer to her front porch, and with an opportunity laid out before me, I abruptly asked, "So, uh, when were you gonna mention you're a mom?"

Audrey sighed, tucking her unbrushed hair behind her ears. "Blake ..."

"Because, I mean, it would've been nice to know that *before* you pronounced us as a *we*," I went on. "Or, did you just expect me to be cool about this? Like it wouldn't matter to me after we've had sex a couple times?"

"I'm sorry. I should've told you sooner, but when I was supposed to bring it up?"

I scoffed, shaking my head. "Oh, I don't know, Audrey. How about last week before we slept together? We were talking all damn night, you had plenty of opportunities. But okay, too soon, I get it. How about last night, then? Shane and Celia were both talking about their kids, you could've at any point mentioned yours. But," I shrugged with passive aggressive and sarcastic flair, "maybe you're right. Maybe there wasn't a good time to mention such a minor detail."

Audrey pulled in a deep breath and stated, "You're annoyed."

I leveled her with a glare. "Yeah. I am. But I'm not annoyed that you have a kid, let's get that straight right now. I don't care that you have a kid, as long as you're not married or some shit—"

"I'm not married."

"Great, wonderful. Good to know," I snapped, nodding fervently. "But you can understand why I'd be a little peeved that this was just sprung on me. I wish you had told me sooner, instead of me finding out about him like this. That's all."

She exhaled and nodded. "I understand. And I'm sorry, you're right. I should've told you, but I hope you can understand why I would've been hesitant. I like you a lot, and I didn't want to scare you away when things were really going somewhere. And believe me, I did *not* expect you to find out like this," she laughed uneasily, shaking her head.

I tipped my head toward my feet and nodded as the irritation dissipated. I found confrontation to be easy with her. I liked it, and for that, I was proud. "Yeah, I get it. I don't know if I ever would've wanted to tell you about Jake, if you hadn't found out the way you did."

"Why are you ashamed of him?"

I lifted my gaze back to hers and shook my head. "Hey," I spat out, hardening my glare. "I am *not* ashamed of him. But my life hasn't exactly been easy by being his brother."

She cocked her head and asked, "But is that his fault, or yours?"

"I …" My mouth was frozen in a position to speak but no words were produced as I stood there on her front porch, unable to talk.

So, Audrey spoke instead. "I got pregnant when I lost my virginity to my first boyfriend," she confessed, and then laughed. "It's still so ridiculous to say it out loud. I had been waiting for marriage, but you know, I was just home from college and we thought we'd get married one day. So, we did it and the freakin' condom broke."

"That fucking sucks," I commented.

She sat down on the steps and welcomed me to sit beside her. "No," she disagreed, shaking her head. "It was Fate. I mean, yeah, it was hard being a new young mom while dealing with my sister being sick and then dying. And yeah, it was hard to get used to working while raising a kid. But I never let Freddy stop me from enjoying my life, Blake, because he *is* my life. So, I include him in it when I can, and I let him make my life better when it's hard." Then, with a smile, she nudged my ribs with an elbow. "And the parts I *can't* bring him into, I drop him off upstairs with my mom and dad."

Her confession coaxed my own as I pressed my elbows to my knees and thrust my hands into my hair. "Jake wouldn't be the way he is if it wasn't for me."

"You keep saying that, but—"

"No," I cut her off, shaking my head adamantly. "Listen to me. It *is* my fault."

"Okay, Blake. I'm listening," she replied softly, giving me the floor.

With a deep breath, I told my story. The one I never told, not even to Travetti. "So, Jake … He was normal. He was so fucking smart—*way* smarter than me. And if you think *I'm* talented with my drawing, his stuff would've blown you away. I mean, even at ten years old, he was winning awards at school and shit. I can't imagine how it would be now … you know, if he could."

I cleared my throat and pushed a hand down to the nape of my neck and squeezed. "I was the wild kid—"

"Can't say I'm surprised," she interjected gently.

Giving her a short chuckle, I nodded. "Yeah. I was always getting into trouble. I drove my parents crazy, but they loved it back then. I kept them on their toes, while Jake kept the peace. He, uh … he kept me out of trouble, too. He'd always try to talk me out of doing shit or keep me from fucking up. Sometimes, I'd listen, other times I didn't …

"So," I went on, folding my arms against my knees, "there was this old abandoned house, down the street from where my parents live. This thing was so fuckin' old and dilapidated, there were literal holes in the floor and the stairs were missing treads. But we were kids, you know. We weren't thinking about how dangerous it was to be in there; we just thought we were cool, breaking into this shitty old place."

249

I stood up and began pacing the length of Audrey's porch. I didn't look at her, couldn't face her, but I felt her eyes on me with every step I took. "Sometimes, we hung out in the backyard and pretended we were explorers. Like, I'm not making it up when I say this place was a jungle, it was so overgrown. And there was this gigantic tree back there with these huge, gnarled branches. It looked like something right out of a Tim Burton movie, creepy as fuck, and it didn't help that there was this old wooden swing hanging from one of the branches. We'd freak ourselves out, making up stories about it, like how it was cursed or haunted, and we'd dare each other to sit on that fucking swing but then we'd chicken out and go home.

"One day, we were hanging out back there and I decided, today's the day I'm gonna sit on that fucking swing, and I told Jake he had to, also. But he was such a pussy." I laughed somberly through my nose, stopped my persistent pacing, and slumped with my shoulder against one of the porch posts. "He told me not to and said some stupid shit about ghosts and whatever the hell else, like something was gonna get me if I sat on the damn thing. He just wanted to go home."

My voice cracked, and Audrey stood. She walked the three steps toward me, but I took a step back, holding out my hand to stop her from getting any closer. I didn't want to be coddled. Not now. Not when it came to this. I needed to feel this pain, this shame, and all this fucking guilt.

"I made fun of him," I said in a low, graveled tone. "I said he was a baby and that if he wanted to go home so

250

badly, he could go. I told him to leave me alone if he was gonna ruin my fun, but he wouldn't fucking leave. He was so legitimately scared that something was gonna happen to me and he didn't want me to be alone when shit went down.

"So, to prove how fucking tough I was, I went right over to the thing, sat down, and nothing happened. It felt sturdy, and I was just laughing at Jake 'cause he made such a big deal out of nothing. So, he says to me, 'Great, now let's go home,' but I couldn't leave it at that, could I? I had to keep pushing shit. So, I started swinging and acting like a fucking asshole, still laughing at him. But then, Jake starts telling me that the branch looked like it was gonna break …"

I pinched the bridge of my nose, still able to hear his frantic pleas for me to stop, to get off the swing, to knock it off and go home. The tears stung the back of my eyes and I tried to steady my lungs with one deep breath and then another. But what was the point? I lost the battle against my quivering chin and burning eyes, and a tear slipped over my cheek.

"There was this sickening noise, this *cracking*, and I could feel the branch begin to give and fall. It happened so fucking fast, but I managed to jump off. I had busted my knee open, but I felt like I had dodged a bullet, it was so crazy. Then, I started to make some asshole joke about it really being haunted or something, when I realized Jake wasn't saying anything. At first, I thought he'd high-tailed it out of there when he saw the thing coming down, but I turned around and found him pinned under it."

"Oh, God, Blake." Audrey could barely speak, her voice coming in nothing more than a whisper, as she stepped closer and wrapped her hand around my wrist. "I don't even know what to say. I just ...," her voice splintered and she cleared her throat, "I just feel like nothing I could say right now would be good enough."

I shook my head and pulled my wrist from her grasp. I expected an expression of hurt, but it didn't come. She just simply watched me, so patient and accepting of everything I was, and I couldn't begin to understand how she could do that.

"Don't say anything," I told her. "I don't need you to. Hell, I don't even *want* you to. I just needed to get that shit off my chest."

"Do you feel any better?"

I shook my head. "No. Not really," I admitted. "I guess it's sort of nice that someone else knows now. That fucking branch hit him in the head and he almost died. Hell, he *should've* died, all things considered, and that's because of *me*. So, yeah, it's my fault I've spent the past ten years of my life doing nothing but whatever I could do to take care of him, because it should've been *me*. Not him—*me*."

In a hurry, I moved away from her, to take a seat once again on the porch steps. Slowly she came to sit beside me.

"Oh, Blake," she said softly, laying a hand against my shoulder, "I understand the guilt, but it was an accident. Your life doesn't have to stop just because—"

"Oh, yeah?" I turned to her. "And what about *his* life? It consists of watching TV, listening to music, and playing with his dog. So, if that's the only life he gets to have, then why should I have a better one?"

Her expression drooped with pity and sorrow as her head shook. "If you had a better life, so would he."

"How the hell do you figure that?"

She offered me a small smile and slid her hand across my shoulders. When her temple touched my arm, I closed my eyes and asked nobody up above to let me keep this. For as long as I could, for as long as I was allowed.

"Part of taking care of someone, is making sure you take care of yourself, and that includes your own happiness. And I know this, because when I'm happy, Freddy is happy," she explained quietly. "So, if you were happy, Jake would be happy, too."

I swallowed the information, letting it settle in my gut, before I tipped my cheek to press against the top of her head. "How do you know that'd work?"

"I don't," she confessed. "But I'm just guessing because God entrusted me to care for Freddy, and He entrusted you to care for Jake."

Chapter Twenty-One

"**T**HIS IS NICE," Mom whispered from beside me.

"Yeah. Sure," I agreed halfheartedly, albeit reluctantly, as we followed Maggie, Shady Acres' Assistant Director, down the hallway and toward the facility's gym.

Shady Acres was the definition of bright and friendly. The staff were attentive, affectionate, and accepting, and after witnessing one of the other residents have a meltdown in the middle of the cafeteria, I knew they were also patient. I knew that if he were to live here, they would care for Jake and do what was best for him, but I still wasn't entirely convinced that living here was the right answer for him.

After my front porch conversation with Audrey, and all of that God talk, I'd hesitantly begun to think that maybe she was right, to a degree. What quality of life had I really provided him by trudging through each day? He knew I hadn't been happy. He always knew my colors, whatever the hell that meant to him, and how could that not impact his mood negatively?

Jake trailed behind us with his headphones blasting his favorite Walk the Moon album. He studied every door, every room, with silent scrutiny, and I wished I could get inside his head to know what he was thinking and feeling. But his expression always remained neutral, unmoved, and that only added to my frustration.

"And here's the gym," Maggie announced, sweeping an arm into the brightly lit room packed with exercise equipment.

"Where does that go?" Dad asked, pointing toward a glass door on the other side of the room.

"That," Maggie began, folding her hands over her middle, "leads to our indoor pool. Water therapy has been wonderful for some of our residents."

"Jake never learned how to swim again," Mom mentioned astutely.

"Oh, that's okay! A lot of our residents don't know how to swim. But," she continued, "the ones who do, really enjoy it."

Dad meandered around the gym, touching the bench presses and weight machines like he was checking for flaws in their quality. Then he nodded approvingly and looked toward me. "This is some nice stuff, Blake," he said. "You should check it out."

"I'm looking at it, Dad."

"Yeah, but you could test it out. Make sure it's good, you know?"

I snorted. "Yeah, Dad. Let me just do a few reps right now for you," I replied sarcastically, but I walked further into the room to get closer to the equipment and make him happy.

While I'd always found it difficult to read my mother, I knew my father had not only been trying to make this easy on Jake, but on me as well. He knew it had taken a lot for me to open up to the idea, so every step of the way, he had sought my approval. From the bedrooms to the rec rooms, he'd always asked what I thought, if I liked it, as though I was the one moving in instead of my brother.

While I appreciated the rare effort, it wasn't making it any easier on me. If anything, it made it harder, as I realized more and more that both of their minds had clearly already been made up.

"So, what do you think?" Dad asked, proving my point.

"It's good, yeah," I replied, brushing my hand along a barbell. "If Jake starts lifting weights, he's gonna kick all of our asses," I made an attempt at a joke, and Dad acknowledged it with a soft chuckle.

"Yeah, right? God help us."

He sidled up to me, tipping his mouth toward my ear. "I think Mom wants to fill out the paperwork before we leave. But what do you think?"

The sinking sensation in my stomach was indescribable, but all I could do was shrug and say, "I don't think it really matters what I think, does it?"

"Don't say that, Blake. You know we care."

"*We*?" I challenged, hardening my glare.

He smiled apologetically and shrugged, answering my question without words.

I sighed, forcing myself to climb down from my defensive anger. "Don't you think you're settling? There are other places. Hell, there are other *options*. And you're, what? Just gonna dump him in the first one you check out?"

He flinched and I knew I'd gotten to him. My words had stung, and that hadn't been my intention. "Sorry," I began to apologize, but he shook his head.

"I'll try to talk to your mother."

Breathing a sigh of relief, I turned to face the door and saw Jake. His eyes were fixated on me as he gripped his iPod in one hand and his headphones in the other. Furrowing my brow, I walked toward him and asked, "What's up, buddy?"

He met my eyes with that knowing gaze of his. The one that never failed to irk me. "You're blue."

"Blue?" I furrowed my brow and he nodded.

"Blue. Like Grover," he stated calmly.

I'd never been given blue before. I'd been so many colors of the rainbow, mostly leaning on the negative side, but never blue. It left me unsettled until I got in the car with Jake and my parents and looked it up on my phone.

Apparently, according to the internet, blue had many meanings, but what I repeatedly found was that blue was the color of intuition and support. The color of someone that others find help in. Someone very generous, in their time and otherwise. My heart thumped as I read, as I connected with the color more and more with every webpage I visited. It was such a vibrant, positive smudge on everything I thought to be me, but it clicked. It fit and it simply worked.

I glanced at Jake, sitting beside me in the backseat. He was drawing, a blue crayon held between his fingers. He circled the outline of a black figure holding a sword and shield, pressing the crayon firmly against the page.

I swallowed at my nerves, as I stared at his picture, and I asked, "Whatcha drawing, buddy?"

"You," he replied simply, not bothering to look at me.

My snorted laugh was forced. "I don't own a sword or shield. That'd be weird."

"You don't need one," he answered, his tone flat as he circled the figure over and over again in blue. "Don't worry, Blake. You'll make it better. You're brave and you're a warrior. You'll make it better."

I smiled, reminding myself that my parents hadn't filled out the paperwork yet, because of me. And even though my color of choice was typically black, blue didn't seem like such a bad color to wear either.

***

"Blake! How are you? Everything okay?" Dr. Travetti asked, opening her office door to me.

"Well, Doc," I began, entering the room and dropping myself onto the couch, "I guess that depends on your definition of okay."

She sat in her chair, crossing one leg over the other. Leaning forward, she grabbed her clipboard from off the coffee table and suggested, as usual, "How about you start with how your weekend went?"

I tipped my head back against the couch and studied the ceiling in search of the best words to describe my weekend. Yet, even with thousands of words in the dictionary, all I could adequately come up with was, "Surprising."

Dr. Travetti urged me to continue, as I knew she would, and I told her about the photoshoot, about how I had called Audrey and invited her to hang out while I had my picture taken. I told her how I then went out with Audrey, Cee, and Shane for dinner, making it the first double date of my entire existence. How I went back to Audrey's place, shared another night of drunken sex, and had woken up to discover Audrey has a kid.

"Wow," she breathed out on an exhale when I was finished.

"Yeah," I agreed. "I really need to stop drinking so much before sleeping with that woman. It's becoming a habit." I chuckled and shook my head at the absurdity of it. I rarely drink, and her experience with alcohol was clearly limited. What was it about spending time together that made us succumb to booze? Was it the need for bravery, for an excuse to act on the obvious attraction?

But Dr. Travetti didn't seem to care much about that. Instead, she focused on the bigger elephant in the room. "How do you feel about her having a child?"

"That's a tough one, Doc."

"I thought it would be," she sympathized. "Do you want to talk about it, or are you purposely avoiding the topic?"

259

I shook my head, drooping forward against my knees. "I'm not avoiding it. I'm just ..." I scrubbed a hand over my chin and met her gaze. "She declared us as a we. Like, together."

A soft smile shaped her lips. "That's wonderful, Blake."

"Yeah, and I'm cool with that. I actually *want* that. I don't know why I want it, especially with her, but I fucking do, you know? And I had thought, hey, she could be my weekend girlfriend. We could do shit together when Jake isn't around, when I have some time off work or whatever. We could *date*." The word rolled against my tongue and I enjoyed its taste.

"Then, this shit drops in my lap, and, Doc ..." I shook my head slowly. "I was pretty annoyed, let me tell you. Like, she should've told me that shit, right? I never thought of myself as someone who could handle kids, you know?"

Disappointment overshadowed her features as she said, "I can understand that, but, Blake—"

"No, hold on," I stopped her. "I talked it out with her, Doc. You would've been so fuckin' proud of me. I had started to get defensive, I could feel it happening, but she wouldn't let me leave until we talked it out."

I thought the good doctor would weep as she nodded. "Blake. You might be my best success story yet."

Barking with a laugh, I said, "Hey, don't get too excited. Maybe it was a fluke, I don't know. And besides, it was pretty hard for me to stay annoyed when I was thinking about that awesome little kid with his *Daniel Tiger* t-shirt and Legos."

"What's his name?" she asked softly.

"Freddy." I smiled, remembering his tough guy attitude. Remembering the things she said to me on her front porch. "She's a teacher raising this cool little kid. She goes out, has a life, and comes home to be a mom."

Something startled the good doctor then. Her gaze widened for a moment, her lips parted, and I thought I heard her gasp. I asked what was wrong and she gave her head a gentle shake. "Nothing. It just reminded me of someone I used to know. But anyway, it sounds like you two have a lot more in common than you thought," Dr. Travetti commented thoughtfully, and I hummed in reply, shaking my head.

"But see, that's where you're wrong, Doc. This girl has never let crap get in the way of her living her life. Her family has dealt with shit, she had a kid, and she still goes out on weekends, and gets inked and drunk and goes after the bitter bastard she likes. She *handles* shit. She doesn't whine about things, she doesn't let them get in her way. She just deals with it and lives her fucking life."

"I see," she replied. "So, you admire her."

"Hell yeah, I do. 'Cause while she's there, handling the shit in her life with patience and a smile on her face, what am I doing? I'm over here, thinking I need to get rid of Jake in order to move forward in my job or to have a girlfriend."

It had been a couple of hours since I went to Shady Acres with my parents and Jake, and the thought of even

261

considering the place bubbled in my gut and left me nauseous. And I admitted as much to the good doctor. "I thought it'd be a good idea," I explained helplessly. "And it's a nice place, don't get me wrong, but ..."

"But what?"

I lifted my gaze to hers and admitted, "I want him to move in with me. I mean, in some ways, it'd be more difficult than it is now, but I think he'd be happier. And it would cut down on our time in the morning. We wouldn't have to wake up as early, and he'd be closer to his school. Plus, I do everything for him now as it is. If he lived with me, I wouldn't get home so fucking late at night. It just ..." I shrugged, suddenly feeling like a moron, "I don't know, it just kinda makes sense to me."

The good doctor's lips spread slowly into an encouraging smile. "I think that's a great idea, Blake. Have you talked to your parents about this?"

I shook my head. "No. It's something I've been thinking about, but this is the first time I've seriously said anything to anybody. Honestly, I don't even think they'd be okay with it. 'Cause the thing is, all these years, I thought I was doing so much better than them. I thought that, because I had gotten him into a program, I was doing more for him than they ever did. But really, we were both just kinda brushing him off."

"So, you have a plan to do better?"

"Yeah," I nodded defiantly toward the ceiling, clenching my fists with determination. "Yeah, I do."

***

"Hey, buddy, I'm just gonna make a call, okay?"

"Okay." Jake nodded, sitting at the kitchen table with his pile of Legos as I cooked dinner. "In your room again?"

He was referring to my phone call with Shane, when I'd slammed the door to get away from him. I couldn't feel guilty for taking a business call, but did I really want him to feel excluded from every matter in my life?

"No," I said, pulling out a chair at the table and sitting down. "But try to keep it quiet, okay? I need to be able to hear."

"Okay, Blake. I'll be real quiet. Like a mouse." Then, he dropped his voice down to a whisper and said, "Like this? Is this good?"

"Yeah, that's perfect." I chuckled and dialed the phone.

The anticipation to hear her voice was enough to kill me. Funny, when just a few weeks ago, I couldn't get away from her quick enough. Now, I was running toward her like my life depended on it. And maybe it did.

"Hey, Blake," Audrey answered, a smile in her voice.

"Hey."

"This is the second time you've called me in three days."

"You're keeping count?"

She scoffed lightheartedly. "Duh. I mean, I might be a grown woman, but deep down, I'm still a girl who has it pretty bad for this really hot guy."

I laughed, shaking my head. "You're crazy."

"Yeah, not so much. Remember, I'd never had anything but a Manhattan until I met you."

"Ah, that's right," I nodded and leaned back in my chair. "*I'm* the bad influence."

She hummed contemplatively, and the sound brought me back to Saturday night on her couch. I pulled in a breath, coaxing my body to calm down and to keep the blood from traveling south, but dammit, I wanted her again. I wanted her now.

"Maybe you're just showing me how to have a good time," she offered, a thoughtful air to her tone.

"Oh, is that all I am to you now? A good time?"

She giggled lightly. "Blake, did you just call me to flirt? Because while I'd love to do this all night, I do have to get Freddy to bed soon."

"Actually," I said, focusing my attention on Jake and less on the stirring in my jeans, "I wanted to know what you were doing tomorrow."

"Well, it's Halloween, and I took off work to take Freddy trick-or-treating, so …"

My grin was unrelenting. "You took off from work for Halloween?"

"Well, yeah, obviously. It's the second most important holiday to Christmas." Then she gasped and exclaimed, "*And* it's your birthday! Did you want to do something?"

I pulled in a breath and wrapped an arm around my middle. "I told you, I don't celebrate my birthday. But listen, if you're taking Freddy trick-or-treating, maybe we could go together."

"You mean, with you and Jake?"

"Yeah." I swallowed, suddenly surprised that I had even come up with this idea in the first place. And to further shake things up, I added, "And hey, um, my parents are coming over tomorrow night to have dinner and cake. If you guys wanted to come by for that, too, that'd be cool."

The line was clouded with dead air while my mind raced with everything I wished she'd say. In the silence, I watched Jake build an airplane out of nothing, without directions or help. He just knew what he was doing, based entirely on a vision living in his mind, and I wondered how he could manage that, while I was blindly tripping through something as basic as a new relationship. Or whatever this was.

It seemed like minutes had passed before she finally spoke, and when she did, her voice sounded stuck in her throat.

"Can I tell you something?" she asked.

It wasn't the reply I'd hoped for, but still, I nodded eagerly because she hadn't hung up. "Yeah, sure."

"I went on a date with this guy about six months ago," and I learned then that I hated the thought of her going out with anybody else as my lips pinched and my fist pumped. "We had a great time, until I mentioned that I have a son. And it would've been one thing for him to simply say he didn't want to get involved with a single mom, but he acted like this was the absolute worst thing I could've told him. He treated me like a pariah and told me to lose his number. So, I did."

"Wow," I muttered angrily, shaking my head. "What a fucking dick."

"Yeah," she laughed. "Honestly, it's part of the reason why I never seemed to find the right time to tell you. I felt like I had to protect myself, and my son, you know? But when you did eventually find out, you never treated me like that."

"Oh, I *am* a dick," I managed to laugh. "Just not about that."

"Because you understand."

My eyes fell on Jake, still building his plane, and I lifted a shoulder halfheartedly. "Yeah. I guess I do."

She sniffled, and I wondered if she'd been crying. "Anyway, I just wanted you to know that I appreciate you thinking about Freddy when you don't have to. And we'd love to come."

Chapter Twenty-Two

"**O**KAY, LISTEN UP, buddy," I said, turning to Jake in the front seat. I laid a hand over his arm to stop him from springing out of the car like a rabbit on speed. In a red sweatshirt and tiger ears, he turned to face me, his expression impatient and urgent. "Remember, we're trick-or-treating today with Audrey and her little boy. You're gonna behave, right?"

"You betcha," he nodded adamantly.

"I'm serious, Jake." I hardened my glare, ensuring he understood just how serious I was. "We can have fun, but no getting mad, okay?"

It wouldn't be the first time my brother had thrown a fit while trick-or-treating. But, at my parents' house and mine, the neighbors all knew him. They understood what he's like and accepted him the way he is. But we were in Audrey's neck of the woods, across town from where I lived. The people here didn't know Jake—hell, Audrey barely knew him, and her son certainly didn't know him at all. I didn't want Freddy's first impression of Jake to be a negative one.

"No getting mad," Jake repeated, continuing to nod.

"Pinkie swear?" I held out my hand, little finger extended.

"Pinkie swear," he said, wrapping his finger around mine.

"Okay," I replied hesitantly. "Come on," and I got out of the car.

Beneath a sky of grey with only a shred of sunlight, I turned to face Audrey's house. The place was even better in the daytime, with the stormy clouds providing an ominous backdrop. I reminded myself again of what a condemnatory prick I'd been when I had first met her, and never once would I have imagined her living in this house.

I rounded the car and steered Jake up to the porch, smiling as he took note of every bit of spooky décor on the lawn and in the number of trees scattered throughout the yard.

"This is Audrey's house, Blake?"

"Yeah, this is her house."

"Do you see the ghosts?" He pointed at a few billowing, white, fabric ghosts swinging from the porch roof. I nodded and replied, "Yeah, buddy. I see them."

I knocked on the door as he commented, "Audrey must really like Halloween, right, Blake? Do you think she likes Halloween as much as me and you?"

Just as I opened my mouth to reply, the door opened to reveal the hottest witch I'd ever laid eyes on. Her velvet, pointed hat, adorned with black and red roses, and matching dress suddenly seemed to suit her more than any of those pastels she always wore. The low-cut

268

neckline accentuated the deep valley between her breasts and, fucking hell, it took everything in my power not to thrust her up against the wall and rip the damn thing off.

"Audrey!" Jake's excitement was abundant and she grinned brightly at the sight of him, seemingly oblivious to the hunger emanating from my gaze.

"Hi, birthday boy!" she exclaimed, reaching out to take his hand. "Look at this costume! Oh, man, Freddy's gonna love you!"

"I'm *Daniel Tiger*," he stated matter-of-factly, gesturing toward his tiger ears, and Audrey reached a hand up to brush her fingertips against them.

"I see!" Then, turning her attention on me, she asked, "And where's your costume? Or are you too cool to dress up?"

"I'm wearing it." I bared my teeth, showing off the vampire fangs I had custom made years ago, and pointed to my eyes to draw attention to the yellow contacts. Audrey's lids drooped with a momentary surge of obvious lust and her lips parted. I laughed hoarsely, shaking my head and dipping my hands into the pockets of my jacket.

"Blake's a lost boy," Jake informed her.

"Like, from *Peter Pan*?" she teased, never taking her eyes off me.

"What do you think?" I smirked, crossing my arms and enjoying our flirtation immensely.

My wandering gaze caught the quick nip of her teeth against her full bottom lip and the movement of her throat as she swallowed. If my brother hadn't been standing beside me, and if her son wasn't in the apartment mere feet away, there would've been nothing stopping me from grabbing her and reenacting the events of Saturday night.

"I think we better get going, Kiefer," she answered in a hushed, throaty tone. "Let me collect the troops."

Raising a brow, I asked, *"Troops*? What?" But instead of answering, she just shot me an apologetic smile and told us to wait a minute before darting back into her apartment.

Jake watched her walk away with a flash of irritation. "Where is Audrey going, Blake? We need to go. It's getting late."

"It's not getting late," I mumbled through my suspicion. "We're fine."

"Where did Audrey go?"

"She'll be right out," I told him, watching the door with expectation.

"It's getting late ..." I sighed as my brother prattled on in the way he did, worrying himself and lowering his gaze. I began to second guess my invitation from the night before, but knowing it was too late to go back now. We were already here, stuck, but my impatience was building, too. I should've explained to her that you can't do this to Jake. You couldn't make plans and then have him wait. He didn't understand the concept of waiting. The word just wasn't in his vocabulary.

But before my frustration could reach its potential, Audrey emerged once again from her door, a purse slung over her shoulder and a small group of people in tow. Freddy walked obediently at her side, dressed as a pint-size Batman, and he was followed by a man carrying a little girl rocking a Tinker Bell costume. I scowled suspiciously at the sight of him and tightened my arms across my chest as he neared the open door.

"Hey, Freddy," I greeted Audrey's son, fighting the urge to glare at the man standing behind him.

Freddy assessed me with a scrutinizing gaze, and then a smile. "Hi, Blake."

"Freddy, honey." Audrey knelt beside him and smiled up at Jake. "This is Blake's brother, Jake. He's going to trick-or-treat with you and Eliza."

The little girl's name was Eliza. I nodded to myself, absorbing the information, as Freddy peered curiously at Jake.

"He's a grown-up. Grown-ups don't trick-or-treat."

"Well, Jake is a special kind of grown-up," Audrey explained. "He's big, like grown-ups are, but he likes a lot of things that kids like, too. He plays with toys and likes *Daniel Tiger*; did you notice his costume?"

Freddy assessed Jake's orange pants, painted with tiger stripes, and his red sweatshirt. The kid sure could scrutinize with the best of them, but I wanted him to like Jake. I wanted the boy to accept him as a big kid in a man's body, and I wanted them to be friends.

Freddy's eyes looked up to Jake's, and he said, "I have a shirt like that, too."

Jake touched a hand to the fabric. "I like red. Red's my favorite color."

"My favorite color's red, too!"

Audrey wrapped an arm around Freddy's shoulders and gave him a little squeeze. "Well, Jake, I think you just made a new friend," she said to my brother.

"I have two friends," he informed her with a nod, holding up two fingers. "David and Ashley. But Ashley is my *girl*friend, she's not a real friend."

My neck jerked to stare at him. "You have a girlfriend?" I spat out the question as a melodic giggle burst past Audrey's lips.

"Ashley's my girlfriend."

"Yeah, you said, but why didn't I know about this?" I crossed my arms, almost forgetting about the guy awkwardly standing and still waiting to leave the house.

He cleared his throat and Audrey chuckled apologetically as she stood. "Oh, gosh, I'm so sorry. Um, Blake, I want you to meet Freddy's dad, Jason. And this," she laid a gentle hand over the baby girl's head, "is Eliza, Freddy's baby sister. This is her very first Halloween, so we have to make it a good one."

Something resembling jealousy worked its way through my veins at the sight of Jason, knowing what he was to her, and I sized him up. He was shorter than me, but still tall. One visible tattoo sprawled the length of his forearm. Clean shaven. Crew cut. He was a pretty boy, that was for damn sure, and a far cry from my personal aesthetic. I couldn't exactly say she had a type, unless *this* guy was her type. In which case, once again, what the fuck was she doing with me?

"So, you're the tattoo guy," Jason said, and I pulled myself from my internal jealous rambling with a nod.

"Yeah, hey. Blake." I reached out over Freddy's head, to offer my hand. "Nice to meet you."

"Audrey showed me the ink you did on her," he said, hoisting the baby higher on his hip. "Pretty wicked, man."

I nodded. "Thanks," I replied, as my mind reeled with the thought that he'd seen it. He had seen *her—all* of her.

I was jealous and territorial, and all I could think was, Dr. Travetti was going to have a field day with this shit. New material to add to her clipboard.

"Okay," Audrey cut in, "you guys ready to go?" Jake didn't bother replying as he turned from the door and started to head down the steps. She laughed and looked to me with adoring amusement. "I guess he's ready."

"He was ready when he went to bed last night," I muttered and allowed myself to grin as I remembered Jake the night before, asking if he could sleep in his costume. Just like every other year.

You're going to miss that when he's not there anymore.

A stab of melancholy burst through the wall of content tainted with jealousy I had started to build around myself and the bricks fell around me in clouds of dust. It dawned on me that this could be my last Halloween trick-or-treating with my brother. It could be the last birthday dinner spent in my house. It could've been the last time I'd deny him the simple joy of wearing his costume to bed, and suddenly I wished I'd just let him. What the hell was the harm in letting him sleep in orange pants and a red sweatshirt? What the hell did it matter if it made him happy?

"Blake?" I blinked my eyes and found Audrey's stare. "You ready?"

I nodded and looked over my shoulder at my brother as he marched down the gravestone-and-bone lined walkway. "Yeah," I muttered, struggling to maintain a tone of positivity and happiness. "Let's do this."

***

As luck would have it, if you could call it luck at all, I found I actually liked Jason quite a bit. He was awkward in his mannerisms and conversational skills, but he was a nice, genuinely good guy. It didn't surprise me in the slightest that Audrey would've once been attracted to him, and from the look in Audrey's eyes, it was clear that affection hadn't left entirely. She still held a deep love for him, and I wondered if I could ever be lucky enough to have her look at me that way. Would I ever be worthy enough?

"I met my wife only a few months after Freddy was born," Jason told me, pushing the stroller.

A flash of heated, lava-like anger, thick and bubbling, rushed through my veins. "While you were with …" I nudged my chin toward Audrey, walking a few paces ahead of us. She had taken it upon herself to supervise as Jake and Freddy went to each door, making sure they were polite, and I found it both endearing and somehow incredibly attractive that she had asserted herself like that with my brother. Our mother acted out in anger so often, while our father looked at him as a stranger, but Audrey wasn't like them. Hell, she wasn't like most people, was she?

"With who?" Jason narrowed his eyes inquisitively and followed my gaze. His eyes widened immediately as he shook his head furiously. "Oh! No, no, nothing like that. She and I broke up weeks after she gave birth. We realized we were better friends than, you know, boyfriend and girlfriend. And as it turns out, we kick butt as parents together. Right, Aud?"

She shot a glance over her shoulder and I caught a glimpse of her smile. "Huh?"

"I was telling Blake that we're awesome parents."

"Oh, yeah," she nodded in agreement and reached out to ruffle Freddy's hair. "I definitely think we do all right."

We came to a stop, to allow Freddy and Jake to knock on another door, and Jason continued telling me the story I never asked to know.

"Yeah, so I met Amy at a teaching supply store, of all places. They say you'll meet the love of your life when you least expect it, right?"

"Sure," I nodded, watching Audrey as she helped Freddy to pick out candy from the proffered bowl.

"I took one look at her and I just knew. It was crazy, man. I've never felt anything like that in my life."

I turned to him, questioning why he thought I cared at all about how he met his wife or how quickly they fell madly in love with each other. But the guy did like to talk, that much was obvious, and so I nodded in reply.

"It's the most bizarre feeling, you know, looking at someone for the first time and knowing they'll be your wife one day." Then, he laughed as his cheeks reddened. "You probably think I'm so lame, talking about soulmates and all that."

I wanted to tell him I didn't believe in soulmates. I wanted to tell him I didn't believe in souls, period. But every time I resisted, a little voice would speak up somewhere in my head. Or, was it my heart? Wherever it was, that little voice said that there was so much about this world I didn't know. I sure didn't know why a thousand accidents had aligned so perfectly to bring me here, to this exact moment. I didn't know how Audrey could be so different from me, yet somehow balanced me out so well. I didn't know what allowed Jake to see a person's color radiating around them, to reveal their innermost secrets. And if I was willing to admit all of those things, I could also admit that I didn't know if there were soulmates, tethered to each other. Maybe even through a thousand accidents, all aligned so perfectly just to bring them together.

"I don't think you're insane," I told him.

He grinned, flashing me a row of straight, white teeth. I didn't swing that way but I could appreciate that Jason was an attractive guy. Sharp jaw, full mouth, friendly eyes, and a symmetry to his face that would make any modeling agency shit their pants. I wouldn't have been surprised if he told me he'd been a jock in school and popular with the girls. A golden boy. A Ken made perfectly to go with Barbie.

"Why didn't your wife come today?" I asked him, while trying to ignore how well he fit Audrey and how much I didn't, despite the sex being good and the company being better.

His smile wilted with a shrug and a glance into the stroller at the sleeping baby Eliza. "She couldn't get off work today. She'd been sick all last week with a sinus infection."

I nodded. "Ah, yeah. Sinus shit has been bad this year."

Jason groaned. "Tell me about it. And with her job, it's tough to take time off work."

"What does she do?"

"She's an adult daycare provider," he explained, completely unaware that he was laying another tile down onto the complex mosaic design of my life.

I turned then, granting him my full attention. "Hold up," I said, and he nodded, tipping his head curiously. "Does your wife work at the Essex Center for Adults?"

Jason's nod slowed to nothing. "Yeah … h-how did you know that?" Now, he looked at me like I was a crazy stalker and shouldn't be anywhere near the mother of his son. But Jason was a smart guy, a quick thinker, and that narrowed glare of suspicion and distrust, was fleeting. The pieces settled quickly into place as his eyes flitted toward my brother. "Jake," he drawled, pronouncing every letter of his name with purpose. "*He's* Jake."

"Yeah," I answered, nodding slowly. "That's Jake."

"Jeez," he muttered. "What are the chances of that?"

I let a long, winded breath whoosh past my lips. "You know, a few weeks ago, I would've said the chances were slim. But now …" I shook my head, looking at Audrey in her form-enhancing witch's dress

277

and her contrasting platinum hair. "I'd say it's par for the fucking course."

Chapter Twenty-Three

EVERY YEAR, Jake would request tacos for his birthday dinner. It wasn't his favorite food, nor was it something he wanted to eat often. He just enjoyed the fun of building his dinner himself, the freedom of putting whatever he wanted together without anybody telling him what he could or couldn't do. I liked to think it made him feel more in control and more like the adult he legally was.

This year wasn't any exception, and after leaving Audrey's house, Jake and I went back to my place to prepare. I had left with Audrey's lips on my bearded cheek and the promise that she'd see me later, and somehow, that simple, gentle kiss felt more intimate than making out. For the hour it took for me to bring up the folding chairs from the basement and get dinner together, I pondered why that was, until I realized it was the first time I'd felt her lips on my body without the influence of alcohol behind our actions. Then, after coming to that conclusion, I was nervous. About inviting her over. About her altogether. What if our attraction was only influenced by booze? Was there anything real about it, then?

My parents showed up before I had laid the taco shells and fixings out on the counter, buffet-style. Mom insisted on helping while Dad sat awkwardly in Jake's room, to avoid helping, I assumed. But I wished he was in the kitchen instead. I wished he had also insisted on helping me, to act as a buffer between my mother and me. But now, left on my own, I just hoped to make enough small talk to fill the minutes until Audrey came. Until dinner. Until they left.

"How was trick-or-treating?" she asked, keeping her eyes on the counter as she filled a bowl with shredded lettuce.

"Good. We had a good time."

"I wish you had invited us to come."

My hand stopped on its way to unwrap the package of shells. "Sorry," I muttered. "Things have been so crazy, I forgot." But had I genuinely forgotten? Or had I subconsciously kept the thought out of my mind, in order to selfishly enjoy the day with my brother, Audrey, and her son?

"It's fine. You just know we like to be included."

I lifted a shoulder in an apathetic shrug. "You never come, anyway." I shouldn't have said that, but it was the truth. Every year, I invited them, and every year, they declined. They were too old, too tired, too busy, they would tell me. I never cared; it didn't matter. I never looked at it as a reflection of their feelings toward Jake or me. It just didn't interest them, simple as that. But now, my mother was clearly hurt, and I was torn between feeling bad about that and being annoyed that I could never seem to do anything right in her eyes.

"Well," she replied shortly, "it's still nice to be thought of."

A knock on the front door ended the conversation abruptly and Mom's gaze shot up to pin mine as she asked, "Who could that be?"

Fuck. I hadn't told them I was inviting Audrey. Hell, they didn't even know there was an Audrey, let alone a Freddy. I pinched my eyes shut and said, "Oh, I forgot to tell you. I invited a couple friends over tonight."

"*Friends*?" She said the word like it was foreign and uncomfortable on her tongue, spitting it out through twisted lips.

I didn't reply as I hurried through the living room to the front door. On the other side was Audrey and Freddy. She had changed, no longer in her witch's costume, but just as beautiful, and Freddy was still decked out in his Batman garb.

"Hey," I answered, then grimaced at how breathless I sounded.

"Hey, long time, no see." She smiled wide, amused by her own lame joke, and my mouth stretched to match.

I welcomed them in, taking her coat and asking if Freddy wanted me to take his cape, to which he declined with more sass than a four-year-old should possess. "So sorry," I replied with deep sincerity, pressing a hand to my chest. "Jake's room is right over there, if you wanna go check out his Legos before dinner."

Freddy looked to his mom for permission, and she said, "Go ahead, pal."

"Cool," he said and darted toward Jake's room. I listened as my dad greeted him with startled interest, and to Freddy's simple reply, "I'm Freddy, Jake's new friend. Are you his daddy?"

"Uh, hi, Freddy," I heard my dad reply. "Yeah, I'm Jake's father."

"You wanna play with us?" Freddy asked him, and I listened as my dad stammered awkwardly, "S-sure."

I laughed as something warmed inside of me as I led Audrey into the kitchen. "That kid of yours is charismatic as fuck," I complimented. She nodded and said, "He gets it from his dad, I think. I'm definitely not."

"Uh, don't take this the wrong way, but you are way more charismatic than Jason is." I shot a wince over my shoulder and she laughed.

"You didn't like Jason?"

"Hey, don't go putting words in my mouth. I never said th—"

"Blake, are you going to continue to be rude or are you going to introduce me to your friend?" Mom's tone was pulled so taut, it was remarkable her vocal cords hadn't snapped from speaking alone.

I stood in the kitchen doorway, mouth open and eyes wide. But, taking a cue from her son, charismatic Audrey stepped forward. "Hi, Mrs. Carson. I'm Audrey. It's so nice to meet you."

My mother offered her hand and as Audrey accepted the gesture, Mom said, "Audrey? Blake never told me about any Audrey."

It wasn't what a woman wanted to hear about the guy she was seeing. Or fucking, whatever. I pinched the space between my brows, waiting for an angry glare or a glimmer of hurt in her blue gaze, but neither came. Instead, Audrey simply laughed easily and turned to flash me with a heart-stopping smile. The kind of smile that makes you wish you had a camera, to take a picture and remember that moment, to look back on when everything eventually turns to shit. Just so you can remind yourself that there was once a time when a gorgeous woman looked at you like *that*. Like it was possible for you to be the center of someone's entire world, even if only for a second.

And it was the best second of my life.

"Blake doesn't talk about much, does he?" she teased, and I rolled my eyes playfully. I was flirting in front of my mother and I didn't even give a shit.

"That's for sure," Mom grumbled, sliding her hand from Audrey's. "He's a tough one, to put it lightly. But if you're here, you must've done something right."

I went back to work setting up dinner, busying myself as they continued to talk. Audrey giggled girlishly and shook her head. "Well, I don't know if it was *right*. I just didn't give him a choice."

***

Mom tapped her fingers against Jake's wrist to grab his attention. He stared at her blankly for a moment before lowering his headphones. "Jakey, music off. We're eating dinner," she scolded gently, taking the headphones from off his neck.

"I like this song. It's not over. It's the One Foot Song and it's not over," he argued, reaching for her hands.

"You can listen after dinner."

She bundled his iPod and headphones together and passed them across the table toward me. I eyed her hands contemptuously and asked, "What do you want me to do with that?"

"Take these into the living room, please," she demanded, urging me to get a move on with a nudge of her chin.

Audrey was sitting beside me and Freddy was sitting beside Jake. They were our guests, and the last thing I wanted them to witness was an argument between my mother and me. But dammit, it was Jake's birthday and if he wanted to listen to his music while eating his birthday dinner, then what the hell did it matter? So, I took the headphones and iPod from her waiting hand and passed them back across the table.

"Here you go, buddy," I said, and Jake accepted gratefully.

Mom gawked at me before her brows lowered angrily. "Should I remind you who the parent is here?"

Pulling in a breath that I hoped would fill me with calm, I replied, "It's his birthday, Mom. If he wants to eat his tacos and listen to music, why can't he?"

"Because it's rude," she disputed.

Any semblance of calm I had gotten from that breath retreated as the anger rolled in. "It's also rude to argue with me in my house, but hey, that never stopped you before," I fired back, raising my voice.

"Here we go," Dad muttered, dropping the last bit of taco shell to his plate. "Don't fight with your mother tonight, Blake. Come on."

"I'm not fighting," I insisted as I reached for my water glass. "I'm just reminding her that when we're in my house, we follow my rules. And if Jake decides to listen to his music on his birthday, then I say he can."

"And that's *exactly* why you're not in control over this situation," Mom spat, taking back the iPod and headphones. "Jake doesn't make decisions. He *can't*," and with that, she shoved away from the table in a huff, stomping her way into the living room. When she returned, his things were missing from her hand, and she said, "You'll get your music after dinner, Jakey. Now, finish eating."

A fire broke out at my feet. The anger-induced flames licked at my heels, legs, and arms. They swept over me, until I was engulfed in a red-orange heat. So hot, so unbearable, and I could hear the bomb in my stomach ticking away, counting down the seconds until I imploded. My fists clenched on the table, pumping and releasing, as I aimed my stony glare at the half-eaten food on my plate. I knew I should let it go. I knew there was nothing to gain from fighting with her. I knew I should just resume my dinner and carry on with the night, but there was nothing left of my appetite and all I felt was mad.

When it finally became too much, I lifted my head, undoubtedly with a face as red as the hot sauce puddled on my plate. I opened my mouth to breathe fire on my mother, and give her a piece of my mind, when I felt a cool, soft hand lay against my wrist. My gaze dropped to those fingers, as smooth as bone and as delicate as a butterfly's wing. She must've sensed my rage, had felt it bubbling over, and now, with just this one touch, I was nudged toward tranquility.

"You know what? I think it's too quiet in here," Audrey spoke up, gently gripping my wrist for just a second before pushing away from the table. "I actually have the Bluetooth speaker I use for class in my bag, so I think I'll turn on some nice dinner music. Blake, do you mind?"

She stood beside me and looked down into my eyes with expectancy while I struggled to pull together the words to reply. "U-uh, no. I don't mind," I barely uttered, my voice gruff and rasped. "That'd be nice."

"Great. I hope that's okay with everybody else," she said sweetly, but before anyone could reply, she ran into the living room.

In her absence, I surveyed the silent table. My father watched my mom with apprehension, his hands clasped against his mouth. Mom seethed from her seat across from me, keeping her eyes on the table and never daring to look my way. Jake continued to eat as if nothing had happened, but Freddy's jubilance had dwindled during the argument and the slow bites he took, the downcast of his eyes, filled me with a guilt I'd never known before. My mother had started it, and I stood by what I'd said, but my behavior had been uncalled for. Now I felt like a raving lunatic, a monster, and with my eyes on this little kid, I was overrun by the desire to do better. To *be* better.

What do you think about that, Travetti?

286

"Hey, Freddy," I said, speaking with a calm softness in my tone, and he cautiously met my gaze. "Your dad told me you really like dogs." His head bobbed gently, shyly. "Did Jake tell you he has a dog?"

Freddy whipped his head to stare incredulously up at my brother. "You do?"

"Mickey's my dog," Jake replied, nodding. "He's a Golden Retriever and a real good boy."

"Where is he?" Freddy demanded to know, jumping up and down in his seat. "I wanna see!"

Walk the Moon's catchy and infectious "One Foot" drifted along the air at a respectable volume and Audrey emerged from the living room. "Goodness, I just love this band," she said, easing back into her seat and meeting my eye. I held onto her gaze, hoping she could hear the 'thank you' resounding through my mind, and when she smiled, I assumed she had.

"Mickey doesn't live here," Jake told Freddy, moving his head to the music, completely offbeat and just as endearing. "He lives at my house."

"I want Mickey to be *here*," Freddy pouted, slumping back into his seat and grabbing his last taco.

"Well," I said, taking a bite of mine, "maybe you and your mom could take a ride with me this weekend. We can go see Jake, and you can meet Mickey."

Mom grabbed a hold of my gaze with a *how dare you* stare. As though I had some nerve inviting them along. And maybe I shouldn't have. Perhaps I should've asked. But wasn't she the one who'd told me to meet someone? Wasn't this why she was taking Jake away from me in the first place, because he was, in her words, preventing me from having a life?

But instead of protesting, she turned to Audrey with a smile. "We'd love to have you, if you aren't doing anything."

Audrey offered her a catching grin and nodded. "That sounds nice, thank you so much." She gestured toward her son. "Freddy really does love dogs, but both his dad and I live places where we can't have any. I'd love to get him one, though. Maybe someday."

I lifted my brows questioningly as I turned to her. "Your parents don't let you have pets where you're at?"

She shook her head. "They don't want the place to smell like animals, in the event I ever move out and they have to get someone else in there. And Jason lives in a pet-free apartment complex."

I nodded contemplatively and glanced at Jake. There had never been anything stopping me from keeping pets at my house. It was mine; I could do whatever the fuck I wanted. Still, I had always used the excuse that I was too busy with work to take care of a dog. But now, I was aware that I kept similar hours to my parents and they managed to take care of one just fine. And now, I couldn't stop thinking how Jake's dog made him happy, more than just about anything else. If I could convince my parents to let Jake stay with me, that would mean the dog would be with me, too. I'd have to make that work, because what kind of selfish prick would keep him away from his pet?

With a decision made to have a conversation with my dad, I settled back into eating as Jake belted out the chorus, wrong lyrics and all. Audrey clapped her hands happily and said to him, "Music makes everything better, doesn't it?"

I took a bite of my taco and nodded as I bumped my arm against hers. "It really does," I agreed.

And apparently, so did she.

***

The candles were blown out and the cake was eaten. My parents and I laid out a stack of presents in front of my brother and we all gathered around to watch him unwrap Lego sets, clothes, a stack of coloring books, and an arsenal of DVDs he'd never get around to watching because he was always too busy replaying *Gremlins*. Audrey shocked the hell out of me when she reached into her oversized tote bag and revealed a wrapped gift.

"Happy birthday, Jake," she said, placing it in front of him.

"Audrey got me a present!" He clapped with exuberance before tearing the paper off to reveal a set of *Daniel Tiger* puzzles. He held up the box, showing it off and ogling the colorful illustrations. "Wow," he drawled, stunned and impressed.

"Do you like it?" she asked, struggling to quell the amusement that crinkled at her eyes.

"You betcha!"

Freddy leaned over to point at the packaging. "I have these, too."

"You can help me if they get real hard," Jake offered, nodding and staring, still transfixed on Daniel and all his friends.

"They're easy," Freddy insisted. "I'll show you. Can I—"

"Uh, hey, pal," Audrey cut in regrettably. "It's getting pretty late and you need a bath. I think maybe you should play with puzzles another day."

I nodded. "Yeah, Jake. You have to wake up early tomorrow, too."

And at that, my parents stood and announced it was time for them and Jake to head home. I helped them carry Jake's gifts to the car while Jake continued to marvel over the box of puzzles. Then, we all stood in the living room as it was time to say our goodbyes.

"It was lovely meeting you, Audrey," my father said, smiling genuinely and bending to give her a warm hug. "You have a great kid."

Seemingly taken aback, but by what, I didn't know, Audrey faltered in her smile and returned the hug. "Thank you so much. And it was very nice meeting you." Then, as she stood back, she added, "And you have a couple of pretty great kids, too."

Dad seemed startled, looking from Audrey to flit his gaze between Jake and me. Something shifted in his gaze as he barely bobbed his head. "Yeah. I guess I do," he replied quietly, still nodding and looking at us both.

Mom's departure was a little chillier but just as genuine, with a gentle grasp of Audrey's hand and a tight smile. "We'll see you this weekend," she said, before lifting her other hand in a slight wave as she added, "See you soon, Freddy."

Jake and I hugged tightly and I told him that I'd see him in the morning. Then, it was just Audrey, Freddy, and me, in a house that, to me, instantly felt more relaxed and airier. But when I turned to face Audrey, to say all the things I'd been holding in since dinner, I found an annoyance I couldn't previously have envisioned her displaying. But seeing it now, it left me disconcerted and eager to fix whatever the hell it was that was bothering her, just to make her smile again. Her face was made to smile.

"What's wrong?" I asked, searching her eyes for clues.

My expectations were set on her not replying or skirting around the issue, the way so many women do. Cee had once spent an entire work day in a pissed off silence, and it was only the next day that she'd told me it was because I had unwittingly used the last roll of paper towels. So, I wouldn't have been surprised if Audrey had taken this opportunity to shut down and make her exit, but she wasn't like other women, was she?

"I thought you were kidding when you said you don't celebrate your birthday." Her voice was strangled by her disappointment and despair, and to make her feel better, I shook my head and replied, "I told you, I don't like to acknowledge it."

That wasn't good enough for her, though. "But your parents should want to," she said, practically whispering against the emotion building a barricade in her throat. "I don't care if *you* don't want to; they should insist on it."

She stood up with an impressive control, taking the cake plate from the table and carrying it to the counter. Then, with her back to me, she continued to say, "I can't believe they didn't even *wish* you a happy birthday."

I glanced at Freddy, who was sitting at the kitchen table with a book from Jake's room, and took the chance to approach Audrey at the counter. It was just over a week since I had stood at this counter and contemplated my next move, before rushing at her with an aggressive kiss. Now, the very thought of kissing her made me crazy with nerves and anxiety, but it still wasn't too far from my mind as I stood next to her, hands on the counter and eyes on the cabinet in front of me.

"They texted me this morning. It's fine."

"Texting you isn't the same as giving their *son* a hug and wishing him a happy birthday."

My fingers moved busily against the countertop. "I don't know why this is bugging you so much. It doesn't matter to me, seriously. I don't care."

With the turn of her head, her golden hair left her shoulder, cascading over her back and exposing the length of pristine skin along her neck. A swarm of attacking bees filled my gut at the thought of leaning in to press my lips there. They stabbed, warned, and reminded me that we were sober, and that she might not want me in that way, not right now.

"It is so sad that you don't care," she whispered, and I replied in a matched tone, "I said it doesn't matter."

"But it *does*," she replied in a voice so harsh it surprised me. "Do you know how much my parents would love to wish my sister a happy birthday, to her face, just one more time? Do you understand what they would *give* to have that chance?"

I shook my head. "No. I can't pretend to know or understand what that's like for them."

Her nod was slow as an unknown understanding sunk beneath her skin. "And I'm telling you that it's horrible for your parents to have allowed you to feel like this."

I scoffed, feeling attacked and criticized. "Feel like what?" I spat defensively.

Audrey lifted the cake back into its bakery box and closed it before facing me with one word: "Unworthy."

Leaving me stupefied at the counter, she put the cake in the refrigerator and left the room, as I slipped into a contemplative void.

Unworthy? It honestly wasn't far from the truth. I certainly didn't feel worthy of celebration or praise, everybody knew that and Dr. Travetti reminded me of it on a regular basis. In fact, as I spiraled through shards of memory, the good doctor's scrawled message zigzagged across my mind, *"Why won't he give himself a chance?"* None of it was a lie, but I'd never once wondered from where this poisonous mindset had come from. Never once had I thought to become a cliché and blame my parents for drilling it into my brain that I was a monster. Not until Audrey said something, and now I wondered, did she see something I'd been blind to for years?

Her footsteps sounded behind me, I'd know them anywhere by now, and she came to stand beside me once again. In her hands was a present, and at the sight of the colorful paper and spiraled ribbon, a wave of nausea and anticipation struck my gut.

"You might not care, but I do."

"You have no obligation to care," I stated, so emotionless, it irked me. "You barely even know me, Audrey. There is no reason whatsoever for you to waste any of your time caring about m—"

"Please shut up," she said, and so I did. "I don't know my mailman at all, Blake, and I wish him a merry Christmas and a happy birthday, because every life, every day, should be celebrated. It's all precious and sacred."

With a sordid scoff, I shook my head, despite hearing her and wanting so much to wrap myself in her words and believe in them. To believe in something. To believe I wasn't a monster, but just a guy who caused a horrific accident over twenty years ago. "Yeah, I bet everybody thought Jeffrey Dahmer was precious and something to celebrate, too."

"Jeffrey Dahmer was still someone's son, and I wouldn't be surprised to learn that she celebrated him every day," she retorted with more warmth than such a sentence deserved. "You don't have to condone the actions of your children to maintain that unconditional love."

"Is that what the Bible taught you?"

She was silent and when my eyes met hers, I found a glare that knocked me down to the level of a snake, slithering on its dirt-covered belly. She shook her head and opened her mouth, that gorgeous, terrifying mouth, to speak. "You can try and push me away with that

294

garbage all you want, Blake. You can even try to make me hate you as much as you hate yourself. But I am telling you right now, it's not going to work."

"You'll give up eventually," I challenged her.

"You'd have to do something really horrible to me, to make me give up on you. And the garbage you say when you're angry isn't gonna cut it."

"Why the hell not?" I asked, unsure there had ever been someone alive more frustratingly gorgeous than her in that moment.

"Because you're wrong, Blake. I do know you. And I know that you aren't the crap you say."

My defenses eased as I relented with a sag of my shoulders. "Yeah? And how the hell do you know that?"

"Because while you think you stole everything from your brother, *he* gave you a heart. And I can see how good and beautiful it is. It's in your art, and in your devotion to him. And those are the most honest things about you."

My lips curled between my teeth, battling the urgency to grab one of the liquor bottles on the shelf within reach. "Even Jeffrey Dahmer had a heart," I pushed out through a startling clot of emotion.

"Yeah," she replied with a somber nod, "but it wasn't Jake's, and there isn't anything impure about that." And that was a point I couldn't argue.

Chapter Twenty-Four

"YOU DON'T HAVE TO open it now," she had said before leaving, "and it's not a big deal. Just a little thing." The present had been left on the counter as she stood on her toes to kiss my cheek. "Happy birthday, Blake."

I could still hear her voice now, hours later. I could still feel the soft touch of her lips against my skin. I stared at the present, still lying on the counter where she'd left it. The last time she had left something at my house, it had felt like a curse, but this gift felt like a shred of hope I wasn't yet sure I deserved. I wanted to feel worthy, though. I wanted to race toward it with open arms, but dammit, I was too old. There'd been too many years of having something beaten into my head, and a couple years of therapy and one good woman wasn't enough to wipe the slate clean. Not so soon.

Now alone, I had the freedom to mull it over. I paced the kitchen and eyed the gift with lingering glances. "You're being fucking stupid," I muttered aloud, shaking my head with disgust and embarrassment over my own hesitation. "Just open the fucking thing," and with that last bit of encouragement, I rushed toward it and tore the paper off before I had the chance to talk myself out of it.

In my hand, I held a notebook. Not a cheap spiral-bound thing or a composition book, like I'd had in school. This was nice, with sturdy binding and thick paper. The kind you might buy at a bookstore. A lifelike skull was emblazoned on the front cover, white on black, and beneath the skull was a quote, scrawled in metallic silver:

To elevate the soul, poetry is necessary. – Edgar Allan Poe

With the book in my hands, I had forgotten my breath, that I needed it to survive, and when I finally had no choice but to breathe, I shuddered distressingly with emotion. I don't know what I'd expected to find inside all that paper, but it wasn't this. This was thoughtful and chosen specifically for me, with my tastes in mind, and fuck if it didn't feel like the most precious thing I'd ever held.

When my bearings had been collected and my heart had settled to a reasonable rate, I flipped the cover open and there, in a bubbly, girly scrawl, was a poem:

What's written here,
Is meant to keep.
When you've crawled,
Into your shadows deep,
When the time you have,
Seems like too much,
When you shudder at,
A lover's touch.

Don't be scared,
To let pain drown,
Just always remember,
To write it down.
And one day,
When that pain is done,
Open this book,
To see how far you've come.
—a.w.

I swallowed at the unrelenting emotional clot in my throat, blinking my eyes and chewing at the inside of my lip, as I stared at the thick, black ink. All of the dots above her I's, all of the T's she crossed. And I knew, without so much as a splinter of doubt, that this was undoubtedly the most precious gift I'd ever received.

***

Me: You shouldn't have gotten me anything.

Audrey: Did you open it?

Me: I did.

Audrey: Do you hate it? I really hope you don't hate it.

Me: Have you been worrying about this all night?

Audrey: Ugh. That question is loaded, and I don't like it.

Me: How do you figure?

Audrey: If I say yes, I sound like one of those clingy, annoying girls. But if I say no, I sound like I don't care, and I definitely do.

Me: I'd say clingy but not too annoying.

Audrey: Oh, gee. That makes me feel SO much better, thanks.

Audrey: So … do you hate it?

Me: No.

Audrey: Are you just saying that?

Me: No.

Audrey: You can tell me if you don't like it, you know.

Me: You're heading dangerously close to annoying territory now.

Audrey: Sorry. Can't help it. I try not to be one of those girls, but I'm still a girl, you know?

Me: I get it.

Me: Anyway, I just wanted to text you to say thanks.

Audrey: You're welcome.

Me: Not just for the present, but for everything today. You helped to make Jake's birthday a really good one and I just wanted to tell you I'm really grateful.

Me: Especially that shit at dinner. I'm particularly grateful for that.

Me: It's not easy for me to say this shit in person. Easier to write it out, I guess. So, yeah. There you go.

Me: Audrey?

Audrey: Yeah, sorry. I'm here.

Audrey: You're welcome, Blake. And you can text me whenever you want.

Me: Cool. Anyway, I'm going to bed. Night.

Audrey: Goodnight.

Audrey: And by the way, next year, Freddy and I are totally singing happy birthday to you. Just so you know.

Chapter Twenty-Five

A S LUCK WOULD have it, Audrey was a horrible singer. Absolutely horrendous. Yet, she didn't seem to give a rat's ass about the fact she sounded like a dying cat in heat, as she ironically sang along to Madonna's "Like A Virgin" from the passenger seat of my car. And that's what I enjoyed the most, how she didn't care. That even when she couldn't hit the high notes, she still exuded confidence.

"I love that song," she gushed with a sigh.

"I don't," I snorted.

"Okay," she drawled. "Then, why don't you put on something you wanna listen to?"

"You don't wanna listen to what I wanna listen to, so don't worry about it."

"You shouldn't assume something like that. You have no idea what kind of music I like."

For a second, I stole my eyes from the road to glare at her. "You won't like my music."

"Try me!"

Freddy groaned irritably from the backseat and Audrey turned to look at him. "Oh, does the peanut gallery have something to say?"

"Yeah," he muttered, "pipe down."

"Yo," I said, glancing at him in the rearview mirror, "nobody tells me to pipe down in my car, got it?"

"Mommy, I want headphones, too."

Audrey laughed, taking a quick glance at Jake, bopping his head to music none of us could hear. "You have them at home, honey. Remember? Daddy got you some for your birthday."

"I want them *now*."

"Well, you don't have them right—"

I reached across her lap to the glove compartment, opening it up to reveal a spare set of headphones. "He can use those. Let him use my phone. I have all of Jake's music uploaded on there, too," I offered, and she gawked at me. I narrowed my glare on the road. "What?"

"You're like, prepared for anything."

"Yeah, have you met Jake? I kinda have to be."

She nodded, plugging the headphones into my phone and setting it up for Freddy. "I'm just remembering when you told me your parents wanted to, um, put him somewhere, and I'm failing to understand why they don't think you're the best option for him. Why wouldn't they just let him live with you?"

I grunted a reply as she handed Freddy the phone and headphones, then she asked, "You disagree?"

"Yes ... no," I shook my head and gripped the wheel tighter, "I don't know. I don't know what I think anymore."

She nodded. "Yeah, I understand."

"I'm just trying to do the best thing for him while I still can. What else can I do, you know?" And right now, the best thing for him was to see my parents and me getting along. To see me happy and doing what was best for me, while keeping him at the top of my priority list. That's what I'd been doing all week, by booking more appointments at the shop, letting him sleep over more often, and talking to Audrey on a nearly constant basis. I had even browsed a few realtor websites, pricing a few vacant storefronts in downtown Salem. It wasn't in the cards just yet, but I knew the possibility would become a reality once my issue of *ModInk* was delivered to the stands. That was only a month away and it took everything in my power not to gnaw my fingernails down to the cuticle.

With all of the changes in my life, I was seeing more of a change in Jake, too. He was calmer and a little more settled. He hadn't had a tantrum in days, a new record for him, and I was beginning to wonder if maybe Audrey really had been right all along. Perhaps my mood really did impact him to such a drastic degree.

Hell, maybe it was a twin thing, who the fuck knows.

I pulled into my parents' driveway and parked the car. Audrey looked out the windshield at the house I grew up in, a smile stretched across her face.

"It's nice," she commented. "Is your room still here?"

I shook my head. "Nah, they turned it into a den after I moved out."

She hummed thoughtfully, pursing her lips. "I bet it was really dark and gloomy."

"I painted my walls black when I was fifteen."

A burst of giggles heaved at her chest as she laid a hand over her heart. "That doesn't surprise me even a little bit."

One side of my mouth lifted in a lopsided smile. "My mom was so pissed, she took my laptop away for a month. So, I dyed my hair black and put that tattoo on my leg instead."

The laughter in her eyes dimmed. "You've always butted heads with her, huh?"

I shifted my gaze to the steering wheel, sliding my hand over the plastic. "Yeah, but mostly since the accident. I mean, we do have our good moments, but they're kinda rare."

Audrey sighed, gazing out toward the house again. "I don't know what that's like. My parents were always great about letting Sabrina and me express ourselves, without letting us go too crazy, you know? Neither of us were up all night at house parties on the weekends, but they had no problem with Sabrina dying her hair blue." A faraway smile tugged at her lips as she added, "Mine was pink. My mom took us both out to the salon for our seventeenth birthday."

"You're lucky," I said, my voice graveled and hoarse.

She offered me a small, sad smile and said, "I know."

***

Early November brought with it a chill that said winter was well on its way. Standing on the back deck of my parents' house with Dad, I held my arms around my middle, keeping my leather jacket closed, as Jake and Freddy tumbled around the yard with Mickey. Mom and Audrey kept themselves busy in the kitchen, getting dinner on the table, and I hoped Mom wasn't giving Audrey a hard time with snippy tones and obtrusive questions.

"You like this girl, huh?" Dad commented, puffing away on the habit he just couldn't quit. With a tip of his head, he sent the cigarette smoke spiraling through the air. The smell reminded me of Cee and my limited experience in her bedroom. I didn't miss it.

"Yeah," I answered, seeing no point in denying it now. The last time I'd invited a girl to my parents' house, I was in my early twenties and I had sworn that I'd never do it again. Apparently, I had lied.

"What about the kid?" It wasn't the question itself that bothered me but what it implied. He wasn't asking whether I liked Freddy but if I liked that Audrey *had* Freddy, and I knew what he expected me to say. But that wasn't me. Not with her.

"He's awesome," I replied, grinning as Freddy tackled Jake and the two landed on the grass with an audible and probably painful thud. I cupped my hands around my mouth and shouted, "Get him, Freddy! Tickle his armpits! He loves that!"

"No way, José!" Jake laughed and scrambled to his feet, running away with child and dog in tow.

"You better not hurt them, Blake," Dad warned under his breath. "You have to be careful when kids are involved."

"I know, Dad." I sighed, knowing that he was only looking out for the woman and her little boy, but I wished that he could maybe look out for me, too. Maybe even consider how much it could hurt, break, or kill me to lose her, even after such a short period of time, and how much it would certainly obliterate my entire existence to be without my brother.

"What's her story, anyway?" He stamped the cigarette into his trusty old ashtray, chuckling as his eyes clouded with nostalgia. "Remember when Jake gave me this thing? He had to have been, God, four? Maybe five? Those were the good ol' days ..."

I eyed the cheap, plastic piece of garbage. "Jake didn't give you that, Dad; I did."

He narrowed his eyes, settling deep in thought, and said, "Huh, I guess you did." Then, he slapped the back of his hand against my arm. "So, anyway, as we were saying. Audrey. What's her story? How'd you meet her?"

I shrugged, shaking away the sting of being forgotten, and said, "She came into the shop about a month ago to get some ink, and the rest is history, I guess."

He jabbed a thumb over his shoulder and lowered his voice to say, "*That* girl has a tattoo?"

My chest rumbled with a chuckle. "Yeah. Believe it or not, she does."

"Has she been married?"

I hesitated. If my mother found out Audrey had a child out of wedlock, she'd judge her, and I didn't want to be the reason for that information being outed. But still, I trusted my dad wouldn't pass it along, and said, "No."

He nodded slowly, processing the information. "She was with Freddy's dad, though?"

"Yeah, they were together for years," I told him. "It was a mutual split, but they're still really good friends. And actually," I went on, choosing to divulge a little more information, "I met him the other day, on Halloween. His wife is Jake's teacher. How crazy is that?"

"Get out of town," Dad gawked, surprised. "That's unbelievable. What a small world, huh?"

"Tell me about it," I muttered, shaking my head.

We stood in silence, watching the boy, man, and dog all run around the yard with an envious amount of energy. I couldn't begin to figure out how it was Jake and I could be the same age, when just the sight of him rolling in the yard and chasing a little boy around was enough to exhaust me. Then again, when was the last time I'd even tried?

So, with my arms still crossed over my chest, I headed toward the stairs and onto the grass. Jake stopped running at the sight of me, a startled expression marring his features. I met his gaze and unlocked my arms, widening my stance, and warned, "Better run, buddy, 'cause I'm coming for ya." But instead of taking off, Jake grinned with excitement and ran straight toward me, slamming his large body against mine. We fell to the ground and wrestled for a moment before Freddy piled on top.

"Blake's ticklish, too!" Jake informed him, digging his fingers into my sides, and as Freddy joined in with devious intent, I don't think I had ever laughed harder in my life.

***

"You boys are *filthy*," Mom pointed out with a sour look on her face.

She wasn't lying. In just ten minutes, I had dirt beneath my fingernails and smeared all across my face, and Jake and Freddy looked even worse. But while Mom never liked us to get dirty, even as kids, Audrey laughed gently and took a shoulder from both Jake and Freddy. "Come on, guys, let's get cleaned up before dinner. Blake, you coming?"

"Yeah," I answered, meeting my mother's eye for just a moment before heading in the direction of the bathroom.

Mom and I hadn't spoken since Halloween, and other than a brief hello when we'd seen each other during the week, our interactions had been minimal. I couldn't gauge whether she was still annoyed or not, but knowing her, she was and would be for some time.

I crowded into the bathroom with Audrey, Jake, and Freddy. Jake sat on the toilet seat while Audrey picked

Freddy up to sit him on the sink's vanity, and I took a place against the doorframe. "What did you guys do out there?" she asked the room, but mostly herself, as she turned on the faucet and grabbed the soap.

"Blake ran," Jake told her. "Blake never runs."

"I rubbed dirt on his face," Freddy informed her, wearing a prideful grin.

She glanced over her shoulder and smiled at me. "I see that."

Audrey scrubbed the dirt from Freddy's hands and face, then kissed his forehead, before placing him on his feet and sending him out of the room. When she moved to work on Jake, I stopped her.

"Hey, you don't have to do that. I got him."

"Oh, stop. I don't mind," she insisted, grasping Jake's chin in one hand and the washcloth in the other.

The act was innocent and mundane, nothing unlike what I or his teachers did for him every day, but this seemed like more. It seemed serious, like real commitment, and I knew I was too close to the edge and in danger of toppling over into a void I wasn't prepared to handle.

As a distraction, I glanced in the mirror and snorted at my reflection. Streaks of dirt lined one cheek like war paint, and on the other, I could make out the distinct imprint of small fingers. "Freddy got me good," I laughed, shaking my head.

"Yeah, he really did," she agreed, scrubbing at Jake's cheeks.

Then, the room was quiet, dangerously so, as she finished cleaning his face. When she was done, I reminded him to wash his hands, and Audrey and I stood back and supervised as he lathered and rinsed.

"Go help Mom set the table," I told him.

His head lifted with a purposeful nod. "Okie dokie," and he was gone, leaving us alone and open to way too much opportunity.

I turned on the water and set to washing my face and hands, while feeling her eyes on my back. All I could think was that she and I hadn't been alone in a week. A week since I was drunk and had kissed her. A week since I had slept with her and then found out she was a mother. A week wasn't a long time, but with her, right now, it felt like it'd been an eternity. All that time, forcing a distance between us, and my hands, wet and working together, begged to touch her again.

"I'm glad you invited us today," she said in a low, quiet voice as she stepped forward to stand beside me. "Freddy's having a really good time. He hasn't stopped talking about Jake all week."

I scrubbed at my fingernails and laughed. "Jake likes him, too. The other day, he told Miss Thomas all about his new little buddy," I turned to her smiling eyes and added, "his words. I guess Jason had told her about—"

"I told her," Audrey confessed hurriedly. "I had called to tell Jason I wouldn't be dropping Freddy off until Sunday and Amy—Miss Thomas—answered the phone. It just kinda came out."

"Yeah, it's fine," I said, shrugging it off.

"I didn't know if you wanted her to know, but I just couldn't keep it in. I know you're kinda private, but—"

"Audrey. Really, it's fine. And anyway, Jake loves it. He doesn't really get the whole stepmom thing, but he thinks it's awesome that he gets to see Freddy's other mom all the time."

She hummed a gentle laugh as her head nodded. In the conversational lull, I focused on washing the dirt from my face, then grabbed a towel from the rack to dry off. Audrey caught sight of me and giggled gently, shaking her head.

"You missed a spot," she said.

"What?" I glanced in the mirror and searched my face until I spotted the smear of black just above my beard. "Fucking hell," I grumbled and turned the water back on.

"Here, let me do it," she insisted, taking the washcloth she'd used on Freddy and Jake, dipping it back underneath the tap before shutting the water off.

I thought to protest and remind her that I wasn't a child or incapable, but the words wouldn't come as her palm cupped my shoulder, leveraging herself as she stood on her toes. The cool, wet cloth touched my cheek with tenderness, and she gently worked the spot off my face. When her eyes lifted, she found my gaze, hooded and affixed to hers. This was a moment, it was ours, and without a word, I took the cloth from her stilled hand and dropped it in the sink. Her fingers spread over my cheek and against my beard, before pushing toward my hair as I framed her face with my hands and pulled her to my anxious lips.

Kissing Audrey had previously been an act of drunken urgency. An insatiable hunger that'd swept us away in a wave of need. I had spent days wondering if I'd ever find the courage to wrap my arms around her while sober, and if I'd ever be brave enough to let her taste the honesty on my tongue without gin to taint the flavor. But I kissed her now with a slow, passionate patience, memorizing every movement of her lips and every pulse of her fingertips against my shoulders and hair. I held her face, holding her to my mouth in a lock I hoped to never break, and her arms looped around my neck to hold me back.

Her mouth opened, welcoming the intrusion of my tongue with a whimpered moan. It was an invitation that I gladly took, while my chest rattled around my frenzied, screaming heart. Telling me this was too good, too real, too sober, and that I needed to back off, back away, far away, before I threw myself into the deep end without learning how to swim. But I couldn't stop myself from pulling her closer, plunging deeper and holding on tighter. I just couldn't let go, and maybe that could be okay, if she was there, to keep me from drowning in her abyss.

"What is taking so long?" I heard the annoyed voice of my mother from the dining room, and I groaned at the premature interruption.

Audrey pulled back and turned her head away from my mouth, but I held on tighter, encouraging her to forget my mother and the world, by moving my lips to her neck. Tasting her skin and inhaling her scent.

"Blake," she giggled breathlessly, pushing against my shoulders, "we need to stop."

I shook my head. "No."

She laughed again and the hairs along my arms stood on end. "I don't want to either, but we have to. They're waiting."

"Please don't make me stop," I muttered against her neck, unable to believe the words coming out of my mouth.

I moved my hands to the small of her back, to press her to my hips and feel the urgency of my situation. She shuddered with a desperate gasp and tipped her head further, exposing more of her neck, and I groaned against the smooth plane of her throat.

"Blake," she whispered, repeating my name. "We have all n—"

"What are you *doing*?!"

I have never backed away from a woman as quickly as I did at the sound of Freddy's horrified disgust. I turned to face the mirror, away from his view, to hide the obvious erection in my jeans as I prayed to a god I didn't believe in.

Dear fucking god, get rid of this boner, amen.

"Hey, honey," Audrey said breathlessly, trying desperately to compose herself as she straightened her rumpled top. "We'll be out there in a second."

"He was eating your *neck*!" he exclaimed, horrified.

Audrey shifted her gaze to glance at me sidelong as she struggled not to laugh, and from the corner of my eye, I winced apologetically as my hand covered my mouth. She was soundlessly asking for backup, but I had nothing to offer, as I struggled to think about anything other than her breasts and thighs and what they felt like straddling my hips.

"Um, no," she admitted, shaking her head. "Blake wasn't ... *eating* my neck, honey. He, um—"

"Then, what *were* you doing?"

"W-well, actually, um ..." She was struggling to come up with something, frantically flitting her eyes around the room to conjure an explanation without telling the truth, but I saw the defeat in her eyes and she succumbed with a sigh. "We were kissing, honey."

"*Why*?" he demanded to know. He sounded angry and I worried this was the end of our budding friendship. After all, he had caught me making out with his mom. That'd piss any kid off, I think.

"Because, um, because," she took a deep breath and settled into her response, "sometimes when grown-ups really like each other a lot, they kiss."

"Oh," he answered, and I heard the confusion in his voice. "Like Daddy and Mama."

Audrey slowly nodded her head. "Yeah," she drawled. "Like that."

Finally, I turned around to watch him shrug and say, "Okay, well ... Dinner's ready." With that, he hurried out of the bathroom and we both exhaled.

"Dodged a bullet there," she said.

Allowing myself to grin, my held-back chuckle now rumbled through my chest. "You should've told him I was a zombie."

She slapped the back of her hand against my arm. "Oh, really, Kiefer? But I thought you were a *vampire*," she teased and sashayed toward the door.

***

"No headphones at *my* table," Mom warned, pointing at the headphones in Jake's hand. Her eyes flashed toward mine for a split second as he lowered them to the table with a pout. I couldn't miss the distinctive glint of triumph in her glare before her attention was back on the plate in front of her.

Audrey smiled at my mother. "This is an amazing pot roast, Mrs. Carson."

Mom barely curled her lips upward. "Thank you very much."

"When my mom makes pot roast, it always comes out so dry and tough," Audrey went on, "but this is absolutely perfect. You'll have to give me your secret."

Mom addressed Audrey with another small smile before diverting her attention to her son. "How do you like it, Freddy?"

"It's good," he answered in a small, shy voice.

"I'm glad," she answered, smiling brighter. "I have something very special for dessert, so eat up."

"Gotta eat it all, Freddy," Jake told him. "You only get dessert if you eat it all."

"That's what my dad says," Freddy said, "but he gives me dessert anyway."

"Remind me to have a talk with Daddy," Audrey laughed, reaching out to ruffle Freddy's mop of hair.

"Are you close?" Mom asked.

I opened my mouth to tell her to mind her own business, when Audrey nodded and replied, "Freddy's dad and I are really great friends, yeah. And his wife, Freddy's Mama, is one of my best girl friends. We're all family," she wrapped an arm around Freddy's shoulders and squeezed, "right, honey?"

Freddy nodded enthusiastically. "Yep."

"I see," Mom answered. "Well, that's great for Freddy, to have you all getting along so well."

"Oh, absolutely," Audrey replied. "That's always been very important to us. But honestly, it's always come easy. Jason and I have been friends for so many years, I can't imagine us *not* getting along."

My mother smiled and dropped the subject by moving onto a discussion about Thanksgiving plans. I never liked Thanksgiving, or the thought of spending time with relatives, but I was trying hard to put myself into a different and more positive mindset. So, I responded to her plan of having our grandparents, aunts, uncles, and cousins over for dinner with a nod and a "sounds good, Mom." She then invited Audrey and Freddy to join us, and while it was more likely out of politeness and less of a genuine want to include them, I still felt my chest fill with warmth and a simple sensation of goodness.

After dinner, as Freddy and Jake played with Mickey, and Audrey helped my father in the kitchen, I stopped Mom in the hallway to ask a question.

"Hey, so I was thinking," I began, keeping my voice low, "if you guys didn't mind, I'd like to keep Jake at my place all week. Mickey, too."

She was startled, but then smiled. "I think that's a good idea."

"Okay, cool. I'll pick them up tomorrow night." I nodded, surprised the conversation had gone so well, so easily. "Anyway, I guess I'm gonna—"

"So, Audrey is still friends with her ex?"

I furrowed my brow. "What?"

A chill settled in her gaze as she shrugged. "I'm just making sure I understood correctly."

"Yeah," I nodded, unsure of where she was going with this and unsure of why it mattered. "Yeah, sure, they're friends. Why?"

"Be careful with that."

"Be careful with what?"

Mom shrugged again. "I don't know, Blake. I'm just saying, if she felt enough for him at one point to have a *child* with him, then there's always that chance she could still have feelings, right? Especially if they're such great friends."

I didn't know what to say or how to react to the blatant accusation. She had just eaten dinner with this woman and her child. She had shared in conversation and friendly banter. And now, she was passing judgment, while said woman was mere feet away, helping to clean up.

My chest puffed with the urgent need to fight and defend, as I shook my head and crossed my arms. "They're raising a kid together," I stated in a flat, firm tone.

"Oh, sure," she relented with a flippant wave of a hand. "I understand that. But I'm just mentioning, you might want to be on alert, you know? Don't get so attached right away."

***

I watched from the car as Audrey dropped Freddy off at his father's apartment. Jason, Eliza, and Miss Thomas— sorry, *Amy*—were waiting outside their second-floor walk-up and threw awkward waves in my direction as Audrey handed Freddy's backpack to Jason. As I returned the friendly gesture with a simple lift of my hand, I thought it probably would've been more polite to greet them with words and handshakes, but I wasn't feeling it. Not after that enraging conversation with my mother, the one that had left me sour and reeling all the way here.

Audrey kissed Freddy's forehead and I saw her mouth move as she said something. *Be a good boy. Remember to behave. Don't give your dad a hard time.* I imagined the things she could've said to him. Things I'd remembered my own mother saying to me once upon a time, before she could only say things about what I was doing wrong or the wrong that could be done to me.

Audrey stood and spoke to Jason, as Amy took Freddy inside. They nodded, smiled, and his hand clasped her shoulder before leaning in to kiss her cheek. A red hot, burning ball of fire instantly engulfed my stomach at the sight I could only read now as intimate, and by the time her hand touched the handle on the car door, I was seething with predatory envy.

We drove in silence against a backdrop of Metallica's "One," a fitting soundtrack for my sour mood. Any time I glanced her way, all I could imagine

318

were his lips on her cheek and his dick in her mouth. All while aware that, had my mother not mentioned it, I never would've given a shit. And the more I drove, the more angry I got, until I knew the night was dead and I should just call it quits before I fought with her over something unbeknownst to her.

"Um …" Audrey looked to me worriedly when I pulled up to her apartment. This wasn't the plan. We were supposed to be back at my place, away from her neighbors and parents.

"I'm not feeling great," I lied, unable to meet her eye.

"Oh," she replied, then turned her gaze back to the house. "Do you want to——"

I shook my head adamantly. "Nah. I should probably just get home."

I expected a nod and a startled expression of rejection and hurt, maybe a kiss on the cheek. I expected her to leave with the assumption that she might never hear from me again.

But she didn't leave.

Instead, she reached across the console, laid a hand against my thigh, and said, "Blake, you don't have to talk to me if you don't want to, and you don't have to tell me what's wrong. But don't leave. Please. Come inside with me."

I don't know how she knew it was my mind that didn't feel well. How she could see beyond my exterior and into the blackness of my brain, I might never understand. But what I did know was, a month ago, I would've ignored her plea. Back then, I would've forced myself out of her reach, despite the screaming in my head to be held and cared for. But that was then, this was now. And right now, I swallowed at the hardened lump in my throat and nodded.

My feet felt heavy as she led me to her door, weighed down by a blossom of jealousy and hot rage implanting its roots through my guts. But with her hand wrapped around mine, warm and sweet, I let the negativity begin to dissipate. Just for now, just for tonight, and by the time we reached her door, I had encouraged her purity to abort all the darkness in my mind. The words of my mother seemed far away, shut outside and in the cold, as Audrey's tight embrace pulled me toward somewhere bright and safe.

Just inside her apartment, she wrapped her arms around my waist and pressed a kiss to the center of my chest. I imagined the vibrations of my heart buzzing against her lips, proof that I was alive, so much more alive with her. I kissed the top of her head and smelled her hair, pulling in the scent and allowing it to push me further toward euphoria.

She slipped her hands from around my waist and tangled her fingers with mine. "Come on," she whispered, tugging me toward a part of her apartment I'd never ventured in before.

"You mean we're not sleeping on the couch tonight?" I teased through a rasped throat.

Audrey shook her head, the corners of her lips curling gently in the darkness. "No, not tonight."

She led me to her bedroom and flipped on the light to reveal a small room with just enough space for her four-poster bed and a dresser. It was cozy and homey. The mattress was covered with a handstitched quilt and a mountain of pillows calling my name, while each of the four posts were draped with scarves, hats, bras, and sweaters. The walls and mirror were littered with pictures and mementos, and the top of the dresser harbored perfume bottles, makeup, and a jewelry chest that couldn't be closed it was so full. I chuckled adoringly at the room, and Audrey leaned against one of the bed posts, cocking her hip and scowling.

"What's so funny?"

I shook my head. "Nothing," I replied honestly, turning in a circle to take in her comfortable little nook. "I just really like your room."

"Oh, you don't mind that it's not a bat cave with black walls and skulls all over the place?"

"No," I answered. "It feels like you. Black walls would definitely *not* feel like you."

"And," I went on, kicking off my boots and flopping onto the bed from where I stood by the door, "I really like that I can jump onto your bed from the door. Very convenient."

Audrey laughed, pulling off her sneakers and crawling over the quilt to lay beside me. "I gave Freddy the bigger bedroom. He needs more room than I do, with all his Legos and toys, and all I really need is a bed and a dresser."

I pointed at the post covered in bras. "No closet?"

She shook her head. "No closet in here. Freddy has one, but it's fine, I have this bed. It's multi-purpose," she giggled.

I watched her let down her curled, blonde ponytail. Her fingers raked through the golden lengths as she sat up, reaching over to the dresser and pulling a drawer open, to retrieve an oversized t-shirt. She pulled off her cardigan, revealing a silky camisole and smooth skin, and as she draped the sweater on a post, my brow furrowed and my smile faded.

Tugging the t-shirt over her head, she noticed my thoughtful scowl and asked, "What's wrong?"

"I've never met anyone like you before," I replied honestly, and she laughed softly, laying back to undo her jeans.

"Well, that's a line," she muttered sardonically.

"No, it's really not." I reached out to brush my fingertips over her smooth, pristine cheek. "I've never known anybody so selfless, not even Jake. You do so much with someone else in mind, and that blows me away a little."

She swallowed against the impact of my words. "I thought you weren't good at talking about this stuff face-to-face," she whispered.

"I'm trying to get better at it."

"You're pretty selfless, too, you know," she said, poking at my stomach.

"And that's another thing I'm trying to get better at."

Chapter Twenty-Six

"SO, THINGS ARE going well with Audrey," Dr. Travetti commented. It was impossible to miss the smile stretched across her lips. She was genuinely happy for me, that I had somehow managed to find something so good in my life, and her joy felt nice.

"Yeah." I nodded, offering her a smile of my own. "At least, I think so, anyway."

"Blake," she tipped her chin toward her chest and eyed me compassionately, "you know, it's okay to admit that something is going well in your life. You don't need to doubt or downplay everything every single step of the way."

"I'm not doubting or downplaying," I insisted, turning my gaze toward the window. "I'm just trying to stay realistic. Things are good, and I like her a lot, but good shit ends. Life gets in the way, *people* get in the way."

"What makes you think that something's going to get in the way of this?"

Scoffing, I shook my head toward the window. "Doc, I've only been seeing her for a few weeks. Come on. There's plenty of opportunity for it all to go to hell. I mean, she's still friends with her ex. Who knows what's going to happen there."

I couldn't believe I said it. *Why* had I said it? My stupid fucking mouth had a mind of its own, and I shook my head at my own stupidity as Dr. Travetti uttered a small thoughtful noise. Then came the scratching of her pen against paper.

"I thought you didn't have a problem with her ex-boyfriend," she mentioned casually, still scribbling.

"I don't," I hurried, turning back to her. "I'm just saying—"

"But why are you just saying? Did something happen?"

I shook my head. "No."

"Then," she lifted her hands in an exaggerated shrug, "where did that come from?"

My lungs deflated with a frustrated sigh. "Nowhere," I huffed. "My mom just mentioned on Saturday that I might wanna watch out for it, that's all. No big deal. Just … keeping it in mind."

"Your mom said that?" She watched me studiously, curling a finger over her upper lip. "What exactly did she say?"

"Just, you know," I shrugged and smacked my hands against my thighs, "that Audrey's friendly with her ex, and that I should be careful."

"Does your mother not like Audrey? Does she have reason to believe she isn't trustworthy?"

"No, she likes her, I think."

"Then, why would she say something like that? I mean, especially when things between you and Audrey are going so well, or at least *I* think so."

I pushed a hand through my hair and leaned into the plush chair. "I don't know, Doc. Maybe 'cause she's my mom and wants to look out for me?"

Dr. Travetti's lips twisted as her eyes flashed with skepticism. It was only for a second, that dull glimmer of doubt, and I bet she thought I hadn't caught it. But I did and I questioned it with a deep furrow of my brow.

"What—" I began only to be cut off as she spoke, "Can I ask you a question?"

"Sure."

She flipped to a new page on her clipboard. "What was your childhood like?"

The snort that came from my nose surprised both of us. "Wow, Doc. Two years into this shit and you're finally falling back on the standard crap. Maybe I've overstayed my welcome."

Canting her head and nodding, she replied, "Or maybe it's that two years into this shit has finally brought us here."

"And where is here?"

"I don't know," she said with an irritating tone of innocence. "Maybe it's the root of your problems, or maybe it's nothing. I don't—"

"You think I had a fucked up childhood," I accused. The tension in my arms increasing as my hands worked to clench and release.

"I didn't say that," she insisted firmly. "I'm just curious about what it was like for you as a kid."

I shrugged, feigning complete nonchalance as my hands smacked the arms of my chair. "My childhood before the accident was fine. Nice house, nice parents. Church every Sunday. You know. Typical bullshit."

"And after the accident?"

"It was an adjustment," I replied shortly.

"Well, it couldn't have been easy for your parents, dealing with Jake."

I shook my head. "Jake wasn't a fucking problem. I mean, it was rough for a while, but he wasn't a problem."

"Were *you* a problem?"

"I ..." I swallowed and reached forward for my cup of tea from Jolie's. "I was a bad kid, I guess."

"Oh, yeah?"

"After the accident, my mom was always pissed at me about something," I admitted easily, surprised that the words could tumble out without any resistance. "I was a troublemaker, and I guess she'd had enough."

"A troublemaker, huh?" Dr. Travetti smiled fondly.

"Well, yeah," I chuckled tightly, forcing myself to nod. "I mean, after all, it was my troublemaking that fucked everything up in the first place."

Dr. Travetti tipped her head back and studied me with a concerned gaze. "It's a long time to be carrying the blame for an accident you caused as a child, don't you think?"

I scoffed and shook my head, but then I wondered about that. Was it too long? Had I really been a troublemaker or such a bad kid? There'd been the accident that had changed it all, yes, and it was unforgiveable, I got that. But don't all kids have their bad moments? They all have a bad day, they all throw their tantrums, and I didn't doubt that I had a few of my own under my belt. But I couldn't remember an incident that ever warranted the *title*. Bad Kid. Troublemaker.

Except that one.

I kept thinking about it periodically as the weeks went by. Another seed had been planted. It was something else to keep my brain busy while I worked, or tried to sleep alone in my bed. But never while I was with Audrey. Shit never got to me when I was with her, at her place or mine, with Jake and Freddy, or without. As much as I had resisted her pull in the beginning, I gave in to it now and silently begged to be sucked in further, into a place where I felt more and more at home.

By the time Thanksgiving rolled around, she and I had fallen into a routine. Our weekdays were spent grabbing lunch, sometimes with Celia, sometimes without. A few nights a week, we had dinner with Jake and Freddy, and come the weekend, when we were both free of responsibilities, we dated as a couple. Sometimes we went out, had dinner, and went to the poetry club. Other times, we just stayed in, ordered pizza, and spent more time devouring each other than eating food. But those nights were the best of my life, nights when I wrapped my limbs around her body and her skin became an extension of mine. And by the end of November, I actually believed I was deserving of this. Something good, something to be happy about, and not once did I think I was too bad for her.

"Where's Audrey today?" Dad asked, as he carved the turkey.

"With her parents," I answered, lifting the biscuits from the baking pan with a spatula.

"And Freddy?"

"With Jason." My mother's speculation about Audrey's relationship with her ex-boyfriend had so far gone completely unfounded, and a smug grin spread across my face at the fact. I showed her, ha-ha.

Dad nodded, dropping slice after slice of white meat onto Mom's hideous platter. "Things seem to be going well with the two of you, huh?"

"Yeah," I admitted easily.

His smile was warm and genuine. Dad had been trying more lately. Audrey seemed to have that effect on him, too. "That's great, Blake. Really, I'm happy for you. It's about time you found someone to make you happy, and—"

Mom hurried into the kitchen in a flurry of aggravation with Jake hot on her heels holding his *Gremlins* DVD. "Jakey, I already told you. We are not putting the TV on right before dinner. It's not happening, so stop asking." She turned to pin my gaze with hers. "And I don't want to hear anything out of you about it, okay? So, don't even think about it."

"I didn't say anything," I muttered. Then, I looked to Jake and said, "Hey, buddy, Dad's cutting the turkey, okay? We're going to eat in just a few minutes. But I promise, right after you're done, I'll put *Gremlins* on."

Jake clutched the box in his hands, eyeing the turkey Dad was almost finished carving. "You promise?"

"Yeah, I promise." Then, I laid the spatula down and extended a hand toward him. "Here, I'll even pinkie swear on it."

Grinning, Jake wrapped his littlest finger around mine and we shook. "Pinkie swear," he declared in a bellow and laid the DVD down on the counter before heading into the dining room.

Dad offered a small smile in my direction. "I don't know what you've been doing with him, but it's like dealing with a whole new Jake."

He wasn't wrong about that. Over the past month, Jake had been less combative and more agreeable. It was easier to reason with him, easier to calm him down, and if I really thought about it, I couldn't remember the last time I'd worried about him becoming violent. It was great and even though I felt triumphant at the praise from my father, I knew I couldn't take the credit.

It was all Audrey.

Well, Freddy, too. But mostly Audrey.

I wasn't the only one she had fixed.

"I haven't noticed much of a difference," Mom all but snickered, crossing her arms and shaking her head. "He still fights with me."

"Well, I'm not saying he doesn't *fight* anymore, he's always going to—"

"Then, let's not act like he's cured, Paul," she snapped, leveling my father with an ugly glare.

Dad lifted the platter and turned to me with the look of a man who'd just had his balls handed to him. "Ready to eat?" he asked, his voice tense and struggling for control.

"Yeah, Dad," I nodded, as I grabbed the biscuits, and I thought again about my conversation with Dr. Travetti. About my role as the bad kid and if it'd been as real as I'd been made to believe. Or if I was just doomed to wear a red mark handed to me after one very, very unfortunate accident.

But that's all it was. An accident.

***

Jake was quietly watching *Gremlins* on the floor in front of the TV, his arms wrapped around Mickey's neck. I came up from behind him with a slice of apple pie, topped with a heaping mound of vanilla ice cream and whipped cream, and asked, "Hey, buddy, want some dessert?"

Jake turned to look up at me with a bewildered grin. "You betcha!"

"Here you go." I passed the pie down to him. "Don't make a mess, okay?"

With both our hands locked on the plate between us, his eyes fixated on mine with that look. The one that managed to work its way through my retinas and into my brain, with the intent of digging deeper and deeper until there was nowhere else to go but to burrow in the pit of my chest and curl up between my lungs. I was frozen and unable to look away, as his smile slowly stretched.

"You're still blue," he seemed to assure me, nodding. "But you're pink also. So pretty and bright."

"Ew, pink?" I twisted my mouth with blatant disgust as my curiosity ignited. "That's gross, man. Don't tell me that."

Jake laughed, taking his pie into his lap. "It's not gross! All the colors are pretty."

I scoffed, crossing my arms and shaking my head. "Yeah, whatever you say, pal."

He shrugged and turned his attention back to the TV. "You should tell Audrey your colors. She put them on you."

Instantly sobered at the mention of her name, I reached down to ruffle his hair. "Maybe I will."

"Tonight."

I chuckled under my breath. "Yeah, I don't think so, Jake. I'm not seeing her tonight, so—"

"You are."

I froze on the spot, startled by the sincerity in his tone. I had no plans of seeing Audrey until tomorrow night, after she and her mother had gone Black Friday shopping. What would make me see her tonight? What reason could I possibly have to change our plans now?

Breaking out of my stupor, I laid a hand over his head and said, "I'll see you on Sunday, buddy." He was quiet now and simply nodded, keeping his attention solely on the movie. I sucked in a deep breath and quickly moved into the kitchen before he had the chance to say anything else. There, I found my parents in conversation with one of my aunts. Quietly, I snatched my keys from off the counter, hoping to make a quick getaway before being roped into the chatter myself, when my mother turned to me.

"Oh, Blake, while you're still here, I wanted to mention something to you."

I caught Dad's somber downward gaze and furrowed my brow. "What's up?" I asked.

"Just so you know," Mom went on without hesitation, "Dad and I went back to Shady Acres earlier this week and signed the papers. We'll be moving Jake over there after Christmas."

It took a few moments for the words to make sense in my head, while the impact instantaneously caused my heart to combust, leaving my chest open and bleeding onto the kitchen floor. I expected my mother to scream at me to clean it up, to demand I get the mop and get to work on making her floor sparkle again. All I could do was reach a hand out to grip the edge of the counter and try to remain steady, to keep myself from falling over into the puddle of blood collecting on the floor.

"Blake? Did you hear me?"

At that snappy tone, I did hear her, and I finally reacted. I curled my other hand into a fist and sent it sailing into the refrigerator door. The sound rang throughout the house and the faces of all my relatives turned to look on at the family drama about to unfold. The refrigerator contents rattled and spilled inside, and the stainless steel did nothing to cool the immediate throb that seared the side of my palm. But that all went ignored as I stared into the startled eyes of my mother.

"You didn't fucking talk to me," I growled through gritted teeth.

"Blake, calm—"

"You didn't fucking talk to me!" I repeated, louder. Angrier.

Mom spread her arms wide, palms open. "Why do *we* have to talk to *you* about anything?"

I uncurled my fist and daggers shot up through my fingers to my elbow as I pointed one throbbing finger at my mother's disbelieving face. "You didn't *say* anything to me! You told me you were *looking around.* You told me you would keep me in the loop. But instead, you went behind my *fucking* back and signed the goddamn papers! How the *fuck* could you do this shit to me? There are other fucking options and—"

"*Options?*" Mom spat condescendingly. "What options?"

And I finally uttered my deepest wishes to the woman who could make them come true. "He could stay with me! He likes my place, he's happy there, he's—"

Her eyeroll cut me off. "You can't be serious."

"Yes, I'm fucking serious! I wouldn't even ask you for anything. He'd be fine, we'd—"

"Should I remind you of why we're in this position to begin with?"

I shook my head, blinking at the burning sensation in my eyes. "Don't you fucking dare. I will fucking—"

"Blake," Dad said, standing up from the table, "go home. We'll talk about this in a couple of days after you've cooled—"

"Fuck you," I shot back, now aiming my finger now toward him.

"Excuse me?" He scowled, crossing his arms.

"I said, fuck you."

"I'm your father," he said, as though that meant something.

"Yeah, you are, and you promised me," I replied, as if that should've meant something to them, and I turned away with my throbbing hand and stormed out of the house.

Chapter Twenty-Seven

AUDREY'S MOM, Ann, a resident nurse, held my hand in both of hers as Audrey grabbed one of the beers she kept for me in her fridge. I winced at her mother's manipulations on my fingers as she slowly studied each digit.

"Well, your fingers aren't broken," she declared, slowly moving her fingers to my palm, and I hissed through my teeth. "But you might've fractured something in here. Might just be a sprain, but you should still get it X-rayed."

I shook my head. "I'm not going to the fucking hospital."

Ann peered at me through a pair of matronly eyes I don't think I'd ever seen before in my life. "Well, I guess you could just leave it alone, and then we'll see how much longer you're able to work after your bones mend improperly."

Groaning, I thrust my other hand through my hair. "Couldn't I just wrap it tonight and go to the hospital tomorrow? I can't even fucking think straight right now."

My voice cracked under the pressure of my emotions and I cleared my throat, instantly embarrassed by how fucking weak I'd become.

Audrey came over with the open bottle of beer and passed it into my good hand. As I drank, she asked her mom, "Where are your bandages? I'll go get them."

Ann sighed and patted my hand before laying it on the table. "Nah. I'll go up. Be right back," and with that, she turned and left Audrey's apartment.

The drive from my parents' house had been done in a blind flurry of rage and desperation. An endless string of curse words and a periodic smash of my fist into the steering wheel had been the soundtrack to my post-Thanksgiving trip back to Salem, and in a single shred of clarity, I knew I couldn't be alone. I knew being in that dark house, alone with all those liquor bottles, wouldn't lead to anything productive or good. I'd turned in the direction of Audrey's place with only one thought in mind: Jake knew. Somehow, he fucking *knew*, and now, I sat at Audrey's kitchen table, shaking my head and pinching the space between my brows, asking nobody how the fuck that was possible.

"How is what possible?" she asked softly, reaching out to touch my arm.

"Jake," I choked, my chest heaving and aching. "How the fuck did he know I'd be here tonight?"

Audrey faltered before replying, "Um ... maybe he just figured—"

"No." I shook my head and dropped my hand to the table. "He *knew* I wasn't seeing you for a couple days, but he was insistent that I'd be here *tonight*. And I just don't fucking understand *how* he could know."

"You don't know the extent of his, um …" *Gift*. I saw the word written on her face, etched into the blue of her eyes and highlighted across the tops of her cheekbones. But she hesitated to say it, knowing how I felt about it. Knowing I'd shake my head and shut her down with an insistence that there wasn't such thing as *gifts*. But right now, I wished she had said it, declaring that's what it was so that I wouldn't have to. The word never left her lips, though. She simply shrugged apologetically, shifted in her seat, and the cross around her neck glinted in the light.

My gaze fixated on the delicate piece of silver, rising and falling with the rhythmic expanse and collapse of her chest. I found a hypnotic calm in its gentle glow and matched my breath with hers.

"No, you're right. I don't know the extent of it," I answered, my voice gruff and rumbling in my chest. Then, I harshly admitted, "I fucking *hate* this shit."

I could've been talking about anything—my pulsing hand, my parents and what they were doing, Jake's *symptom*, that fucking cross—but Audrey didn't ask for clarification. She just simply nodded somberly and said, "I know."

I could've gone on to elaborate. About the breathing anger I held toward my mother, nestling deep inside my gut and turning sour with my Thanksgiving dinner. Or the conflict between my brain and heart over what the hell I believed. And the weight of my helpless and broken heart, crushing against my chest and splintering my ribs. I wanted to tell her everything I hated about it all, but the words failed me as I looked into her eyes that seemed so impossibly blue and kind.

"What the fuck are you doing with me?" I asked, shaking my head.

"What do you mean?"

"I mean," I went on, reaching out to take her hand, "I can be such an insufferable, angry piece of shit. I'm a total fucking mess. And I still cannot understand why, after everything these past couple of months, you still want to be with me."

Audrey cocked her head as those delicate fingers intertwined with mine. "You always say this like I have a choice. Like I could just walk away."

"Well, yeah," I replied. "'Cause you can."

Shaking her head slowly, she smiled so sweetly and so adoringly, the weight against my lungs was lifted. Just a little. "But I can't."

"Oh, no?" I challenged. "And why not?"

"Because …" She hesitated, as though choosing her words carefully, before going on, "Because there are certain things in our lives—certain *people*—that are just supposed to be there. We don't choose them, or what they'll mean to us; they're just a part of who we are."

My old instincts said to laugh, snicker, or belittle her insistence that this wasn't all one big accidental misunderstanding. But I couldn't give in to them when that voice, getting louder every day, told me there was something to what she was saying. Something honest and true and so fucking terrifying, I could hardly stand it.

"And what is it you think I am to you?" I asked instead, surprised to find my voice so hushed, I could barely hear it myself. And without hesitation, she answered, "You're the man I'm meant to love."

A simple four-lettered word had never choked me up as much as it did in that moment. And it wasn't that it had never been given to me before. My brother loved me and often told me so. Sometimes Cee admitted to a platonic love, while giving me a hug or in parting. Yet, this love from Audrey was new and strange and one I had never felt worthy of before. But with her hand holding mine, I knew it was the truth. The Real Deal.

You're still blue. But you're pink also. So pretty and bright.

You should tell Audrey your colors. She put them on you.

"I—" That one word caught in my throat and I choked around its sound.

As I coughed awkwardly, Audrey unleashed a smile that left me breathless and convinced I'd die in this moment, finally a happy man. She held my gaze as she said, "You don't have to say anything," and it occurred to me that she didn't believe her feelings would be reciprocated. And how was it that she could seem so perfectly content in settling for something so sad and mediocre?

The remainder of my bricks fell with the crushing realization. Ignoring the pain in my busted hand, I reached out to lay my palm against her cheek. "Jake told me to tell you that you put the colors on me," I confessed.

"What colors are those?"

"Blue," I told her, and with a deep breath, added, "and pink."

Audrey's recognition hit her in small doses. First, with the lift of her chin, and then, the parting of her lips. She nodded slowly and whispered, "That's the color of love."

I nodded, knowing nothing else needed to be said, but needing to say it anyway. "For the first time in my life, I made the decision to feel hurt and angry with someone else and not alone. You make me so fucking vulnerable, Audrey, and I hate it so much. I fucking hate that I don't have a choice in any of this shit, and that nothing makes sense anymore. But I love you, and I guess that's all that really needs to make sense."

Her smile wobbled as her emotional control slipped away with tears that flooded her eyes and slipped over her cheeks. I brushed away what I could with sweeps of my thumbs, but the battle was impossible and I succumbed to the defeat, settling for a kiss instead. I relished in the wet warmth of her tears against my face, the salt that moistened her lips and mine, and the taste of passionate joy on her tongue as she kissed me with the strength of every confession she held in her heart.

Nimble hands gripped my cheeks and inked hands gripped hers, and when her forehead touched mine, she whispered, "Thank you, Blake."

"The hell are you thanking me for?"

Shrugging, she smiled and smoothed the hair at my temples. "For letting it happen."

I choked on a gruff chuckle. "I don't think I ever had a say."

"But you stopped fighting it," she pointed out gently.

Audrey's mother announced her presence with an awkward clearing of her throat. Unable to control her smile, Audrey released my face and went to change into her pajamas, leaving her mother to wrap my hand. Ann worked in a gentle silence, periodically taking a glance at my eyes to smile. Her touch alone was a healing agent, soothing and softly affectionate. I watched as she weaved the bandage meticulously and tightly, but not so much it cut off the circulation, and I could understand why she'd chosen to care for people for a living. It's who she was. But whether it was simply her professional bedside manner, or a true affection toward me, I relished in her touch and in being cared for.

When she was done, she gave my bandaged hand a soothing rub before laying it on the table. "You should be fine until tomorrow, but you're going to the doctor whether you like it or not, got it?"

With an obedient nod, I replied, "Got it."

"No more punching refrigerators, okay?" She smiled warmly, crinkling her eyes.

I chuckled. "I'll try not to."

Her smile slowly faded as she packed away the rest of her bandages in a zippered bag. Then, with sincerity, she turned to me and said, "I don't know if it's my place to say something, but after the way you showed up here tonight, I feel like I should."

"Okay," I said, nodding and permitting her to continue.

Folding her hands against the table, she went on, "I don't know what the situation is with your family, but I do know how close you are with your brother. What your parents are doing to you is abhorrent. But not just for you, but Jake as well. As a mother, and knowing how you two are together, I couldn't imagine separating you."

I sucked in a deep, controlled breath before saying, "I guess they think they're doing what's best for him. And I don't know, maybe they think that keeping him out of my place is going to help me, so I guess—"

"Honey," she stopped me with a term of endearment that made me want to crawl inside her chest and call her my own, "it doesn't take a doctor or specialist to know what's best for the both of you."

The comment was sobering. Eye-opening, even, and I began to wonder if it really was that obvious to everyone. And if it was, then why didn't my parents see it, too?

Or did they?

"I always knew what was best for my girls," Ann continued, revealing in her sorrowful smile the perpetual sadness of losing one of her daughters. "Did Audrey tell you Sabrina was a lesbian?"

I shook my head. "No, she didn't mention that."

Ann nodded and fiddled with a ring on her middle finger. "It was an adjustment for her father and me. Truthfully, we didn't take the news all that well, and now, I look back on that night with so much embarrassment, because why does it matter, really?" She shook her head at the rhetorical question before going on, "But even still, when I met the woman she had fallen in love with, I fell in love with her, too. Because I knew right away that she was what was best for my daughter."

Then, she reached out and tapped my good hand once. "That's how I felt meeting you for the first time."

Snorting, I replied, "Oh, I'm sure that was great for you."

"It was," she answered without hesitating. "The way Audrey looked at you, I knew you were exactly what she needed. She was broken for a long time after losing Sabrina. We all were, but she took it the hardest. She hid it well—she had to, to be what Freddy needed—but deep down, she was battling something dark. You put the light back in her soul."

I could only nod, absorbing her words and knowing there was truth in that for me as well. Audrey had glimpsed the darkness in my chest and lit a match. She'd started a fire and given me the reason to believe I could, in fact, have a soul. Something bound only to flesh in this life, something with the capability to move from this world into another. It felt crazy, but wasn't everything?

Ann laughed gently. "And no, maybe you're not who I would've picked for her. You're a little more, uh, decorated," she tapped one of my fingers, "than I maybe would've preferred. But God doesn't always package the best ones in what we'd expect. That's what makes them harder to find. And more worth the wait."

"Hm," I grunted contemplatively, lifting one side of my mouth into a lopsided smile.

"I bet she's not exactly what you expected either, huh?"

"Nope," I laughed.

Audrey returned to her small kitchen, freshly showered and wearing a pair of shorts and a sweatshirt I'd left behind a couple of weekends ago. At the sight of her, standing there in my shirt, I felt ragged and worn, exhausted and ready to curl up in her warm bed. To forget about this day for just a few peaceful hours of sleep.

Ann excused herself with one last pat against my hand, and the moment the front door was closed, my shoulders slumped and my eyes closed against the weight of weariness sitting heavily on my back. Audrey wrapped her arms around my shoulders and pressed my head to her chest.

"What the fuck am I going to do?" I asked, in hopes she had the answer.

"I guess that's for you to decide," she replied, stroking her fingers through my hair.

"What do *you* think I should do?" I wrapped my arms around her waist, holding on tight to the only anchor I'd ever known.

"Well," she went on, pressing her chin to the top of my head, "if you really want my opinion …"

"I do."

"Then, I think you should take all that pent-up anger and frustration that you're no longer wasting on us, and put it toward the real battle," she said, hugging me tighter.

I sighed exhaustedly. "It's too late. They've already signed the papers," I told her, shaking my head and still unable to believe that this was happening. "I just don't fucking get it. He's been doing so well these past couple of months. Why the fuck would they still think this needs to happen?"

"I don't know," she admitted in a hushed tone that reverberated in my ear. "But it's not too late, Blake. It's never too late, as long as you're still able to fight. And Jake is worth fighting for."

Chapter Twenty-Eight

"AUDREY, YOU DON'T need to be here," I muttered in the radiologist's waiting room. "I'm fine. Go shopping with your mother."

"I'll go shopping with my mom later," she insisted, wrapping her arms around mine. "Besides, I like getting to spend more time with you."

"You already spend a lot of time with me."

"And yet, it never feels like enough," she replied sweetly, before kissing my cheek.

I grumbled a reply as I heard my name being called. Picking my head up, I answered, "Yeah?"

The technician approached with a kind smile. He probably looked like that all damn day. Always smiling, through the good and the bad, delivering some optimism even in the crappiest of times. I could never survive in a job like this. I'm too real, too bitter.

"You sprained it, but there's no break," he said with a goodhearted nod. "Keep it wrapped up and use it sparingly. You can take some ibuprofen if the pain and swelling gets bad."

"Got it," I replied, nodding. "Thanks a lot."

"Of course." He turned his smile from me to Audrey and added, "Tell Ann I said hi, all right?"

Audrey grinned sweetly as she pulled her purse onto a shoulder. "Oh, I will. Have a great day, Jeff."

"You, too," Jeff said and turned toward the door from which he came. Then, with a look over his shoulder, he pointed a finger at me. "Oh! And no more punching refrigerators!"

I forced a chuckle, lifted my bandaged hand and replied sardonically, "Learned my lesson, Jeff. Thanks."

We left the radiology building and stepped into a cold late-November morning. Audrey hugged my arm to her side and asked what I was going to do for the rest of the day while she hit the stores with Ann. I shrugged as I unlocked my car and replied, "I don't know. Might go home and get some shit done."

"What kind of shit?" she asked, climbing in.

"Well, someone's been a bit of a distraction," I shot her with a wink and she blushed, "so I'm a little behind on cleaning and laundry. Should probably do some of that."

"You want me to come over and help?"

I narrowed my eyes as I started the car. "I've been cleaning and doing laundry for a long time. I really don't need any help."

"Yeah, I know," she replied innocently. "I just didn't know if you'd like the company, or um …"

I glanced at her with accusing eyes. "You're afraid I'm gonna drink all the booze and *really* fuck up my hands."

Audrey grimaced apologetically. "I'm sorry. I just know you're hurting and I'm worried about you being alone."

I've never been one to open up about my emotions. Hell, that was why I'd started receiving therapy from Dr. Travetti in the first place. To get it out and have an outlet. But Audrey was changing that. With her, I felt I could be open and honest, and so I replied, "It feels good to be worried about for once, but I'm fine. I swear."

"Okay," she said, almost satisfied, and I started the car.

***

The house suddenly felt hollow thinking there'd be no chance of Jake living here full-time. I never noticed that before, during the weekends when I considered the time away from him as a welcomed reprieve. But now, as I realized our regular time together was running out, the silence came to me as a scream before dying as a pathetic whimper in the pit of my chest.

I dulled the noisy quiet by keeping busy. I vacuumed the living room, swept the kitchen floor, and dusted the shelves. I loaded the washer and managed to fold some of Jake's clean clothes with my busted hand. Two hours of chores flew by without too much thinking, but once there was nothing left to do and I sat down on the couch, the eerie hush came for me again.

Our pictures were everywhere—the drawing of the two of us and the photographs on the mantle. Jake's puzzles were stacked on a shelf beside the TV, and his

DVDs were on a shelf below that. Coloring books, board games, and buckets and buckets of Legos cluttered another set of shelves, and as I looked at all these things, I wondered how empty my house would be once it was all gone. How despairingly sad. How pointless.

This house had always been with Jake in mind, and without him in it, what was its purpose? It was home, but only together, in whatever capacity that meant. Without him, it would be a tomb.

"I can't let them do it," I said to no one. "I can't let them fucking do it."

Without a moment's hesitation, I grabbed my phone and dialed my father's number. He was the more reasonable one. I could talk to him, apologize for my outburst last night and discuss things like an adult, like a man. And by the time he answered, the determination was buzzing through my veins.

"Blake," he said curtly.

"Hey, Dad."

He didn't respond, probably thinking I was calling for Round Two, so I hastily added, "I'm not gonna fight with you."

"Well, that's good to hear." His tone was just as flat as before.

Nobody said this battle was going to be easy, I told myself as I let loose a strained breath. "So, I'm sorry about last night. Mom caught me off-guard. I just wish she'd told me soon—"

"Your mother and I don't have to tell you *anything*."

My jaw gritted at the verbal blade held to my throat. "I know that. That's why I'm apologizing—"

"You should be apologizing to your mother, not me. You really upset her last night."

"Fine," I replied, struggling to keep my cool. "Is she around? Put her on."

"Let me see if she'll talk to you."

I forced my sardonic chuckle to remain locked in my chest as my father asked my mother if she had it in her to speak to me. I heard her reply but couldn't make out the words, then Dad replied, "I don't know what he wants." They spoke about me like I was the last person they'd ever want to hear from. Like talking to me was a painful chore, like I was worth nothing and my existence was a burden.

And it wasn't lost on me that not so long ago, I felt the same way.

Mom muttered something and Dad spoke into the phone, "I'm going to put you on speakerphone."

"Okay," I replied, taking that over nothing, and waited.

"Why are you calling?" Mom asked bitterly.

"Hi, Mom."

"I'm not in the mood to chitchat," she snapped in reply. "Just say what you called to say."

Wetting my lips and thinking about the booze in the kitchen, I swallowed at the vile, angry words begging to be said. "I, um … I called to say that I'm sorry."

Mom guffawed. "You don't get to apologize and expect we're just putting it behind us. You embarrassed us last night, do you not understand that? You humiliated and belittled us in front of our family, like a *child*. It's bad enough this is the type of thing we deal with from

Jake, but you? You're a man, Blake, and it's about damn time you acted like it."

My stomach churned and my lips screwed up with distaste. "You know, for someone who didn't want to talk, you sure have a lot to say."

"And there you go with that mouth of yours. Doesn't take much for you to show your true colors."

The abrupt wobbling of my chin surprised me. I never used to be one to get emotional, but this was too much. Too much to handle, too much to wrap my head around, and far too much to take all at once.

"Mom, I just called to apologize and see if—"

"If, what? If there was anything you can do to change our minds?"

I sucked in the snot that began to accumulate as I shook my head. "That's not—"

"You know what, Blake? I don't want to continue this conversation. I'm done. I'm just done with you right now. I've had enough."

Pushing a hand through my hair, I stared at a stain on the living room carpet without seeing its ugly, muddy brown and only hearing the disgusted tone in my mother's voice. "How the fuck can you talk to me like this?" I managed to ask.

"I've been asking the same thing of you your entire life and you don't see me throwing temper tantrums over it."

My hand lowered to my side as I stared at that matted brown spot. "The fuck are you talking about?"

"You have made my life a living hell since the day you—"

"Diana," Dad finally spoke up from the sidelines. "That's enough now."

"If it weren't for *you*, none of this would've happened in the first place," she went on. "We wouldn't even be having this conversation, Jake wouldn't be the way he is, we—"

"Diana! Enough!"

My mouth fell open with a sudden zap of clarity. Hidden memories, buried beneath the rubble, came to the surface in a torrential wave. The stain morphed, turning into something I hadn't seen since I was ten, shortly after the accident. Jake's spilled glass of milk, and Mom's screams at me to clean it up. The spot shifted, now it was ice cream, smeared on the kitchen floor after a tantrum Jake had thrown. Mom, grabbing my arm and pulling me along to mop it up.

Another shift, another spot, another spill. I was sixteen, hanging out with my friends. Jake couldn't hang out with us, he couldn't skateboard or rollerblade, and he'd thrown a fit out of jealousy and rejection. There'd been chocolate milk everywhere. I'd told him we could hang out later, told him that we'd build Legos and watch *Gremlins*, and the bargain had been enough for him. But not for Mom. She had scolded me in front of my friends, treating me like a child, and had thrown my skateboard in the trash. Because, as she'd said, Jake came first, before friends and skateboarding. Before me. It was the least I could do, after everything. After what I'd done.

"You resent me," I quietly stated. "You … you have spent over two decades making sure I'd hate myself as much as you hate me—"

"Good Lord, Blake, where are you getting this stuff from?" Mom huffed exhaustedly. "Tell me this is some garbage that girl's feeding you. You know she doesn't like us."

Anger battled with my heartbreak as I growled, "Don't you fucking dare talk about her."

"Oh, for crying out loud, you barely know the girl!"

Another realization struck me and I blurted, "You don't want me to be happy. Fuck, you've *never* wanted me to be happy. You—"

"All right, Blake," Dad intervened. "That's enough. I think we all just need a little time to calm down, okay? We'll talk to you on—"

"Why the hell did you let her do it?" I asked my father candidly. "You became a fucking zombie and let her manipulate me. You let her treat me like shit over a fucking accident. You let her make sure I'd grow up to hate myself and—"

"Don't be dramatic, Blake. Come on," Dad cut in, sighing as Mom said, "That's what he does."

My vision re-focused with a crystal-clear view of what my life had been like. We're all taught that our parents are here to protect us, pat us on the back, and tell us how proud they are to call us theirs. To ensure that we grow into happy, confident adults. But my parents never did, and I am the miserable, broken result of that.

Now, I'm blue. And I'm pink. I can fight, and I can love, and I decided then that I would fight them. And maybe, despite it all, I could learn to forgive them. But I couldn't see any room for love.

"I'm hanging up," I announced calmly.

"Okay, that's a good idea," Dad said. "Maybe we'll come over for dinner—"

"No," I interrupted. "You won't. Neither of you are welcome in my house for the foreseeable future. I'll see Jake on Sunday." And I hung up.

***

"Hi, Blake, what can I do for you?"

Dr. Travetti's voice was a lifejacket held too far from my reach. I coached my breaths in and out of my lungs until I could reply. "Hey, Doc. Sorry to disturb your shopping day."

She laughed lightly. "Don't apologize. I do all my Black Friday shopping online."

"Smart."

There was a brief lull as I struggled to find the words I needed to say and how to say them. The more I struggled, the more I wondered why I had called her at all. What the hell was she even going to do for me? What was she going to tell me that I didn't already know myself?

I tipped my head back against the kitchen wall and eyed the shelf of liquor bottles. The numbness kept within the multicolored vessels pulled at me with a temptation I'd never known before. It worried me, how desperate I was to succumb to the black nothingness, but what worried me more was to allow this pain to swallow me alive.

"Blake?"

I cleared my throat and replied, "Yeah, Doc?"

"Are you okay?"

"Would I call you if I was?"

"Fair point," she said, immediately sympathetic in her tone. "What's going on? Is it your girlfriend?"

Girlfriend. Dr. Travetti had been the only one to call Audrey my girlfriend in the time we'd been seeing each other. It was nice; it made me smile, even now.

"Nah," I said, shaking my head and wishing she had never left me alone. "I haven't fucked that up yet, apparently. She loves me."

"She told you that?"

"Yeah …" Fuck. My eyes watered, remembering the moment from last night.

"Oh, Blake," Dr. Travetti said, her tone lilting whimsically. Chicks fucking love romance. "That's so wonderful. You have no idea how happy I am for—"

"My parents signed the papers to send Jake away," I cut in. Because while Audrey's love for me was certainly worthy of joy, there was a greater, darker force looming over my head, robbing me of all the light I'd recently found in my life. "They didn't even fucking talk to me like they said they would."

"I don't know what to say, Blake." My heart felt the burden of her tone, coated so heavily in sympathy. "I'm so sorry."

"I got into a fight with my mother last night and went to Audrey's, because I didn't want to be alone," I went on, eyeing a particularly appealing bottle of vodka. "But today, she went shopping with her mom, so I came home. I ended up calling my parents to apologize for last night and to try and work this shit out—"

"That's something the old Blake wouldn't have done," she commented, speaking to me like a proud mama.

"Yeah, well," I snickered sardonically, "I wish I hadn't. 'Cause you know what I learned today, Doc?"

"What's that?"

That bottle was looking more and more like a thing of need. "My mother despises me. And get this—*she* blames me. How fucking funny is that? All this time, I've been blaming myself, and it turns out, she's been doing the same fucking thing."

"How do you know this?" Dr. Travetti asked, speaking slowly and eerily calm.

"Oh," I laughed with cynicism, "believe me, she didn't try to hide it. She just came out and told me. Did you know that God punished her by giving her me?"

She exhaled against the phone. "Blake …"

"Yeah," I nodded, licking my lips, so parched and desperate. "That's funny, right? I mean, I always thought I was punishing myself because there *is* no fucking god, but as it turns out, the bastard used *me* to punish *her*. And then I guess she decided to take it upon herself to make my life miserable, because I made hers a living hell by existing and ruining Jake. Or some fucking shit, I don't fucking know."

"Blake," her voice nipped at my ears, in an attempt to snap me out of it, "I need you to breathe—"

"No. I won't fucking *breathe*." I pushed away from the wall to lurch forward and take the few strides to the shelf of booze and snatch that damn bottle. "My own fucking mother hates me. Who the fuck hates their own kid? Who the fuck takes their anger out on a fucking *kid*? Who the fuck …"

My breath was ragged and the sob escaping my lungs surprised me. As my hand tightened around the bottle's neck, I leaned forward, smacking my forehead against a cabinet door. "Goddammit, Doc," I cried into the phone, all at once noticing the tears on my face and the trembling in my voice. "They're taking him away from me. I don't want them to take him away."

"I know, Blake," she spoke to me in that tone meant to drag me from off a cliff, "and I am so, so sorry this is happening to you."

I smacked my head again, barely holding onto the phone with my bad hand, as I demanded, "Tell me what to do. You're always telling me what I should do, so tell me something now. Tell me what the fuck I can do."

"Blake, I need you to listen to me," she said, coddling in her tone. "I am not a lawyer. I don't know how it is you could battle something like this, other than to say I'm sure there is a way. But right now, you need to calm down because you're not helping anybody by acting out in rage, okay? Let's calm down."

"How the fuck am I supposed to do that?"

"Well," she said, "why don't you tell me about what happened with Audrey?"

Chapter Twenty-Nine

THE PHONE CONVERSATION with Dr. Travetti had calmed me down, and that night, Audrey came to stay. I was grateful she hadn't seen me at my worst, because she only deserved my best, and together, we decided I'd talk to Amy, Miss Thomas, the next chance I got. Audrey was certain she would know what I could do, and I felt a calm in knowing that I had a plan.

I spent the weekend buried in her arms and between her legs, in some attempt to drown my anxieties in something that wasn't alcohol. She and Freddy agreed to accompany me to hang out with Jake on Sunday and acted as a buffer between my parents and me, knowing they wouldn't attempt to get a rise out of me with her there.

Come Monday, everything seemed back to normal. Jake and I went about our morning as though our days weren't numbered, and there was a real bittersweet sadness in that. When I dropped Jake off at daycare on the way to work, I pulled Amy aside and simply asked how I could go about getting legal guardianship over

Jake. She was surprised to learn I wasn't already his guardian, and I briefly explained our personal situation. I omitted the details about the mother I only recently acknowledged had been abusing me my entire life and the father who'd allowed it all to happen by turning a blind eye.

Curiosity glinted in her gaze as she had said, "Well, I guess you could always talk to your parents—"

"No, that's not an option at this point. I just need to know how I'd go about doing this from my end, without getting them involved." Until I saw them in court, I'd also neglected to mention.

Slowly nodding her head with unspoken understanding, Amy went to her office to retrieve a few pamphlets regarding disability law and obtaining guardianship. Then, in a quiet voice, she'd said, "And Blake, if there's anything I can do, please don't even hesitate to ask. Jason and I are always here."

I thought about what she'd said a number of times in the days that followed. About the support system I'd developed in the time since I'd met Audrey. The kind of people who I had kept at arms' length, until she had entered my life and acted as the bridge between me and everybody else. Connecting and pulling me from the private island I'd banished myself to.

Had I ever deserved being exiled?

I no longer thought so.

On Friday, I was no closer to having a plan than I had been before, but otherwise, I was happy. My issue of *ModInk* had hit the stands, and with the excitement of having my name in print, the turmoil of the previous weekend had dissipated. Audrey insisted that we should invite Cee and Shane over for dinner to celebrate, and that was how I found myself flipping pancakes and grilling sausages for a table of six.

"Blake," Shane said, coming up behind me, "your brother is fuckin' awesome, man."

I chuckled, shaking my head. "Please don't feel obligated to say that."

He scoffed. "The fuck? Why would I feel obligated? I've never seen someone build with Legos so fast in my life."

"Oh, he showed you, huh?"

"Hell yeah, he did, and honestly, it doesn't really surprise me. I mean, with your talent, I guessed he'd have to be artistic, too."

I nodded contemplatively, thinking about his obsession with Legos and how it hadn't existed before the accident. He might've lost his talent for drawing, but he hadn't completely lost his artistic ability. It'd just manifested differently. "I guess I never thought about that before."

"And hey, man, what's up with that color thing? He told me I'm tan, and dude," he glanced down at his all-black attire, "I ain't wearin' any tan."

Flipping the pancakes onto a plate, I chuckled lightly. "Yeah, he sees, uh …" I pinched my lips, considering how to explain it to him, then simply said, "He sees auras."

"No shit?"

"Yeah, it's a, um, a gift, I guess. He's good at reading people, knows who to trust." I handed him the

360

plate and noticed his worry expressed in the clench of his jaw. I smiled assuredly and said, "Tan's a good one. It usually means you're friendly."

Shane gave an approving nod. "Damn straight." Then, he faltered, squinted one eye and asked, "So, that means he likes me, right?"

"Yeah," I said. "You're good."

Shane headed toward the table with the plate of pancakes and said, "Hey, you know, you could actually work that into your ink."

I dropped the sausage links from the pan onto another plate and narrowed my eyes as I worked. "Huh?"

"I mean, you could still do your gritty shit, man; it's your signature. But, think about it. How cool would it be to incorporate just a splash of personalized color into someone's ink? Kinda like the butterfly, but it doesn't have to be the same."

"Huh," I muttered, granting the thought permission to seep in. "It's not a bad idea." In actuality, I loved it.

"You could work with Jake," Shane pointed out, and the reminder of why that wouldn't work struck me as a lance to the gut.

"Yeah," I said, not allowing my emotions to reach the surface. "It's definitely something to think about," and I left it at that.

***

Audrey came out from the kitchen with four beers pinched between her fingers. She handed them out to Shane and Cee, then came to perch on my lap while passing a cold bottle into my hand. Settling her back against my chest, I wrapped an arm around her shoulders and took a pull from the bottle. With my eyes closed and my temple pressed to hers, I listened to Jake and Freddy playing animatedly down the hall, tasted the beer, and in this moment, this brief and satisfying moment, I was happy.

"My God, they're so cute," Cee commented, and I opened my eyes to see her nudging the neck of her bottle toward the hall just as Freddy squealed and Jake declared he was "gonna get him."

Audrey nodded. "They're totally B-F-F's."

I eyed her with skepticism. "I dunno about that. Freddy mentioned something to me about another kid at his school."

Smirking with a dash of seduction, she shook her head and grasped my chin in her hand. "Nuh-uh. Freddy told me the other day; Jake is his best friend." Then, with the gentle quality I'd come to expect from her, she kissed me lightly. I took a breath, like I always did when her lips were on mine, as if that was the only time I was permitted to have air.

"Well, I guess we better get going, since these two obviously need a room," Shane teased.

Audrey pulled away just in time for Cee to whack Shane's chest lightly with her hand. "I'm finishing this beer first, thanks," she retorted with a laugh. Then she looked to Audrey and said, "My ex has the kids for the weekend. I'm gonna take advantage of it."

"Girl, there's a case of twelve in there with your name on it," Audrey replied, laughing and settling against me once again.

"Hallelujah!" Cee knocked back the beer with a hefty gulp before raising the bottle to me. "I love your girlfriend, Blake. She gets me."

With a sincerity building in my chest, I waited for Shane and Cee to find a distraction in what was happening on the TV before putting my lips to Audrey's ear and whispering, "I love my girlfriend, too."

She hummed gently, smiling and layering her arms over mine. "You're getting soft."

"Yeah, maybe," I replied, "but is that really such a bad thing?"

"Well, I'd say it's one of the best things that's ever happened to me, so," she turned and touched her lips to mine once again and said, "I'd say, no."

***

The house was dark and quiet. With their sleeping bags rolled out in the living room, Jake and Freddy were fast asleep while *Gremlins* continued to play for the second time that evening. Audrey moved slowly into my bedroom and closed the door behind her, leaving it open just a bit in case Freddy needed her.

"Jake's never had a slumber party before," I mentioned, pulling my t-shirt off. "Well, not since the accident, anyway."

Audrey kicked her shoes off as she nodded. "You've told me he didn't have a lot of friends."

I shook my head. "No. He didn't have *any* friends. The ones he did have ditched him," I corrected her, dropping my hands to the studded belt around my waist. "When I've told you that my parents did nothing for him, I mean, they did *nothing*. He hardly left the damn house. They thought it'd make it easier on him, on them, if he didn't go out. So," I pulled the belt free in one aggravated tug, "the only time he'd see other kids our age, was when I brought people over."

"And he wasn't allowed to play with you?"

"When we were younger, he did." I undid my fly, watching her intently as she removed her yellow shirt in a way that appeared almost as a dance. Her movements were so delicate, so graceful, and with the fluidity of water, I watched the fabric, as it drifted to the floor. "But as we got older, my friends didn't like having him around."

"That's not their fault," she interjected softly. "They were just kids."

"Nah," I shook my head, "I know. I never really thought it had anything to do with him being, you know, different. It was always more that he was into stuff we didn't like, or even just the fact that they weren't his friends, you know? They came over to hang out with me, not my brother."

"That used to happen with Sabrina and me. We didn't share a lot of the same friends."

Dropping my jeans and sitting on the bed, I nodded before faltering and saying, "I feel like I'm insane."

"Why do you say that?"

Raking my fingers from both hands through my hair, I hung my head and stared at the floor. "Because I was always so convinced that these people hated him, when they didn't. My mother told me that they did, that's why they weren't allowed over, and not once did I ever think to question it."

Stepping toward me, Audrey took my hands in hers and held them tight. "Look at me," she commanded, and I did. Even now, when such ugliness threatened to shroud every sliver of light, she was there, glowing and beautiful. "This is the last time I ever want to hear you blame yourself, do you understand? Nothing that happened was your fault, absolutely *nothing*—not even the accident. You were a victim, simple as that."

"And what the fuck am I now?" I asked, nearly snickering. "Damaged goods?"

"No," she said, stepping forward and straddling my lap in nothing but a few flimsy scraps of lace that begged to be torn off. "You're a warrior. And a survivor."

"And you know what you are?" My palms pressed to the dip in her back, holding her against my needy body. She shook her head, threading her fingers through my hair, and I said, "My savior."

Thrusting my mouth against hers, we kissed feverishly, desperately, as I lowered my hands to her panties, suddenly too cumbersome and far too much in the way. I pulled at them, stretched them, and groaned with my tongue in her mouth at the increasingly annoying fact that the damn things wouldn't rip. Audrey giggled in her girly way and mumbled against my lips, "You can just ask me to remove them."

365

"Yeah, but where's the fun in that when I can try ripping them off?" I replied, rolling quickly to lay her back against the bed. She let out a high-pitched shriek at the sudden movement and I pressed my finger to her lips. "You better keep quiet. Don't wanna wake them up. Freddy might think I'm actually trying to kill you this time."

"Oh, my Lord." Audrey clapped a hand over her mouth before giggling wildly. "He would be traumatized for life."

"Then, you better be very, very," I lowered to my knees and pulled those damn underwear off, "*very* quiet."

I devoured her as if she was my last supper, feasting as though I'd been starving since the day I was born. I pushed her closer and closer to the edge, with an encouraging tongue and coaxing lips, until she prayed to my name and pulled at my hair. And just when her body stiffened beneath my hands and her back curved like she'd been possessed, my phone began to ring.

"Blake," she whispered hoarsely, coming down from the high without actually coming.

"Ignore it," I demanded, gripping her thighs and delving deeper.

But the phone persisted. "Blake," she groaned, propping up on her elbows. "Just answer it, it's fine."

"Fucking hell," I grumbled with a sigh and reached for the damn thing to find it was my boss. "It's Gus. What the fuck does he want at eleven o'clock on a Friday night?"

With lustful eyes, she watched me hungrily and smiled. "Better find out, Kiefer. And you better do it quick, 'cause you still have a job to finish."

Grunting, I nodded and answered the phone that'd begun to ring again. "Yeah?"

"Were you just getting laid?" Gus asked immediately, his voice lilting with amusement.

Rolling my eyes, I asked, "Fuck off, man. Why the hell are you calling me so late?"

"Sorry," he said apologetically. "I normally wouldn't, you know that, but you'll never guess who I got a call from just now."

"Nope, probably not," I muttered, pulling myself up to sit on the bed.

"Does the name Devin O'Leary mean anything to you?" Now he just sounded excited.

I wrinkled my nose and shook my head. "Nope. Can't say that it does."

Gus sighed. "Blake, do you live under a fucking rock?"

"I guess I must." I wiped a hand along my brow. "Gus, just tell me what the hell is going on, okay? I'm tired."

"Okay, okay. I just got a call from Devin O'Leary's manager. He's a fucking rock star, man; he's *huge*. He and his band are playing a show here on Sunday, but they're rolling into town tomorrow and they want some ink done."

My gut bottomed out. I didn't know who the fuck this Devin O'Leary was, but given the exuberance in

Gus's tone, I had a feeling this was a major opportunity. "Well, holy shit," I uttered on an exhale.

"Yeah. And guess who they requested?"

"Jesus, fuck," I wiped a hand over my mouth as Audrey sat up and wrapped her arms around my shoulders. Curiosity blanketed her stare as I asked, "How many of them are there?"

"Five guys in the band, but only four want ink."

"That doesn't exactly lighten my load here," I said, thinking about it now in a more realistic light. "How the hell can I design four tattoos and get them done in less than twenty-four hours?"

"Well, that's the best part," Gus went on. "They're giving you free reign. They want you to decide whatever you want, could be flash, could be shit you already have buried somewhere in all your diaries, I don't know. Whatever you wanna do, man, it's up to you."

"I'm not sure that's supposed to make me feel better," I laughed sardonically.

"Blake, really, if you think it's too much, I won't tell you to do it. But I just want you to realize how big this is for your career."

I smiled and nodded adamantly. "Yeah. Yeah, man, I'll be there."

"Fuck, yeah," Gus replied. "I'll see you bright and early."

I hung up the phone and told Audrey what had happened. Her jaw dropped at the mention of Devin O'Leary's name and she'd asked in teeny-bopper fashion if she could meet him. Mild jealousy bloomed in my gut as I laughed and told her I didn't see why not, and she proceeded to bounce excitedly on the bed.

We made love in a way that felt like art. Delicate, meticulous strokes, gentle swoops of hips and brushes of hands. A painting, playing out only in my mind, vivid and bright with every color of the rainbow. We collapsed on our canvas and twisted in the aftereffects, sighing and drifting toward a dream I hoped she'd be in. And all I could think was, this was a good day.

Chapter Thirty

SATURDAY MORNING and Salem Skin could only be described as a madhouse. Even at seven o'clock, a mob had already formed around the front entrance. Excited onlookers crowded around the two tour busses, parked on the street without any effort for discretion. Instantly overwhelmed, I parked the car and took in a trembling breath, gripping the steering wheel with my white-knuckled hands.

This is what I wanted, I told myself. I wanted change, and I wanted to be better. I wanted to live a healthier, happier, and more successful life, for myself and my brother, and now, I was doing it for Audrey and Freddy as well. This—the celebrity clients, the thriving crowd, the attention—this was the consequence of that, of trying, of making an effort and putting myself out there.

"This is crazy," I muttered.

Audrey had schooled me on who Devin O'Leary was while I scrambled to get ready for work. She'd played a few of his songs for me—not my thing, but it was clear the guy was talented—and I'd quickly learned enough about him to get a grasp on what to do for him. I'd have to play it by ear for the other guys, so to speak, but according to Audrey, Devin seemed like the guy to impress.

Audrey had stayed back at my place, to help Jake get ready for his weekend at our parents' place and she was dropping him off before taking Freddy to his dad's. Then, finally, she'd be here. I wished she was here now.

With a deep breath, I got out of the car and approached the back entrance of the shop. Gus threw the door open before I could reach its handle and stared at me with a reasonable dose of shock.

"Damn, kid, look at what you're doing to us!" He clapped a hand against my back and went straight to business. "I already took the liberty of cleaning up your space. I'll let them in while you get your shit set-up, okay?"

"Anybody else coming in today?" I asked, walking through the breakroom to my station.

"Kara and Matt, yeah, but not until later. Why? You think you're gonna need them? I'll tell them to come—"

"No," I shook my head, as I pulled out my machines. "Better they're not here at all. I want to get these guys done before anybody else comes in. They're *celebrities*; they don't need other clients gawking over them or some shit."

"O-oh," Gus stammered and scratched his bald head. "Shit. I didn't even think about that. Maybe I should tell them to cancel their appointments for the day."

I met his eyes with an unintended incredulity. "Uh, yeah," I said, nodding. "I would."

"Fuck. Okay. Yeah, I'll call them up right now."

As Gus hurried to the phone, I called after him, "Yo, let them in first, man!"

Clearly flustered and in over his head, Gus smacked a hand over his eyes. "Jesus Christ. I'm not cut out for this shit. Okay, okay, calm the fuck down," he pushed out a few deep breaths and nodded slowly, "okay."

Then, he opened the door.

The applause and cheers from the crowd outside wasn't unlike a barreling train whizzing by. They were so boisterous in their excitement, but maintained a healthy respect and distance for the group of men, as they hurried from the buses and into the shop. Gus locked the door and drew the curtains, allowing them privacy. He busied himself with introductions and a brief tour as I sat down to ready myself and quietly observe these guys before meeting them myself.

They were all heavily inked except for one. It was funny, like one of those *Sesame Street* segments from back in the day—*one of these things isn't like the others*, or some shit like that. I wondered how the hell he'd managed to get roped into a touring gig with these guys, but then again, what must people think when they saw me with Audrey?

Their personalities differed from sagely to quiet and reserved to boisterous bordering on obnoxious. That was the one who approached me first, a blond guy with his hair tied back in a knot. Considering the size of his big arms and a lean everything else, I guessed he was the drummer. Obviously the outgoing one of the bunch, he sauntered over with his hands in his jean pockets, wearing a smirk.

"Blake Carson, I presume," he greeted me, not yet offering his hand.

I nodded, unraveling a roll of paper towels and tearing them into sheets. "That'd be me."

"Too cool to come say hi to us, huh?"

My eyes met his. "I don't give anybody special treatment," I replied, not caring who he was or what he did for a living.

"Well, that's pretty fucking rude."

This day was already off to an amazing start. I was devoting my Saturday to ink these hotshot rock stars who had the audacity to call the night before they wanted to come in, and now this guy was giving me an obnoxious attitude.

Furrowing my brow, I cocked my head and began to speak, "Well, sorry to—" But I was cut off by his laugh and a smack against my shoulder.

"Holy fuck, dude. *Relax.* I'm just messing with ya," he said, gripping my arm and giving me a friendly shake. "I'm Sebastian and I like to fuck with people, it's what I do."

"Kick him in the balls if he pisses you off. He likes it," another guy said, approaching me. He spoke with a more southern accent.

"Noted," I said, allowing a laugh as I opened a drawer to pull out some inks.

"Anyway, I just wanted to thank you for making time for us. We don't usually pull the celebrity card."

"'Cause we're not dicks," the southern guy added, "I'm Chad, by the way."

"Nice to meet you guys," I said.

"We grabbed this month's *ModInk*, saw your shit, and had to stop by while we were in the area," Sebastian explained.

"Which is only for the weekend, unfortunately," the tallest of the bunch tacked on as he headed into the back. This one I recognized as Devin, the ringleader and the head honcho. "Although a few of us don't live too far. We could've come up if you couldn't fit us in."

I shook my head. "Nope, you guys are good," I said, standing up to snap my gloves off and finally shake their hands. "Blake."

"Devin," he answered, but I already knew that. I expected he realized but introduced himself anyway and I liked that. It was humble and relatable, to not assume that the world would instantly know his name.

I was introduced to the others—Tyler and Jon, the tattoo virgin—and I set to work, briefly consulting each of them to get a feel for what they'd like. I didn't have time to sketch anything out, since I wasn't working with a whole lot of time. But when I told them I was going rogue with some freehand work, they seemed even more enthusiastic and ready to get started. And so was I.

My cell rang in the middle of the first tattoo, a sooty moon and stars on Chad's shoulder blade. It was Audrey and I apologized for the interruption as I pulled my gloves off to answer.

"I'm so sorry," she immediately said, sounding breathless. "Jake needs you for something and he's—"

374

"Is he giving you a hard time?"

"Oh, no! Not at all. But he's being a little, um, resistant and says he needs you. I told him you're working, but he's really adamant. I'm so sorry," she repeated.

I glanced around at the shop full of guys. Strangers who didn't know me and didn't understand my situation. But intuition told me they were good men with big hearts and I quickly made a decision.

"It's fine. Bring him over here."

"Are you sure? We don't have to. I can distract him."

"No, it's okay. He'll never let it go if you don't, and then he'll give my parents a hard time." The thought was tempting, but the last thing I wanted was for them to punish him for it. "Just come down. Text me when you get here and I'll unlock the backdoor."

"Okay," she relented. "We'll be there in a couple of minutes."

I hung up and Chad glanced over his shoulder as I pulled a fresh pair of gloves on. "Your girl?" he asked knowingly.

"Yeah," I nodded, picking my machine up and situating my foot on the pedal, "she has to stop by with my brother really quick. I hope you guys don't mind. He just needs to—"

"Dude, we're good," he replied with a smile. "It's nice enough you came in. None of us can expect your life to just stop 'cause of us."

I chatted with him for a bit before Audrey came by. He was a dad of two, married to his best friend, and currently adding a third bathroom to his house in Texas. He explained briefly that with his chronic illness, Ulcerative Colitis, he felt he needed one to himself. "But livin' with three women, I'm thinkin' about adding a fourth," he laughed and shook his head, "one for each of us."

The more we talked, the more I found I liked and understood him. It struck me hard that, after years of tattooing in near silence, I'd been missing out on so many stories from my clients. The different walks of life, the varying circumstances that'd brought them to my chair. It was a shameful moment, to realize all of those wasted opportunities, and I made a split decision to change. Again.

Audrey texted me that they were there, and I announced apologetically that it was time for a momentary break. Chad insisted it was cool and took the moment to grab his phone and text his wife.

I unlocked the backdoor and Audrey, Jake, and Freddy walked inside.

"Hey," she greeted me, standing on her toes to press a kiss to my jaw.

"Hey, guys. I can't talk for long."

"Did you hear your brother, Jake? We can't be here long," Audrey spoke to him with a kind firmness. "Remember, Mickey is in the car. He's waiting. Okay?"

"We won't be here long. Not long." Jake nodded and glanced through the breakroom to the open workstation. Right in his line of sight was Chad and Jake pointed. "He's blue like Blake."

With that mention, I thought about the piece I was working on, the moon and stars. I remembered the idea Shane had pitched the night before and in a trance, I moved through the breakroom and stood above Chad's shoulder, assessing and working out the details in my mind. I visualized a splashy watercolor background, a muted blue mixed with grey, to highlight the grit with something beautiful.

Nodding slowly, I asked, "Hey, Chad, you mind if I add some color to this?"

He glanced over his shoulder at me and shook his head. "You're the artist, dude. I'm your canvas. Do whatever you wanna do to me."

"Awesome." I grinned, finding a new excitement in my work, and turned to find Jake standing in the breakroom doorway. He was eyeballing the shop full of strange men, Devin specifically.

"He's purple," he announced, pointing. "Bright, bright, bright purple."

"Oh, yeah?" I asked, remembering that purple auras typically belong to spiritual, creative types.

Devin lifted his head from the tablet he was using and smiled at Jake. "Well, now there's two of 'em," he said, making the typical twin comment. Then, he looked to me and asked, "What's with the color thing?"

"Jake sees auras," I told him.

Devin nodded. "So, my aura is purple?"

Sebastian laughed. "He matches his wife's hair! How fucking cute."

"That's actually kinda crazy," Devin said, still nodding thoughtfully. "Add some purple to mine. That'd be cool."

And so, Jake went around the room announcing their colors to me. Tyler was green, Sebastian was orange, and Jon, the quiet tattoo virgin, was pink. Every one of them treated Jake with gratitude and kindness and all shook his hand. Audrey stood back with her hands gripping Freddy's shoulders, keeping him from interfering as the two of us inadvertently worked with Devin and his band.

When we'd been around the entire room, I brought Jake once again to the back exit. Audrey asked if he still needed to tell me something, and he thought about it intently for a moment, before shaking his head.

"That was all," he said with an affirmative nod.

"So, you *knew* you had to come here to do this?" I asked, crossing my arms and trying so hard to figure this shit out.

He nodded again. "Yes. That's why Audrey drove Mickey and me and Freddy here."

"I see."

"You do now," he stated with sage and wisdom, and I didn't bother to fight it as I replied, "I do now."

Reaching out with both arms, Jake pulled me in for a big, encompassing hug that caught the breath in my lungs and tripped the heart in my chest. Overwhelmed by an emotion caught between contentedness and concern, I hugged him back, touching my nose to his shoulder and patting his back.

"Love you, buddy," I whispered, bringing my hand to touch the back of his head.

"I love you, Blake." He rocked from side to side, an act leaning toward playful. Then, he said, "It's going to be okay. Don't be sad. Don't be worried. It will be okay."

My heart stopped with the eerie tone in his voice. "What?"

"Don't be sad. Don't be worried. It—"

"No, I heard you," I pushed away and gripped his shoulders in my hands, "but what are you talking about?"

Jake smiled and mimicked me, pressing his palms to my arms. "Don't be sad. Don't—"

"What's gonna happen, buddy?"

Then, just as quickly as the smile appeared, it vanished. There was nothing left of his happiness, and all that was left was the disturbing look of clarity as he replied, "When I go away again."

***

I finished the band's tattoos with the difficult distraction of Jake's words hanging heavily over my head. I managed to chat through the guilt and anger corroding my veins and smiled through the constant reminder that he knew. He knew our parents were sending him away and that they were putting him in a facility. *He knew*. And, he'd spoken as though he had accepted it with such a simple ease, like that was the only option we had, and maybe it was. Maybe I needed to accept it myself, move on with my life, and settle into a new normal. But I didn't have the faith he had, in somehow knowing everything would be okay. Because in the deepest pit of my gut, I knew it wouldn't be.

Audrey had come back to the shop and kept herself busy by chatting with the guys as they waited to get tattooed or for the others to be finished. She unabashedly gushed over Devin's talent and the piece I had done on his calf, a sketchy black daisy on a backdrop of purple-grey watercolor. She giggled relentlessly as the day went on, filling the air with something other than Gus's music picks and the warnings spiraling through my head. And when the day was over, she asked if anybody was hungry with an offer to grab some food if we were interested.

Devin shook his head apologetically. "We have dinner in the bus but thank you. It's been a real pleasure hanging out with you guys today." Then, he handed me a card with his personal number. "Let me know if you ever wanna come to a show, man. We got you covered."

"And don't you worry," Sebastian chimed in. "We'll be back for more ink. I still got some space … somewhere."

They left and Gus slinked from his office. He exhaled exhaustedly like he'd been the one doing back-to-back tattoos for the past twelve hours. When he clapped his hand against my back, he said, "You did good today, kid. You handled yourself way better than I could. You should be proud."

I was surprised to find myself nodding, because dammit, I *was* proud. I had done some of my best work yet on those guys, they'd all had a positive experience, and I'd made in them repeat customers. There wasn't much more I could ask for than that.

Audrey wrapped herself tightly around my arm and asked if I was ready to head home. I didn't know if she meant her place or mine, but it also didn't matter. They both felt comfortable, both felt like home, so I nodded.

"Yeah," I said, leading her toward the door. "Let's go."

Chapter Thirty-One

"HAVE YOU EVER been in a serious relationship before?" Audrey asked over dinner, gripping her burger in two hands and smirking mischievously. "I mean, besides this one."

"Oh, is that what this is?" I lifted a brow before taking a bite of my grilled chicken wrap.

"We've already exchanged I love you's. That's pretty serious," she pointed out.

"Hmm," I nodded thoughtfully as I chewed. "You make a good point."

"So?"

I shrugged and laid my wrap down to exchange it for a fry. "Not really. I had a girlfriend in college for about a year—"

"A year? That's not exactly a short period of time," Audrey laughed, wiggling in her seat with excitement. "What was she like?"

"You really want to hear about my ex-girlfriend?" I somehow doubted that. I'd always been under the impression women didn't care to hear about previous relationships. Yet Audrey nodded eagerly, and my cheeks puffed with my exhale. "Okay, well, her name was Lori. She was an art major and we met in one of our shared classes. Things were good, until I brought her home to meet my family."

"What happened then?"

I shifted in my seat and diverted my gaze to look out the window. It was snowing. The world was layered in a thin blanket of white dust and looked nearly picturesque from inside the restaurant. The conversation, the memories it inspired, made me want to be out there in the numbing cold and wintry hush. But Audrey believed it was better to face the pain than to bury it alive, and I felt her hand against mine, ripping me away from the urge to run.

"Blake?"

"Yeah?"

"What happened?"

"My mom talked me into breaking up with her," I stated simply before I could think better of it.

Audrey appeared taken aback as she lowered her burger to the plate. "What do you mean?"

"She, uh … she initially acted like she was cool with her. You know, she talked about how nice she was, how pretty, whatever. Until she saw that I actually liked her, like, um …"

"Like it could last?" Audrey offered gently.

"Yeah," I nodded, "exactly. That was when she cornered me and started mentioning all these things I should be careful about. Like the fact that she, uh … that she … um …" I stalled, faltering as I remembered the dinner at my parents' house, when Mom had mentioned being concerned about Audrey's relationship with her ex. I shook my head and clapped a hand over my eyes as I muttered, "I am the biggest fucking idiot on the goddamn planet."

"What are you talking about?"

Dropping my hand to the table, I looked her in the eye and said, "She did the same thing with you."

"With *me*?"

"Yeah. She told me to be careful of you, because you have a good relationship with your ex."

Audrey's mouth fell open in shock. "I don't ... what the ..." She closed her mouth and shook her head before beginning again. "You don't really think that, do you?"

"Hell no," I replied and meant it. "But that's what she's always done. And I don't know if it's that she doesn't want me happy, or if it's because she sees outsiders as a threat, or what. I have no fucking clue. I just can't believe it's taken me so long to see what a fucking evil witch she is."

"I think it's sad," she admitted quietly.

"Yeah," I nodded, "so do I."

"You know," she went on, "just because things aren't great right now between you two, doesn't mean they never can be. She's still your mom, and maybe one day, when this is all behind you, you can find it in your heart to forgive her."

I scoffed, shaking my head. "I spent a long time hating myself because she manipulated me to do just that. You think I'm ever going to find an inch of forgiveness for her, at any point in my life?"

"I'm just saying, you never know."

I smiled affectionately at the nearly innocent look of hope on her face. "You have way more faith than I'll ever have."

Audrey returned the smile and took another bite of her burger. "All I'm saying is, you never know."

***

I woke up abruptly to a dark room and an eerie quiet. It was midnight and the house was still around me and Audrey still slept soundly beside me with her arm over my chest and her leg wrapped around mine. Snow pattered outside, landing in whispers against the window. Everything seemed calm and perfect, and yet, nothing felt right.

I focused intently on my body. Maybe it'd been something I ate, maybe the food had been bad. Yet my stomach was fine, without nausea or pangs. I didn't have a headache, backache, toothache, or any other kind of ache to speak of.

With a deep breath, I closed my eyes and tried to go back to sleep. I urged my worried mind to find contentedness in the woman at my side, the comfortable bed at my back, and the peaceful lullaby of the snowfall outside. It was winter, the season I loved about as much as autumn, and the brunt of my life was good. There was nothing to be worried about in this moment, and I just needed to go back to sleep.

But I couldn't. It seemed impossible to find the calm I so desperately sought, and the longer I laid there, the harder my heart began to beat toward a panic. Finally, I let out an agitated huff and sat up in bed. Audrey's arm dropped from my chest and I scrubbed my hands over my face.

"Fuck," I muttered, pulling my knees up. "What the hell?"

"What's wrong, Blake?" Audrey asked groggily, now curling her arm around my waist.

"I can't sleep," I explained weakly, as I laid a hand against her hip. "Sorry for waking you up."

"No, it's okay," she assured me. "You want some tea? Maybe that would help."

"Yeah …" I nodded at the idea. "Yeah, I think I'll do that."

She nodded in her sleepy haze and rolled away. "Okay, I'll get the kettle boil—"

I chuckled and caught her before she could leave the bed. "No, you go back to sleep. I got it."

Humming, she nodded again. "Don't be gone long."

"I'll come right back," I promised.

In the kitchen, I waited for the water to boil, desperately trying to ignore the trepidation making itself at home in my gut and mind. It felt insane, how unsettled I was over absolutely nothing. The house was fine. Audrey was fine. I was fine. Everything was fine. I gritted my teeth, planting my palms firmly against the counter as I repeatedly chanted in my head. *Everything is fine. Everything is fine.* The mantra was on a continuous loop, in hopes that something would click, and I'd manage to shake this horrific dread I couldn't pinpoint.

JAKE. The microwave clock read 12:22 when the thought hit me as I poured the boiling water into my mug. It came as a bellowing shout, presenting itself in big, bold letters as black as the water surrounding the tea strainer of loose leaves. My hands started to shake and I put the hot kettle down on the counter before my vision blurred too much to see what I was doing.

I ran from the kitchen to grab my phone, but when I got to the bedroom, it was already ringing. Audrey was sitting up in bed, bewildered as I burst into the room and snatched my phone from the nightstand to find my dad calling.

"Blake?" she asked, her voice trembling. She was scared.

So was I.

I didn't respond to her as I quickly answered the phone. "Dad?"

I waited for his voice to say something to me, anything, but it didn't come right away. First, I heard someone else. Someone I didn't recognize.

"Ma'am, I understand. I need you—"

Then, my mother's voice, shouting, "Don't you tell me to calm down! I can't ... I can't ..." She was crying, sobbing, and unable to control herself.

My heart couldn't possibly beat any harder, or any faster, without exploding. "Dad?" I repeated, once again going ignored.

"Diana," Dad spoke, forcing a calm that wasn't coming naturally. "Go with them. I'll meet you there. Okay?"

Then, he acknowledged me. "Blake, listen to me—"

"What the fuck is going on?" I blurted, my voice strained and choked. "Dad, I want you to tell me right now what—"

"Listen to me!" he barked without the intent to be cruel, but to shock me into shutting the fuck up. "I don't have time right now, Blake. I just need you to get to the hospital. Okay? Are you listening to me?"

My legs felt weak, so tired and fragile, and I dropped to sit at the edge of the bed. Audrey hurried to kneel beside me, wrapping an arm around my shoulders and wiping her hand against my face, and it was then that I realized I was crying.

"Dad, what the fuck happened?"

"Blake, *please* just do what I'm telling you," he begged exhaustedly, his voice cracking.

"What happened?" I pleaded with him.

Dad sighed, clearing his throat and coughing before saying, "Jake …" The name came out fragmented, splintered with pain, and I laid a hand over my eyes to catch the dripping pieces of my broken heart.

***

The world was a blur of white snow and bright lights, a palette of blinding beauty, muddied by the chilled, ugly black eating away at my heart. Audrey drove to the hospital, careful to remain calm and not speed, but I still caught her stepping on the gas a few times as she struggled to keep her composure.

We didn't know what was going on. My father hadn't confirmed, when I demanded to know, if Jake was okay. He had simply told me to get to the hospital as quickly as I could, and so that's what we did. We were barely dressed when we ran from the house and into the car, with Audrey in her flimsy pajamas and me in a pair of sweatpants and my leather jacket. She had at least thought to grab her flip-flops, while I was only in socks but did I care? Did I feel the cold seeping through the cotton to freeze my heels and toes? No.

Because all I could think about was, I should've been there. I should've never let him go back to my parents' house. I should've been more attentive, more aware, more proactive in keeping him separated from them. Why hadn't I gone to the cops the moment I knew my mother had been a manipulative bitch for so long? What could the cops have even done? I didn't know, but it seemed like an appropriate response to finding out I'd suffered emotional and mental abuse for over twenty years. Why couldn't I have been a better brother, a better protector, a better ... a better ... better...

Why couldn't I have just been *better*?

"Blake," Audrey cut through the deafening silence with urgent concern and reached out to grip my thigh.

I was shaking all over. My teeth clacked together, my hands clenched and trembled, and my legs jounced relentlessly. I willed my limbs, my jaw, my lungs to find calm and resume control but they wouldn't stop, they couldn't stop. They would never stop until I knew what the fuck had happened to my brother.

"Blake, talk to me."

I shook my head. I was scared to speak, or even to open my mouth, scared to know what might come out.

Would I puke all over the dashboard? Would I scream like a broken animal? Would I speak with an unsettling amount of control?

"We're almost there, okay?"

I nodded and a fresh batch of tears welled in my eyes. Fuck. I wanted to be there, wanted to know what had happened, wanted to know what was happening *now*. And yet ... I didn't. I didn't want to face whatever the fuck was going on. I didn't want to be at the hospital. I didn't want to see my parents, didn't want to find Jake hurt or—

"W-w-what if he's d-dead?" I spoke aloud for the first time since hanging up on my father. I turned to face her, eyes wide and wild, without any attempt to stop the tears from spilling and soaking my face. "What i-if he's fucking *dead*?"

"Blake," she whispered, then swallowed. Her eyes glassed over and she blinked rapidly. "Don't say that."

"What if he is? What the fuck do I do?"

"Don't think about it right now," she commanded, hardening her tone.

"I-I'll fucking kill them. I will fucking crush them, Audrey. I'll fucking b-b-break their goddamn necks and—"

"*Blake!*" Her hands smacked against the steering wheel. "Blake. Let's just try to calm down and find out what happened, okay? Please, just ... just try to calm down. Just breathe."

"Breathe," I repeated, snickering and shaking my head. And why the fuck could I not stop crying? How the fuck did I have so many tears in me? How the fuck had they not dried out yet? "I can't fucking breathe."

But somehow, I managed, sucking in the air and puffing it out, and by the time we pulled into the hospital parking lot, I had calmed my lungs to something manageable. Audrey parked the car and held my hand as we hurried through the sliding doors into the emergency room on legs that moved too slow.

We found my father meandering aimlessly in a corner of the large room, full of people waiting and complaining. Their voices all blended together into an annoying cacophony as I released Audrey's hand, ignoring her insistence to hold on, and moved quickly with my sights set on my dad's straight face.

"Blake!" Audrey shouted, alerting a few people to our presence. "Stop!"

"Where the fuck is he?" I demanded, grabbing my father by the arm and forcing him to look me in the eye with a jerk.

"Mom's with him," he replied, emotionless.

My grip tightened on his arm, yanking him closer to me. "Answer my fucking question! Where the fuck—"

"Blake," he interrupted, shaking his head. "It's not good."

I continued to hold his arm but my fingers loosened. "Don't say that. Don't you dare—"

"Mom got into a fight with him," Dad explained, looking right through me, his stare was so blank. He was in shock, barely blinking and barely breathing. "He wanted to go home, he said. He wanted to be with you, he only ever wanted to be with you. He said he hated us,

391

and Mom sent him to bed. We didn't know he was gone. We didn't know he left. He took the damn dog. That fucking, fucking dog ... Jesus, Mickey ..."

I watched in crippled horror as my father fell apart, his face crumpling as he stumbled forward to lean against my trembling body. His arms wrapped around me, hugging so tightly, I thought he'd crush me. Tears hit the leather on my shoulder, pattering rapidly as he cried and struggled to catch his breath.

"I-I'm so sorry. I'm so, so, so sorry. My fucking God. I'm so sorry." Who he was apologizing to, I didn't know. It could've been me. Could've been Jake, Mickey, or even God, for all I knew. But it didn't matter. What mattered was that he was sorry, and he was in pain and so was I.

I hugged him back. I held him and he held me, holding each other up when otherwise we'd fall. I forgot Audrey was there, standing behind me, until her hand gently touched my shoulder.

"Blake," she whispered, afraid to penetrate the moment that was so simultaneously heartbreaking and precious.

Quickly, I stepped away from my father, as I wiped at my eyes, and saw my mother enter the ER waiting room. She looked about ten years older from the last time I'd seen her on Thanksgiving, all frail and ready to shatter. She approached us like a ghost, her feet barely moving along the floor, until she stood in front of us. Her eyes moved from my father to me, and then to Audrey, when she curled her lips into a snarl.

"Why the fuck are you here?" she spat through gritted teeth.

"Don't you talk to her like that," I immediately reacted, raising my voice and stepping between my mother and girlfriend.

"She shouldn't be here. I never said for her to be here." She turned to my father, replacing her hurt with anger, and snapped at him, "Why the hell is she here, Paul? She's not family!"

"Diana," he muttered, lowering his gaze to the floor. "Just stop. Please. Just stop. Tell us what's going on."

"I won't say a damn thing in front of her."

I moved forward and backed my mother into a wall boasting a poster about keeping the ER clean. She gasped as I towered over her, and I realized that she was scared. Scared and terrified of her own son, and all I could think was, *good.*

"We wouldn't even be here if it weren't for you!"

"Blake, stop," Audrey said, grasping my arm and pulling me back.

I shrugged her off but didn't say anything else as I waited for my mother to speak. "Don't you dare blame me. Don't you dare put this on me! You are the *last* person who should be blaming me!" she cried as tears zigzagged along her cheeks and dripped into her mouth. Then, she sputtered, "Don't you fucking—"

A throat being cleared grabbed our attention, and we turned to face a doctor. He wore an expression so grim, I thought of him as an angel of death, here to deliver the bad news.

"Mr. and Mrs. Carson," he spoke to my parents, eyeing me warily. "I'm afraid I—"

"Oh, God. Oh, no," Mom pushed out between trembling breaths, and to my astonishment, Audrey rushed to her. She wrapped her arms around my mother's shoulders, holding her tightly, and Mom didn't shove her away.

The doctor stood, patient and waiting, before continuing, "It doesn't look good. He flatlined and we thought we'd lost him." I choked on an immediate surge of bile, rampaging through my throat to meet my tongue. Swallowing and gasping, I pinched my eyes and forced myself to listen. "We brought him back, but I'm afraid it doesn't look promising. As of right now, the machines are all that's keeping him alive."

My mother combusted with a sob, holding on to Audrey and crying. My father backed into the wall, using it to hold himself up before he gave in to the need to collapse. My eyes remained affixed on the doctor, on the cold, clinical look on his face as he spoke of my brother, not by name but by his gender. He spoke of Jake like he was just a body, a body on a table to try and save. And if he couldn't, oh well, there were others. There'd always be others. But Jake wasn't just a body, he was my fucking brother, and this asshole with his white coat and nametag was standing here, instead of saving his fucking life.

"So, why the fuck aren't you saving him?" I fired at him, tensing my fists at my sides.

The doctor shook his head. "Sir, we've done all—"

"Don't tell me you've done all you can do!"

He sighed morosely. "I am telling you that, because I promise you, I have. It's up to him now."

I shook my head and looked away. At a time when I was so dangerously close to shattering into a thousand pieces, I felt unreasonably proud that I'd turned around to face the wall, instead of thrusting my fist through his face.

Dad cleared his throat and wiped at the tears staining his cheeks. "Can we, um, can we see him?"

"He's in a coma," the doctor informed us. "But yes, you can see him."

The words rose to my mouth and I spat them out through clenched teeth. "He has a name."

"What was that?"

I whirled on my heel, forgetting I was only wearing socks—*why the hell hadn't I grabbed my fucking shoes?*—and nearly fell on my ass as I faced him. "I *said*, he has a fucking name, you son of a bitch."

The doctor's face was now etched with a sympathetic pain that told me maybe he had a heart inside his cold, crisp exterior. But still, he said, "Sir, I understand what you're going through, but if you can't calm—"

"You're not listening to me," I shouted, stepping toward him. I hardly noticed that Audrey had released my mother and was now turned to me, reaching out to grab my arm and saying my name. "He has a fucking name. Just use his fucking name. None of this he, him bullshit; use his fucking *name*!"

The doctor swallowed as he nodded once. "I understand. But if you cannot calm down, I'm going to need you to leave."

"Oh, my God," I laughed darkly. "You can't just say his goddamn name. Do you even know what it is? Do you even care what it is? Does anybody fucking—"

"Sir, I'm gonna ask you to come with me," a deeper, authoritative voice said from behind me. I looked over my shoulder at the security guard with his hand resting on the taser at his belt.

I never stopped to realize that I was behaving like a raving lunatic. I never once took a look at my own erratic behavior and thought to stop. Neither of my parents said a damn thing as I left the emergency room of my own accord, walking with an angry purpose to drop myself on the curb just outside of the sliding doors. The cold was bitter in a dark world full of bright snow where the slush accumulating along the sidewalk seeped through my socks and to my feet. Yet, I didn't feel it. I felt nothing but the agony chewing its way through my skin and tendons and bones, and I felt it all so deeply. So internally, beyond my physical self, that I knew, without a doubt, there was more to me than this sack of skin and bones. I was so much more and it took my brother lying on what could be his death bed for me to realize it.

The quiet slapping of rubber against concrete broke the wintry hush around me. Audrey approached in her unseasonal flip-flops and sat beside me on the curb. "Blake, I talked to them. They said—"

"I want you to leave," I blurted out, hanging my head.

"No, you don't."

I sucked in a deep breath that I hoped would bring me clarity, but it didn't. "Yes," I nodded, "yes, I do."

"You're upset," she stated.

"No fucking shit, Audrey!"

She laid a hand against my shoulder. "Oh, God, Blake, I'm not attacking you."

I thrust my hands out against the backdrop of buildings and sky and shouted, "The whole fucking *world* is attacking me! This entire fucking universe has been attacking me since the day I ruined my brother's life, and all I've ever wanted to do was keep him safe. That's all I was ever supposed to do. That's it! And the *second* I stop to be fucking selfish and live my fucking life for myself, this is what happens."

"Blake, you have no idea what you're saying."

"Jesus fucking Christ, I know exactly what I'm saying!"

"No. You don't," she stated firmly, leaving her hand on my arm. "Why don't we go back inside? I talked to them; they understand. You can come back in and see Jake, but I need you to calm down, okay? Please, just try to calm down."

I shook my head with such a bitter taste in my mouth, I spat bile onto the sidewalk. The world around me felt weird. Unreal and cruel and nearly post-apocalyptic. I looked at the sky through a bleary haze of existential rage and silently asked what the fuck Jake had ever done to deserve this shitty hand he'd been dealt. What the fuck did he do? What the fuck did he ever do to deserve a brother who stole from him, a mother who denied him normalcy, and a father who had turned a blind eye? What the fuck could he have possibly done?

Audrey stood, wrapped her hands around my arm and tugged. "Come on, Blake. Come with me."

Slowly, I shook my head, turning from the sky to look at her and catching a glimpse of that goddamn motherfucking tattoo on her chest. And suddenly, it was so clear, so transparent, and I lifted a finger to touch it. The delicate structure of her sternum was ungiving beneath my touch.

"It all started with *this*," I said to nobody, then I looked at her. "You never knew how to leave me the fuck alone."

"Blake, let's—"

"You could never just leave me the fuck alone! You've always been following me, hounding me, refusing to fucking leave, until I finally give in, and what happens? Everything goes completely to hell!"

She finally let go. "What?"

"Just leave me the fuck alone, Audrey!"

"Why would I do that?"

"Because I'm fucking begging you to," I pleaded through gritted teeth. "I need you to go the fuck away and leave me the fuck alone."

Swallowing, she slowly nodded. "I'll leave," she whispered, cautiously relenting. "But I'm not gone, Blake. Do you understand? I'm not out of your life, I'm just going home."

Home.

I wanted to be home. I wanted to be in my bed and in her arms. I wanted my shoes and blanket, all my things and my tea. I wanted sleep, and above everything else, I wanted my brother. I wanted his music on my stereo. I wanted his movies playing on the TV, Legos all over the living room floor, and pancakes every fucking night for dinner. I wanted his stupid fucking dog shedding all over my house, drooling on the couch, and getting his food on the kitchen floor. And at the thought of Mickey, my hand drooped to my side, scraping my knuckles against the concrete.

"Where's Mickey?" I spoke, my voice rough and broken.

Audrey sank to her knees in front of me. "Mickey died, Blake."

I shook my head furiously. "You don't know that."

But she nodded and reached out with a trembling hand. Her palm grazed my cheek, her fingers aimed for my hair. "Your dad told me."

A sob broke through my lips as I continued to shake my head. "Fuck," I blubbered. "He loves that fucking dog."

"I know ... I know," she whispered, collecting me in her arms.

She stroked her fingers through my hair and listened to me cry and wail. She coddled me, rubbed my back, and rocked with the gentle wind, never mentioning that she was cold and shivering. Never complaining that my fingers were bruising her back. Never letting go until I had settled in an exhausted heap against her shoulder.

Then, she kissed my cheek, my temple, my forehead, my lips, and said, "You're gonna go inside and see your brother. I'm gonna take your car and go home. Do you have your phone?" I could only nod in reply before she continued, "Okay. Call me when you want me to come get you. Okay?"

I nodded again and her lips touched my forehead once more. "Fight for him, Blake," she whispered, and left me alone on the sidewalk.

Chapter Thirty-Two

JAKE HAD TAKEN Mickey and his backpack, filled with his *Gremlins* DVD, iPod, headphones, and stuffed dog—the necessities. Wearing his *Mickey Mouse* pajamas and a black coat, he'd walked two blocks away from my parents' residential neighborhood before reaching a main road. Visibility was low and the roads hadn't been plowed yet. They were slippery from the snow and ice, and by the time the driver saw him and the dog, she couldn't stop fast enough.

She'd hit Mickey first, and according to her account of the accident, Jake hadn't reacted. He'd probably been stunned, frozen, completely unsure of what to do, and she hit him with her Jeep.

The time of impact had been 12:22 in the morning.

The driver, a kind woman named Lacey, had escaped with not a scratch on her body, but a gaping gash across her heart. After calling 9-1-1 and the number on Mickey's collar, Lacey had sat in the snowy road, cradling Jake's bleeding head in her lap, until the ambulance arrived. My parents came shortly after, and that's when Dad had called me.

Now, in a curtained area of the hospital's Intensive Care Unit, I sat with my parents in a foggy silence, caught somewhere between being asleep and awake. I stared forward at my brother's lifeless body, wrapped in bruises and bandages, and thought, that's what I'd look like if I was dying. It was so fucked up and morbid, but fuck it. That was the truth. That's exactly what I'd look like, and God, how I wished it really was me instead of him.

As angry as I'd been, the doctors really had done everything they could. They had repaired his lung, punctured by two fractured ribs. Had sewn up the cut across his forehead and stitched all the minor scratches on his face and hands. They'd also set and casted his broken leg and ankle, with a warning that he'd likely need further surgery if he pulled through.

If he pulled through …

It was the head injury that really had them worried. The swelling and bleeding on his brain had been alleviated as much as the doctors could, but to say they weren't hopeful for his survival was an understatement. And even if he did make it through the morning, they'd said, there was no guaranteeing that he'd wake up. "If he does get very lucky—and I mean, very lucky," the doctor had said, "there's no telling how much damage has been done, especially given the condition of his brain before the accident. Something like this would likely be catastrophic."

Considering that Jake's luck hadn't been all that great since the ripe old age of ten, I wasn't so confident in his chances now, but I was hoping. I was hoping, and hoping, and if anybody was out there to hear me, I hoped it was paying off.

Dad glanced at me from his chair. "Why don't you go home and try to sleep?"

Looking from Jake's body to Dad's face, I gestured toward the bed. "You're kidding, right? I can't sleep right now."

"I know," he replied, "but you should try. Call Audrey and have her pick you up. We'll tell you if anything changes."

As I looked back to Jake and heard again the whoosh of the machine pushing air in and out of his lungs, my throat tightened and my chest immediately felt like it'd burst. Fuck, I didn't want to cry, not again, but how could I even think of sleeping in my comfortable bed while he was fighting for his life? That's what I should've been doing, that was my job. But what the fuck could I do now?

"I don't wanna leave him," I admitted in a broken whisper.

Dad reached out and gripped my arm. "I know, and he knows that, too. But you're no good to him when you're so tired."

"What about you guys?"

"We'll take shifts," Mom said softly, meeting my eyes with something close to affection.

So, reluctantly, I nodded and called Audrey. I stayed at Jake's side as I waited, just in case, hoping he'd wake up or show some sign of life, but there was none. When Audrey texted to let me know she was there, I held his hand, leaned in close to his ear, and whispered through a throat clotted with tears, "You better not die on me, buddy, you got it? I love you. Don't fucking die."

I slumped into the car and kept my eyes on the sunny sky. It was uncharacteristically warm on this winter day and all the snow had melted. If this was some kind of a joke, it wasn't funny.

"How is he?" Audrey asked quietly, turning down the volume of her music. Some country station she insisted on keeping programmed in my car.

"Still alive," I muttered.

"That's something," she assured me, reaching out to rest her hand against my leg.

We drove toward Salem and I began to think about all of Jake's things. His toys, movies, and puzzles. Mickey's bowl in the kitchen. I swallowed at another build-up of emotion and said, "I don't think I can be in that house right now."

"Okay," she replied. "We can go to my place. You have clothes there."

Clothes? I glanced down at my sweatpants, socks, open leather jacket and bare chest beneath. Jesus Christ, I hadn't noticed I'd been like this since arriving at the hospital nearly five hours ago. I laid a hand over my eyes and shook my head, overwhelmed by her thoughtfulness, patience, and unwavering kindness.

"I don't deserve you," I muttered.

"I love you."

"You shouldn't," I insisted. "I'm a fucking wreck."

"Well, I still love you."

"I can't imagine why you'd want a psychopath who can't keep his crap together," I said, remembering how I screamed at her outside of the hospital. "I can't imagine why you'd want a guy who gets so defensive and flips out when shit really hits the fan."

"But that's who you are," she whispered, glancing at me. "You fight hard and love even harder, and that's what I want. I want *you*."

I relented with a silent nod and she drove us the rest of the way to her house. Her mother was surprised to see us pull up to the curb, and upon seeing my disheveled state, asked urgently what had happened. Audrey promised she'd talk to her later, but first, she led me to her bathroom and helped me undress like I couldn't do it myself. Hell, I wasn't sure if I could. She ran the shower, took off her clothes, and pulled me under the spray of water to wash my hair and scrub away the morning's tears and pain. She dried me off, helped me into clean clothes, brought me to her bed and ordered me to lie down. I listened and waited as she made me some toast and tea, with an insistence that I should get something in my stomach. When she returned, I could only stare at her, feeling both bewildered and unworthy.

I hadn't asked her to do this, none of this, or any of the things she'd done in the months I'd known her. But she did it anyway, and with so much grace and selflessness, that through knowing her, I knew God must exist. Because while someone as fucked-up as me could exist in this world, there was also her, so brilliantly flawless and beautiful, to love me in spite of it all and to

405

balance out every one of my imperfections. And that was perfect, and only a perfect being could make sure of something like that.

"I'm glad you didn't leave," I said frankly, as she crawled into bed beside me.

"What do you mean? When?"

"Ever," I stated, wrapping my arms around her and burrowing my face against her chest.

"I left you today," she whispered, guilt-ridden and apologetic.

"But you didn't really. You gave me space. That's not the same as leaving altogether," I insisted, allowing her heartbeat to lure me toward sleep. "Don't ever leave me."

"I won't," she promised, stroking her fingers gently through my hair.

"I fucking love you."

"I love you, too, Blake."

**

I woke up disoriented and alone. The room was veiled in darkness and the clock beside the bed read that it was eight at night. How long had I been sleeping? Was it even the same day?

I laid there for a few moments, allowing cognizance to settle in, and when it did, I bolted upright with only one thought on my mind: Jake. Logic told me someone would've woken me up if something had happened, so that wasn't necessarily bad, was it? It meant there hadn't been any change, which was neither bad nor good. And at least he was still here. If he was here, that meant there was a chance and any chance was better than none.

I left the room to find Audrey and her mother sitting on the couch with plates of pizza in hand. Ann looked at me, laying her plate on the coffee table, before standing to approach me.

"Oh, honey, I don't know what to say, except that I'm so sorry," she said, reaching up to wrap her arms around my neck.

Hugging her, I nodded and admitted, "I don't know what to say either, so … thanks."

"You let me know if you need anything, okay? Anything at all. You need dinners? I got you covered. Laundry? Cleaning? Just let me know. Please."

"I will," I assured her, continuing to nod.

Audrey stood up, empty plate in hand, and asked, "Are you hungry? You wanna eat something?"

"Um," my stomach grumbled in reply and I nodded, "yeah, I think I could eat."

She hurried into the kitchen to grab me a slice. Ann released me from her grasp and encouraged me to take a seat. But I'd been laying down for so long, I still wasn't sure how long I'd been sleeping. I needed to do something proactive, something useful.

"Hey, Audrey, where's my phone?" I asked, sweeping my gaze over the living room.

"Oh, it's right here," she called to me, and a few moments later, she came back into the living room with a slice of pizza and my phone in hand. "I charged it while you were sleeping."

407

I thanked her sincerely, kissing her forehead before finally taking a seat. I ate, surprised to find myself so hungry, as I checked my phone for messages. Both of my parents had texted me periodically, giving me the infrequent updates throughout the day.

"How's he doing?" Audrey asked, sitting beside me.

After reading the last message and breathing a sigh of relief, I told her, "Well, he's still in the coma, but the swelling on his brain has gone down significantly."

"That's good!" Ann chimed in optimistically.

"Yeah," I nodded, "Dad said that, even though Jake's definitely not out of the woods, things are looking better than they did before." I put the phone down and scrubbed a hand over my chin as I went on, "I mean, even if he pulls through and wakes up, there's no guaranteeing what kind of damage has been done, but—"

"Stop," Audrey cut in gently, moving closer and propping her chin on my shoulder. "Take the good news and let yourself feel happy about it before you shoot it down."

"I'm just being realistic," I replied, touching my head to hers.

"Yeah, honey, I know," Ann said. "And I know you don't want to get your hopes all the way up either, but it never hurt to be just a little hopeful."

They were right, I knew they were, so I allowed myself a moment to read the text from my father again. The one in which he told me the swelling had decreased and things were looking better, complete with a praying hands emoji. Dad never used emojis and I took it as a good sign.

Signs. Souls. Fate. Gifts. God.

Jake's ability to see auras had been a gift. Audrey said so, and I believed her now. A slew of breadcrumbs—*signs*—had brought Audrey and me together, and I believed that now, too. I believed that Audrey herself, was a gift to me, the perfect mate to my imperfect soul, and if I believed all of this, then I knew I must also believe in God.

And if I believed in that, then there was a chance that something, whatever it was, was listening. And maybe they—He, Her, It, whatever—would care about what I had to say.

Chapter Thirty-Three

"**B**LAKE," Dr. Travetti greeted me, rushing toward me as I walked into her office forty minutes late. She surprised me with a hug. "God, I'm so sorry."

"Hey, Doc. Doesn't this violate some kind of doctor-patient code or something?"

She stepped back with a roll of her eyes. "I think we can make an exception this time," she quipped, attempting a smile I knew she didn't feel. "I guess it's a stupid question to ask how you've been."

"Uh, yeah," I nodded, walking toward the chair I saw as mine. "I'd say that'd be a pretty stupid question."

"How is Jake? Any improvements since your call last night?"

I shook my head solemnly. "No. He's still on life support, but he's alive."

"Well, that's a good thing," she encouraged. "How are you handling everything?"

I pursed my lips and considered the question before replying, "I completely lost my shit initially."

"Of course."

"But, I don't know. I guess I've had a little time to process. Or maybe I'm just numb."

She nodded slowly with understanding. "That's perfectly normal, Blake. Everything you're going through is *absolutely* normal."

Then, I asked, "Is it also normal to wanna pray?"

Cocking her head with curious intrigue, she slowly nodded. "Yes. I would say it is."

"What about you?" I continued, questioning. "Have you ever prayed?"

"I have, but, Blake, this—"

"I don't know how," I admitted. The confession left me feeling embarrassed for some silly reason. "I thought about asking Audrey, but old habits die hard, I guess, so I'm asking you first."

Dr. Travetti smiled ruefully. "Blake, we've known each other for a long time now, and I realize you don't know much about me. It would be unprofessional for me to sit here every week and delve into stories about *my* day or *my* past, so I don't. But, given your question and what you're going through right now, I think I can make an exception."

Leaning back in my chair, my curiosity piqued, I gestured for her to go on. "I'm listening."

Setting aside her clipboard, she crossed her legs tightly and began, "I lost someone very special to me a few years ago. We didn't have the bond that you and Jake have, this person wasn't my brother or sister, but I believed they were my soulmate. They were also sick, and I knew what I was getting myself into when I met them. But it didn't matter at the time, because we were so in love and I had myself convinced that love alone could keep them alive. But it couldn't, and they died."

Dropping my gaze to my clasped hands, I swallowed at my emotions and uttered, "Fuck, Doc. I'm so sorry."

"You can't plan for how much it's going to hurt to lose them, even if you know ahead of time that it's coming," she went on, casting another shred of light over her hidden past. "And after they were gone, I felt very alone and distant from my patients. I, um, had a hard time talking to people when all *I* wanted was to talk to someone. So, because I didn't have many people in my life at the time, I talked to God instead.

"I told Him about my pain and my problems. I asked Him to send messages to … this person I had lost. I begged Him to send me a sign, to make me feel like I had a purpose again, and …" She cleared her throat and rubbed at her nose, obviously stalling.

"What happened? Did He answer?"

Dr. Travetti nodded as she shifted uncomfortably in her chair. "I actually, um … I actually believe He sent me you."

Furrowing my brow, I asked, "Huh?"

She let loose a watery laugh, and dammit, I actually thought she might cry. "I was at the end of my rope. It had been almost a year since she … this person had passed away and I had received nothing. No signs, no … messages from beyond, absolutely nothing. So, one night, after having quite a bit to drink, I yelled at God and told Him that if he couldn't bring Sabrina back, I needed him to give me something, *anything*, to make my life worth living again. And do you know what happened?"

"What?"

With pen in hand, she pointed at me. "You called me the next day, saying you needed someone to talk to. You didn't have a reason, not at the time, but you just needed someone. And so did I. And I believe that you were my sign."

Slowly nodding, I allowed what she was saying to sink in. "So, that's why you got all testy when I told you I didn't believe in that shit."

Dr. Travetti's cheeks pinked just a bit. "I'm not in the habit of pushing my personal beliefs on patients, but it did make me a little sad, yes."

"I get it," I replied, twisting my hands around each other and trying to think of what to say next. The woman had divulged a piece of herself, something that must've made her feel so vulnerable to me, and I hadn't a clue of what to say back. And then, something hit me. Something so seemingly small, and maybe it was, but I asked anyway. "Wait, what was her name?"

Dr. Travetti shook her head and shooed the question away with a lift of her hand. "I shouldn't have—"

"Seriously, Doc. Please, what was her name?"

Sighing, she tipped her head with impatience and embarrassment coloring her cheeks. "Her name was Sabrina."

My heart began to march in my chest. "I might be overstepping here, but was she Sabrina *Wright*?"

In that moment, Doctor Vanessa Travetti revealed a side of herself to me that I'd never seen before. Her face burned a glowing, bright red, the color of her defensive rage, as she tightened her grip around the pen. Her mouth formed a terse line as her spine went rigid, and all that gave away her blatant hurt underneath, was the glazing of her eyes.

"Blake, how dare you," she pushed from her lips, her voice pulled so tight against the strain in her chest. "How do you know that? Have you been digging up information about me?"

"No," I stated simply and honestly. "I—"

"Why would you do this to me?" she demanded. "Why would you—"

"Doc," I told her hurriedly, "Audrey is Sabrina's sister."

"Audrey? *Your* ... Audrey is ... Audrey Wright?"

As I nodded, Vanessa pressed one hand to her chest as the other dropped the pen to the floor. She covered her mouth to stifle a gasp as her eyes stared blankly toward me, almost as if she'd just seen a ghost. My first instinct was to hug her, to console her, to tell her that this shit was just par for the course in my life, but maybe it wasn't. Maybe this was just the final piece of one big puzzle, all coming together to create something giant and beautiful in the most confusing, unbelievable, and fucked-up way. But, I didn't hug her. She was still my therapist and we were still on the clock.

But, instead, *she* hugged *me*.

"Oh, my God, how is she? How is everybody?" she asked, holding onto me tightly, now realizing I was her only connection to the family of the woman she loved.

"I think you already know how Audrey is," I managed to laugh.

"Oh," she stepped back and cleared her throat, "right. I guess I do."

"This is weird," I was the first to say, and she laughed, nodding in agreement. But then, she added, "It doesn't have to be, for now, but I think you might want to find yourself a new therapist eventually."

I pondered that for a second, considering myself with someone new after all the years I'd been seeing the good doctor. I wondered if I even really needed the therapy anymore, now that I had Audrey, and the truth was, I didn't think so. I no longer thought it was necessary and probably hadn't been for a while, but the thought of not having Dr. Travetti in my life left me feeling off. I didn't want to say goodbye.

"Maybe," I answered. "We'll see what happens."

She nodded understandingly. "With Jake."

"Yeah. Exactly."

"You'll keep me posted, of course."

"Come on, Doc. You know I will."

The session felt over, and so I stood up. I told her I'd see her the following Monday, or maybe sooner, depending on where the week went, and I headed toward the door. She stopped me with my name, and I glanced over my shoulder.

"Blake, about praying …"

"Yeah?"

"Maybe He listens most when you get angry."

I nodded and smirked as I said, "Well, I got plenty of anger to spare."

"Oh, I know," she offered me a smile. "Put it to good use."

I walked the rest of the way to the office entrance, when something Audrey's mom had said weeks ago struck me, the night she'd told me about Sabrina's girlfriend, about how much she'd loved her. I bet she missed her, too.

"Hey, Doc?"

"Yeah, Blake?"

"You should give them a call," I said. "I think they'd really like to hear from you."

Vanessa didn't reply for a few moments, but I waited with my hand on the doorknob, ready to leave. Finally, she coughed and cleared her throat, before saying, "Thank you, Blake. I think I might."

***

Time passed in a monotonous drag, with every day bleeding seamlessly into the next. Audrey had taken the liberty of cancelling all my tattoo appointments for the foreseeable future, until we had a better idea of what was going on, and I was grateful for it. That gave me the freedom to spend every day at Jake's side, watching for the flutter of an eyelid or the twitch of a finger, and when the chair became too uncomfortable, I crawled wearily back to Audrey's place, never mine, to collapse in her bed. It'd become my new routine, but after a week had passed, I found that not having a distraction was a dangerous thing.

I had too much time. Too much time to think, dwell, and obsess. I'd find myself glancing over Jake's body to stare at my mother. The woman who'd seldom acknowledged my existence in the time we'd all been at the hospital. She looked at me like she was sorry, but if she really was sorry, then why couldn't she make more of an effort to make things better? She could've thanked Audrey for dropping off dinner every night. She could've smiled at Freddy when he told her he was sorry. She could've looked me in the eye when she said she'd see me tomorrow. But she never did, and I was pissed.

"Maybe you shouldn't go to the hospital tomorrow," Audrey suggested hesitantly.

I stared at her incredulously. "Are you serious right now?"

Ann ladled beef stew into the bowl in front of me and said, "It's not a bad idea, honey. You've been there all day, every day, for the past week. You need a break."

"Yeah? And what if he wakes up and I'm not there?" I challenged, my tone teetering toward irritation.

"Your folks will call you," Audrey's father, George, assured, meeting my eye and holding my gaze.

"He'll be scared though, and if I'm not there, it'll make it worse."

Ann looked to Audrey for backup, who covered my hand with hers. "You're right, and we know that. But, sweetheart, sitting in that room every day for hours on end isn't helping anything."

I shook my head as my resolve began to buckle. "But if he wakes up—"

417

"Then you'll hurry over there to be with him. But in the meantime, you should at least go home and get some other clothes to wear." She grimaced apologetically, lowering her gaze to the hooded sweatshirt I'd been wearing for nearly a week.

I'd been avoiding my house ever since the accident. Jake was everywhere within those walls, and the thought that he might never walk again, let alone through the door, tore at me in a way I don't think I can describe. I was so afraid that seeing all his things would rip at the wounds and make them deeper, that I would've been all right to never step foot in there again. Still, I knew Audrey was right. My clothing options at her place were limited to only a couple of t-shirts, one pair of jeans, and the sweatpants I'd been wearing the night of Jake's accident. I needed to suck it up and go home, if for only a little while.

"I'll go with you, if you want," Audrey offered.

"No, it's fine." I shook my head, keeping my gaze on the steam curling up from the bowl. There was no way I'd let her take time off from work so close to her holiday break, just to hold my hand while I collected some clothes from my house. It was absurd, even if it did sound tempting.

Ann sat across the table from me and gestured at my dish. "Aren't you hungry, honey?"

"Oh, yeah," I nodded, offering her a smile as I dipped my spoon into the dish. "It smells great."

"Mom likes to add Guinness to her stew," Audrey mentioned.

Pressing a hand to my chest, I said, "Woman after my own heart."

Ann brushed the flattery away with a scoff and a wave of her hand. "Oh, stop it. It's not like I came up with the recipe myself or anything."

"Well, it—"

I was cut off by the chime of a cellphone. Audrey glanced at me anxiously and I shook my head in answer. "Not mine."

"No, it's mine," Ann said, getting up from the table.

"Ann, we're eating dinner," George grumbled, glowering at his wife's back as she headed toward the kitchen counter and retrieved the ringing offender.

"It could be the hospital," she replied pointedly. But then, she gasped and hurried back to the table with the phone in hand. "Oh, my ... George, look at this."

He glanced at the screen and uttered an "oh, wow" as Audrey lifted her head with concern and asked, "Who is it?"

"It's Vanessa," her mother whispered, her face sheet-white, and I lowered my spoon to the table.

I hadn't told the Wright family about Dr. Travetti, not wanting to excite them with something that might never come. I'd left it up to Vanessa, and I was glad she'd made the decision to reach out.

Audrey looked to me with shock and whispered, "She was Sabrina's girlfriend."

Slowly, I nodded as Ann answered the phone. "H-hello?"

The conversation was painfully one-sided as Ann asked Vanessa the usual questions. How she was, how was business, how was the family. But when Ann's voice strained with emotion until it broke, she hurried out of the dining room, and we heard nothing at all.

"I can't believe she called," Audrey whispered as though afraid to speak.

"When was the last time you talked to her?" I asked.

George rubbed his bearded cheek with a palm. "Oh, boy, I guess … I guess it was the funeral." He glanced at Audrey. "That sounds about right, doesn't it?"

Audrey nodded sorrowfully, slowly paddling her spoon through the stew. "Yeah. We didn't see or talk to her again after that."

"Such a shame, too," George went on, sighing and leaning back in his chair. "Her office is right over in Derby Square. She works with a team of doctors now."

Audrey was smart. It was one of the things I loved about her, and I knew that at the mention of the location, she'd put it all together. And she did, making it clear with a quick turn of her head to stare at me with a wide, teary-eyed stare.

"You did this."

"Huh?" George asked as I shrugged and said, "I only made a suggestion. I didn't know what she'd do."

"How did you know?"

Lifting my mouth in a smirk, I shook my head, refusing to tell her with a mutter about doctor-patient confidentiality. Ann returned to the table, her hands clutched around her phone and tears drying on her cheeks. She told George and Audrey that Vanessa wanted to see the family for Christmas Eve, if that was all right with everybody. As Audrey and her father answered with enthusiasm, I silently excused myself from the conversation and returned my attention to my food.

This felt like a family moment. And I wasn't family.

But George lured my attention back by saying, "And we'll plan on you being there, too, Blake, but of course, we know you have to take things day by day right now."

With my mouth open in an embarrassing display of shock, I stammered, "W-wha ...," before swallowing and asking, "I'm sorry, what?"

"Christmas Eve," Audrey clued me in, laying her hand against my back.

Slowly nodding, mildly confused, I answered, "Oh. Right. Yeah, sure."

"Which reminds me," Ann said, grabbing her spoon, "Blake, what size do you wear? I mean, I'm not saying I'm buying you clothes for Christmas, but—"

George snorted. "But she's saying she's buying you clothes for Christmas. And if I were you, I'd keep that information locked up tight."

Ann's jaw dropped in mock offense. "What exactly are you saying?"

"He's saying there's no way you'd pick out anything Blake would actually wear," Audrey said, corroborating with her father.

"You don't know that!" Ann reached across the table and patted my hand. "I mean, how hard can it be? All he wears is black!"

"Hey," I said, having finally collected myself enough to chime in. "I'll have you know, I actually own a red sweater my mom made me wear on Christmas a few years ago."

"Oh, well, excuse me!" Ann laughed, lifting her hands from the table. "I stand corrected."

The exchange was silly, and I assume, damn near meaningless for the average person, but I'd only seen things like this on TV and in movies. If my family had ever shared in moments of playful banter, I couldn't remember them. It was nice, to feel included and wanted. To feel cared for. I found myself smiling, despite the lingering sadness looming overhead, and I relished in the brief reprieve, hoping I could keep it for a while longer.

Hell, maybe I could even keep it for good.

***

"Good night, sweetheart. Love you," Audrey said to Freddy as she hung up the phone. She tucked her feet underneath the blanket and laid beside me. Draping her arm over my chest, she kissed my shoulder and whispered, "Thank you."

I slid my arm beneath her and around the curve of her waist. "What are you thanking me for?"

"Vanessa," she said, her voice just as hushed as before. "I know you won't talk about it, and that's okay. But I just want you to know how much it means to us."

"I just did what anybody else would've done."

Anchoring herself with a hand against my chest, she propped up abruptly and shook her head with furious adamancy. "No, Blake. A lot of people wouldn't have. I mean, I like to think that the majority of people are good, but they're also selfish. They don't step outside of themselves; they can't. But you are a good man, and I love you for it."

She pressed a kiss to my lips and I closed my eyes, holding on tight to what she alone had made me believe that I was—a good man. And hell, maybe I always had been. Maybe all of that guilt and blame had been for nothing, and I just needed this woman to show me that. Everything, all of the good that had come to me these past few months, all the sanity I've managed to hold onto during this week without my brother—it was all because of her. Only her.

My hands sought her face and held on tight as I whispered, "I love you" against her lips. I had said it to her before, and I had meant it, but this felt so much more like an eternal truth. Like what I felt now was too deep and too settled to ever leave. It went beyond my body, beyond the pumping organ in my chest, and made itself at home in the core of my being, made of color and stardust. And fuck, I found it so hard to breathe, so hard to do anything but grip my fingers in her hair and hold on for dear life. Like she was all that was keeping me from drowning.

I parted my lips and coaxed hers open, swallowing her air to keep my lungs working. Her moan was small and delicate as she swung her leg over my hips.

"Is this okay? Are *you* ..." She started to ask if *I* was okay, if my mental state could keep it up, but she didn't have to. The past week had been sexless and cold. But now, I needed it, proven hot and hard against her hips, practically begged for a distraction, a release, anything but the worries flurrying around in my head like the snow glittering the sky. Words wouldn't form on my tongue, it had other things in mind, but I gripped her ass in my desperate hands and pressed her to me until she groaned and devoured my mouth again with a gentle nod of her head.

The open fly of my pajama pants proved to be little hinderance as I pulled Audrey's underwear to the side. We fitted together easily, so comfortably tight and warm, and I sighed with the relief of coming in from the bitter cold. If I had allowed myself to think too much, I would've hated myself for needing sex so badly, while my brother was fighting for his life, but I couldn't let myself think that. Not when this was too good, too soothing, and too necessary for my sanity, as I let her use my body however she wanted. I stared up into her blue eyes, dipping into their oceans and streams to float serenely on my back, until they closed and so did mine. I wondered about her neighbors and parents, and how much they could hear, as I was forced to cry out and her hand clapped over my mouth.

Audrey giggled like we were younger and this was forbidden, taking her hand away from my lips and leaning forward to press her mouth to my ear. "I love you, Blake," she whispered, her words broken with the impact of her climax. "I love you so much, I forget to breathe sometimes."

I pulled in the scent of her hair and nodded, kissing her cheek and her chin and finally her lips. "I know the feeling."

424

"I feel like I should be scared of this," she whispered, now resting her head on the pillow behind my head, her body still covering mine.

"Why?" I threaded my fingers between hers and kissed her knuckles, her palm, her wrist. Just to touch her and remind myself of her warmth and life, to hold onto when I felt cold and so alone in the solitary confines of my tomb of a house.

"Because I know this is it for me, and I don't know if you feel the same way."

My eyes met hers in the darkness. "What if I said I didn't?"

She swallowed hard and gripped my fingers. "I'd still love you, anyway."

I chuckled and shook my head, still unsure of how someone could love me so much. Hell, not even my own mother could manage. "You're something else, you know that?" I laughed, kissing her again.

A thoughtful sound vibrated against my lips before she asked, "So, then what am I?"

"You'll laugh if I said it."

"I promise I won't."

Sighing, I rolled my eyes to the ceiling and lifted a shoulder. "Maybe you're my angel."

I expected a giggle, or even hysterical laughter, but all I heard was that noise again. Thoughtful and contemplative. "Sent to Earth to save you?"

I nodded. "Yeah. Maybe."

"You were the better twin to save Jake, and I was the better twin to save you."

"Maybe we're the surviving twins," I found myself saying, and my voice caught in my throat, unable to believe I'd say the words aloud, "to save each other."

Audrey nodded. "That sounds more likely to me. But that'd make you an angel, too."

I laughed. "Well, now we know it's all bullshit."

"Not necessarily." She laid her head down, finding a comfortable place for her forehead against my temple. Her yawn was infectious and I wrapped my arm around her, accepting the luring hand of sleep. "Remember, Lucifer was an angel, too."

Snorting as my eyes drifted shut, I muttered, "So, I'm the devil now."

"Maybe, Kiefer," she said, using the nickname I had once found lame but now loved, "but whatever you are, you're mine."

"Yeah, I am," I agreed, sighing contentedly and wrapping my other arm around her shoulders, "and I'm not going anywhere."

Chapter Thirty-Four

"ARE YOU SURE you don't want me to come with you?" Audrey worried as she got ready for work. She buttoned a white cardigan over her teal camisole and added, "I mean, it's just one day. It'd be okay for me to call out sick."

I shook my head, crossing my arms tightly over my chest. "Stop, I'm fine." And, I actually meant it, too. After sleeping well for a solid seven hours, I now felt prepared to face what awaited me at home. But Audrey clearly wasn't convinced, turning her bright blue eyes on me while she chewed her bottom lip with disdain.

"I just feel really bad making you go alone."

"Don't feel bad," I assured her, unraveling my arms and stepping forward to kiss her forehead. "Go to work. I'll be here when you get back."

Guilt washed away the worry. "Blake, if you really want to go to the hospital, then—"

"No," I stopped her, pressing my lips again to her forehead. "I'll go tomorrow. You were right; I need one freakin' day outside of that room."

So, after Audrey left for work, I got into my car and headed across town through a path of dead leaves and speckles of snow leftover from the night before. Pulling into my driveway felt like a slice of déjà vu from a past life, and I swallowed at the worry that maybe I *couldn't* do this after all.

The door opened with a groan and the floors welcomed me with untimely whispers. I swept my gaze over the living room, taking in Jake's Legos and stacks of puzzles and movies, and the exhale that came from my mouth felt like my last. It left me empty and starved for air in that shell of a room, and I hurried to my bedroom to find my breath.

Behind the closed door, I set to work, grabbing clothes from my closet and stuffing them into a duffel bag I hadn't used since college but had kept anyway. I wasn't sure how long to pack for, and how long I'd be at Audrey's place, so I mindlessly shoved in as many clothes as the bag would hold. Then, I scurried around the room, grabbing miscellaneous things I'd been missing over the week, when my hand brushed against the information pamphlet I'd been given at Shady Acres, still standing on my drafting table. It stopped me in my tracks and I stared at the smiling faces of their residents as I remembered my parents' plans.

Whether he woke up or not, Jake would be leaving anyway.

"Son of a bitch," I muttered, snatching the smooth piece of paper from the table. My eyes bore through the crisp letters and vibrant colors as I repeated, louder this time, "Son of a fucking bitch."

It came on quick, the tornado that began in my gut and moved its way to my heart. A swirling frenzy of rage and despair, unleashed through my hands as I crumpled the pamphlet and chucked it across the room. It was too light to go far, and fluttered to the floor only a few feet away. That wasn't good enough. I needed more, and controlled by my blinding emotions, I picked a book up from a nearby shelf and threw it at the opposite wall. It made impact, rattling the window and leaving a scuff mark. I picked up another.

"You motherfucker," I growled, throwing the book. I picked up another. "You son of a bitch. What the fuck did I ever do? What the fuck did *he* do?"

I didn't have time to feel silly or stupid as I tipped my head back and looked to the ceiling. "Well, asshole?! Where are your fucking signs now, huh?"

And as I had suspected, I was met with nothing but silence in the vacant house.

"Yeah," I muttered, swiping the back of my hand under my nose. "That's what I fucking thought."

I grabbed the duffel bag from off my bed and rushed down the hall to the living room, when I was stopped in my tracks by the vibrating of my phone. It was ridiculous to think the Almighty could've been giving me a call, absolutely absurd, but my hand shook anyway as I took it out.

Surprise, surprise—it wasn't God.

I took a deep breath, allowed myself a second to feel like a jackass, then answered, "Hey, Gus."

"Hey, Blake, is it a bad time?"

"Not really," I lied, wiping a hand over my brow.

429

"How's your brother?"

"Still in the coma." I hadn't meant to sound so sardonic, but what the hell? He'd know if there were updates. This was small talk, and not the kind I wanted to have. So, I repeated once again, "What's up, man?"

Gus took a deep breath and began, "Well, I know you've got a lot going on right now, Blake. I get what you're going through, but you've been getting tons of calls lately and I got to thinking—"

"Are you firing me?" I cut in, panicked and strained. "'Cause, dude, if you're firing me, I'll—"

"Fire you? Jesus Christ, Blake, calm the hell down. You're too quick to fly off the handle, you know that?"

I groaned and shook my head, remembering the many times Dr. Travetti had pointed that out. "Yeah, sorry. Working on it."

"Anyway, I got to thinking about how things have been lately. You know, how your career has been really taking off—about damn time, too, by the way—and how I'm not getting any younger ..." He trailed off and cleared his throat. "Kara's pregnant, did I tell you that?"

"No, you didn't mention that." My voice was hoarse, as if it'd been unused for a while. I dropped the duffel by the door and headed toward the kitchen for some water.

"Yep," he answered, unable to contain his pride. "She and Matt came over last weekend and gave us the big news. I'm gonna be a grandpa."

"Congratulations, Gus. That's awesome," I told him as I went to the fridge and took out a bottle.

"Thank you," he replied with an abundance of gratitude. "The thing is, Blake, I really want to be there for my grandkid, you know? I want to be that kickass grandpa who babysits their grandkids while their parents are working. I wanna be able to take him or her to Disney World, the aquarium, and all that cool shit."

Uncapping the bottle, I nodded thoughtfully. "I feel you, man."

"Now, I know that's sort of why you've been reluctant to take on more of a workload, but you've been managing, right? You got that pretty girlfriend of yours and her little boy now, and of course your brother, and you've been good. Right?"

While I took a swig of water, it slowly began to settle in why exactly he was calling, and after lowering the bottle, I answered, "Well, I mean, this past week—"

"Well, obviously, we're not talking about that," he assured me. "That's a whole other situation, but I just mean, in general. Things have been going well."

"Yeah, I guess so. Sure."

"Right. So, how would you like to take over?"

"Take … over," I drawled, pursing my lips and considering what that meant. "Would the, uh … would the place be mine? Or …"

"Well, I thought we could be co-owners," he suggested. "But you'd manage the place. You know, handle business your way."

I considered rejecting the offer right away. The dream of having my own tattoo shop never involved taking over Salem Skin. I'd always wanted to own a place in Derby Square, in the heart of the town and in the middle of the crowds. But Salem Skin was my home away from home. Gus had taken me under his wing and changed my life. The guy was more of a father to me than my own dad, and suddenly, I couldn't imagine ever wanting to be somewhere else.

"You wouldn't wanna ask Kara or Matt?"

Gus pulled in a breath, hesitating in his reply, before saying, "I love those kids, you know that, and they like what they do. But you have a gift, Blake."

I snorted at that word. "A gift," I scoffed, shaking my head.

"Yeah! A gift!" he shouted impatiently. "God, kid, I shouldn't have to tell you this, but there's a lot of people tattooing out there right now, and a good chunk of them are decent at what they do. But it's a lot less common to come across the ones that are artists, honest to God *artists*, and you're one of them. So, take credit, for fuck's sake, and take over the shop."

I cast my gaze over the kitchen floor and spotted Mickey's water bowl in the corner, still full and never to be used again. Seeing Jake's stuff scattered all throughout the house hadn't tempted my emotions as much as I thought they would, but that damn bowl forced a lump to rise in my throat and I struggled to maintain my composure.

"Okay, Gus," I croaked, then clamped my lower lip between my teeth as my eyes pinched shut.

"Okay? To which?"

I laid a hand over my eyes. "Both."

"Well, that was easy," he commented, chuckling lightly.

I wished him a good day and promised I'd call if there were any updates on Jake's condition. Then, I stared at that dish and fought the bout of tears that begged to leak from my eyes and drip into my beard as I muttered, "You giveth, and you taketh away."

***

"When's Jake gonna wake up?" Freddy asked Audrey that night while she put him to bed.

"I don't know, honey," she replied solemnly. "Hopefully soon, but it could take a while."

"Mama said she misses him at school," he told her.

Audrey glanced over her shoulder at me and offered a weak smile. *Hang in there*, it said, and I tried. "I bet she does. I know he's very special to her," Audrey replied, and I knew that was true. When I had called Jake's daycare after the accident, Amy hadn't even tried to stop her tears as she cried into the phone with promises to pray, hope, and whatever else she could do to help him wake up and to make him better.

"Get some sleep, okay?" she said to her son and kissed his forehead. She stood up and headed to the door, meeting my eye with a sympathetic glance.

"Night, Freddy," I said, waving into the room, before he stopped me.

"Blake?"

"Yeah?"

"What are you getting me for Christmas?"

The question brought me to laugh and I shook my head, stepping into the room. "Well, if I told you, it wouldn't be a surprise, would it?" I asked, crouching at his bedside. "Why? Got any requests?"

"I want a tattoo. Like you and Daddy and Mommy."

I chuckled even harder. "Ah, well, I don't know about that, kiddo. When you get older, I promise I'll give you all the tattoos you want, but you're still a little young. I think your mom and dad might get mad at me if I did that."

His eyes widened with fear. "Would Mommy make you leave?"

Nodding assuredly, I replied, "I'm pretty sure she would."

"I don't want that."

"Good. Neither do I." I reached out to ruffle his shaggy brown hair. "Get to sleep."

I began to stand when he stopped me again. "Wait. There's something else I want."

"Okay," I drawled, squatting back down. "What's that?"

"Bring Jake back. I don't want him to be at the hospital anymore."

Pressing my lips into a firm line and fighting the tears that stung the backs of my eyes, I nodded. "I'm trying, kiddo," I said, while being unsure if yelling at the sky and throwing shit against the wall could really be considered trying.

"Okay," Freddy replied, offering me a satisfied nod. He reached out a hand and patted my shoulder. "Night-night, Blake."

"Night, Freddy."

I stood with a sigh and focused on not slumping my shoulders as I walked past Audrey. She closed the door behind her and instructed me to sit in the living room while she made us some tea. As I sat down on the couch, I remembered the first time I'd been here in her apartment. It wasn't that long ago, only several weeks or so in the past, but it felt like years since I'd first come here, drunk and confused. I'd been so resistant to what I thought I'd always known, and now, I couldn't leave. She was my salvation and my belief that there was something more to all of this. Leaving would've meant to turn my back on the only comfort I had left, and maybe it was enough. Maybe I'd be okay if Jake were to die. I could go on with the hope that he was in a better place, if only I had this woman and her child to need me, to depend on me and to love me.

"Fuck," I muttered under my breath, running a hand over my mouth and through my beard.

"Here you go." Audrey came into the living room with two steaming mugs and handed one to me. My mood must've been written plainly on my face as hers contorted with concern. "You hanging in there, Kiefer?"

My hand wobbled in gesture. "I'm getting there."

I took a sip of the tea and immediately sighed at the sharp note of bergamot, warmed by the sweet vanilla. It was a simple comfort and I gladly welcomed it to make itself at home in my belly. Audrey asked if it was good, as if there was a chance at all I'd find it bad, and I nodded. "Very good," I assured her and put the mug down on the coffee table.

"So, Gus called today while I was at the house," I began, rubbing my hands against my jeans. "He wants me to take over the shop."

The brim of her mug had barely touched her lips before she pulled it away with an excited gasp. "Blake! That's amazing! What did you say?"

"He didn't give me much of a choice," I laughed uncomfortably.

Her face reluctantly fell. "Oh ..."

"I want it," I said with sincerity, and her eyes lit up again with excitement. "I'm just having a hard time feeling happy about it."

She didn't reply. Instead, she just reached over and scooped one of my hands into hers and held on tightly. It wasn't long ago when I'd need to call Dr. Travetti and release my troubles to someone who would listen and write things down for analysis. It was funny that now I felt content with simply having someone to listen and hold my hand. It felt like enough.

We drank our tea and went to bed, lying side by side and kissing lazily with our hands clasped and our hearts marching to the beat of the same drum. With a sigh, I laid my head on her chest, my ear pressed to the butterfly I'd carved into her skin, and I was lulled toward the safety of slumber in her arms. I imagined every night of the rest of my life ending this way, after a long day at Salem Skin, and after eating dinner with her and Freddy as a family. I imagined her and me, together in this bed, or maybe mine, and feeling nothing but contentedness that this was our life and that it was as good as a life could be. It'd be all I ever dreamed of, all I never knew I could have, and all I never knew that I could even deserve. I would fall asleep with a gentle smile on my face, knowing this was ours and how nothing would take it away.

But the fantasy was wiped away with the reminder that Jake was alone, trapped in a prison he couldn't break out of, and I wasn't able to help him. I couldn't rip him out, I couldn't do a damn thing, and I held in my tormented hurt as I silently begged anybody who would listen to do what I couldn't.

Please. Please, for fuck's sake, help him. Whatever you need to fucking do, just save him. Please.

Chapter Thirty-Five

ON NEARLY A daily basis, the doctors mentioned the eventual possibility of turning Jake's machines off if there was a stop in brain activity. But after weeks, it still hadn't come. Not yet, anyway. He just seemed to be stuck in a permanent state of limbo. Not quite sleeping, yet not dead, either. Audrey was convinced that it was his body's way of healing after the accident. And maybe she was right. We all knew it'd be next to impossible for him to cope with the doctors' orders of taking it easy while his bones mended. It was a nice thought and I wanted to believe her, but I was forever the realist and I wasn't convinced that his body just simply hadn't let go yet.

Still, I hoped she was right.

What I did find amazing, was how we'd all settled into this new normal way of life. After a week and a half had passed since the accident, I had gone back to work, needing the daily reprieve from the monotony of sitting within the hospital walls without any end in sight. I'd spent my days tattooing and daydreaming about what I was going to do with the shop once Gus and I made my status as shop manager official. And I never let my phone out of my sight. Just in case my parents called.

Now, it'd been about three weeks since Jake's accident, and it was a few days before Christmas. I'd gone to bed early, exhausted after a day of work, then sitting at the hospital, and cooking dinner and doing laundry with Audrey. She was out of work for the holiday break and we had plans to do some last-minute Christmas shopping before I went down to see Jake, and when I woke up, she was already missing from what I'd begun to think of as our bed.

Stretching my arms overhead, I relished in how refreshed I felt. It'd been weeks since I had slept so well and there was only a faint twinge of guilt in regard to that. I opened my eyes to stare at the ceiling, listening to the sounds of the old house, and smiled when I heard Audrey's singing voice come from the kitchen. With the assumption that she was making tea and breakfast, I sat up to rub the sleep from my eyes, with all intentions to join her. But before I could press the heels of my palms against my face, I was stopped, rendered stupid and stunned, at the black and yellow figure of the butterfly.

So small and perfect in its design, it was perched precariously at the bed's footboard and apart from the gentlest twitch of antennae, it was motionless and almost looked fake. My heart hammered wildly in my chest as I reached out slowly for my phone and quickly texted Audrey, telling her to get in here right now to make sure I wasn't completely losing my fucking mind.

439

It was possible. I hadn't seen Dr. Travetti for some time, not since the session where I told her to call Audrey's family. My condition could've deteriorated in that time, whatever the hell my condition even was exactly. Things felt too okay while still being so bad, so I could see where my mind would start conjuring these simple delusions. Why the fuck would a butterfly be here, in my girlfriend's bedroom, in late December? How the hell was it even alive?

The more I sat there, frozen solid, the more I thought about it. And the more I thought, the more I began to think I really was seeing things. There was no possible way there was a butterfly in here right now, and just as I began to feel self-assured in my ability to talk myself away from the brink of insanity, Audrey entered the room and stopped with the smallest of gasps.

"Oh, my Lord," she whispered, clapping a hand to her chest.

"Wait, you see it, too?" I answered, my voice hoarse and embarrassingly shaken.

Audrey nodded and quietly tiptoed to the bed, climbing on to sit beside me. "How long has it been there?"

"I don't know. I just woke up." Then, I turned to her and shook my head. "How is *that* your first question, and not how the hell it's here in the first place?"

"Because I know how it's here," she replied simply, keeping her eyes on the butterfly that hadn't yet moved.

"Oh, really? How?" I challenged, narrowing my skeptical glare.

"It's a message."

I didn't mean to roll my eyes but I did, accompanied by a steady shake of my head. "Audrey, come on …"

Her eyes met mine then. "I get that you have an explanation for everything, and that's fine. But what could possibly be your explanation for this, if it's not that?"

Sighing, I turned toward the butterfly again. It still hadn't moved from its spot on the footboard, but its wings lifted and dropped in a slow rhythm, almost in time with my breath.

"I …," I'd begun to speak, but I was stopped short by the reality that there was no logical explanation for this. Whatever I could say would sound just as ridiculous as her assumption of it being a message from someone or something, and so I closed my mouth to shrug.

"That's what I thought," Audrey jabbed, accepting the victory with little grace.

"I'm not agreeing with you," I pointed out. "I just don't know what else it could be, other than a freakish thing." And it really was a freakish thing. The butterfly was nearly identical to Audrey's tattoo, and if she wasn't going to point that out, neither was I.

"What do you think it—" I began, when my phone started to ring, and Audrey grasped my wrist. Her gaze was full of fear and dread as she stared at the device in my hand and the butterfly flew off in a fluttering frenzy around the room. And I knew why.

My dad was calling.

A swirling mess of nausea, sadness, and hope tangled through my gut and veins as I stared, shaking and scared, at the phone. I couldn't move. My brain screamed for me to answer the call, to pick up the fucking phone, but my fingers wouldn't comply. I could hardly blink, let alone get my hands to behave the way I needed them to, and finally, Audrey had to take it from me.

She put it on speakerphone and said, in a quivering voice, "H-hello?"

"Put Blake on," Dad said urgently.

"He's here. You're on speaker," Audrey replied.

"Blake?" he asked, as if he didn't believe her.

Somehow, I managed to coax my vocal chords into saying, "Yeah, Dad. I'm here."

"We need you here now," he rushed, nearly breathless and shaken.

I blinked rapidly, too tempted by the tears stinging at my eyes. "Wha-what's going on? What's happening?"

He was too quiet and hesitated for too long. My heart hammered, my head spun, and my jaw hung open so loosely, all I could do was cover my mouth with a hand to ward off the uprising of bile in my throat. Audrey's hand was against my back as she reminded me to breathe, saying my name and saying other things I couldn't hear. But my father's voice sliced through the torrential wave of panic, saying, "He's waking up, Blake," and I heard him. I heard him loud and clear, and thank God for that.

***

Walking through the hospital felt otherworldly. With Audrey's hand in mine, I tugged her toward my brother's room with urgent desperation. I needed to see him, know

442

he was alive, and ensure that my parents weren't just pulling some sick, cruel joke on me.

I heard him before I'd even reached his door at the end of the hall. He was shouting for everyone to get away from him, to not touch him, and to let him up and let him leave. I released Audrey's hand and took off at a run, zigzagging between carts and irritated hospital personnel, until I reached his open doorway.

Crowding around his bed was a handful of nurses and a couple of doctors, all struggling to keep him still while they took his vitals and blood. My parents noticed me first, as I barreled my way into the room, calling his name through a dream-like haze.

"Blake, Blake, Blake," my brother answered through his panicked outburst, tugging his arms out of their clutches. The IV line snagged on the bedrail and he cried out in pain, only to tug harder.

"Oh, God, he's gonna rip it out again," one of the nurses muttered. "We need to sedate—"

"No!" I shouted, hurrying to his bedside. "Don't you dare!"

She twisted her face and looked like she was about to protest, when I finally got to him, clasping his face in my hands and collecting his tears in my palms. "I'm here, buddy," I assured him, barely breathing as I leaned over to press my forehead to his. "I'm here."

Jake grappled for my shoulders, holding onto me with enough force to crush my chest. "I wanna go home, Blake. I wanna go home."

"I know, buddy, I know," I soothed, smoothing his hair away from his forehead, dotted with sweat. "But

443

listen to me, okay? Can you listen to me?" He nodded furiously and I continued, "You need to listen to these people, okay?"

He shook his head, keeping his gaze on me as though that alone could make the room disappear. "I don't like it here. I don't like them. Don't like them at all."

"Yeah, I know, but I promise, they're only trying to help you."

His frantic resolve settled a bit as he exhaled. "Don't leave."

"I'll be right over here," I swore to him, pointing behind me.

"Pinkie swear?"

Sniffing back a sudden rush of emotion, I nodded, reaching for his hand and wrapping my smallest finger around his.

"Pinkie swear."

***

I kept my promise and stayed in the room with my back glued to the wall, overseeing every move the nurses and doctors made. Jake mostly kept his bewildered gaze on them, but every now and then, his eyes darted in my direction. Making sure I was there and that I hadn't left. Audrey had slipped out sometime during my dutiful watch. She hadn't said anything, and I hadn't noticed, but I knew she understood.

After what felt like hours, the room was finally emptied of medical staff, taking the air with them, and it was just my parents, Jake, and me—a family that no longer felt like one. Mom hurried to Jake's side and wrapped her hands around his, but he jolted from her grasp.

"I wanna go home," he said, turning to me with urgency before repeating, "I wanna go home, Blake. Let's go home."

I didn't know what to say. Now that he was awake and the prognosis was miraculously good, I wasn't sure what my parents' plans were and I didn't want to lie to him. Still, I did want to comfort him, so I laid my hand over his and said, "I know, buddy. Soon."

We let him fall asleep and when his snores filled the room, I felt a cool hand on my forearm.

"Blake," my mom said, so soft and weak. "Can I talk to you?"

Exhausted and ragged, I laid a hand over my eyes. "Mom, I really don't want to fight right now."

"Neither do I. Just … please, I want to talk."

Reluctantly, I turned my eyes from Jake's sleeping figure and followed my mom out into the hallway. She asked if I'd like to get some coffee from the cafeteria, to which I replied coldly, "I don't drink coffee."

She responded with a sad smile. "I guess I never knew that. What about tea?"

"I like tea," I concurred with a nod.

"So do I."

***

We sat in the cafeteria, hot paper cups of tea between our palms. It was weak, nearly flavorless, and at the first sip, both of us screwed our lips with disgust. Mom caught my expression and laughed lightly. I couldn't remember the last time I'd heard my mother genuinely laugh, but there it was.

It was nice.

Then, she began to speak. "Do you remember when you were a little boy and you'd run around in your underwear with that plastic sword and shield?" I shook my head at the question, while remembering a particular drawing Jake had made weeks ago. "You were always my brave little warrior. Always up for a fight, always getting into something, and your father and I were always waiting for you to get hurt. We didn't wish for it to happen, but we expected it, I guess."

She kept her eyes on the table as she continued, "I hated that you boys hung out at that house, but I couldn't control you. And Jake …" She sniffed lightly. "He would follow you to the end of the world, so there wasn't any controlling him either. But there was also a comfort in knowing he was there, to look out for you. Even your father would say, 'He's okay, Jake's with him,' and that always seemed good enough. That made me feel better. So, when it was *you* running home, telling us you killed Jake …"

She lifted her head to meet my gaze then and said, "I didn't know what to do with that, Blake."

I recalled that moment with tiny bursts of hazy memory. Me, bursting through the door of my parents' house, knowing the blood was trickling down my leg but not caring. Then, gasping through my hysterics, and telling them over and over that I'd killed my brother.

"I was terrified, and I guess my fear manifested into anger. God, Blake, I was so, *so* unbelievably angry, and no matter how many times I told myself that it was just an accident, I couldn't stop myself from feeling that rage. In just a few, stupid seconds, my beautiful, smart, talented, sweet boy was taken away from me—"

"He's still Jake," I finally muttered, knowing it didn't make anything better and that it was damn close to being a lie.

Mom tried to smile but failed as she shook her head. "Yes, but he's not the boy I knew for ten years, and I guess … I guess I've been mourning that boy for a long time, and I needed something to blame for losing him." Her glassy eyes, swimming in apologetic agony, met mine and she said, "It was so easy to blame you. It shouldn't have been. God help me, it *really* shouldn't have been, because you're my son and I love you—I always have—but it was still just so … *easy*. And I pulled away from you and ruined everything, I know I did, and I'm not sure I could ever apologize enough for what I've done to you."

I wiped a hand beneath my nose and struggled to say, "I don't know either."

Her nod was sharp and broken. Her hand fluttered awkwardly, touching her hair and temple and neck. "Well, I, um, I was hoping I could at least begin to try, if you'd let me. I want to do better. I want to *be* better, Blake. I want to fix this—Lord, I want to fix this so badly. I hate what this family is now, and I see how

447

much better you're doing, how much better you're being with Jake. Hell, even your father is making an effort. And after this past month, I feel like ... like I'm *finally* opening my eyes again, and I'm realizing how much time I've wasted being angry. And Blake, I don't want to waste anymore of my life being mad about something that was never, *ever* your fault or his. I don't. I just want my family back."

Exhaling, I slowly nodded, knowing exactly who to thank for everything good now in my life. My happiness and newfound faith and Jake's contentedness. Dad's attempts at acceptance. It was the same woman who'd also suggested there could still be hope for my mother and me, hope that we could forgive and reform a relationship that had died two decades ago. I hadn't thought it was possible then, hadn't even wanted to entertain the idea. But now, sitting across from her and seeing the tears that trailed over her cheeks and around her untouched cup of tea, I found myself wondering if it really was possible. Not to forget, but to forgive and maybe head slowly toward something resembling a family.

"I'm not gonna pretend like I know what it was like for you," I spoke through a throat so constricted and graveled. "I can't put myself in your shoes, and I don't want to. Fuck, I can't even empathize, because all I can think about is the fact that I was your kid, too, and you didn't give a shit about how much you were hurting me. You didn't think about how I'd grow up or how fucked up I'd be."

Her sob almost startled me. "Blake ..."

Holding up a hand, I continued, "You and Dad were so consumed by what you lost, that you never for a second took the time to look at what you still had. You neglected *both* of us, and I can't ever forget that. Hell, I'm not even sure I can ever forgive you for it," I folded my arms on the table, leaning forward and fixing my stare on hers, "but I'm not you, I'm not gonna waste twenty years of my life being pissed off, so I guess I can try."

Sniffling and nodding, she wiped her hands against her cheeks. "That's all I'm asking you for."

"I know a good place you can start."

She nodded adamantly. "What? What can I do?"

"Don't dump Jake in that place," I told her, furrowing my brow and feeling my stony walls crumble as I began to plead. "Please. Don't do that to us. Let him live with me. You guys can see him whenever you want, but just please, don't—"

"Okay."

I narrowed my eyes. "That was too easy."

She shook her head. "Your father and I already called Shady Acres a couple of weeks ago. We weren't going to send him there, he made it very clear he didn't want to go and only wanted to be with you, so …" She offered me a wobbly smile. "Okay."

"You didn't say anything."

Dropping her gaze and offering a slight shrug, she said, "We didn't know if he'd ever wake up."

Then her arm reached out and a hand covered mine. I considered pulling away. I thought about yanking my hand from beneath hers and tucking it into my lap, denying her the affection she'd denied me for too fucking long. That's what the old Blake would've done. The angry, bitter, vibe-less Blake. The one who'd wondered if the world would've been a better place if he just ceased to exist. But he was gone, and in his wake was me. A strong man deserving of family and love, even from this woman sitting across from him. Because hadn't we all been broken, in our own way? That accident twenty-four years ago had shattered us all and sent our pieces swirling in a chaotic wind. But maybe with time, those fragmented bits could come to settle in the same place. Maybe we could rebuild. Maybe we could become something better, something good.

"He's better with you, Blake," Mom admitted confidently. "I'm done fighting that."

Then I allowed myself to smile. Because it felt like a step in the right direction.

Chapter Thirty-Six

"I WANNA GO HOME," Jake said for what must've been the three-thousandth time in just a couple of days.

The doctors were keeping him in the hospital for the time being, to undergo rehab and observation, before being discharged. By some unbelievable miracle, he hadn't suffered any further brain damage, and now his mobility needed strengthening after weeks of lying in bed. Otherwise, he seemed to be okay, all things considered.

To be honest, I'd seen more unbelievable things happen recently and nothing seemed to surprise me anymore.

"I know, buddy," I said, laying my hand on his leg. "Soon."

I hadn't told him yet that he'd be staying with me. Not for a prolonged visit or a sleepover, but permanently. It was for his own good to remain in the dark for now. Knowing would've made him more impatient, which only meant he'd be even more difficult for his nurses and doctors. Still, keeping the secret had been tough for me, and even now, my legs jounced with the excitement.

My eyes darted quickly to my phone as I checked the time. Dad caught the motion and asked, "Do you have to get going?"

Reluctantly, I nodded. "Yeah. I have to be at Audrey's place soon, and I still have to change before I can head over there."

"I wanna see Audrey," Jake whined. "And Freddy."

"They're coming by tomorrow, buddy, remember?" I assured him, patting his leg.

Then, I stood up and faced my parents. "You guys good here?"

Mom assured me with a sturdy nod. "We're fine. Dad brought over a Lego set to do with Jake. You go, enjoy dinner. Tell Audrey and Freddy we said hi."

"I will," I said, watching as Dad positioned Jake's table over his bed. He smiled at my brother in a way I hadn't seen in years, and I could've wept at the sight of him ruffling Jake's shaggy hair. Something in that told me we'd be okay. We still had a long way to go, but I allowed myself to believe that we'd get there.

"All right, buddy," I said, and Jake gave me his full attention, despite the temptation of Legos. "I'll see you tomorrow, okay?"

He caught my eyes and grinned. "You betcha."

***

In a black sweater, black leather jacket, and black pants, I felt I looked the part as much as I was ever going to.

Meeting members of the family and dressing to impress … It was never going to be my thing, but for Audrey, I was willing to put in more of an effort.

I was nervous, though. Tonight, I'd be seeing my shrink, Dr. Vanessa Travetti, as strictly Vanessa, the girlfriend of Audrey's late sister. I didn't know what to expect from that or how I was supposed to behave. I wondered if I should style my hair differently, to make myself less like the Blake she knew inside her office. But I resisted the urge and decided I was fine, before heading over to the other side of town.

Passing by St. Peter's on the way to Audrey's, I smiled at the Christmas Eve Mass crowd, blocking the view of the crowded headstones behind the wrought iron fence. Maybe next year, I'd find myself there, with my parents and brother, the way we used to. Maybe I'd even bring Audrey and Freddy along as well, despite her insistence that she didn't need Church to feel close to God. But for now, I just looked up high, to rest my gaze on the cross within the bricked exterior and nodded my head in thanks.

When I got to Audrey's place, I grinned at her house, decorated to the nines in twinkling lights, plastic reindeer, and a wooden Nativity scene, among other decorations. If these people loved Halloween, they were absolutely obsessed with Christmas, and that didn't surprise me much. I burrowed my hands in my pockets, moving up the walkway toward the porch, when Jason stepped outside with his baby daughter, Eliza.

"Hey, it's the Tattoo Guy!" he bellowed excitedly, extending a hand. "Good to see you, man. Merry Christmas!"

"Merry Christmas," I greeted him, as we shook. "What are you guys doing out here?"

"Just getting a little fresh air," he said, rocking Eliza gently. "I was so happy to hear Jake's doing well."

I smiled at the sentiment. "Thanks. Yeah, he should be home soon."

"Amazing. Talk about a Christmas miracle, right?" His smile was infectious, and I allowed my grin to broaden.

"Yeah. Seriously."

Clapping a hand against his shoulder, I told him I'd see him inside, before pushing through the door, heavily adorned with garland and lights. The house was packed with neighbors, friends, and what little I recognized of her family—more specifically, her cousins, Regina and Nicole. I hadn't seen them since that night at the poetry club, but they noticed me right away.

They rushed toward me with drinks in hand, wishing me a merry Christmas and saying it was so nice to see me again.

"We've heard you've made quite the impact on our girl," Nicole commented, brushing her arm against mine. "I bawled like a baby when she told me you love her. I can't handle that type of shit right now. Not until I get this kid out of me, at least."

I chuckled. "I'll assume that's water in your glass, then."

Wagging a finger at me, she tsk-tsked. "Pretending it's wine, thank you very much."

Regina nudged her head over her shoulder toward the stairs. "Audrey's upstairs, if you're looking for her. She's been driving herself crazy all day, getting ready for this shindig, so lay the compliments on thick, okay?"

Chuckling again, I nodded. "Noted."

I headed upstairs to her parents' part of the house. There, I found Audrey and her mother, bustling around the kitchen in aprons and oven mitts, while listening to a rendition of "Have Yourself a Merry Little Christmas" I'd heard a time or two before—I think it was Coldplay. I leaned against the doorframe and watched her, in her cranberry red velvet dress and glistening curls, until she turned and spotted me through startled blue eyes.

"Good Lord, Blake!" she shouted, pressing her hand to her heart.

"For someone so big, you're pretty quiet," Ann commented, smirking in my direction.

"I told you, I'm a vampire," I joked as Audrey came to stand closer to me. I slipped my hand around her waist and pressed a kiss to her forehead.

"How could I forget?" she whispered, standing on her toes to kiss my jaw. "Kiefer."

I smiled fondly at the nickname and asked, "Can I help with anything?"

"Yeah," Ann said in a demanding tone, "you can take this one and get her the hell out of my kitchen."

"Mom," Audrey began to protest, but Ann was hearing none of it. She leveled her daughter with a stern glare and said, "You've done enough. Now, go. I'm fine in here."

With a pout, Audrey threw down her mitts and apron and allowed me to steer her out of the kitchen and down the stairs. She took control then and pulled me into her apartment, closing us off from the party outside, and when I asked what she was up to, she told me she wanted to give me one of my presents.

Raising a brow and grinning suggestively, I asked, "You wanna do that right now? With all those people out there?"

Audrey shoved playfully against my arm and rolled her eyes dramatically. "That's happening later. But this can't wait. Honestly, I've waited long enough," and then, she hurried to the mantle in her living room and produced a notebook. She handed it to me in a way that felt reluctant.

"What is this?" I asked, eyeing the worn cover.

"It's Sabrina's journal."

Wide-eyed, I swallowed, clenching the book in my grasp. "You're *giving* this to me?"

"Well, not exactly," she said slowly, then took it back into her hands. As she flipped it open and thumbed through the pages, she explained, "Sabrina always kept journals, ever since she was a little kid—I was the poet, she was the writer. After she died, my parents gave me her box of journals, thinking I'd want them, but I couldn't bring myself to read them. She treated them so privately while she was alive, so reading them after she was gone felt too much like snooping through her secrets, you know?"

"Hm," I grunted, nodding and continuing to watch her flip through the pages.

"But after I met you and Jake, seeing your relationship with him made me miss Sabrina so much, I wanted to feel closer to her."

"You didn't tell me that," I muttered, almost defensively, and she smiled into my eyes.

"I'm not sure you would've listened to me then," she replied pointedly, and I couldn't help but chuckle.

"Touché."

She opened to a particular page and continued saying, "Anyway, I started reading her journals a couple months ago. At first, it felt like prying, but then, it just felt nice, to see her handwriting and to read her thoughts. But then, one night, I came across this entry, and I knew you needed to read it." She turned the book around to face me and passed it to my opened palms.

Eyeing the scrawled scripture, I asked, "Why?"

"Because you asked why she got the tattoo."

My breath whispered from my lungs as I held the book in my hands and turned to her couch. Deaf to the chatter and laughter behind her front door, I sat down and braced myself. I don't know why I felt I had to. Maybe it was just the finality of having a definitive answer to a question I'd had months ago, assuming I'd never get one. Or it could've been the fear of a letdown, a mundane explanation for something that had quite literally changed my life in every possible way. But whatever it was, I swallowed my apprehension and began to read.

"God, what a mixed bag of a day.

It started with a doctor's appointment. I don't feel well, I don't feel <u>right</u>, and I told the doctor as much. But all he could tell me is everything looks the same and that I have nothing to worry about. But come on. I'm dying. I know I am, I can feel it in everything I do. Like this could be the last time I write in this book and that wouldn't be a surprise to me. It's a feeling I have that I can't help, and I'm not sure I'd even classify it as a scary one. It's just weird. And a little sad, too, but only because I'm worried I won't do everything I need to before this part is over.

I can't talk about this to Vanessa anymore, though. She cried so much tonight. It's like she's already mourning, and I hate that. I mean, I get it—I'm not sure I'd be any different, if it was the other way around—but I'm still here. I worry so much about what'll happen to her after I'm gone. I worry she'll close herself off, and I just hope someone walks into her life who can give her purpose. She needs that.

Ugh. Okay. Too heavy. Let's get to the good stuff.

I got my tattoo! I wrote about the idea a while ago, but I finally did it tonight. And it is <u>gorgeous</u>.

I fell in love with this artist on Instagram. His name is Blake Carson and he works at Salem Skin. His work is breathtaking in this gritty, gothic sort of way and it's a total understatement to say I've been drooling over his work. I mean, I've been completely and utterly obsessed with his artwork for <u>years</u>, and I've wanted to get something done by him for about as long. Honestly, it's stupid that I haven't done it sooner, but I guess I just thought I had time. But today I woke up knowing so *affirmatively that my days were severely numbered, and after Vanessa went home, I went over to Salem Skin. I didn't even make an appointment, even though his Instagram page strictly says he works by appointment only. I just walked in there, told this girl with dreadlocks that I needed to see him specifically, and when he came out from the back, I got the most bizarre feeling. I wish I could adequately express how I felt, but all I can say is, I knew that meeting him meant something. I don't know how or why, but I just knew. So weird.*

Anyway, Blake asked me what I wanted to do and when I wanted to come in, and I told him I needed to do it right away. The look he gave me made me laugh, like I had some audacity making demands, and he said I could make an appointment and come back another day. But I wouldn't leave."

I looked up from the book laid open in my lap and met Audrey's eyes with an urgent, sincere recollection. "I remember her," I declared with clarity. "Holy shit, I actually remember her. She was so fucking adamant, telling me she needed this tattoo done *right now*, and I was just thinking, who the fuck does this chick think she is?"

Audrey laughed, swiping her fingertips beneath her eyes. "Yeah. Sabrina was pretty intense sometimes. She came on pretty strong."

"You have that in common," I told her, smirking gently before turning my gaze back on the book.

"I told him it was very important I get the tattoo done right away, because I wasn't sure how long I'd be around. I didn't clarify what that meant, but his

459

demeanor changed and he looked at me as if he knew. Then, he just nodded and said in this really cool way, 'Okay, let's do it.' He didn't even ask what I wanted. He just agreed to doing my tattoo, whatever it was, and took me into the back.

I knew I liked him before, but that really solidified it.

So, when he did ask what I wanted, I explained it to him. I wanted a black Swallowtail, one half in color with its yellow markings, surrounded by a splashy watercolor sapphire blue. And then, the other half entirely in black and white, with his signature grittiness. I wanted it to blend seamlessly from color to black and white, from pretty to gritty, and I swear I thought he'd say no at that point. Because this isn't what he does. I don't know what happened, though, because he was just nodding slowly while I described it to him, and then he grabbed his sketchbook. He didn't ask questions, didn't protest, didn't even make a face. He just drew it up and we got to work.

I can safely say that it's the most gorgeous thing about my stupid, broken, dying body.

I didn't tell him what the butterfly means, but he didn't ask either. Honestly, I've only told Audrey. I won't even tell Vanessa, because I don't think she can handle it. But I'll write it here: it's life.

In the beginning, we are born in our purest form. We then become ourselves during the stage between caterpillar to butterfly, so colorful and full of beautiful possibility, and we believe, with the blindest of hope, that we'll be perfect forever. That time is endless. That there is a multitude of chances, of opportunities. Until one day, *the reality of mortality settles in deep and dark, and we suddenly become aware of how limited we are. It is all so black and white. There is no grey. We live and we die, and there's nothing more to it than that.*

But God, isn't it still so beautiful?

Oh! And one more thing: The no-questions-asked compassion from this guy was so unlikely, considering his tough-as-nails exterior, and all I could think was, he'd be so freakin' perfect for Audrey."

I closed the book with an irritating lump sticking relentlessly in my throat. Try as I might, I couldn't dislodge the damn thing as I sniffed and regained my composure, before my eyes met Audrey's again.

"I didn't remember the tattoo," I admitted again. "I don't even remember doing it on her, but I'm glad I at least remember her."

"You don't remember why you did it? Not even now, after reading that?"

I shook my head regrettably. "I really wish I did. But the only thing I can think is, her insistence had been so urgent, I knew it was really important; it had to be. That meant more than my ego."

Audrey nodded as she slipped the journal from my hands and held it to her chest. "I'm glad you could make her happy. I'm so glad that, of everybody she could've gone to, it was you."

"So am I."

Then, I stood and cocooned her in my arms. "Thank you for letting me read that."

"You're welcome," she whispered against my chest, and then she sniffed a gentle laugh. "And Sabrina was right; you really are so freakin' perfect for me."

***

Audrey told me she was worried Vanessa wouldn't come, but when we exited her apartment, I spotted a familiar face through the stained-glass window in the door. A gasp escaped Audrey's glossy lips as she unwound my arm from her waist and hurried toward the door to throw it open. There stood Vanessa Travetti, already with tears in her eyes at the sight of Audrey.

"Oh, my God," Audrey could barely say before throwing her arms around Vanessa. "I can't believe you're really here."

"I can't believe it either," Vanessa admitted, weeping gently and hugging Audrey tight.

Her gaze crossed the foyer to where I stood, still in the doorway where Audrey had left me, and she smiled gently as she mouthed, "Hi." I lifted a hand in a wave before approaching the door with hands in my pockets and a smile gradually tugging at my lips.

"Blake," Vanessa greeted me as she took a step back from Audrey's tight embrace.

"Doc."

She grinned and shook her head. "I think you can call me Vanessa here."

Shaking my head, I wrinkled my nose and said, "Nah. You'll always be Doc to me."

She hugged me then, wrapping her arms around my neck tightly and I wrapped mine around her waist. She pressed her cheek to mine and whispered, "Merry Christmas, Blake," like it was a secret, a sentiment shared only between us. I nodded, hugging her tightly, and whispered back, "Merry Christmas, Doc."

To anyone else, that hug would've appeared as nothing more than an embrace between friends, close friends even. But to us, it was the end of a very long journey, one of anger, disbelief, and a deep-rooted sadness, too heavy to carry alone. It felt like a goodbye, but ... maybe it wasn't. Maybe it was simply the beginning of something else—a friendship, maybe even a family. But for now, we hugged and hugged until Audrey laid her hand against my shoulder, and I found myself laughing as I took a step back. I wrapped an arm around my girlfriend, my savior, and pressed a kiss to her temple, as Vanessa smoothed her hands over her sweater and smiled fondly into my eyes.

"Well," she said, "I guess I'll go say hi to Ann. Is she upstairs?"

Audrey nodded. "Yeah, you want me to take you up there?"

Vanessa shook her head. "No, I'm fine. I remember the way." There was a bittersweet melancholy in her smile as she took Audrey in, standing at my side, and she said, "I wish Sabrina could see you so happy."

Audrey's smile faded as she tightened her arms around my waist. "She does. And after all, none of this would've happened in the first place, if it hadn't been for her."

I thought about that all throughout dinner, sitting at a table full of Audrey's family and friends. I thought about how wrong I'd been all this time, assuming that it was all Audrey's doing, and her tattoo. Her refusal to leave me alone and her presence in my life ever since. But where it all began, where it *truly* all began, was with her sister.

A dying girl who wanted a tattoo of a butterfly.

Chapter Thirty-Seven

"WHOA, WHOA, WHOA! I don't think so, mister!" Audrey shouted from the kitchen before racing into the living room.

Looking up from cutting our Christmas 2.0 ham, I found Jake in the middle of an attempt to get up from the couch on his own. Audrey slid her shoulders beneath his arm, holding him up while coaxing him to sit back down. His leg was still in the cast, with at least another month and a half to go. Jake was dependent in so many ways, ways even he didn't understand, but mobility had never been one of them. It had easily been the most challenging thing about having him home. In *my* home.

I dropped the knife and fork to hurry over to assist Audrey. "Hey, buddy, what do you need?"

His eyes shifted to Audrey, then back to mine, acting as though he had a secret to tell. She immediately got the gist and smiled at us before returning to the kitchen. Now alone, Jake whispered, "I gotta pee."

"Okay," I said, nodding. "Of course, you just gotta say something."

"Audrey said I can't stand up. I stand up to pee, Blake."

"We'll figure it out," I told him. We'd been figuring it out for over a week now, and I'd say we were doing pretty good.

The doctors had given Jake clearance to leave after he'd spent six weeks in the hospital, with him being awake for about half that time. It'd been tough keeping him content there, if you could call it content at all, but my parents and I had managed while taking turns sitting with him. It became a full-time job in itself, albeit a temporary one. The worst part was hearing him talk about Mickey and how excited he was to see him again. Telling Jake that Mickey had passed away, while he was still in the hospital, would have upset him too much, so in a jointed effort to keep him as calm as humanly possible, we'd agreed to keep the painful secret to ourselves until he was home.

He'd taken the news about as well as I thought he would, and that was after I'd lied to him about how exactly his dog had died. It would've destroyed me to have him know he'd unwittingly killed his pet that night. So, instead I had told him Mickey passed away peacefully in his sleep while he was also sleeping. Jake had nodded sagely, absorbing the information before the tears began, and said, "He wanted to try to find me, but he got lost."

I had wondered if maybe Jake knew the truth of what'd happened to Mickey and just went along with the story. But that was just one of those things I'd never know, nor did I want to know, so I'd just hugged him and let him cry.

To soften the blow of losing his dog, we had decided to have a second shot at Christmas, since Jake had missed it the first time around. So, before he came home, I brought out the tree that I'd neglected to put up in December, decorated the house with stuff Audrey picked up on clearance at Target, and on a cold day in mid-January, Audrey and I woke up early to make Christmas dinner. Again.

Now, after helping Jake to pee and dropping him off in his room to play with Freddy, I headed back into the kitchen to find that gorgeous woman, who I still wasn't sure I deserved, listening to country music and mashing potatoes. She rocked her hips to the beat, singing along to lyrics about legends and Heaven or something like that.

"What the hell are we listening to?" I grumbled over her endearingly off-key voice.

"Kelsea Ballerini," she answered shortly before continuing to croon and sway.

"What was wrong with my music?" I challenged, taking purchase against the counter beside her, crossing my arms over my chest and glowering down at the top of her head.

"Oh, nothing," she replied innocently with a gentle shrug. "I just wanted to hear this song."

"You just don't like my music," I accused teasingly.

Her blue eyes met my smirk. "I never said that."

"Really? Then, you won't mind if I just turn Korn back on?"

"Um …" Her lips pursed with consideration, and I laughed.

"It's fine. You hate my music. That's cool," I brushed it off, feigning hurt and hugging my arms around myself.

"No, it's just so, um … violent. And that's not very Christmassy."

Lifting my lips in a smile, I shook my head. "Why can't you just say you hate my music? It won't hurt my feelings. Believe me, I've taken worse."

She let go of the potato masher, leaving it in the bowl, and her arms snaked around my waist. "I'll never use the word hate when talking about you," she said, resting her chin against my arm. "Even if your music does suck."

"Wow," I uttered on a long exhale, unwinding one of my arms to wrap it around her shoulders. She sighed at my touch and relaxed against my side. "Never's a really long time. Quite the commitment."

"It is," she agreed, nodding as her lips slowly spread into a grin.

"I mean, if you're willing to say something *that* crazy, maybe you should, I don't know, consider staying here more often, or uh, leaving some stuff—"

"Kiefer," she stopped me with my favorite nickname. "Are you asking me to move in?"

I shrugged in a noncommittal sort of way and replied, "Well, I mean, I didn't actually say that, but if you wanted to take it that way …"

468

"And Freddy, too?"

I rolled my eyes to the ceiling and sighed. "No, Audrey. I thought you'd leave him at your apartment alone until he's ready to go to his dad's place. Of course, Freddy, too."

She nodded slowly and replied in a soft, quiet voice I could barely hear over Chelsea's twangy singing—or was it Kelsea? "I like that idea."

***

"We will never host another holiday," I later warned her through teeth so gritted it was amazing they hadn't shattered.

My small house, that Audrey had once described as cute, didn't feel so cute right now, packed full with more friends and family than I ever realized cared. They had all brought presents for Jake and not an inch of space beneath the tree could be seen. The sight thawed my not-so-frozen heart just a little more, with the realization of just how lucky he really was. Hell, when I really thought about it, we were *both* lucky. Because despite it all—the accidents, the self-loathing, the proclamations of potential suicide, and the parents who once made their own suffering a higher priority than their kids—we had turned out all right. Jake was loved and so was I. And we deserved every fucking bit of it.

Still, I was never going to have another massive get together in my house, and I loudly repeated the sentiment to Audrey.

469

"Yes, we will," she insisted, wrapping her arms around mine and seemingly enjoying this far more than I was. "Look at how happy he is."

She was right about that. Jake's grin outshone every bulb on the tree and could've easily been in competition with the sun. He loved all the attention and company, and that alone was enough for me to relent with a sigh.

With dinner already out of the way and dessert being handled by our mothers, I made the quick decision to slide my arms from Audrey's grasp to lift my hand. I waved at my father, standing across the room by the front door, and after he caught my waving fingers, his head bobbed with a barely noticeable nod before he slipped out the door.

I stepped away from my girlfriend to perch on the arm of the couch beside Freddy, who sat beside Jake with his tablet, and I nudged the little boy's shoulder with my knuckles.

"Hey, guys," I said, grabbing their attention.

"Hi, Blake," Freddy muttered, looking up from the game he was playing.

"Blake, Blake, Blake," Jake chanted, pointing at the screen. "Freddy's showing me how he plays. He plays real good, right, Freddy? You play real good."

"Yep," Freddy confirmed with a deep nod.

"Awesome," I appraised. "But, hey, could you put the game away for a couple minutes? I think it might be time to do presents."

Jake's attention was immediately diverted with a clap of his hands. "Okie dokie!" He reached out toward the pile of gifts, not quite brushing his fingertips against the brightly colored wrapping paper and ribbons from his seat on the couch, and he groaned in frustration. His gaze whipped toward me with a hot demand scorching his eyes. "You told me to tell you when I needed help, like when I have to pee, and I need help right now!"

A murmured chuckle blanketed the room as I scrubbed a hand over my jaw. "Yeah, I'll give you a hand in a second. But, uh, before it gets too late, I think my present really needs to come inside first."

"What is it?" Jake's excitement was urgent and contagious, and dammit, I couldn't help feeling it myself. I'd been waiting over a week for this moment and I could hardly stand how slow my dad was being about bringing it inside.

But then, I saw his distorted figure behind the door's glass, and I didn't have to wait anymore.

"Okay, listen up, guys," I said to both my brother and Audrey's son, "I need you to keep your cool, got it? Don't get too excited or loud or—"

The front door opened and Freddy jumped off the couch as he shrieked, "A puppy! Mommy, look! It's a puppy! A real-life puppy!"

"I see that," Audrey said through an unstoppable burst of giggles.

A sentimental hush laid heavily over the room as the squirming bundle of fluff cowered in my father's arms for a moment as the excited little boy jumped at his feet. I felt a tightness in my lungs and I realized I hadn't taken a breath since Dad had stepped inside. It all came out now in an exasperated whoosh, before I turned to look at Jake, to see his reaction and whether or not this was a good thing or if I had just literally ruined Christmas by essentially replacing his beloved friend. Even though that's not how it'd felt to me, when I had visited the shelter.

Celia had told me a litter of puppies had just been dropped off and before I realized what I was doing, I was ditching work to check them out. I hadn't anticipated becoming attached or signing any papers, but within just a few minutes of meeting the little guy, I knew he needed to come home.

Call it intuition or whatever.

Jake's wary eyes were pinned on the puppy—a Border Collie and Labrador mix with the friendliest brown eyes I'd ever seen. His chest lifted and fell with short, shallow bursts of breath before his freshly-shaven chin wrinkled and began to quiver.

My gaze flitted quickly to find Audrey's as my heart plummeted straight into my stomach, only to meet the back of her head as she knelt on the floor with Freddy. It was a fleeting moment of selfishness, but dammit, I needed her to turn around and see that I needed her help. I had fucked up. But what else is new?

But then, in a voice so small and quiet, Jake asked, "Is that puppy really mine, Blake?"

I turned back to him as my momentary panic startled to settle. "Yeah, buddy. He is. Well, I kinda thought we could all share him—you, me, Audrey, and Freddy—but he's really yours."

"Is he a real good boy?" A tear slipped from his eye and dripped from his chin. "Like Mickey? Like Mickey is in Heaven?"

I hadn't planned on getting emotional, but fuck, it was hard not to. "Yeah," I rasped through a throat too constricted to breathe. "He is."

After a long pause and a careful assessment, Jake finally nodded and said, "I wanna hold him now."

Dad carried the now-excited puppy over to the couch, sat beside Jake, and passed the little guy into his lap. My breath held still in my lungs as the anticipation of how they'd connect skittered through my veins. I guess I hadn't quite realized how important this moment would be, and now that I was there, it was almost too intense. Almost too much. I felt like I was waiting forever for that little puppy to tilt his head and stare into the gentle gaze of my weeping brother, overwhelmed with a cocktail of happiness and grief. Then, he hopped up onto his hind legs, resting his forepaws on Jake's chest, and his tongue lapped out to bathe Jake's cheeks with kisses, and I relished in the relieved breath that could finally leave my lungs.

"I think he likes him," Dad laughed, his eyes flitting toward mine.

The lump in my throat was burdening and I swallowed hard against it. "Yeah," I croaked, grinning. "I'd say so."

"What are you going to name him, Jakey?" Mom asked, making me aware that she'd been standing nearby, and for how long, I had no idea. When I looked at her, I found her eyes shiny with emotion and her hands clasped to her chest. Her gaze met mine and we shared a smile. She was trying, and so was I. It was the best we could do, and for now, that felt like enough.

473

"Blue," Jake stated assuredly and sputtered with laughter when the puppy licked over his own lips.

Dad nodded thoughtfully. "Blue, huh?"

Jake hugged the puppy—Blue—just tight enough and turned to meet my gaze. He smiled softly, his eyes taking on that look I knew so well. His head nodded sagely and said, "Blue for you, Blake. Blue for you. Because you're better. All better now. Right?"

My lips pinned between my teeth as I slowly nodded and replied, "Yeah, buddy. All better now."

Epilogue

"THAT'S A LOT of candles," I muttered to Jake.

"Because we're a lot of years old," he replied simply.

"You make us sound ancient."

"Ancient means old."

I laughed, shaking my head. "And you think we're old?"

"Older than Freddy," he pointed out, and with a snort, I replied, "Well, you're right about that."

Audrey hadn't lied when she said she'd sing to me on my next birthday, though I'm not sure I ever doubted her. It didn't stop me from wanting to run away though, when the enormous cake was laid in front of us. There had never been another time in my life when this many eyes had been on me, and I wondered if it was at all possible to crawl inside yourself and never come back out.

"Don't look so nervous," she practically scolded me as she lit each of the candles. The flames danced wildly, setting the cake aglow.

"I don't look nervous," I argued. "I look like I wanna get the hell out of here."

"You're going to get through it, and you're going to be fine," she insisted with a gentle smile. She finished lighting the candles and gave my shoulder a reassuring squeeze.

Then, in the only way she knew how, Audrey carried the crowd into an off-key, rousing chorus of Happy Birthday. I cast my gaze downward, away from every set of eyes pinned on my brother and me, and Jake slipped his hand into mine.

Everyone sang, and I lost myself in a distracting torrent of reflection.

What a year it had been. I had found myself, found love and a peace I never thought could be unearthed from the rubble of my life. And amidst it all, I had almost lost Jake … again. But he had come back to me, where he belonged, to live with Audrey, Freddy, and me. And for the first time since I was ten, everything felt good.

Damn near perfect in fact.

Audrey's cool hand against mine brought me back to reality, sitting in the renovated Salem Skin, with all of our friends and family surrounding us at the front desk.

"Make a wish, guys," she whispered.

"What should we wish for?" I asked Jake, and he scoffed.

"We can't make a wish together, Blake. I make my own and you make your own. But we have to keep it secret. Don't tell anybody your wish, Blake, or it won't come true," he lectured with adamancy.

"Jeez," I muttered, shaking my head, taking in all the army of flickering flames. "Okay."

Then, I took a deep breath and blew.

***

The cake was eaten and the guests were gone. Cee, Shane, Audrey, and I cleaned up while Jake and Freddy hung out with an episode of *Daniel Tiger* on the waiting room TV. Then, we all left the shop with hugs and final birthday wishes, all too ready to wind down. At home, Audrey got Freddy settled in his room, freshly furnished and decorated to his liking, while I made sure Jake was set for bed, teeth brushed and face washed. When he was comfortably huddled beneath the blanket with Blue at his side, I eagerly retired to my bedroom, flopping onto the mattress to wait for my girlfriend.

It was a good day, I reluctantly admitted to myself, allowing the smile to spread slowly across my face. It wasn't something I'd expected, but throughout the day, I had found myself grinning and thinking about how nice it was to be celebrated. Even to have my parents there, offering a birthday card with a bit of money they knew I didn't need. But they had wanted to give it to me, they had wanted to show some affection and love with a gift, and I had accepted with a hug.

Things weren't perfect, but our path to recovery was lit with hope. And I'd be lying if I said I wasn't enjoying the journey.

Dr. Travetti hadn't come the way I'd hoped she might. She was invited, both by Audrey and me. I wanted her to meet Jake. I also wanted her to see the progress I'd made since our last session so many months ago. But she hadn't come. She called instead with an apology and an explanation.

"I got my closure at Christmas, and I'm worried that seeing Sabrina's family again will reopen the wounds that have finally begun to heal," she'd explained regrettably. "But I wanted to call and let you know, I am so proud of you, Blake. If I haven't said it enough, I really am, and I do hope I see you again."

I didn't think I ever would, but I hoped, too.

Audrey quietly entered the room and closed the door behind her, barely allowing it to click shut. "Oh, my Lord," she whispered, shaking her head. "I didn't think that kid would ever go to sleep."

"He's excited," I offered. "It's been a long day."

"Oh, I know." She climbed onto the bed beside me, sitting with her legs crossed. "I just couldn't wait to get in here with my birthday boy."

Her porcelain fingertips made absentminded circles along my bicep while she held my gaze with a quiet affection. Round and round, up and down, her eyes hooded and lips curved into a small smile. A full heat puffed inside my chest, coiled through my throat, and licked with pressing insistence against my tongue until I asked, "How the hell did I get so lucky?"

"I ask myself that question a thousand times a day."

We had a good life and a good routine. It was an easy, comfortable blanket, wrapping us up in a warm security and reminding us with gentle smiles and gentler touches that this was *it*. She was it for me, and I was it for her, and I couldn't create a more imperfectly perfect pairing if someone paid me to.

"I have something for you," I said, losing the staring contest to look away and grab a book from the drawer in my nightstand.

"It's not *my* birthday," she protested with a giggled laugh.

"Trust me, this is a present for me, too."

I handed her the book, something she immediately recognized with widened eyes and a soft separation of her lips. When she cracked the spine and opened the pages, she let out a whispered gasp.

"What?" I asked, amused.

"I didn't think you'd write in it," she admitted quietly.

"Why not?"

Audrey smiled and cocked her head exhaustedly, like the answer should've been obvious. "You're a *little* hard to please."

Snorting, I gestured toward the book, encouraging her to read, and she did.

There wasn't much between the pages, admittedly. Poetry was something I succumbed to only when the inspiration struck, and that didn't happen often. Only when life got too loud, too hard, or too much, did I feel the itching need to put pen to paper. But I had, when inspiration called, and I kept every single one.

There was a poem for my birthday last year. One for Thanksgiving and for Jake's second accident. The prose scribbled on those lines were laced with pain and written with a shaking hand. But then, there were the others that came after. The one I wrote after Audrey and I had made love. The one I jotted down quickly while unpacking her boxes. The one about having dinner with my parents, so overwhelmed by the absence of bitter words and sour faces. The one I woke up to scribble in the dark, about watching her sleep, so overrun by love and the good things I never thought I'd have, or ever deserve but always wanted.

"Blake ..." Her hand pressed hard against her chest, fingers splayed.

"I've come a long way," I replied as she continued to read.

"You have," she agreed.

"That's because of you."

Audrey looked up, blue eyes swimming in crystal lakes, and shook her head. "No. It's because you let it happen. You got tired of standing still, of living in the past with all your guilt and anger, and you decided to start moving. *You* did that. I was just there, hoping to come along for the ride."

"Well, it was a bumpy road," I laughed bitterly.

While clutching the book in her hands, she leaned in, kissed my lips, and whispered, "The ones worth taking usually are."

Acknowledgements

MY LIFE HAS BEEN a complicated maze of coincidence and fate, and all of it has somehow led me here.

Somehow, around thirty years ago, I met a kid who's mother planted the first seeds of my future. She told me then that my books would one day be on the shelves of the library. I wish I could tell her now that she was right.

Somehow, fourteen and a half years ago (at the time of writing this), I met a guy of impeccable artistic ability. I had no idea then that this guy would one day be my partner in crime, the father of my baby (brewing right now as I type this), my future husband, and the creator behind all of my covers.

Somehow, somewhere around ten years ago, while making beauty videos on YouTube, I met a gal from New Zealand. I had no idea then that this gal would one day be one of my greatest friends and the editor behind all of my stories.

Somehow, over the years, I've met an army of people—authors, friends, and readers alike—who have all played a part in putting me where I am right now.

Somehow, several years ago, I discovered these guys, Ryan and Matt Murray, a set of identical twin brothers in Salem, MA. They are both extremely talented tattoo artists, heavily inspired by the history of Salem and the dark, gritty macabre of life and death. I have followed their work for years, and because of them, I felt the pull to write a story about twins living in Salem. While they didn't do much to inspire Jake Carson, their style of tattooing and physical aesthetic played an enormous part in the creation of Blake. So, thank you to them, for sharing their art with the world. One of these days, I'll get to The Black Veil Studio and have them carve a piece of themselves into my skin.

I don't know where I'd be without any of these people. I don't know where I'd be without you, Dear Reader. I certainly wouldn't have written this book, that's for damn sure, but I'm so glad that I did.

About the Author

Kelsey Kingsley is a legally blind gal living in New York with her family and a cat named Ethel. She loves music, makeup, tattoos, and Edgar Allan Poe.

Kelsey is a Slytherin. She curses a lot and she fucking hates cheese.

For more from Kelsey, please consider checking out her website at: http://www.kelseykingsley.com

More books from Kelsey

Holly Freakin' Hughes
Daisies & Devin
The Life We Wanted
Tell Me Goodnight
Forget the Stars
Warrior Blue

The Kinney Brothers Series
One Night to Fall
To Fall for Winter
Last Chance to Fall
Hope to Fall